SOME REVIEWS OF GARRY KILWORTH'S BOOKS

His characters are strong and the sense of place he creates is immediate. (*Sunday Times* on *In Solitary*)

A subtle, poetic novel about the power of place – in this case the South Arabian Deserts – and the lure of myth. It haunted me long after it ended. (*City Limits Magazine* on *Spiral Winds*)

The Songbirds Of Pain is excellently crafted. Kilworth is a master of his trade. (*Punch Magazine*)

Atmospherically overcharged like an impending thunderstorm. (*The Guardian* on *Witchwater Country*)

A convincing display of fine talent. (*The Times* on *A Theatre Of Timesmiths*)

A masterpiece of balanced and enigmatic storytelling...Kilworth has mastered the form. (*Times Literary Supplement* on *In The Country Of Tattooed Men*)

An absolute delight, based on the myths and legends of the Polynesian peoples. (Mark Morris on *The Roof Of Voyaging*)

THE SOMETIMES SPURIOUS
TRAVELS THROUGH
TIME AND SPACE
OF
JAMES OVIT

a science fiction novel in three parts:
Stopwatch
Ring a ring o' roses
Memoirs of a Monster

by
GARRY KILWORTH

infinity plus

Published by infinity plus

www.infinityplus.co.uk

Follow @ipebooks on Twitter

ISBN-13: 978-1540692375
ISBN-10: 154069237X

This novel is for Colin and Sue Waters –
for the many pleasant hours spent with them
aboard their yacht the *Hilda May*.

BY THE SAME AUTHOR

Novels

Witchwater Country
Spiral Winds
Standing on Shamsan
The Iron Wire

Science Fiction Novels

In Solitary
The Night of Kadar
Split Second
Gemini God
Theatre of Timesmiths
Cloudrock
Abandonati

Fantasy Novels

Hunter's Moon
Midnight's Sun
Frost Dancers
House of Tribes
Roof of Voyaging
The Princely Flower
Land of Mists
Highlander (novelisation of film script)
A Midsummer's Nightmare
Shadow-Hawk

Young Adults' Books

The Wizard of Woodworld
The Voyage of the Vigilance
The Rain Ghost
The Third Dragon
The Drowners
Billy Pink's Private Detective Agency

The Phantom Piper
The Electric Kid
The Brontë Girls
Cybercats
The Raiders
The Gargoyle
Welkin Weasels Book 1 – Thunder Oak
Welkin Weasels Book 2 – Castle Storm
Welkin Weasels Book 3 – Windjammer Run
Welkin Weasels Book 4 – Gaslight Geezers
Welkin Weasels Book 5 – Vampire Voles
Welkin Weasels Book 6 – Heastward Ho!
Drummer Boy
Hey, New Kid!
Heavenly Hosts v Hell United
The Lantern Fox
Soldier's Son
Monster School
Nightdancer
Faerieland Book 1 – Spiggot's Quest
Faerieland Book 2 – Mallmoc's Castle
Faerieland Book 3 – Boggart and Fen
The Silver Claw
Attica
Jigsaw
Hundred-Towered City

Horror Novels
The Street
Angel
Archangel

Short Story Collections
The Songbirds of Pain
In the Hollow of the Deep-sea Wave
In the Country of Tattooed Men
Hogfoot-right and Bird-hands

Moby Jack and Other Tall Tales
Tales from the Fragrant Harbour
Dark Hills, Hollow Clocks
The Fabulous Beast
The Best Short Stories of Garry Kilworth

Fantasy Novels as Kim Hunter
The Red Pavilions Book 1 – Knight's Dawn
The Red Pavilions Book 2 – Wizard's Funeral
The Red Pavilions Book 3 – Scabbard's Song

Historical Fantasy Novels as Richard Argent
Winter's Knight

Historical Sagas as FK Salwood
The Oystercatcher's Cry
The Saffron Fields
The Ragged School

Historical War Novels
Jack Crossman series
The Devil's Own
Valley of Death
Soldiers in the Mist
The Winter Soldiers
Attack on the Redan
Brothers of the Blade
Rogue Officer
Kiwi Wars

Ensign Early series
Scarlet Sash
Dragoons

Memoirs as Garry Douglas Kilworth
On my way to Samarkand: memoirs of a travelling writer

CONTENTS

A science fiction novel in three parts:

Part One:

STOPWATCH

1

...AND I AWOKE ON A cold hillock in Hyde Park.

Naked and bemused, but nevertheless cognizant of my reasons for being in this situation, I stared around me. Unfortunately the trees obscured all but the highest buildings beyond the park and those peaks that were visible were only silhouettes against the dark sky. I climbed to my feet. It was close to dawn and I remembered I had to make my way to the bridge over the Serpentine. We had chosen this venue with the fair certainty that this particular feature in this particular London park would still be in evidence.

I found the lake and began to walk along the shoreline. My heart was pounding in my chest. Would there indeed be someone on the bridge to meet me? If there were not, I would be in desperate circumstances. Indeed, during the time I was not present in this city invasions could have taken place or there could have been a radical change in government. Was there a foreign power in charge now? Or did we have a dictator, one of our own kind grown too powerful to eject? Any political situation I could dream up was certainly possible.

Shivering with the chilly breeze – if my journey time had been accurate enough it should be early spring – I stumbled along and eventually found the bridge. My heart dropped down to my gut and the panic began. There was no one in sight. They were supposed to be standing in the middle of the bridge waiting for me. This was indeed the nightmare I had been dreading. All along I had said to them, 'Are you sure you can have someone waiting for me? There can be no mistake. I must have someone to meet me.'

'James Ovit?'

I jumped and whirled. A tall man stood there with a bag in his right hand. He smiled at me. 'Sorry to startle you.'

'Are you my contact?' I croaked. 'You're supposed to be in the middle of the bridge.'

'Indeed. I was heading that way when you appeared. You're a little early.'

Relief coursed through me, warming me.

'Thank God you're here though.'

At that moment I almost collapsed with the stress. Indeed, I started trembling uncontrollably and tears streamed down my cheeks. He reached out and with a strong hand under my right arm held me up for a few moments. He said, 'I can understand why you're feeling shocked. You must have had a journey. Here, put some clothes on. Then we can go and find a coffee somewhere. Do you drink coffee?'

'Tea or beer, normally – but I have had coffee.'

'Good.' He let me go.

He stood well away from me, not watching, as I dressed in the strange clothes he gave me. Strange not only because of the style, but because of the texture. I don't think I had ever felt a material quite so soft and smooth. And it was all one, not several pieces. A sort of tightish fitting overall in a dark blue. I had trouble finding out how to do up the front, which was flapping open. My companion came to my aid.

'Here.'

He ran a light hand from my stomach to my neck and the two halves sealed themselves. No buttons, nor any zips that I could detect. Just two strips that ran along the edges of the material. Once on, I felt warm and snug, even though the layer of clothing was quite thin. I noted in the growing light that my helper had on a similar garment.

'What is this stuff? What's it made of?'

'That? Oh, Slinke. Most clothes are made of Slinke these days. You can still get wool, cotton and other materials here on Earth, but Slinke is in favour.'

'Good descriptive name for something so silky.'

'Oh, no. I mean, that's not why it's called that. Just a coincidence I suppose. Slinke is the man who invented it. Wolfgang Slinke. A Bavarian.'

'A German.' In my present mood I had no love for that nation. 'A German invented it.'

'Well, yes – as I say, a Bavarian though, not a Prussian.'

The distinction was lost on me, but I didn't feel like pursuing the subject any further. I was given a pair of slip-on shoes, thinner than my old carpet slippers, and these too felt very comfortable. They had looked too small at first sight, but actually fitted well.

'You knew my size? In shoes?'

'Not really – they fit any size.'

'Oh.'

The man then handed me a small haversack.

'You'll find money and other necessary items in that bag,' he told me. 'Once we've had coffee, you won't see me again.'

'No, that's what I was told. What's today's date by the way'

'17th May.'

'2055?'

He grinned. 'I should hope so.' He then looked at me strangely. 'Yes, I suppose they have a different calendar where you've been.'

The last sentence took me aback a bit, but I felt I ought to proceed with caution. Take things very slowly. It was possible to make some very silly mistakes, else. Therefore I didn't question his unexpected addition to my straight question. Indeed now that I knew that my journey had been successful I felt more buoyant. I was dressed and warm, and had in my possession the means to stay alive in my old city.

My helper led me down a street which, if it had been noticeably different in my own time, did not shock me with its changes. Yes, there was a lot more steel and aluminium, and chrome that shone so brightly in the morning sun it hurt my eyes, but I suppose the centres of cities don't change that much. There were quite a few new buildings, that towered over their surroundings: architecture that was new to me. But I didn't feel like a stranger in a strange land. There was much that was familiar.

So, as to the city having been transformed into something unrecognisable, that had not occurred. There were buildings far older than a man's lifetime here and in any city of consequence: many of them would no doubt still be there in another century, two centuries or even a millennium hence. The one thing that did astonish me was the lack of traffic on the road, which appeared to be a precinct walkway. The cars, or vehicles, whatever they were, seemed to be floating smoothly high above the streets with no apparent engine noise.

We entered a cafe where the coffee smelled delicious.

'Did you have coffee up there?' asked my friend.

Up where?

'Oh, yes.'

He went to the counter and ordered the beverages, paying for them with a rod or baton which the man serving him slipped into a slot and then returned to him. There was a big shiny machine at the back,with tubes going everywhere and steam issuing from a tap. The server pushed a couple of coloured buttons in a row of the same and I deduced that somewhere inside that glittering engine my coffee was being made. Indeed it made all the appropriate noises from hisses to gurgles to clanks: coffee-making has never been a simple operation.

My friend sat down. 'Looksay, I've ordered you a *giallo ocra*, with rich-cream milk, I think you'll like that.'

'To be honest, I could drink muddy puddle water so long as it was warm. That was a rude cold awakening back there in the park.'

The drink was indeed delicious and lived up to the promise of its aroma. So often coffee can smell wonderful and then spoil itself for the drinker by having a bitter harsh taste. This was smooth and silky, and went down easily. There was also some buttered toast on the side, which looked no different to the toast I had eaten as a child. I wolfed this down, following each swallow with a sip of the dark yellow nectar.

While the coffee was being made one or two people had entered the cafe and ordered their breakfasts at the counter. They were dressed similarly to my friend and me and used the same method of currency, the short batons, which were always returned to them. The upper part of their clothing had slots into which they slipped the batons once the server returned them. The patrons then sat at tables where they took out small round objects about the size of a saucer. I watched as a man placed it flat on his table and was amazed to see tiny figures and buildings spring from it like mushrooms. These toy-sized colourful scenes continually altered: a dancing, fairy tableau vivant which shimmered and shape-changed as I gaped in awe.

'Catching up on the news on their slices,' said my companion casually, nodding at the other patrons. 'You'll soon get used to things. Now, let me tell you that in your haversack you have enough money on your stick to carry out your mission – more than enough – but please be careful. Try to remain inconspicuous, at least for the first year or two. You'll find a communicator, with instructions, in your pack. It contains all the information you'll need to survive on this world.'

'On this world,' I repeated, feeling I really had to take this further. 'As opposed to...'

He smirked. 'Your own planet, of course. Look, I'm just a messenger. I've been told nothing, really – it's all *need to know* – so I'm thinking that you've been somewhere a long way away and have come back. My best guess is another planet. My task is simply to meet you and to hand you the survival pack. I really shouldn't even be having coffee with you, but,' he smiled and sipped from his cup, 'I do need a good infusion of the brown stuff to lubricate my engine in the morning and why not ease you into life down here on Earth.'

'Yes, yes of course. Do you know the name of the, er, planet from which I am supposed to have come?'

He shook his head. 'No, they didn't tell me. My instructions came from my department head. There was no face-to-face meeting. It came in the form of an authenticated message. I know as little about you as you know about me. However,' he leaned back and looked at me quizzically, 'they can't stop me surmising and I've decided you were sent out to a distant planet, oh, probably light years away – and now you're back.' His eyes were shining as he took another sip of his coffee. 'I've been visiting that bridge every morning for the past week waiting for you.'

'So, why do you think I was sent – to another world.'

'You work for the government, don't you? You've probably brought something back.' His hand went up and he laughed. 'Oh, you don't need to tell me what it is. I guess we'll be informed, soon enough. A new world for people to live? A new Earth rich in food and minerals? Whatever it is, I'm sure I'll be one of the first to know. After all, if it hadn't been for me, you'd be walking the streets naked as a babe.'

This last remark was made a little too loudly and two of the other patrons of the coffee shop stared at us.

'Well,' I said, 'you could be right – or you could be wrong. Obviously I'm not permitted to divulge anything to you at this point in time, but I'm sure you'll be told eventually.'

'Maybe or maybe not,' he said, pursing his lips between the clauses of his sentence, 'but it's probably the same place the Angels come from.'

My mind buzzed.

'Angels?'

'Ah, you probably left before they arrived, am I right? They came here about a year ago. Just appeared among us. They estimate there's several dozen of them, thereabouts anyway, but they don't seem to club together like you'd expect. They're not herd animals. You only see them wandering around alone. No one knows where they came from or why or how. Suddenly they were among us, quietly getting on with whatever they do when they're not out walking the streets. Angels.' His face took on a distant dreamy expression. 'Yep, angels all right.'

'Angels aren't real,' I pointed out. 'They're mythical.'

'Yes, but they look like angels. You know, like the pictures.'

'Lots of different ones. What are they? Cherubs? Clones of St Michael? Raphael's angels? Durer's angels?'

He shrugged. 'You'd know if you saw one. They're, well, they're quite beautiful to look at. I can use that word, because they're not human of course. Seven feet tall, slim, delicate features. Weird eyes though. Sort of pale grey eyes that seem to look right into you, right inside you. You have the feeling they know what you're thinking, though that's not been proved one way or the other. No wings, of course. Or halos. That would be stupid, wouldn't it? Just a general appearance.'

'Dark or light?'

'Hair or skin? Well, some have blond hair and some are jet black. I mean, really blond and really black. As for their skin colour, sort of olive-brown.'

'Does anyone have any idea where they came from? What makes them angelic anyway? Surely not just good looks?'

He coughed, then said, 'Looksay, they don't have sexual organs. They're…blanks. Yes, that's what they are, blank.'

That seemed to sum it all up for my companion.

'And,' he continued, 'as to where they came from, there's been all sorts of theories. Outer space. Under the sea. Another dimension. A parallel world. And of course, one of the Heavens of the many religions. You name it, someone's put it up as an answer. The Angels themselves won't say, or can't say. No one speaks their language and while they've learned a few of our languages they're reluctant to talk about themselves. They seem eager to learn, but not to teach.'

'But they could be the vanguard of some invasion force?'

'Yep, that they could, but what do you do about it, eh? Put them in a concentration camp? The world's moved on from solutions like that. Apparently they're watched, very closely, by secret service agents – but so far no one has any complaints about them. They don't do anything wrong. They don't do anything at all really. They're just *here*. Another thing, all of them have this sad expression on their faces, as if they really want to be somewhere else. Maybe they do?'

'Do they work? Do they have jobs?'

'Not to my knowledge. You're wondering how they live, because in fact they do need clothes for warmth, shelter from the weather and they do eat food and drink drinks. Well, it may not surprise you to learn there are all sorts of people providing for them. People who think they actually are angels and others who become fans of anything exotic and don't even care or want to know where they're from originally. You just have to be different and mysterious in this world and you'll gather a fan base prepared to fund any lifestyle you choose to enjoy.'

'Now,' I said, 'I've been away a long time. No communication because it was too far – ah, several thousand parsecs. So perhaps you'll be able to fill me in on a few details. Nothing that will compromise your position as a messenger. For instance, what's the political situation? Who's in charge of the UK now?'

His head went backwards a little. 'UK? Oh, the *United Kingdom*? We haven't been united for 30 years.'

'So which country left the union?'

'Scotland, Northern Ireland, Wales, Cornwall and Yorkshire. All independent countries now. The world's decentralised in the last few decades. Basques have their own country. Catalonians. Valencians. In America most of the states have seceded from the union and are unitary. India, Russia, Pakistan, all broken up. China's fragmented into several different nations: Canton, Shanghai, I don't know how many others. The world is now a huge jigsaw of little countries.'

I was amazed. So that's why earlier he had been at great pains to point out that Slinke was a Bavarian, not a Prussian. The two were now separate nations.

'Look, when I left there was talk of a world government, some time in the future.'

'Oh, we've got that, all right.'

'But you just said the globe has decentralised.'

'Ah, yes. I suppose when I said *countries*, I should have said federal regions – nations. We've got the Government of Earth – GOFER – but to be quite honest it doesn't have any teeth. It sort of oversees the world in a benign and quiet way, laying down rules and laws which no single nation takes much notice of and just go their own sweet way. Some, like the Prussians, always take notice of GOFER's rules and regulations, but they're unusual.

Always been a bit stiff and starchy, the Prussians, eh? Even before you left for your unknown planet.' He winked.

'So, there's still an England – and this city, London, is still the capital?'

'Oh yes, can't see that changing, can you?'

Now I had another question, since this man before me seemed to think I had been to a far distant planet. 'And travel to the stars?'

'Well, you'd know better than me about that. There's no real information about starships – you know, going out beyond our solar system. I expect that's all kept secret. Everyone suspects it's going on – which of course it is – but only those who work in the business know for sure. There's the two Moon colonies of course, and a brand new station they've set up on Mars. We're told about those. But as to places way out there, amongst the twinkle and tinsel, that's kept under wraps.'

I asked, 'Why would they do that?'

'Looksay, rivalry. Every little country on the planet wants to be the first to discover an Earth-world. I'll bet when you report in, they won't tell anyone what you've found for a long while.' He nodded and smiled again. 'I found you naked and cold in Hyde Park, so I'll be watching and listening, knowing I played my part in it all.'

'But,' I pointed out, 'I didn't step out of a spaceship.'

'Matter transmitter. You were teleported, weren't you? I'm not silly.' He tapped the side of his brow with his forefinger. 'Teleportation. The government thinks we don't know about these things, but we're not stupid.'

2

WHEN I CAME TO MY senses there was a blurred face just inches away from my own. I could feel hot, odorous breath on my cheeks as the owner of those features peered into my eyes. I think I let out a groan of despair, wondering for just a split moment if I was still alive. However as I moved my head to one side, to avoid the smell of the exhalations of the person scrutinising me, I became aware that I was steeped in my own sweat and that my left leg still had that deep dull ache around the ankle from when I injured it on falling out of the trees.

'You speaking English?'

The face had withdrawn to a position about five feet above my own. Indeed, the owner had straightened and was looking down on me with a sympathetic expression. It was a pleasant countenance, light brown in colour and with small crinkled lines around the corners of the eyes. Not a face to be feared. Certainly not a demon from Hell, though not an angel from Heaven, either. A Malay. A tribesman or farmer. I smiled at him and he smiled back, his brown eyes shining.

I went up on my elbows and stared at him, noting his spare but muscled frame. He was wearing a longi which covered his legs to mid-shins. On his upper body was a Marks and Spencer soiled white vest. The vest was back to front and inside out: I could see the 'Rainbow River' label.

We continued to stare at each other in silence for a few more minutes, during which I could hear a cockerel crowing and chickens clucking somewhere outside the hut we were in. Then I remembered he had asked me a question which had so far gone unanswered.

'Yes, I am English.'

I spoke simply, slowly and precisely as I had been told to do, if ever I was shot down and forced to deal with the local population.

'Good.' He smiled again. 'You no Japan soldier. Listen, I speaking not good English, but little.'

'That is good for me, because I speak very little Malay. *Satu, dua, tiga, empat, lima.* I can count to five and say please and thank you, but that's all. *Terima Kasih.*'

'*Sama-sama.*' He came back with the traditional repost. Then, 'I find you in forest. You have hurt leg.' He pointed to the limb in question. 'Broken? Yes, I think so.'

There was a noise from a dark corner of the hut and then I realised someone else was in the room. Peering into the gloom I could see a young woman doing something with some pots. She too looked up and smiled at me, then continued with her work.

'My wife,' said my host. 'She get ready to make dinner.'

'In here?' I looked around me. It was a typical kampong dwelling, probably on stilts, with wooden floor and walls, and palm-leaf roof.

'No, no, sir. She make it outside. In here would catch fire.'

'That's what I thought.'

I stared at my left foot which was still pointing at a very peculiar angle. When I moved it, it hurt like hell. I pulled up my trouser leg and saw that the swelling around my ankle had gone down a little, but it was still puffy. However, now that I had the leisure to study the injury, I could see the twist was right on the joint. Perhaps not broken after all?

'I think it's dislocated,' I said.

'Is what?'

'Not broken, the joint has come out.'

'Not broken? Good. But I fetch our doctor now, yes?'

Doctor? I wondered what that meant, but this was no time to ask questions or protest. I lay back as he tripped away as light as a lizard. So feathery on their feet, those natives. Delicate movements. I could hear him skipping down the wooden steps and so knew for sure that the hut was on stilts. His wife left shortly after him with another quick smile at me before going through the doorway. She appeared very young, not much more than a girl of fifteen or sixteen.

Not long afterwards my host was back. A large woman was with him. The hut swayed as if acknowledging the presence of an important person as she walked across the thin wooden floor. This was obviously no real doctor as I had suspected, but someone in the village who probably practised natural medicine. Without any formalities or questions she immediately knelt down and gently lifted my ankle up to inspect it. I gritted my teeth expecting pain, but she lay the foot down very soon afterwards with just as much care. Then she spoke to me in Malay. I looked at the young man for assistance.

'Lady doctor say you foot out of proper place,' said my host. 'You wish her to put back again?'

I thought about this. 'I don't know. Has she done this before?'

He laughed. 'Many times. We climb trees and fall down. We dive in river and hit rock. Many, many times.'

'All right. What do I do?'

The woman nodded as if she understood my acquiescence by my expression and straight away took an object out of a bag she was carrying. It was a half-deflated ball. She pushed it between my teeth. I think it was an old tennis ball she had got hold of from somewhere. It had probably been used for throw-and-fetch with slobbery-mouthed dogs. It tasted slimy and well-used. I wondered how many mouths it had been in, besides mine, and how many germs were embedded in its worn surface.

It was while I was thus surmising that a sudden ball of pain travelled up the length of my body from my ankle and exploded in my head. I let out a gargled groan and found myself biting down hard on the rubber. A minute later the foul thing was taken from my mouth by the small man. He held it fastidiously between two fingers confirming my fears about its former usage.

'All done. Finished. Foot now better.'

Hardly better, but when I stared down at it, the sweat dripping from my head and face, I could see it was back in the 'proper' position for a left foot. The big woman was beaming at me. Then she reached forward, felt my brow with a large calloused hand, slapped my face gently, tweaked my nose, then said something to my host.

'She go now,' he said. 'Work done.'

I gasped. 'Please – please thank her very much – I'm afraid I have no money to pay for her services.'

He looked aggrieved. 'Money? Money not necessary. She come back tonight to sleep with you.'

I blinked rapidly at this, looking at this huge bulky female who was probably in her fifties, but my friend grinned too quickly.

'See, I make joke. All Englishman like make joke. I know this, I work in Singapore for Tuan Simpson. All time, they make joke. Now I leave you for sleep. You have little sleep. Then we eat. Good?'

'Yes, thank you. *Terima Kasih*. Your joke was very funny.'

'I think so. Yes, I think so. But shocking. You no tell wife.'

'Of course not. She would definitely be shocked.'

'Yes, she is very strict person. Dragon lady.'

It was hard to imagine that the pretty young woman I had seen was in any shape or form a dragon, but I nodded, lay back and tried to banish from my head the hellish ache in my throbbing ankle.

THE AROMA OF SOMETHING SIMILAR to stew wafted up between the floor boards from below. I lay there staring at the woven-leafed ceiling. A large black cockroach was making its way amongst the crispy fronds, no doubt smelling the same cooking as I was myself. The place was alive with wildlife of course. Nothing of any real harm, up here in the hut, but arachnids and insects aplenty. When I had been a small boy, they had been frightening to me, but no longer. I had lain in the jungle for two days before these Malays found me and in that time had been crawled over by countless ants, spiders and other small creatures.

Three days previously, on the 15 December, 1941, I had been navigating a Catalina sea plane for my captain, Flight Lieutenant Peter Standish. We had flown from Bombay to Singapore to deliver mail and other cargo, and had taken off again. On the way back to India, we were expected take a short flight northwards and make a supply drop over Kota Tinggi where some Australian troops had been encircled by the invading Japanese. As we were flying over the jungle we came under fire – just small arms stuff, machine guns and rifles – but they hit our fuel tank which exploded in flames. Peter told me and the rest of the crew to bale out. I let the others go first and stayed with my captain until he ordered me to go a second time. So I jumped. I don't think he followed because the aircraft crashed just a few minutes later into a thick nest of trees. Peter, I was sure, was dead, while the rest of the crew had baled out leagues away from my landing place.

I descended into treetops where my parachute caught in high branches. I was left dangling until I decided I had to cut myself down and take my chances of a soft landing on the forest floor below. It was indeed spongy with moss, but I twisted my foot as I hit the ground.

With my leg out of action I tried crawling, but after a while it seemed a futile thing to do, for I was finding nowhere better than where I was at that moment. So I propped myself up, my back against a tree, and realised that I had to be found by someone – my own people, the locals or even the Japanese – if I were to survive.

No one came.

The pain in my ankle turned to a nagging ache which never left me. I thought about making a splint, but there seemed to be no suitable wood about. The undergrowth was all ferns and light bushes with no substantial branches. After a while I grew apathetic and simply sat there like an idiot, wishing, praying for a passer-by. None came, of course, even when I started yelling for help.

I slept and woke, slept and woke, and after two days decided I had to find food and water especially or I knew I would die. A terrible thirst took control of my faculties and drove every other thought out of my head. Finally I got to my one good leg and hopped from tree to tree, using them to support my weight for a few moments. Finally I came across a small river. There I fell on my face and drank and drank until I passed out, probably from over-hydration.

Therein lies the history of my drop from the sky.

THE DAY AFTER MY ANKLE had been righted I was told by an anxious and worried Mamat (my host) that the Japanese army was swarming down through the country and was heading towards Singapore. I got to my feet with the aid of a bamboo rod I had been given and hobbled to the doorway of the hut.

'Shall I leave now?' I said. 'I must try to get to Singapore.'

'No, no, sir – they are all about now. Japan soldiers. They killing everybody. You stay here, see what happen. Maybe Singapore soldiers fight Japan soldiers and win? Then you go. No one will go with you now. I am forbid to go away by my Siti. She tell me, no, you no go. You stay here with me or Japan soldier come and do bad thing.'

I could see her point and sympathised with Mamat's dilemma. His young and beautiful wife was more important to him than an injured British airman, obviously, and if she were afraid of being raped or killed were he not there to protect her, then it was his duty to stay, even though his presence would not make any difference one way or the other, should the Japanese visit the village. The enemy were infamous for their behaviour towards the local population and Mamat would be shot out of hand were he to resist any attempts to defile his wife.

So I stayed, since it was almost impossible for me to walk to Singapore without assistance, especially with the rainforest crawling with Japanese soldiers. It seemed they were making rapid progress on foot and on bicycles, towards their goal. Mamat told me they had tanks too, I could hear them in the distance, grinding along an old dirt road some miles from the village. I knew that General Percival's army had no tanks and no doubt they had been flushed southwards by the rapidly advancing better equipped Japanese army.

The time of the 'star-led chieftains' came and went and we were soon into January. Japanese soldiers had come to the village three times since my arrival. Each time my hosts hid me in a small make-shift bunker covered with bracken and leaves. Each time when I emerged I was swept through with guilt on learning that the Japs had taken men from the village to work elsewhere on the peninsula. I wondered if their families would ever see them again. The Japanese were already notorious for working people to death in this war. Women too, had been taken. One

31

was shot and decapitated when she raked the face of her rapist with her fingernails. Yet I had been protected by these good people.

At least Mamat's wife had not been violated or abducted yet. She had something of the actress in her and was good at disguising herself as an old crone. I was amazed at the skill with which she disfigured herself into a bent old woman, her charcoal-blackened face screwed into a mask, her hands wrinkled with talented use of river clay, her hair greyed with ash from the fire. However, others soon began to copy her and I feared that next time the Japs came they would be suspicious of so many hags in the village, some of whose disguises were not that well done.

'You will destroy all Japanese men soon,' Mamat told me. 'British Army is never beat for long time. Always they win in the end. British soldiers in Singapore will drive Japanese from Malaya – you see.'

I wish I could have shared his faith. Perhaps it was time for the British Empire to call it quits? Luckily for us, the Americans were now well in the war, and they were a gung ho bunch of warriors. I couldn't see the Japanese holding out forever against the British, the Americans and all their numerous allies. At Pearl Harbour the Americans had been dealt a foul blow and they were absolutely incensed by it. So perhaps Mamat was right, maybe we would win in the end, but oh, what a depressing experience, to be part of this defeat on the Malayan Peninsula. I felt humiliated for my country and my heart bled for those who had been captured and the treatment they would receive, unless our army in Singapore could manage to retake this jungled landscape.

My ankle was still very weak, but by January I felt that I could walk a good distance, at least to reach the river and take a canoe down to Singapore. However, by the time I had made up my mind to make the journey, Mamat came back and reported that

Singapore had fallen. The British army and their allies in the Lion City had surrendered to the Japanese. There was nowhere safe to go to. I was absolutely stunned and emotional on hearing this news. It was difficult to accept such a terrible turn of events. My blood pounded in my head and I was physically sick, vomiting on the ground where I stood. Singapore fallen? Just like that? How could that be? I kept questioning Mamat, even getting angry with him for giving me the answers I didn't want to hear.

'Don't be stupid, man. Are you sure? Surrendered? But we had more than 100,000 men. Why would they capitulate so quickly?'

Mamat stood there looking upset and helpless, as if it were his fault the British had given up so quickly.

I sat for a whole day staring into the flames of Siti's cooking fire, wondering what on earth I was expected to do. It was without doubt that Indonesia and the Dutch East Indies would be the next to fall to the soldiers of the Rising Sun. Thailand was already occupied. Where could I run to? I was surrounded by countries that had either been conquered by Japan, or with governments sympathetic to them. I could now start walking, but where the hell to? How far would I get? Yet if I stayed in the village I would put the villagers in grave danger of their lives and would probably be branded a coward by my own people once the war was over.

I later learned that though at one time General Percival had had around 135,000 men, almost a third of those had been killed or captured in the retreat down through the Malay peninsula. Another 15,000 were non-combative personnel, leaving Percival with an exhausted remnant of his army, almost out of ammunition and out of water. They were said to have been defeated by only 30,000 Japanese, but that figure was simply the front line troops. There were many more coming down through Malaya to reinforce those who had taken Singapore. Percival had no reinforcements, no tanks and had little choice but to surrender.

For the first time in my life I was completely indecisive.

3

SOMEONE HAD, THROUGH THE INTERVENING years, thought to keep the notes and equipment left for me by the original team up to date. There were people out there in the city who knew I had arrived, but this was an experiment and they wouldn't contact me unless I got into serious difficulties. They wouldn't be the same people who sent me of course. Those poor bastards were all dead unless they had learned to live at least one-and-a-half centuries. None of the original team had been younger than fifty years of age when I left. So anyone around now had been passed the task by predecessors and would not know me personally.

I learned from the notes on my 'Instructions and Information' on the slice that the sale and purchase of all property was now handled solely by a government department. There were no estate agents. I went along to the Housing Trust and told them I had been out of the country for a long time, having been doing ecological work in the Ecuadorian rainforest, so would they please be patient with my ignorance. (Thankfully there must have been some rainforest left, for no one looked at me in astonishment. That, or the people at the Housing Trust were not very knowledgeable about foreign climes.) Indeed, a young woman in the tightest coverall I had yet encountered was extremely patient with me and even showed me how to use my 'currency stick' to secure the apartment I wanted to rent. Halfway through our transaction however a very tall dusky-looking creature entered the open office and simply stood there, his gaze travelling over the whole room.

All work stopped instantly. The place went absolutely silent as men and women looked up and gawped at the stranger. It reminded me of one of those cowboy films where a gunfighter enters the saloon and everything goes eerily quiet and still before the shooting starts. However, I don't think there was fear in the air in this situation, but there was certainly a palpable tenseness. For my own part I had never seen such a beautiful human being – tall, serene-looking, majestic – except of course he, she or it was not human, but an alien from a distant planet.

No wonder everyone had stopped what they were doing. The charisma the creature exuded was astounding. It flowed in invisible waves across the room. It was tangible. I could have stood and stared at this exquisite creature all day and not tired of the exercise. The allure of its presence held me breathless with a strange yearning that gripped me within and I almost squirmed with desire to make myself known to it, to walk up and touch it – just a handshake or a stroke of its hair – anything to make it notice me and perhaps smile, if such a gesture were possible for a being that came from another world under a far-off star.

I suddenly broke the silence as if it were made of thin glass.

'Jesus Christ!'

The words had exploded from my mouth involuntarily, I was so astonished and amazed by the being who stood in the doorway I could not help the expletive. Everyone then turned to look at me, including the extraterrestrial. For a few extremely uncomfortable seconds I was the sole object of attention. Then the tall immigrant to our world spun on his heels and almost glided through the doorway, ducking a little to get under the door frame. The stillness remained for a half-minute longer, then everything returned to normal: voices, desk machines, feet walking, all the usual sounds. My young lady however remained staring at me.

'That's a funny expression,' she said.

I blinked. 'What is?'

'Your exclamation.'

I thought for a second, then said, 'Oh, sorry, yes, my oath?' I suddenly realised such an outburst might be regarded as a serious profanity in the society of which I was now a member. I had no idea how religion had developed or not since my time. 'I'm sorry, it just slipped out. Are you, er, a strong church-goer?'

'Nothing like that. I just haven't heard the name used in that way before. It was almost like swearing.'

My neck prickled. 'Yes, I suppose it was – the, er, natives in Ecuador used it quite often unfortunately. I picked it up, having been there so long. I was close to the headwaters of the Amazon, you see – the Rio Napo – and they're full of profanities in that area…' I babbled ridiculously for a few minutes while she continued with the paperwork. Actually, there was no paper, it was all done on a flat screen on the top of the desk, her fingers flashing over it and creating words and figures as if by magic. Eventually she was satisfied with everything, then showed me how to pay for it with the 'stick', and I walked out of the building with a voice codeword that would open the door to my new possession in Theobald's Road, Holborn.

The apartment was furnished in the latest style, which appeared to be retrospective. It had a distinct flavour of the art deco, without lending itself totally to that mode. I quite liked it. For the first time I felt a little more at home. My mother had enjoyed art deco and I had grown up in a house which paid homage to the style. There were hidden extras of course. The viewing area which covered one wall called the 'vita'. The vita had amazing perspectives and showed what I would call 'films' in three dimensional form. You could swear that the figures were solid and the scenes in them stretched back to the horizon. In another wall recesses appeared at a touch of the finger in which there were devices that produced cooked food, coffee, tea, and other delights. You had to load the devices with packages of the same of course, but it was eating and drinking made easy. No fuss. No bother.

Whenever I went out I ordered on the apartment cleaner which gently sucked all the dust and dirt – what there was of it – into mouth-like slots in the skirting. Where it went to after that I have no idea. The bed was amazing. I could have slept blissfully for weeks in its soft folds that cuddled me like a warm, furry creature. It always woke me gently if I was having a nightmare or an anxious dream, having I suppose recognised my distress from the movements I was making. I could have left on the device which soothed one with soft, pleasant phrases on those occasions, such as 'There you go, there you go, nothing to be alarmed about – just a nasty dream wafted away by Luxidrift Incorporated,' except that I decided to mute a speaker which worried me more than any nightmare at three o'clock on a deep dark morning. In any case, a simple voice command would turn on mellow lights and any rapid beating of the heart brought under control within a minute or two.

Two days after moving into the apartment the Electronic Butler (Elburt) announced there was someone approaching the apartment. I ordered the door to one-way transparency which revealed the caller. At first I didn't recognise her and was loath to let her in, but then it came to me: she was the woman who dealt with me at the Housing Trust. For the last several days I had been studying my slice which contained all I needed to know in order to live in this new world and for the first time I gave Elburt an order to open the front door to admit a stranger to the place. There was no hesitation on his part. The door slid back neatly into the left side wall and I found a young woman smiling at me.

'Good morning,' she said, brightly.

I was worried. The one thing I didn't want to do was arouse any curiosity about myself. I remember reading a line in a Raymond Chandler novel: *The man was about as inconspicuous as a tarantula on a piece of angel cake.* That's how I felt every time I left the apartment and went to do something amongst the citizens of London. What had I done wrong in this instance? Had I given myself away with that silly story about Ecuador? Surely this woman was suspicious of me.

'And a very good morning to you too, but is there something wrong? Do I need to verify anything?'

'No, no.' Her smile broadened and her face shone. She really was very pretty, with her short blonde curls and blue eyes. 'You looked a bit at sea when you came to us at the Housing Trust. I'm off duty at the moment and I thought you might like someone to show you the city, since you've been away so long in South America.'

'Ah – very kind. Very kind of you. But I think I'm fine, you know. Cities don't change that much.'

'Hmm, you obviously haven't lived in China. Hong Kong. Shanghai. They change every day there. You can wake up and find you're lost before even leaving your own building. Do come on. I have nothing important on today and it would be nice to show you how our parks have improved over the last few years...'

Then I said a very true but very stupid thing, which even as it left my mouth I was regretting it.

'I'm married, you know.'

Her expression changed instantly. She looked offended.

'Ah,' I managed to blurt out, before she spoke again, 'that was an idiotic remark. There's no reason why we couldn't spend the day together without any romantic ties developing. That is…'

'How strange you are,' she interrupted, her eyes narrowing a little. 'What an old-fashioned thing to say. *Romantic ties*. You really have been in the jungle for a long time, haven't you? Looksay, I just thought you seemed a bit lost and lonely, but I'm obviously mistaken.'

'No, no, you're right. I am feeling a bit at sea – now there's another antique expression, so I'm not the only one who uses them. The, er, only books I got to read out there, in the Amazon, were some very old paperbacks left by a priest who used to work among the local Indians. Georgette Heyer historical novels set in the Regency period. Romantic nonsense, really, about aristocratic ladies falling in love with dukes and earls.' I recalled some of the slice's information and laughed. 'Thank goodness we don't have any of those left, these days – the nobility, I mean.'

'Oh, I think it's a bit sad. There's still a lot of titles about, but no one takes them seriously any more, I agree.'

'And no new ones.'

'And no new ones. Looksay, I don't want to upset your wife.' She peered into the apartment as if expecting to see one. 'You didn't say it was a dual occupancy. You'll have to come into the office again and we'll alter the contract to suit the circumstances.'

'She's, ah, still there. Still over in Ecuador. We're – we're sort of separated. It's very claustrophobic, working together in a place where you are the only Europeans for a thousand miles. She's very understanding anyway, about relationships between men and women. That is,' I was beginning to perspire on managing to get into deep philosophical waters again, 'she believes in friendships between the sexes, without any…without any…'

'Romantic ties?'

I stared at her. 'Would you like a cup of coffee. Please do come in. I'm such a fool sometimes.'

Now she smiled again. 'I find that endearing. Yes, wouldn't mind a coffee. I'm Sonja by the way. Sonja Svenlik.'

She knew my name from the rental contract, so I didn't respond in kind. Instead I said, 'Hi!' and proffered a hand, which she eventually took and shook with a twinkle in her eyes and then responded with the remark, 'Lo! You are *very* funny.'

I laughed then. 'Yes, I am, aren't I? There's always something a bit pathetic about being old-fashioned, but at least it's harmless.'

She took off some slim lilac gloves, the only addition to her indoor wear that I could see, and looked around the apartment.

'It's very sparsely furnished, isn't it? I'm sorry. I should have given you a wider choice.'

'Oh, it's fine for me. I'm a minimalist.'

Elburt made us some coffee almost instantly and I took them still steaming out of the niche in the wall. We sat each in one of the two armchairs, the coffee table between us.

I said, 'You mentioned the parks. Have they been renovated recently?'

'They're always undergoing some sort of improvement. Shrinking of course, as those fucking politicians grab bits for their housing developments.'

I blinked at the language, but knew that the word had become so inoffensive and innocuous in today's society it was used as frequently and casually as the 'bloody' or 'bugger' of my own childhood.

'Do you believe they're corrupt – the latest politicians?'

She wrinkled her nose, sipped her coffee, and after a few more moments' thought, said, 'No worse than usual, I suppose. There's always *some* corrupt ones, aren't there, in any society.'

I nodded, then said, 'Can I ask you a personal question?'

She shrugged. 'If you like.'

'You're not married or engaged yourself, are you?'

'Engaged? Do people still do that? No, I'm not married. Are you worried about some irate husband bursting in us?'

'No, just inquisitive. Bad manners, I know, to be curious about your personal life. It seemed to me, when I left this country, that the estate of marriage was still thriving, but from what I learn from the news, hardly anyone gets hitched these days. I have yet to meet a married person. You all seem to enjoy being single.'

'Enjoy? I don't think it's so much enjoyable, it's just more convenient in today's world. Looksay, people don't want to get tangled up with other people. There's too many of us around now. I only have to call someone and I've got company, so why should I lock myself to another person for life? It doesn't make sense. It doubles the things you have to do to keep on track and interferes with one's career.'

'What about love? A lifelong love?'

'Oh, we're back to romance again,' she teased, taking another drink of Elburt's perfect brew. 'Well, yes, people do still fall in love in today's London society, but few of them seem to need a formal declaration. They just get on with it until they find they don't need it any more and then they get back to normal life again. Love is an inconvenience, James. It starts to take up all your time, like owning a boat or a second home. There's always something to do that wouldn't need to be done if you were just on your own. I'm sorry, I sound like a cynic, don't I? But you'd be surprised to find how many people agree with that view. Love just gets in the way of getting things done. Time is so precious, isn't it? We're only here for a century – if we're lucky, that is.'

I couldn't really dispute her philosophy on marriage without getting tangled in an argument which might take an age, so I said nothing to this except to acknowledge that she had a point. Then

I accepted her offer to show me 'the improvements' to the London I had known 'before I went to the Amazon'. I didn't want to get too close to this woman however. I was on a mission and that had to take precedence over everything else. I didn't know how much my Ecuadorian trip camouflage actually worked. Was there any rainforest left, for example, and was Ecuador even called Ecuador these days. I had invented a story on the spur of the moment the details of which I was woefully ignorant. I should have researched it and got it off pat, instead of stumbling through a half-baked fictitious history with no substance behind it.

I did enjoy the day out though. The stress of my mission fell away as we walked the streets and she began pointing out various new building landmarks. We took the underground railway, which was still called 'the tube' but which was nothing like the underground of my youth. It had high-speed trains which had no walls or doors between the carriages. You could see right from one end of the train to the other: a sea of heads, many bent forward, reading. There were holograms everywhere, showing the latest news or advertising something: it was hard to concentrate on conversation with so much going on in the background. Twice she had to snap her fingers in front of my eyes to regain my attention.

On the streets of the city there were no vehicles. These were now high above us, zipping wingless through the air. I had read about this in my notes which stated that they remained aloft through very clever use of magnetism. I have not, nor ever have had, an engineer's brain. Even though the information had been simplified for people of my ignorance I really had difficulty in understanding the principle. Then again, when I had owned an early television set I was never really knowledgeable or even interested in the workings behind the screen. I love the mathematics of navigation and cartography, but devices with hidden workings leave me cold. You open them up and all you find is a nest of wires and other bits. Their secrets remain their secrets, unless you've had a long course in how to decode them.

At the end of the day we had a meal together. She suggested we might go to a show sometime and I sort of half-agreed, but said I was going to be busy for the next week or two. This didn't seem to put her off at all, for she told me brightly she would call me in a fortnight and would I allow her to choose the entertainment? In the end I acquiesced and we parted, me going back to my apartment, she to hers. She had wheedled the address of my slice out of me and so I had to expect I would hear from her again.

Nothing of London I had seen that day had really shocked or amazed me in any way. Yes, there were new structures and certain licentious entertainment houses seemed to have found their way into law-abiding society. I suppose the aspect of this future London which upset me the most was the noise level. Indeed, in my own time the streets had been filled with noisy traffic, yelling news vendors, church bells, chiming clocks and other sound makers, but now almost every building had three-dimensional animated tableaux on their roofs or platforms. These were advertisements consisting of multi-coloured figures whose extended necks allowed their inflated heads to swoop down to ground level, so that they could stick their faces into those of passersby and yell loudly into their ears that 'Jissips' was a superb pain reliever or 'Slurppp Beer' was drunk by millions.

A thousand voices and tunes filled the streets and buildings of London, played at such a volume that the music was heavily distorted: ragged, blaring, harsh, ironically heard by very few because the majority of the population had a chip in their heads with which to listen continuously to their favourite music. I hated the sounds that bounced off the walls of alleys and flowed down the main streets of the city. They gave me the most tremendous headache. Even the '40s blitz could not compare with this cacophony.

4

WHEN I WAS A CHILD there was no need to roam far away from one's own home because the world came to your front door. The baker, the vegetable man, the coal man, the milkman, the pedlar with his pans and knife-sharpening tools. They all delivered their wares, often on a daily basis. And it wasn't just the tradesmen needed for basic living: people brought luxury items too. There was the ice cream van, hot-chestnut sellers, the tally man who had a vehicle full of cheap dresses which he hoped to sell to housewives, the rag'n'bone man who would give me a goldfish in a jam jar in exchange for any old unwanted items (even rabbit skins from the kitchen waste), the God-people handing out tracts and Sunday-school colouring books, the lemonade man with his cart full of bottles of fizzy drinks, many, many others. Then, of course, there was the rent collector and the man who managed the Christmas Club and the money lender who wanted his investment back plus interest.

They came into the village at one end and left at the other end. The world flowed through our main street, shedding its precious cargoes and picking up dues. Provided you had a reasonable job with a more-or-less living wage you could survive in a state of comfortable stasis.

Until I was ten years old, I had not even visited the next village, two miles away. Then my father died of gangrene of the leg, when his scythe sliced away part of his calf. He was drunk at the time, having been drawn into the pub on his way back to the hay cutting after dinner one Saturday. He patched himself up, without washing the wound, and finished his day's work. On finding it did not heal, he again treated himself. We could not afford a visit to the doctor believing it would eventually get better on its own. He didn't want to worry his family over a 'scratch'.

''S nothin',' he said. 'Don't you go frettin' about me woman – it's just a small sprint in me ankle.'

He meant a sprain, but eventually the gangrene must have swept poison through his body, because he went out one day looking very ill but defiant in the face of my mother's enquiries and was found in a ditch the following morning, his body frozen iron-hard, his blind eyes staring belligerently at the skies.

That was when I got a before-school job as a paper boy, which took me into the two neighbouring villages. I would walk more than 10 miles before going to school. Then one day I was delivering a paper to the Big House just outside our village when I found a man lying on the ground. He was dressed in good clothes, Tweeds, and had a dog running round him, barking. At first the dog would not let me get near him, but after two sharp commands the animal sat and stared at me.

'Are you hurt, sir?' I asked.

He snapped, 'Of course I'm bloody well hurt, you idiot. I've twisted my ankle, can't you see? Help me get to my feet. I need to get to the bell over there.'

Although I was only eleven years of age I was reasonably strong and I let the man climb up my body. The dog, a border collie, watched, its head cocked on one side. Leaving the bag of newspapers and magazines on the ground, I was the injured man's crutch to the gate of the Big House. Its real name was The Grange but everyone in the village called it the Big House, because that's what it was. He pressed a bell on one of the gate's pillars and soon a man appeared, a gardener I think, who strolled at first until he saw the old man, then he began running. The dog squeezed through the bars of the gate and scampered towards the servant, fussing around his heels as that person's feet crunched on the gravel drive. The gate was opened, the servant took over from me, and I went back to pick up my bag of newspapers.

As I bent down to grab the strap, which had fallen in a puddle and was soaked in muddy, brown rainwater, the old man yelled, 'What's your name boy?'

I turned to look. He was resting heavily on the servant's shoulder, but he was facing in my direction.

'James – James Ovit, sir.'

Without another word or acknowledgement, he turned back to face the house, hobbling alongside his helper.

Two days later there was a shiny new bicycle standing outside my front door, delivered from the nearest town, Southend-on-sea. My mother was arguing with the man who had brought it.

'What's it for?' she said. 'You can't just leave that here. We can't pay for it.'

'Already paid for,' came the reply. 'Mr Swanson at The Grange asked for it to be delivered here. Said it was for a James Ovit.'

'James,' cried my mother, her arms folded under her chest in the cold morning air, 'what've you done?'

'Just helped a man who was hurt, that's all. He'd twisted his ankle, Mum. I just gave him a hand.'

'Why's he sent you a bike?'

'For helping him, I suppose.'

My mother was very proud. She didn't approve of charity.

'It don't seem right. That's an expensive machine. Is that all you did, help him to his feet?'

'And to his gate. Then he rang the bell and a bloke came running.'

The van man delivering the bicycle said, 'Oh, Mr Swanson – he's got money comin' out of his ears. It won't be much to him, a bike like this one. He could buy the whole shop if he wanted.'

'It still don't seem right.'

She was wavering now, staring at the chrome handlebars which glinted in the sun. I stared too. It was a beautiful thing with a bright red frame and a single brake under the right hand grip. Not only did it have a brake, it had a silver bell and a black lamp on the front. It had a nicely oiled chain and black pedals that had not seen the foot of man. I gathered it all in with my eyes, the whole wonderful machine. Mine. This bicycle was *mine*. No more walking between villages to deliver papers. I could do it in a flash on these superb two wheels. Life was looking up. I was going up in the world. Other paper boys had bikes, of course, but I hadn't seen one so new it could have been fashioned by angels.

'I want a go.'

The voice was petulant. A stamping of the foot on the stoop added the full stop to her sentence.

My sister, Saviour, had appeared in the doorway. She was one year older than me.

'You can't have a go on this one. It's mine,' I crowed. 'I helped the man at the Big House and he sent me this as a present.'

Saviour glowered. 'Mum, I can use it too, can't I?'

Mum unfolded her arms and waved them in the air.

'I knew there'd be trouble. I knew it would bring trouble.'

She went indoors, leaving me to sign for the bike, while Saviour rattled away in my ear about sharing things.

'I'll take you on the crossbar,' I said, to get rid of her, 'but it's not a girl's bike. You can see that. It's a boy's bike, with a crossbar. Girls can't actually *ride* bikes with crossbars. It's a known fact that it does somethin' to their fannies.'

'That's rude! I'm going to tell Mum you said *fanny*.'

'Now you've said it too, Sav,' I pointed out.

'I'm allowed. I'm a girl.'

But she didn't say anything, once we got indoors and sat down to toast for breakfast. Later I gave her the ride I promised. Saviour was all right really. We used to fight a bit, but mostly she totally ignored me, so we got on well enough. She was always down at the swings with the other girls, larking around. Occasionally she joined in the cat-calls when us boys went past her and her friends, but for the most part we left each other alone. She was called Saviour because Mum said she saved her and Dad's marriage when Dad was a wild man. He was always a bit of gambler and something of a drinker when he was younger, so Mum said, but when Saviour came along he discovered responsibility. He still got drunk very occasionally, but not every night, like before.

After I got the bike I became a free bird, flying everywhere and anywhere, especially at weekends. I would cycle miles out into the countryside, explore the creeks along the River Crouch and around the corner of the Thames. I would go out as far as Paglesham along the seawall paths, through tree-canopied winding lanes, skirting the salt marshes and the mud pockets of the Dengies. There were two other boys who had bikes in the village: James Black and Albert Spencer. Al, Blackie and I would set off after our paper rounds on a Saturday morning and not reappear in our homes until darkness fell across the land. Our adventures were not startling, but they were exciting to schoolboys who had hardly ventured a mile from their own front doors before then.

The day after my 13th birthday Blackie, Al and I cycled into Southend and I went to the pictures for the first time – the Electric Palace Picture House – and saw the film *King Kong*. We came out stunned by the magic of the cinema. How did they make that giant gorilla look so real? Everything looked like it really happened!

Blackie, the most sophisticated of our small gang, who had already been to the pictures before that day, was as awed as the rest of us.

'Did you see how that Fay Wray sort of looked up and up and up on the boat, starin' at nothin' really, though o' course she was told to imagine somethin' really scary there in front of her? Then her face changed to a really frightened look and she screamed like hell as if there actshully was a giant monster there, when there was nothin' but thin air really. Do you think she somehow guessed she was going to see a whacking big ape later on, when they got to the island?'

This was a bit deep for Al and me. We stared at Blackie and finally nodded. 'I 'spect so, Blackie. She must've,' I said. 'What do you think, Al?'

'Yeah, definitely.'

But I think what we all went home with, and pondered on deeply in our beds that night, was the fact that there was an astonishing world out there and it wasn't out of reach. We had all read fairy tales and other such literature when we were younger. I still found a certain amazement in the comics I read. But there was more, much more out there, to feed the empty pockets of our imaginations with magical worlds. It was probably that experience, that first visit to the picture house in Southend, which set me up for accepting the assignment which I would undergo as a man in my thirties: the mission which changed my life forever.

When it came time to leave school for good, I felt I knew everything about everything. At fourteen I went to work in the same shop from which my cycle had been purchased four years previously. I loved it. Blackie had gone into his father's garage and was apprenticed to be a car mechanic and Al went into a grocery store. I didn't envy Blackie. I much preferred the simplicity of bikes to cars. Nor was I jealous of Al's larger wage packet. Fitting and maintaining bicycles was easy to learn and soon I was proficient at something others found a mystery. Middle class ladies would bring their cycles to the shop to have the brake blocks replaced, or a puncture mended and would praise my work. Bicycles were my life at that time. Beautiful shiny machines that did not cost a mint to purchase or maintain, yet carried the owner to exotic locations within an hour or two. I now had a racing bike and still went out on weekends to remote destinations: pubs out near Creeksea or Bradwell, or to Latchingdon and Burnham-on-Crouch, both the latter places good hunting grounds for girls who had the nice accents and pretty manners absent from most of the village girls I had grown up with.

At 18 I met the 19 year-old daughter of a doctor who found something in me to like. However, after a few dates she started to take me in hand and mould me into something a little more acceptable to her friends. She told me I didn't actually engage with life; that I just let things happen to me rather than making things happen. When I thought about it, I decided she was right. I didn't go out and get things, I waited for them to come to me. I was dreamy and cloud-headed, definitely, but promised myself I would pay more attention to life, to what was going on around me, to what was going on in the world at large. I would become sharp and attentive, and take in all that I saw and heard.

I didn't mind being taken in hand. I was happy to learn the right way to hold a knife and fork and all those other small actions that separate a yokel from a man-about-town. Amanda taught me how to greet someone, what to wear to a garden party, not to scoff at poetry, how to nod thoughtfully and talk about 'the clever use of colour' when shown an old oil painting, and – most importantly – encouraged me to go to evening classes to get an education. It was at those evening classes that I became interested in astronomy, and so when the war came and I was assessed on entering the Royal Air Force, my knowledge of the stars helped to get me on a navigator course and eventually into the cockpit of a Catalina seaplane.

Becoming aircrew did not enable me to hold on to Amanda's affection. She, like many young women, preferred Spitfire pilots to seaplane navigators. I didn't blame her. There was a craze among young women, my own sister included, for fighter pilots. If she couldn't get a Spitfire man, she next went for a Hurricane flier. The times were like that. The poor bastards – I mean the fighter pilots – didn't last long anyway. Most of them were shot down within two weeks of finishing their training. No wonder the girls loved them. They were dashing heroes sent out in a blaze of glory to die young. Anyway, both the women in my life, Amanda and Saviour, went dippy over the fighter boys and I was fortunately left to concentrate on the navigator training course, which was a good thing, since I didn't find it easy. I scraped through and came out with sergeant's stripes on my arm.

They sent me first to Canada, to finish my training. It was the first time I had been out of England, but Canada was no great culture shock. That came afterwards when I was posted to India. There I was appalled by the poverty and the heaving mass of people who lived cheek by jowl in shelters made of rags. There were those who had money of course, but they were few and far between. Mostly the population seemed to surge back and forth in brown waves of quiet despair, looking for some way in which to feed themselves and their families.

There were dead bodies left in the street, which circumnavigated by passersby. There were children with stick-thin limbs who begged with saucer eyes. There were old men and women crouched in dark corners from which they would probably never again emerge. The whole scene shocked me to the core. I had thought we, my mother, sister and I, had been poor, but what we had considered poverty bore no comparison to the deprivation I witnessed in India.

The poverty aside, I found India an amazing, exotic place, full of colour and excitement for a young man. The heat bothered some of my comrades, but I loved it. The local food was strange and difficult to get used to at first, but once I got the taste for it I couldn't get enough of the curries and flatbreads they served from the roadside stalls. I loved the babble of the languages, the markets, the nodding heads, the coffee, the tea, the brown raptors that perched on high walls, the kingfishers that zipped here and there even in the cities, the camels and painted elephants, the pi-dogs, the vendors of bizarre ornaments.

I loved everything but the poverty – but in the end of course, I even became inured to that.

5

AT THE APPOINTED TIME I stood on the bridge in Hyde Park and awaited the second traveller. I expected a woman named Alice Toop and she would arrive as naked as I had myself. So, to save her as little embarrassment as possible, and from the cool of the morning, I had a blanket ready. When she came, however, running through the dawn's gloom, she declined the blanket and dressed immediately in the suit I had brought. Once that had been achieved we shook hands and nodded.

'Alice?'

'Yes of course. And you're James.'

'We need to get you back to the apartment,' I said. 'It's not too far from here. Once there we'll get you a hot drink and something to eat.'

'I'm not desperately hungry, but I could do with a cup of tea,' she said, smiling.

We had never met before and we both sized each other up in a polite way. Alice was a broad-faced woman in her late thirties. She had brownish hair and blue eyes. Her frame was stocky and muscular for a female. There was humour in her bearing though and my first instinct was to like her. Something in her expression told me she would be easy to get on with and that I wouldn't be pestered with complaints or petty requests for instructions. We started walking for the gateway.

'How tall are you?' I asked. 'If you don't mind me asking?'

'Is there a reason for the question?'

'No, just curious. You can be as short as you like for this work. There's no height restriction. It's not the police.'

She laughed. 'I'm five foot, two.'

'Ah, same height as my mum. By the way, the system is metric now. No one talks in imperial measurements.'

'I'll have to remember that.'

I could see her staring around her, as we walked through the streets.

'It's changed a lot, on the surface,' I said. 'Many of the buildings we knew remain though. It's only a hundred years, after all. The old and new are intermingled as they always have been.'

'What strikes me straight away,' she remarked, 'are the traffic signs – there doesn't seem to be any.'

Very observant.

'That's because the cars don't use the streets any more. They fly – up there.' I pointed to a taxi navigating its way through the high rise buildings. 'It's a lot safer. Something to do with magnetism. And they never crash. They bounce away from each other, quite violently sometimes I admit, but the two metal shells never actually touch.'

'Interesting. And aircraft?'

'Still plenty of those around. Rocketships too, going back and forth to the Moon and Mars. That's as far as they've got, those two heavenly bodies. However, I have to tell you straight away, there are people – we think they're people – from space. They call them Angels because they're sexless and rather beautiful. Very tall and elegant, and seemingly always completely calm and of a peaceful nature. Perhaps they're not in the same shape they employed on their home world, but were able to copy our form once they saw what we looked like. Anyway, it's not an invasion from outer space. They're not hostile. No one actually knows where the aliens are from, but they think it's somewhere light years away – not near, not from our solar system.'

'How exciting.' Alice's eyes shone. 'Angel-people! Not from this world! Wonderful. I knew it would be very different. Marvellous. That's why I volunteered for this, you know, because it *will* be different. The austerity back home was getting to be rather boring.' She looked up at me. 'I was chosen out of a thousand applicants.'

'Yes,' I said, 'we are the chosen few.'

'It makes you feel special, doesn't it? Exclusive.'

I didn't think so, but I agreed with her to stop the conversation from going any further.

'We're here,' I said, ordering the outer doors to open. 'You have to use your voice for everything these days. It opens doors and locks them again, produces hot meals, turns on the home entertainment – you name it, your voice has command over it. Elburt, the Electronic Butler, does most of the work. You have to produce an initial vocal pattern of course. Once you have, it can't be duplicated, even by the cleverest mimic. Once that's laid down on your master key, you simply use it to control everything that needs to be controlled.'

'Mechanically?' she asked. 'Can your voice be duplicated by using a recording device?'

'I'm told it can't be duplicated in any way. It's like a fingerprint – or DNA.'

She looked puzzled. 'What's that? DNA?'

'Ah, I was forgetting. Well, you'll soon find out. I don't want to go into all the latest inventions and discoveries. It would take too much time. There's been a huge surge in technology. A vast number of electronic inventions, which recently have – luckily for us – been incorporated into one small device about the size of an old-fashioned tea-cup saucer, but flatter and slightly thicker. You can do just about everything with that device. It's called a *slice*. Mostly it's used for sending and receiving messages, with or without three-dimensional pictures…'

She interrupted me. 'This is really a super time, isn't it? Where they've sent us to.'

It seemed my sturdy new little companion was a romantic.

'If you say so.'

At that moment Elburt said, '*Someone approaching.*'

'Transparent,' I ordered.

Through the now one-way-viewing door I could see Sonja standing uncertainly on the other side. She could not see us of course and she spoke into the comm.

'James? Are you there?'

My companion looked at me and shook her head.

'Hi Sonja,' I responded. 'Sorry, I'm very busy at the moment. Could you come back later?'

Sonja stepped back from the door and stared as if she was trying to see through it from her side.

'Just a coffee,' she said, softly. 'Ten minutes, that's all.'

'I can't. I really can't.'

Still she stood there with a frown on her brow, then finally turned on her heel and walked away. Before she entered the lift, Sonja took one last glance backward at the apartment, then she was gone. My palms were sweating as I ordered the door to opaque once more. Sonja's timing could not have been more awkward. Not that I had anything to hide from anyone, but I would have preferred to have dealt with my first new traveller without interruption. I'm a man who likes things to go smoothly, without any need for superfluous explanations. I'm not good at social interaction and I like to be in control of things. Now I was on the back foot, probably having to explain something redundant to the operation. Something that was private and nonessential.

Indeed, Alice said quietly, 'Who was that?'

'A friend,' I replied, sharply.

'Really? A friend? Is that allowed?'

I had been pretending to busy myself with straightening a chair, but her remark infuriated me. I rounded on her.

'Who are you, the time police?' I growled. 'Mind your own bloody business.'

Alice went very pale and for a moment I thought she was going to burst into tears. Immediately I felt guilty. There was no reason for me to yell at her like I had done, but it had annoyed me intensely to be questioned.

'Look,' I said, in a softer tone, 'we're both stressed. It's that kind of a situation. I'm sorry if I sounded…well, I *did* sound angry and I am really sorry. It's been difficult, trying to fit into this world, this time, while still maintaining I'm part of it and at home here. On the surface the people here are much the same as those we left in 1955, but you only have to spend five minutes with one of them to find they're very different. The fact is we have to get to know some of them to find out what's what, yet at the same time not allow them into our secret. What I find *really* strange is that no one has mentioned time travel, which doesn't make sense.'

She looked calmer now and in control of her emotions and my respect for her professionalism was in place again.

'That's true,' she said, nodding. 'If we had time travel in the 1950s, it would be passé by now, wouldn't it? Yes, it was a top secret discovery in our day, but surely over the last hundred years it's become public knowledge.'

'Well, it hasn't – at least, I don't think it has. I haven't asked anyone outright, but I think it's time I did. Discoveries and inventions don't get lost to human knowledge, certainly not over a single century. I can't imagine how they've managed to keep it under wraps, unless they decided they had to because something went terribly wrong with the initial experiment – the first time travellers – *us*.'

She frowned. 'You think our efforts might end in failure?'

'I don't know. I just don't know. There's nothing we can do except carry on doing what we're trained to do, what we're supposed to do. My job is to manage a safe house for those following behind me. You're the first. Once I've brought you up to speed on life, the world and as much as I know about 2055, then it's your job to go out into that world and implant yourself among its citizens. I expect eleven more like you, then I hope they'll recall me back to our own time.'

'But – but if no one admits to there being time travel now, then how are we going to get back?'

'There's got to be time travel. We're proof of that. Someone, somewhere knows the secret. When you are all installed I'll make myself known to the government and then I expect they'll take me away somewhere, interrogate me at some length, make sure I'm not some loony, then introduce me to the cabal who are privy to that secret. As I've just said, you can't uninvent something. I wouldn't be surprised if we're expected. Perhaps when I reveal myself they'll say, "Ah, James, it's about time you made yourself known to us." Now,' I said, nodding, 'we should get on with your education. Have you any questions before we wade into the heavy stuff?'

'Yes – why does almost everyone in the street look as if they're a million miles away in their heads?'

'Implants. They have a small disc the size of a thruppenny bit in the nape of their necks. They're either listening to music or some broadcast or other while they're walking along. It doesn't impair their judgement at all – or doesn't seem to. They just like being entertained while they're moving from one place to another. The disc also works as a telephone and as a memory aid – all sorts of things in the same vein.'

'My goodness, that's amazing. Have you got one?'

'No – I'm not here to be entertained. I've got to concentrate on my mission, just as you have to.'

She pursed her lips before saying, 'Yes, yes of course.'

6

I CAME TO THE REALISATION that I could no longer sacrifice Mamat and his tribe to the danger of being massacred by the Japanese. They were a dignified people: upright, proud and determined to protect a stranger even at the risk to themselves and their families. I wasn't worth all of that. In my ragged shirt and trousers, hardly a uniform any longer, I left the village and made my way downriver in an old leaky canoe. I hoped to somehow find a way across to Indonesia.

That first night I stopped in a place where the foliage overflowed into the river, dragged my canoe up onto the bank and fell asleep beside it. I was prodded awake the next morning and found myself pinned down by four or five of those long bayonets the Japanese soldiers fitted to their rifles. A ring of stern faces stared down at me. I knew only one word in Japanese.

'*Konnichiwa*,' I said, smiling up at them.

They kicked the shit out of me and dragged me to their camp by my ankles. At first I thought their officer was going to behead me. Indeed he drew his sword and swished it around my shoulders several times, yelling and spitting, probably for the benefit of his soldiers. but finally he let out a triumphant toothy laugh and sheathed the blade again before kicking me in the direction he wanted me to go.

I was taken to Changi PoW camp, a jail with high walls the tops of which were decorated with machine gun posts. In that infamous place I spent the whole rest of the war until the

Japanese were finally beaten and cowed, and had slunk back to their devastated islands. They had executed and starved many of my fellow prisoners and those who had survived were skeletal and undernourished, riven with dysentery and other diseases, and hardly fit for human society again. Yet we did go home and did fit back in with our fellows, though the nightmares never really went away.

All of us found it a difficult transition and none of us forgave the army that had incarcerated us, humiliated us and had treated us worse than they would have treated animals. What angered me the most was that their top general was greeted as a hero when he returned to Tokyo. This man, who had murdered the citizens of Singapore – Chinese, Malays and Europeans – murdered them wantonly in cold blood, went on to write a best-selling book about his conquest of the island and the Malayan mainland, thus making him a rich boastful man. My disgust with those who allowed this abhorrent injustice to take place filled me with a bile that never really went away.

I had no idea what I wanted to do now that the war was over, but luckily the Royal Air Force still required navigators and I decided to remain a commissioned officer with my one wing on my chest. So I took up where I left off, flying in a Shackleton around the coastal waters of Britain. It was an easy life. I was fed and watered, the pay was not exceptional but it wasn't meagre either. I had comrades for companionship and enjoyed the company of young women who still found aviators exciting, even though they were no longer in a highly dangerous occupation. By the early 1950s I was enjoying life again. I had decided I never wanted to marry, especially after witnessing my sister Saviour produce a whole handful of noisy children who seemed to demand constant attention. That was not for me. I liked a quiet life, a pint or two with friends in a pub, a game of darts now and then, and trips to France or Italy when I could afford it. It was a pleasant existence, with few ripples, and I was happy to let it continue as long as possible.

In September of 1952 I received a letter from the Air Ministry telling me to report for special duties to an office in Holborn. I duly went along to a building in Theobald's Road where they sat me down with a hundred other military types and set me a questionnaire. I was never told the result of that paper but presumably I had impressed my superiors with my answers because they then set me a series of further tests, along with a remnant of the group that had taken that first questionnaire. Gradually the numbers were thinned. Eventually we were down to a dozen souls.

Finally I found myself in a room with three scientists all of whom beamed at me while the bushy-browed one in the middle told me I had been chosen as the best of those whom they had examined for the momentous task which they required me to undertake.

'And that would be – what?' I enquired.

'A journey through time. A voyage into the future.'

There was silence as all three of the white-coated eggheads stared at me, waiting for my reaction, which when it came was a raucous belly laugh.

'No, seriously,' I said. 'What do you want of me?'

'Young man,' said the head scientist sitting before me, 'this is no joke. I – *we*,' he gestured with his hands to include his compatriots on either side of him, 'we know that it sounds ludicrous and we understand your disbelief, your scepticism, but we are deadly serious. You must be aware that during the war many new inventions and discoveries came about through necessity, the mother of such things. While we did not set out to find what we have, it revealed its amazing capabilities accidentally during the search for a code breaking device.' His blue eyes were penetrating. 'You must be aware that so very often marvellous inventions and discoveries come about by accident?'

'I suppose so,' I said. 'But still…'

'But still you find it difficult to believe? Quite understandable and you must be given time to absorb what you have learned today, which must of course never leave this room. I hardly need to say that it's a top secret project and were anything to leak out denials would follow, not to mention a charge of treason for the man responsible. Am I clear?'

'Perfectly clear, sir.'

'Good. As I say, for the moment you will leave here with nothing but the knowledge that time travel *is* indeed a possibility. I'm sure you'll eventually come to acknowledge that fact, once it has been allowed to permeate through the layer of scepticism that forms a shell around every human being's natural credulity. Once you have come to accept what we have to say, you must then begin think on this – we would like you to volunteer to be part of an experiment. We need men and women willing to be projected into the future – pioneers as it were, to prepare the frontier of what is to come for others to follow. For myself, I think it is a great honour to be chosen for such a mission and I hope you will come to feel the same.'

I was in a daze when I left that room. It would indeed take me a while to accept what I had heard from these three sages (though in truth, only one of them had spoken the whole time) but there was another concern. I had fallen in love. The girl – well, hardly a girl, she was a woman of 23 glorious summers – was a WRAF officer who was stationed with me at RAF Coltishall, in Norfolk. No longer flying, I was now the Communications Officer on a fighter station which boasted Hunters and Javelins, both beautiful combat aircraft. Joan Dunn came originally from Surrey and while I had at first winced at her plummy Oxbridge accent, I came to love it as much as I did the woman who spoke the words. She wasn't beautiful in the classic sense, being a sturdy lass, but she had character and intelligence, both of which I admired in a woman, clear blue eyes, a tight mop of bronze curls, a nice complexion, and she could hit a tennis ball with all the strength and savagery of a lioness.

We actually met on the tennis court, where she beat me hollow. That evening in the mess we sat and talked over drinks before one of the fighter boys came and whisked her away. I remembered the Spitfire pilots and how they got all the girls during the war. Nothing had changed. Hunter pilots were just as much sought after by post-war females. However, to my great surprise and delight she ditched her escort within an hour and was back at my table before midnight. 'My ex-boyfriend,' she explained with a wry smile. 'He still thinks there's a chance.'

'And there isn't?' I said, sipping my whisky.

Candidly, she replied with a smile, 'Not now I've met you.'

I remember taking a mental step back at this point. I wasn't used to such forward females. However, Joan was different to any other girl I'd met before and very soon I had fallen for her in a big way. We played tennis, walked the byways and alongside the brooks of Norfolk, went dancing at the Samson and Hercules Ballroom in Norwich, had picnics in dreamy meadows – the whole works. I was – we both were – smitten.

Coming home from Changi prison camp and the war had been both good and bad. Britain was jubilant with its victory over Hitler's Germany and the Japanese, and the euphoria was difficult to ignore. There had been the horrors of the death camps to assimilate into the national conscience and whether we could have done more to prevent the ghastly loss of life. Then of course there were the terrible twin aspects of the atom bomb. This invention had ended the war more quickly than otherwise, but then we were stuck with a weapon of mass destruction and couldn't uninvent it. It was like having a monster in the back shed which might at any moment escape and turn on those who had employed it for their own ends.

The gratitude of a nation towards the man who had pulled them through their darkest hour had not extended to voting him into the office of Prime Minister in 1945. Winston Churchill was a Conservative and Clement Atlee's Labour Government came to power promising social change and a swifter path through the austerity which was bound to come after the new American President, Harry Truman, ended abruptly the lend-lease agreement they had had with Britain during the war. Harry S. wanted payment up front for any food imports in the future.

Do I accept the mission that's been offered me and go off into the unknown future on what will probably be another ill-thought-through experiment by scientists and politicians, or do I stay where I am, relatively happy and looking forward to a lifetime with a woman I love deeply?

Excitement and adventure, or fireside and slippers?

Which?

6

ONCE I HAD TAKEN THREE days to brief Alice and had sent her on her way I went to see Sonja. I knew where she lunched and found her in her usual corner restaurant. She did not look pleased to see me.

'Hello,' I said. 'Look, I'm sorry I was abrupt the other day.'

Sonja stared at me. 'Who was she?'

I raised my eyebrows. 'How did you know it was a woman when I didn't let you in?'

'I waited for her to leave.'

I could feel the irritation rising in me again.

'I'm sorry – you mean you were spying on me?'

'If you want to call it that. Who was she?'

'You know, she asked me the same question about you, after I sent you away from my door – I told her to mind her own business.'

Sonja said nothing to this, but again stared directly into my eyes, before turning her attention to her lunch.

'Am I missing something here?' I asked quietly. 'Are we friends or has the situation moved on from there? Do I owe you explanations when I meet with people? I wasn't aware that our relationship went any deeper than meeting, talking and sharing trivialities.'

'Listen,' she said, after swallowing a mouthful of vivid green sludge, 'there's something strange about you. You'd better be careful. That woman was strange too. She didn't seem to know what she was doing. She looked lost. I don't know whether you heard, but last night the Morningstars sabotaged another skyplatz – destroyed its gyro and sent it spinning down into the business district. Killed three people.'

The Morningstars were a group of terrorists intent on returning the world back to nature. They had some vain hope of bringing back the forests and fields and providing a world where the birds could sing again – a landscape not of chrome and glass but of ditches, hedges and meadows. It was all pie in the sky of course: an impossible cause that would only result in the destruction of property and the deaths of a few innocent people. These lunatics were willing to die themselves of course, in the their insane quest for green grass.

'Sonja, I am not a Morningstar.'

'Well, you would say that, wouldn't you?'

'Yes, especially when it's true. Look, why don't we take in a show tonight – one with *real* people and hang the expense. We usually enjoy each other's company, don't we? The woman in my apartment this morning was one of my colleagues in Ecuador, that's all. She was bringing me news that my wife wants a divorce. I still think you have no right to ask such questions, but there it is. She is, of course, unused to city life coming as she did directly from the South American rainforest – but she is not strange. Neither am I. No stranger than any other mad eco-scientist.'

This drew a smile from her. 'Oh, all right. I'm sorry, I just felt you were extremely rude. I'm not impolite to other people so I don't like it when someone is offensive to me.'

'Understood. I'm sorry too. I apologise for my jungle manners.'

And that was that. We were back to being friends again. I actually needed Sonja quite badly. She kept me sane in this world of the future which I knew I could never come to like. It was all too brash and gaudy for my taste. It ran on wheels too swift for my taste. Too slick. Too – well, too futuristic. I was beginning to yearn for the simpler, quieter life of my own time. Not only was I beginning to crave for my old life – a beer in a pub, a drive out into the countryside on summer's day, a film on a Friday night, an evening in front of a coal fire reading Agatha Christie or listening to Dick Barton on the wireless – I was also desperate to get back to the love of my life, Joan, that stalwart and cheerful lass who had really only just come into my life and brought with her a whole lorry load of sunshine. Joan Dunn was my future, not this racy world of insentient devices.

Indeed, I sympathised with the aims of the Morningstars, though I found their methods – as I did with all terrorists – abhorrent. Apart from being ineffective, wanton destruction and death does not bring in a better world, nor a juster one. Sonja was a little island in a sea of mayhem by simply being a listener and a source of insignificant chit-chat.

On the news that evening, before I left for the theatre, came a startling revelation. They had at last discovered what the aliens were doing on Earth. It seemed they were castaways. The vehicle or method of travel they had been using when they passed through our solar system suddenly failed them and left them shipwrecked, as it were. They were merely able to travel a short distance to the only habitable planet within reach. Some perished in the descent, in the way meteorites burn up in our atmosphere, but the majority made it to the surface of our small globe.

This would not have been so bad, said the grave newscaster, if one or more of them had been engineers or scientists of some kind. Unfortunately all the survivors to a male, female or android, were the equivalent of accountants or insurance salesmen. There was not one among them with the expertise to build another transport which would take them back to their own world, wherever or whatever that was. They were stranded, lost in themselves, and without any compass for finding a life on Earth which would give them any sort of comfort or happiness.

I was so glad I was not in the same position as the alien Angels. I had been promised a return to my old life. The very words had been, 'Once your mission is over you will find yourself in your own time again.' I was beginning to look forward to that now. I still had some weeks, perhaps months, to go. There were eleven more travellers who needed to pass through my hands, use my safe house, and only then could I look forward to a return to the life and the love I left behind in 1955.

7

WE WENT TO THE SHOW – a glitzy review with songs that grated on my nerves and flashy dances which did nothing for the art of movement – and afterwards had a meal at a small restaurant. There, at a corner table, with only robotic waiters who could not care less what we were saying, Sonja dropped a bombshell.

'James,' she said, staring intently into my eyes, 'do you love me?'

I was taken aback but the suddenness of the question. I tried to make light of it. 'I thought you said love was an inconvenience? Got in the way of life?'

'Don't laugh at me,' she said, fiercely, her eyes shining with the intensity of her manner, 'do you love me, James?'

'Love you? I – I'm very fond of you, Sonja.'

'Yes, but we are in love, really, aren't we? I mean, we don't say it, but I think we both know we are.'

'Sonja…' I paused, knowing I was going to upset her. '…Sonja, I'm in love with someone else. I have been for some time.'

Her face hardened and her eyes narrowed.

'It's her, isn't it? That woman in your apartment.'

'No, definitely not. It's someone else. Someone I went to college with.'

'What's her name?' was snapped back.

'Joan.'

72

'Sounds a very stupid old-fashioned name to me – is she stupid and old-fashioned?'

'Sonja, please. She's not stupid and I like old-fashioned. I'm old-fashioned myself. Now, I think I need to go home. Do you want me to see you back to your apartment? I'll give you a call in the morning, when we've both had time to think. I'm very sorry if I've given you the wrong impression. Forgive me. I'm not very good socially. You must have seen that in me. I probably gave out the wrong signals and I've hurt you.'

She snorted. 'Oh, don't worry about me. I'm fine. I think I've had a lucky escape really. You're quite a boring man, you know. Off you go then. Don't bother to call. I think we've taken things far enough.'

And that was that. I left the restaurant and decided to walk home through the noisy city streets. By the time I reached my apartment I was feeling relieved. All right, I wouldn't have a companion to talk with when I felt lonely, but I had to be fair to Sonja who obviously wanted much more than that – a lover not a friend – and I had been an idiot to expect otherwise. Men and women are forever looking for someone to share their life with them and to expect her to waste her time with me when she could be out dating someone who could fulfil all her needs was wrong of me.

Elburt made me a beverage and I went to bed feeling wretched and confused. It was a long time before I dropped off to sleep and I don't think I was in that state for very long before I felt a hand shaking my shoulder. I sat up abruptly and made some sort of alarmed sound. The lights were on and three large men stood by my bed dressed in uniform.

'Mr Ovit? You must come with us.'

'What…who are you? How did you get in?'

'Police. Get up and get dressed. We need to talk to you.'

'Talk to me? What about?'

'Get up! Now!'

I got up and dressed very quickly. I had a feeling Sonja had something to do with this. The police – one of them I saw now was actually a woman – stood and watched me impassively. Once I was ready they frog-marched me to the elevator and thence we went to the roof where a police vehicle was hovering. None of them spoke to me on the journey across the rooftops of London, until we docked at a large oblong grey building.

'Follow me,' said the policewoman.

I duly followed her. She led me down to a room in which sat an older flabby-looking man with a lugubrious expression on his loosely-fleshed face. There were two chairs, but no other furniture. My fat-headed interrogator nodded to the chair he was facing and I sat in it feeling frowsy and not a little worried.

'Now, James Ovit, isn't it?' he said. 'Tell me what you know about the Morningstars.'

Subtle? Soi? The police hadn't changed much from my own time. 'We know you done it, so you might as well fess up!' This was going to be an interview conducted with bluntness, I could see that, and I could probably get through it without too much use of my intellect. But I had had enough. I had in my armoury a name which I had been told to use if I ever got into deep trouble in the future world of 2055. I felt it was time to use it. Although I had not completed my mission I was thoroughly depressed by it all. I could see no sense in it. What was it all for? So they had planned to send a baker's dozen of us a hundred years into the future – but for heaven's sakes for what? What was the central purpose of the project? Was it simply a Mount Everest? To climb because it was there? Or was there indeed an important goal, a good reason for the exercise?

'I would like you,' I said to my interrogator, 'to contact Sir William Longsbury, if you will.'

The policeman jerked upright. 'Who?'

'Sir William Longsbury.'

I expected him to say that there was no such thing as knights of garter in this enlightened modern age, but he didn't. He frowned, darkly and spluttered, 'Is that your lawyer?'

I went for broke.

'If you do not inform Sir William that I'm in this position, you'll be an extremely sorry man. I take it you enjoy being a policeman?'

'A threat?'

'Not at all. Sir William will explain. Please get him here as soon as possible and you'll find this mess will go away.'

'It isn't a mess.'

'It will be if you don't do as I ask.'

Miraculously the man did it. He went out presumably to find out how to contact Sir William Longsbury, who I had never met. Longsbury was just a word to me: a codeword perhaps, which would produce help? Did the nobility still exist at all? I had no idea whether the name I had been given before I was sent into the future was viable or not. Was there such a man and how did they know he would be alive and well a century after their time? That part of the equation did not make sense to me at all and I was fully expecting my interrogator to return with a sneer on his face to tell me there was no such person in existence.

I was left sitting in the small room with other policemen wandering by and glancing in at me through the transparent walls. No doubt I was an object of curiosity and there were many speculations as to whether I was a terrorist who was trying it on, or whether I was an undercover member of the Secret Service, or whether I was just plain innocent of all and everything, though the latter choice would be the last thing on the minds of policemen hopeful of a wonderful coup.

A very smooth and suave-looking man in his forties entered the room after an hour of me waiting. He had the sleekness of a seal and the eyes of a shark. He extended a hand for me to shake.

'James Ovit, I presume.'

I caught the allusion, even in my mental agitation.

'Is that a joke?'

He nodded. 'An attempt at one. I should have called myself "Stanley" rather than Longsbury, shouldn't I? The latter's an assumed name, anyway. You don't need to know my real one. Well, well,' he looked me up and down, 'our traveller from the past. So, you found you couldn't run the whole course, eh? Never mind, no doubt we've learned a lot from your experience. Now, let's get you out of here and back to your apartment. Expect another visit tomorrow, from some old friends. In the meantime I'll have a chat to Mr Plod and sort things out here.'

I was taken back to my apartment in the same vehicle that brought me, still in a dazed state, wondering what the hell was going to happen next. I knew one thing: I was going to request to be sent back home. They had promised me it was possible and my homesickness had reached desperation level. This was not just another country, another place, it was another time. I was a stranger in a strange century and I was stumbling and bumbling along without any real purpose or destination. I wanted to go home. I was desperate to go home. I *had* to go home. My sickness for home had reached trauma level and I think I was heading for a breakdown.

8

THE NEXT MORNING A TERRIBLE shock walked through the doorway to my apartment. I think I knew as soon as Elburt let them in that I was never ever going to go back to that place and time I thought of as home. The three scientists who had originally interviewed me in 1955, the men responsible for sending me on this mission, entered and sat down before me, taking out their slices. They were dressed in ordinary 2055 clothes and looked very much as if they belong to this century.

Their spokesman, the middle one, lifted his head and peered at me quizzically, before saying, 'Now, James, how are you feeling?'

'I think I'm going mad,' I said, unable to unravel my thoughts. 'I'm certain of it.'

He gave me a fatherly smile. 'Yes, I know, it's all very confusing, isn't it? I'm sorry we had to do it this way, let you believe you were a time traveller, but for the experiment to work it was necessary. You will now undergo some psychological tests. The object is to find out if you have suffered any real trauma in travelling through time. You haven't done that of course, but you *believe* you have, which is much the same thing as far as the mind is concerned. It should be very interesting, very revealing.'

'I still don't understand. I was born at the beginning of the last century. I was raised there, went to war there…everything,' I finished helplessly. 'Oh God, I think I'm drowning.' I began to sob, burying my face in my hands, unable to take in what was happening. A man in white Slinke came from another room in the apartment. He had obviously came in behind the three scientists. He pressed something against my forehead, warm and metallic, injecting me with something. A calmness came over me after that. The same man wiped away the tears from my face with a soft cloth and then nodded at the three wise men who nodded back as he left the room.

'Let me explain what has happened and perhaps you'll feel a lot better,' said the spokesman. 'You were part of an experiment to examine the psychological effects of time travel. Obviously before we send someone hurtling into the future it's best we find out whether the subsequent experience is going to damage the mind in any way. So we ascertained you were willing to take part in the experiment, then we wiped your mind clean of all memory, inserted new memories, those someone might have experienced back in the early years of the 20th Century. You were led to *believe* you were from that time, actually you're a Londoner of this century, born in Tottenham in 2021. Your mother, Polkinghorne, still lives there and is very much looking forward to seeing you again.' He turned his head right then left towards his companions. 'Her stage name is Stevene. Quite a beauty in her younger years. Still is, of course. She's only in her forties now, but she hasn't been on the stage professionally for a long time now, not since her third husband…'

I interrupted. 'I knew that I was not going to travel through time? Before you wiped my mind. You told me what would happen?'

The two silent partners of the spokesman chuckled, while the head man said, 'Yes, of course. It would have been illegal to put you through such an ordeal without you knowing what was going to happen. We have your permission on record.'

'Is – is my name James Ovit?'

'Oh yes.'

'But my mother's name is Polkinghorne.'

A smile. 'Her fourth husband's surname.'

'And what about Joan?' I asked, desperately. 'Is she real?'

More smiles from the wings.

'Oh no. She's one of your figments. One of many.' He gave me a schoolmasterly look. 'You surely guessed that she wasn't real? "*Joan Hunter Dunn, Joan Hunter Dunn, furnished and burnished by Aldershot sun...*" The poem by John Betjeman "A Subaltern's Love Song"?'

'I must have missed that one. What was my degree in?'

He studied his slice before saying, 'Ah yes, Engineering. That would explain it. However, the young lady you've been seeing since you, er, arrived in 2055...'

'Sonja?'

'Yes, that young woman – she's real.'

'Oh good,' I said, without enthusiasm. 'What about Alice? Is she another one who will have to be psychologically assessed?'

'No. She's a member of our team. You're the only one we have actually put through a mind wipe. All the rest were, are – would have been – actors.'

I felt weary. Used and weary. Now it seemed I had to be mentally probed and prodded, put through a mind-grinder. I wondered if I would ever come out sane at the end of it all.

'One of your team.'

'Yes, but the good news is, you're seven years younger than you think you are!'

He seemed pleased with this revelation and expected me to feel the same way. Right at this moment I could not care less how old I was. In fact I felt a hundred.

'So,' I asked, apathetically, 'when do you put me right?'

'Put you right?'

'Yes, when do I get my real memories back? When do you replace these "figments" as you call them?'

All three scientists exchanged knowing looks.

'Ah,' said their spokesman, 'as to that…unfortunately it's not possible to return you to your original mindstate. We have learned — some tragic earlier experiments — that the brain can only be wiped clean once. After that the brain loses its retentivity. If we wipe it again there's no memory skin left to absorb, or I should say, cling to any reinserted memories. You will be left an idiot without a mind. A cabbage.' Something occurred to him at the moment and and turning to his colleagues, he added conversationally, 'Though indeed there is a recent theory — Professor David Travino-Jacklin's — that like several plants the Brassicaceae family and even Crucifers do have the shadow of a vegetable brain.'

'You're telling me,' I said, the bile rising, 'I'm stuck with the mind of a man who lived a century before my time?'

The spokesman sighed and shrugged his shoulders.

'What about sending me back as I am? You do have time travel, don't you?'

Again all three men exchanged knowing looks, then their spokesman said, 'We're getting close. We're getting *very* close.'

9

AFTER THEY LEFT MY SPIRIT felt bleak and empty. There was a big hard lump in my breast that sat there like a rock. The shock I had received had left me with a physical pain that was quite unbearable. I spent the evening and most of the night alternately weeping pathetically and smashing things in a great rage. How could they think this was acceptable? To rob a man of his real memories and replace them with false ones? It was inhumane. The next day I informed them that I absolutely refused to cooperate with their psychological assessments. They would get nothing from me. Even were they to try to force me to undergo tests I would resist with all my will power. You can't *make* a man tell you his true feelings.

A week after the ordeal I paid a visit to my biological mother, the serial monogamist having four husbands behind her already.

'Did you know your middle name is Winston?' she told me. 'I called you that to remind me who your father was – these things are easily forgotten, you know.'

I hadn't known. I had no idea I had a middle name.

'But there's my surname?'

'I married two Ovits,' she countered, smiling.

Despite my disapproval of her lifestyle, I liked the woman. She was a stranger to me, naturally, the mythical, fictitious mother being paramount in my memories, but she seemed a nice, sympathetic, mature, effervescent woman. And I could see why men with power and money found her vivacious and attractive.

She told me she was relatively rich and moved in the higher circles of society. Each time she had married she had moved up the social scale a few notches. She told me if I wanted money I had only to ask: she was happy to supply me with my needs.

'Also,' she said, brightly, 'have you considered a career in the diplomatic service? You were a meteorologist before they sent you away, but you never seemed to enjoy the work. I'm not surprised. Controlling the weather might be fun at first, but people always want the same thing, don't they? Rain at night, sun during the day and snow on Christmas morning. It must be very boring, especially since there is no longer the same threat of global warming that they had in the last century

'Now, being a diplomat is easy work and there's lots of good things about it – banquets, balls, visits to foreign places – and all you have to do is talk to people. You can do that, I'm sure.'

'Don't you need a brilliant education and contacts for that kind of work?'

'Oh, you went to a very good school and I've got all the contacts in the world.'

'I'll think about it. Thank you, Mother.'

The last word was hard for me, but as I say, she was a nice person and it wasn't her fault I didn't recognise her for who she actually was.

Over the next few weeks I tried to get my head in order. One of my mistakes was to contact Sonja and begin an affaire. It could never have worked. I was too abstracted, my mind buried in a lost world. We parted amicably a month or two later, remaining friends. I had a few of those from my previous life of course, but since I recognised none of them it was difficult to meet them on the same ground. They knew me and expected me to know them. But they were indeed strangers and if I were to take up with them again I would have to do so on that basis. It seemed that most of them, if not all, were irritated by my lack of warmth.

The government did indeed try to get me to a debriefing session, but I told them they could punish me in any way they thought fit, I was not going to undergo any examination and they could go to Hell. They backed off, but I think they're simply letting me have a cooling off period and will probably come to me again in the future.

Things didn't personally get any better for me. My head was stained with anguish and I knew I would go mad if I didn't get help of some kind. I was securely trapped. Forever a captive in an world that was completely foreign to me. Locked in a prison cell to which not only was there no key, but there was no keyhole to put one in. The anguish of being helplessly and agonisingly wrenched from a familiar world and abandoned in another was brutal and spiritually crippling.

TODAY I JOINED A THERAPY group for those who are sure they belong in the past. I sat down with patients whose minds have been warped by stress or some genetic weakness who sincerely believe they are from a time gone by. Their torment at coping with life in 2055 is similar to my own. Like me they pine for a time and place that is beyond reach. We are a wretched, helpless set of individuals and our only comfort is to share our distress in the hope that it will give us some relief from what feels like a constant, unabating physical pain. I was disappointed to find that with me it failed to work. So too, I think, for another individual trapped in a world far, far from its homeland. One of the aliens, an Angel, sat opposite me and the desolation and misery in its expression was harrowing to witness.

Garry Kilworth

Part Two:

RING A RING O' ROSES

1

IN THE END, I DID get to travel through time, but I wasn't *sent* to the future. It was the other way around. I was snatched from the past. It turned out that my mother's latest husband, number four you will remember, was an eminent scientist. His specialisation was energy compression. He could cram enough power into one energy brick to last a nation a whole year. Unfortunately he wasn't taken seriously in the 21st Century and his theories were ignored. He was a man before his time. This was partly due to jealous rivals pooh-poohing his ideas and partly due to the fact that his brain was larger than most men alive and there was no one who really understood his equations. He tried, of course, to explain them, but being an egghead he did not have the tools to communicate with minds simpler than his own and his ideas went to waste.

Went to waste, that is, until future scientists found his notes and being that much more advanced than the dodos of the 21st Century, they recognised in his scribblings the enormous potential for the transportation of energy. The notes were not complete enough for even future readers to make sense of the theory, so they decided to bring forth the professor himself. A time travel device had indeed been invented by that millennium and though used very sparingly it was possible to send people back in time, or fetch them forward. They reached back into the past and grabbed Professor Polkinghorne, whipping him into their era to assist them with their problems. Only trouble was, he refused to help them unless he could be with his wife, my mother of course, and he added that her son James would have to accompany her or she would create an almighty fuss and reject the marriage bed.

Thus it was I was in bed one morning moodily playing footsy with a sleeping woman I'd met two weeks before and the next moment standing completely naked before a group of time machine operators, some of whom stared and smirked, and some of whom looked pointedly away. One of them was a woman who would become my lover in a very short while. She, incidentally, was not one of those who had shown good manners, but member of the smirkers' group.

So, here I was, in the far distant future, along with my mother and her number four, whom she divorced fairly quickly to marry a man of the new millennium. I did warn the fresh one that he probably wouldn't last very long, but either he had an ego the size of Jupiter or he didn't mind being short term because he took absolutely no notice of me. I don't know what it is about my dear mother, but older men seem to lose all sense and sensibility when it comes to having her exclusively. To give her her due, she was never unfaithful to the man she was betrothed to at the time.

My mother Silvia's new husband was a powerful politician with high connections and I was able to gather up my metaphorical pick and shovel, and continue with my old grind in a future diplomatic service which hadn't advanced an inch since 2056, silky talk being still silky talk, and smooth manners and false smiles the continued tools of the persuasion and arm-twisting trade. However, one positive side-effect of the time-jump was that it caused my false implanted memories to fade into thin, misty dreams and the real memories of childhood and early manhood were reawakened and came to the fore once again.

2

'YOUR ORDERS HAVE COME THROUGH, James. You're being sent to the planet Sylvanus, one of the more important posts. Rather appropriate given your mother's name."

My boss, Per Erik Johansson, seemed pleased for me. I had of course heard of Sylvanus. It was the only world which produced LC3, a source of energy on which the world into which I had been thrust relied totally. Without it, Earth would be switched off. Yes, we still had solar, wind and wave power, but not nearly enough for our needs. Other sources had long since been abandoned: fossil fuels and nuclear energy. Indeed, Sylvanus was an important post, but it was also a dangerous place. LC3 radiated corrosive rays and spending too long on such a planet might possibly result in cancer. It was not a post that was sought after by established staff, though for someone like me, young and inexperienced and looking at his first overspace posting in the diplomatic service, it could be regarded as a brilliant coup.

'Am I to be the Governor's assistant?' I asked, my mind running over the list of governors of outworlds, wondering who I'd be working for. 'What's the duty?'

Per Erik smiled. 'Keep up, James. Sylvanus declared independence two months ago. You're to be the new ambassador. You'll need to set up the whole shebang. You take most of your staff with you of course and, well, there you have it. An *ambassador* at twenty-seven years of age? Your mother will be proud, eh? By the way,' Per Erik coughed into his fist, 'give her my fondest regards when you see her, eh?'

Per Erik too? My mother was insatiable.

Earth's Ambassador to Sylvanus? My heart started beating fast. It really *was* a coup. Such an important planet surely needed someone with vast experience? Why me, brand new to the rank? It was hard to take in. Still, I composed myself, they must have their reasons. I only hoped it was not because of who I knew, rather than for what I knew. (Damn, who was I kidding? Of course the influence of friends and – ah – relatives had to come into it somewhere.) Should I turn it down because I did not believe myself worthy? Anyone who thought I might do that did not know me. I was puffed up with my own importance, confident, ambitious. In more common parlance, I was full of myself. There was no way I was going to turn the post down because of my slight misgivings as to experience. I was a capable man. I learned quickly. I would soon overcome any difficulties that might come along.

Sylvanus is what we call an Earthworld. It's very similar in many ways to the planet of my birth. Round about the same distance from its twin suns, a breathable atmosphere, a twenty-five-and-a-half hour day and therefore years marginally longer. However, all in all, not far off a copy of good old Gaea. It seemed though, when I looked it up, that life, evolution, had taken a slightly different turn on Sylvanus. No fish had crawled out of the ocean to become reptiles, birds or mammals. There are no fish, no reptiles, birds or mammals. Only insect-like seeds, which seem to have developed from the complex plant life.

I imagine that in the early history of a newly-cooled Sylvanus seeds detached themselves from primitive plants and floated off to fertilize barren soils. They then gradually developed more complex kite structures which enabled them to travel further and further. Finally they started using flat projections, much like those on the seeds of our own sycamore trees, as wings to carry them over landscapes and seas. These seeds transmuted over millions of years to became many varieties of vegetable-based insects, very like an animal-based insect, but definitely flora not fauna.

Thus, Sylvanus became a vegetable world. (The media have dubbed it BC – the Big Cabbage, a term I dislike intensely.) There are thick lush rainforests, dense jungles, sweeping grasslands and oceans clogged with underwater plants. Sylvanus is a tangle of vines and trees. A garden gone mad.

I couldn't wait to tell my mother of my good fortune, though I was pretty sure she would already know. Indeed, she would no doubt make a good pretence at being surprised and ecstatic. The latter emotion would probably be real, since she would be getting rid of her critical son for a longish period. My mother was an outrageous woman who was still having marriages and affaires at the age of seventy-six, with men half her age. Surgery had allowed her to keep a semblance of her earlier good looks and once upon a time I had hopes that she would settle down with one partner. After my father had divorced her he had then managed to get himself killed filming wildlife. My mother then had swept from one husband or lover to another. I believe she was trying to punish my father for leaving her: a useless exercise once he had been eaten. It became a lifetime habit and I think she would be glad that her son was not around to lecture her on her behaviour.

I would also gain by not being around to witness her inappropriate conduct. My new posting would suit us both. I determined to call her with the news as soon as I left Per Erik's office in the Shanghai Spire building.

Out in the street, crammed with shoppers, business people and those on their way to oblivion in the side alleys, I made that call on my mobile dansefloor, hoping that my mother had her device powered up. Like many older people she took time to get used to new methods of communicating.

'Ah, James – I'm with someone at the moment. What is it?'

Surprise me, I thought, but I actually said, 'Oh, sorry, Mother – look, I've got my first posting. Sylvanus. And listen to this. I'm to be their first Ambassador from Earth. What do you think?'

There was a rustling sound in the background which raised images I didn't want in my head. Then the dansefloor revealed the sharpish features of my only parent. She was indeed in the act of tying the sash of a black silk robe covered in pink dragons. Then followed a silence which seemed to last a long time, but was probably only a minute or two. Finally my mother spoke and the worry in her tone surprised me. Perhaps I was wrong about her influencing people to get me the post?

'James, isn't that the place where all those people died?'

'What do you mean? When?'

'When they first colonised it. All the people who went there caught some horrible disease and died, didn't they?'

I nodded at the dansefloor. 'Yes, they contracted a particularly virulent form of cancer – one we had no cure for at the time – before the discovery of LC3, the cause of the disease. Their children are still alive. It's believed this second generation developed an immunity to the rays in the womb. Ten thousand original colonists went and they left behind them around eighteen thousand children, who are now all healthy adults. In fact they're more than grown up, more than healthy, since they're several hundred years of age and have never suffered a day of illness, any of them. They're not only immune to the cancer, they seem to have discovered the secret of ever-lasting life without resorting to an elixir. They believe themselves immortal.'

'The parents all died before their time and the children live on forever,' she said, wistfully, 'that doesn't sound very fair, does it? Do we know how they manage it?'

I tried not to guess what would be my mother's reason for wanting to live forever. To continue to have these endless empty affaires that seemed to give her no real spiritual satisfaction? I could not fathom my dear parent. She would ever be a mystery to me. I knew her to be intelligent and wise, yet here she was living this shallow existence. However, I had long since ceased to question her, which was always regarded as criticism from me, and though I did mention from time to time that I thought she needed a hobby, I knew I couldn't change her lifestyle. That had to come from herself, when and if ever she was sated with leaping in and out of countless men's beds.

'No one yet knows why they've lived so long, Mother.'

'Others have died too, though, haven't they?'

I had to admit that some visitors to the planet had ended up with the particular kind of cancer that LC3 generates. Those cancers previously suffered by Earthians had been conquered, but certain new strains, from new worlds, were still to be overcome.

'I shall take all the proper precautions, you can be sure of that. No one's contracted the disease recently. You know me. I blub if I cut my finger. I'm very keen on survival, Mother,' I joked. 'Perhaps I'll find the elixir they have hidden away and we can both live forever? Though you probably won't want me around raining on your parade, so if that happens I'll have to get another posting to the far side of the universe so that you can enjoy yourself without my disapproving face around.'

She ignored the banter. 'You will be careful, won't you, James? I know I'm not a great parent, but I do love you.'

'I know you do. Look, I don't have to leave for a few days. How about dinner one night?'

'I would love to, darling – but I'm on Mars and don't get back until next Thursday.'

'Ah. I'll be gone by then. Well, I'll call you from Sylvanus.'

'Yes, do that sweetheart, and congratulations of course. Ambassador! Your father, whatsisname, I've forgotten, would have been extremely proud of you. I know I am. You're quite young for such an exalted post and that makes me a very proud mama. Now, remember what I say, do look after yourself, won't you?'

'I will.'

A man's voice in the room behind her called out, 'I've found my shoes, now what the hell did we do with my socks? Oh, sorry, you're on the…'

Silvia cut the connection before the end of the sentence, but not before I had caught a glimpse of a clergyman's collar.

3

NOT LONG AFTER MY MOTHER and I arrived in this time I met Jocinda Perez.

'Scottish,' she told me at a party, 'can't you tell by the accent?'

'Yes, I know, but what side?'

'The posh side,' she said, smiling. 'East coast.'

An Edinburgh lass. Apparently the Perezs were an old Scottish family from back in the 23rd Century. We got on well together, both being keen on yachting (my interest having been miraculously formed a few minutes after she had told me of hers). Her father owned three yachts – a sailing catamaran, a motor yacht and a sailing yacht – which she had, all three, taken out on her own at various times. There was little danger in that, even for a novice, since every boat on every ocean was tracked by computer and there were numerous safe-haven floating harbours around the wet parts of the globe in the event of a storm.

'You're very lucky,' I told her. 'I've hardly had a chance to – to indulge my own passion for the sea.'

'You must come out with me sometime.'

'I'd like that.'

We talked about our parents next. Hers were fabulously wealthy. My mother was not poor, of course, but nothing to match the Perez clan. My dead father, Winston Ovit, I knew very little about. I probably did before my mind was wiped by the state, but now I have no memory of him whatsoever. I did meet him once, by accident in a cafe in London in the June of 2058. I didn't recognise him of course, but he made himself known to me. He seemed a pleasant, ineffectual man, but I had felt no emotional filial ties to him and never took up his offer to contact him again. Not that it mattered to me, but it might to Jocinda, coming from a family like hers, but I don't think Winston Ovit was either well off or very far up the social ladder of his time.

'My dear sweet mother's fine,' I said, inwardly wincing at the thought of her string of male friends, 'but my father was killed by a wild animal.'

'Oh, I'm sorry, where did that happen?'

It sounded rather lame to just say "Africa" and this woman had no idea I was from the past, so I lied with, 'Bakersworld, one of the newer planets.'

Her eyes opened wide. They were marvellously brown.

'They make bread there?'

I laughed. 'No, no, the planet was discovered by someone called Baker – you know.'

She did know. There were many worlds like it. Smithworld, Abdulworld, Mitsuworld. You find a planet, you name it after yourself, and by the third generation of colonials they've forgotten you. The name stays, but the man or woman who was behind the discovery is consigned to a chip in Istanbul's 'Hall of Offworld Records'(the acronym is pronounced as *whore*) that mighty digital store of names and other mundane bureaucratic information.

'How did your father die?'

'Torn to shreds by a lion – um, an *alien* lion, that is. I've seen a picture of one. Cat-like creature, quite beautiful in its way. As for my father, there were only a few bloody ribbons of flesh left hanging on the lower limbs of a tree he tried to climb to get out of reach.'

'Oh. Did you manage to get to the funeral?'

'I could have got there, but they said there was very little to cremate, just the few scarlet ribbons, so it wasn't much of a funeral. More of a memorial service, really. The lion ate the rest of him, lock, stock and liver. I didn't know him that well, anyway. He left my mother when I was five and showed no interest in seeing me again.'

'That's sad.' She stroked my cheek with the back of her hand and a tingling went through my whole body. I began to wish I had several fathers who'd rejected me as a child and had then been eaten by wild beasts.

Jocey and I did not go to bed straight away. We had several dates – the theatre, the opera, the cineplatz – and then one night, after a very romantic meal at *Chez Frasier's* on the Isle of Capri, we found ourselves in the sack together. Later I met her dad and he invited me to join the family on their yacht.

It was a disaster. I had taken several poems with me – not mine, but others written by professionals long since gone to dust – and intended to read them to her while we rocked gently on the ocean under a full moon. This did not happen. I was seasick the whole time, hanging over the rail thing, whatever it's called on a boat (the fact that I didn't know what to call parts of the craft weighed heavily with her when she came to decide whether to continue the relationship) and depositing the meal she had cooked for us in the water. Colourful and unusual fish came to investigate the contents of my stomach, a fact which I later pointed out to her, but this did nothing to sway me back into favour.

'It wasn't even stormy,' she blazed. 'There was hardly a ripple on the surface.'

I tried to get away with saying I had been unwell *before* the voyage, but she was having none of it.

'You weren't too sick to wolf down the stir fry I cooked for you – I've never seen such a disgusting display of manners.'

Now that I was *persona non gratis* of course, everything I did, had done, had said, was offensive to her. She no longer found my quips funny, decided that a little joke I had played on her about not being able to swim when I could actually cut through the pool like a fish, had been intended to demean her, humiliate her, and generally make her look like a silly fool. I was a liar and a fraud, and she wanted nothing more to do with me. Thus my first love, my only love until I was sent to Sylvanus, trotted off down the street, the steam coming out of every orifice. That's how I wanted to imagine her, anyway, the image making me laugh rather than cry, which is actually what I did when I went home.

4

MY RISE THROUGH THE DIPLOMATIC corp has been particularly exceptional. In fact, I am probably the youngest ever ambassador to head an offworld embassy. Why was I so successful? Firstly I was good at my job, secondly, my mother had been with more than one or two of the senior men in the service and strangely enough they all thought the world of her and honoured the promises given during pillow talk. It secretly irked me to know that I owed my meteoric rise in part to the sexual exploits of my dear parent, but I wasn't going to say no when they offered me plum posts and rapid promotion.

I was back in Per Erik's office, getting the low-down on my staff.

'Who's my second in command?' I asked.

'Your chargé is an experienced man who's served at four different missions – a man named Randolph Ng. Have you met him?'

'Not that I recall.'

'Well, you will, this evening at the opera. I've got several tickets for tonight. It's Verdi by the way. He's a little older than you, I hope you can handle that. Ten years your senior.'

I nodded. 'So long as he can.'

'Randolph is very flexible, I assure you. Anyway, your second – your Minister – is Charlotte Umboko. You've met Charlotte, I'm sure?'

'Yes, we served together on one of Juno's moons.'

I liked Charlie. She was a no-nonsense person, ambitious, but not thoroughly ruthless like some of the diplomats I had come across. She would never stab you in your back to get promotion. In your chest, yes, but she'd let you know it was coming before the knife plunged into you. She was confident and assured. The ones to beware of were the under-confident members of staff, whose irresolution often led them into making insidious attacks behind your back in the hope that it would get them noticed by someone above as equally insecure. I had met a few of those in my time and I was pleased Charlie was not one of them.

'And of course you'll have the usual staff below, to take care of such things as security, communications, etcetera. You'll be employing local staff for the mundane things like cooking, cleaning, making beds – all the day to day routine stuff that actually you don't need to know about, so why am I telling you? Ha, ha. Did your mother mention me at all? When you passed on my regards?'

I gritted my teeth, but not so that Per Erik would notice.

'Yes, she returned your regards with pleasure.'

'Ah, good. Always liked Silvia. A fine, elegant lady with such impeccable taste in…in…clothes.' I swear for a moment I thought he was going say 'men'. 'Now, James, I'll meet you at the Sydney opera house at 8 pm. Is that all right for you?'

'Yes, I'll see you there.'

I went home and later in the day changed into black tie, black shoes, black socks, trousers and dinner jacket, before going into a teleport office and sending myself halfway around the globe to dine on my own in that great Australian city. I had got used to eating alone. I spent the time observing the other diners, wondering about their lives, their relationships, and whether they were happy or not. Given the restaurants I frequented they would without doubt have money, but health and happiness needed to be gauged by studying them with their partners. I never bothered wondering about loners like myself. We were a sad lot and though I was not *unhappy*, I was not ecstatically wildly joyful either. I was comfortable with myself and my life and indeed, there were changes to look forward to. Travel is a wonderful balm to loneliness. One imagines that a new relationship is just around the next exotic corner of the universe.

Per Erik was holding forth in the opera house bar that was reserved for 'Fellows and Members of World Culture'. Charlie was there and waved to me as I entered, a big smile on her pretty broad face. Standing next to her, drink in hand, right elbow on the bar, right foot on the brass foot rail, was a thin man with bushy red hair. He stared at me in a not unpleasant way as I crossed the room, but there was no vivacity in that look, merely a studied enquiry. He was measuring me up, as subordinates almost always do when they first meet their boss, wondering if I were going to be trouble or whether he could handle me.

I shook Per Erik's hand, then kissed Charlie on the cheek, as she whispered fiercely, 'I always knew you'd make ambassador.'

'Oh,' I said, in a normal voice, 'you've met my mother, have you?'

She kicked me playfully on the calf.

Per Erik chose not to notice to this exchange, but instead opened his palm in the direction of the other man and said, 'James, I'd like you to meet your *Chargé d'Affaires*, Randolph Ng.' The Ng stuck in Per Erik's throat, as it does in the throats of most English speakers. Randolph did not look particularly Chinese, but like my own, his ancestry obviously held a grandfather whose origins were Asian. The world population was such a mixture, a great blend of races, it was doubtful if any nation could claim to be original to the country of their residency. Even the tribes of the Amazon forests, the trees long gone and replaced by appliances which divided the separate elements of seawater, had long since been swallowed up by the rest of the human race.

'How do you do, Your Excellency?' he said.

I took his thin hand in mine and answered, 'Oh please, we're an informal party this evening. Just call me Mr Ambassador.'

I saw a hardness enter his eyes and I realised my flippancy had not gone down well.

I said, 'Sorry, that was meant to be a joke. What are those things on your face, by the way?'

'These?' he pushed the device up on the bridge of his nose with his right forefinger. 'These are spectacles. Sometimes called *glasses*, though I can see how that can be confusing in a bar.'

I knew what they were, of course, from my false memories of an artificial childhood, but I wanted to test his tolerance with my impertinence. 'Ah. And what do they do?'

'They correct my vision. I have a genetic disorder – my eyes are imperfect.'

'Why not get them corrected surgically?'

'I prefer to wear spectacles.' His features were expressionless as he continued with, 'I expect you see that as pretentious, Mr Ambassador?'

'James. Really, James. No, not at all. I would be hypocritical if I did. I still listen to my music through earphones and often I can be seen wearing a fedora hat in the park on Sundays.'

Now he glared. 'Are you making fun of me, sir?'

'I'm making fun of myself, number two. Please, don't let's get off on the wrong foot. Charlie will tell you I'm not someone who gets his kicks humiliating his staff. When I'm off duty, I'm a bit of a schoolboy. On duty, I become what I'm supposed to be, a diligent and industrious diplomat, skilful at handling the locals and firm but fair with my subordinates. Here, we are enjoying ourselves, a few drinks and a night at the opera, and I hope you and I will have a good working relationship.' I did not add that as sure as hell we would not have a relationship outside of work, since I knew we were as different as rats were to birds. I'm not sure which one of us was the rat and which the bird, but it didn't really matter.

'I'm sure you two will hit it off like a house on fire,' interrupted Per Erik, 'won't they Charlie? Now, what will you have, James? Malt whisky? My shout...'

The rest of the evening didn't go too badly, considering the start I'd made with my new Chargé. Charlie was a bubbly as ever, hiding that keen intellect and sharp intuition that would eventually get her the ambassadorial post she craved. I could almost see the moving parts of her brain analysing the situation between the three of us and working out how to use it to her best advantage. I had no illusions about Charlie, but fortunately she and I were made of the same clay and though we might scheme and plan our way up the next rung, we never compromised honour or integrity. I wondered about our new recruit, but determined to give him the benefit of the doubt, until he proved otherwise.

5

TELEPORTING TO A DISTANT WORLD is not a lot of fun. Not for people like me who get scatter-sick. We didn't go directly of course. We did it in manageable hops. But still, my atoms do not like being streamed and they make a fuss when they're all crammed back together again in their ordered places. Once we reached Sylvanus I went to bed for two days to recover. The journey didn't seem to have affected my two subordinates, who immediately got stuck into the work. Charlie visited me twice, I suspect just to make sure I wasn't on my deathbed. She always had that one eye on the next rung up the ladder and was not sentimental, even when it came to people she knew well. She wouldn't kill anyone to get there, but natural causes were regarded as serendipity.

Once I was on my feet I went to see the President of Sylvanus, a man who was boss not of a country, but of a whole planet.

Olaf Jung had been elected on the day Sylvanus declared independence from Earth. To date the mother planet has colonised some 240 outworlds and at the time of writing this 207 had declared independence. Some were so far away they were not worth us Earthians bothering about: deep, deep in the blackness of the universe. Others, like Sylvanus, are close enough to still have strong ties to the mother world. Sylvanus has no manufacturing and everything on this world has **Made on Earth** stamped on it somewhere. Earth had a special relationship with

Sylvanus, which is rich in a mineral unique to the that planet. LC3, from which sheaves of energy rods can be fashioned, were sent only to Earth. Goods, luxury and otherwise, were transported to Sylvanus in return. We had gone back to the old barter system of yore, the Sylvanians having no need of money, only of devices, machines and other commodities.

One thing Sylvanians did not require was food. They could feed themselves from their abundant crops. There is no indigenous large animal life on the planet – no fish, mammals, birds or reptiles – plenty of insects, many of them a lot bigger than the insects we're used to, but more on that later – and the inhabitants had all been raised vegans. I was going to miss my bacon sandwiches, that's certain. There were no special arrangements for embassy staff. We had to live like the locals or starve. All this I knew from my research, but now I was going to have a talk with the person in charge of the planet and learn from him.

'Ambassador!' he exclaimed, rising from his seat behind an enormous desk and extending a hand. 'This is an historic occasion.'

'Mr President. It's very good to meet you.'

It was like shaking hands with a lump of bread dough.

He was a smooth-faced corpulent man (you can't call presidents 'fat' – at least not in print) with a silky-looking skin. In most ways President Jung resembled an Earthian, but there were subtle differences. I have said above he was 'smooth-faced' rather than 'clean-shaven'. That's because Sylvanians did not grow hair anywhere on their bodies. Transmutation. They had, over the past 400-odd years, adapted to their environment in various ways. Why hair was deemed unnecessary by the conditions on their world, I have no idea, but they were all bald and hairless. No eyebrows, no eyelashes, no pubic hair, nothing. It made him look kind of washed out and limp.

'So,' he said, as I took the imported chair opposite him, 'you're our first ambassador?' He was studying me carefully through red-rimmed eyes.

'You think I'm too young,' I said, smiling. 'I hope you don't think I'm going to be a pushover if there are any disagreements?'

He laughed. 'You do look young, but then I'm nearly 500 years of age, so everyone from your world is young to me. I shouldn't think we'll have many disagreements, Mr Ambassador. The arrangements we have with Earth are perfectly satisfactory. You get what you want and we get what we want. We're not an avaricious people. We're happy with our lot. You know why the planet is called Sylvanus, of course? Heaven. It's a perfect world. The Garden of Eden, found.'

'And immortality.'

'We believe so. No one has died a natural death yet. We had several fatal accidents in the early years – from killer plants and trees, poisonous fungi spores, acid sap, that sort of thing – but after that we were very careful. The whole population lives in this beautiful city, inside this protective sti-glass dome, and very little danger presents itself. Machines do the mining. Robots service them. We have devices for everything we need to do or have done, thanks to the mother world. Yes, we believe we will live forever, boring as that may sound. Actually, we're not bored. We love life and hope it will never end.'

'I should envy you,' I replied, 'but I don't. I'm not sure why. I'll probably learn that while I'm here.' I paused for a moment, before continuing. 'I've always been fascinated by the colonisation of outworlds. Especially that of Sylvanus. Your parents, the first colonials all died of some kind of cancer, is that right?'

'Correct. No one at the time knew about the effects of LC3 ore, the fact that it radiated energy harmful to humans. Within thirty years, all the original colonials had passed away. Only the children remained alive and well, apparently immune to the radiation. And here we are, still as healthy as we were as infants. None of us suffer illness, not even what you would call "a cold". Consequently we have no need of doctors – though you were wise to bring one of your own with you.'

'You're a very lucky people.'

'We are indeed.' He laced his fingers together on the top of his desk and I sensed by the tone of his reply that he was about to become more serious. 'Now,' he continued, 'I'd like your opinion on the business of Lars Peterson, in your capacity as the Ambassador, of course. Sylvanians are very unhappy about it, but I'm sure you can give me a reasonable explanation for the conduct of your government which I can pass on to the people of this planet.'

I stared at his round face, utterly mystified.

'This business of Lars Peterson?' I repeated. 'What business? Who is Lars Peterson?'

Now it was his turn to stare at me.

'You surely must be joking?' he said, finally.

I shook my head. 'I have never heard of a Lars Peterson.'

The fingers unlaced themselves, then laced again.

'Well, I know the dissection was carried out in some secrecy, but I would have thought they would bring their first Ambassador to our planet in the loop. Extraordinary. Sometimes the behaviour of your officials leaves us here on Sylvanus baffled, but then we're a very naive people, I have to admit.'

I felt an anger growing within me, against my government.

'I'm sorry to be so stupid,' I said. 'I can assure you it's no fault of mine that I haven't been briefed. Could you explain?'

'Certainly. Several years ago we banished a citizen of this planet to one of the outer moons. Over the centuries he has been a huge nuisance to us and we've put up with his antics, but more recently his behaviour entered the criminal. Peterson was subject to uncontrollable rages and while he never killed anyone, he injured several citizens and caused a lot of damage when he went on the rampage.'

I interrupted. 'Did you not try medicine? Calming drugs?'

He spread his hands now. 'They made no difference. They didn't even slow him down. We have no prisons here, as you well know. Finally, everyone had had enough of him and we decided to put him out of harm's way. A station was built on Iago, our nearest moon, with a supply of air and water, and food was teleported to Peterson regularly. However, quite unknown to us he walked out of his safe environment one day and suffocated through lack of air. Iago is deadly cold and his body froze solid within a very short time. The reason why he decided on suicide has gone with him to the grave. He left no note.'

Now it was coming back to me. I did remember hearing about a man who had created a problem on Sylvanus. I also vaguely recalled something about the banishment.

Olaf Jung was peering at me. 'So you do know?'

I was flustered for a moment. 'Oh, I was just remembering about something I heard on one of our news programmes, but still the name means nothing to me. So, what's your problem with my government? What have we done?'

'Peterson's frozen remains were taken from Iago and teleported to Earth. I have no idea how it was done, but by the time we found that the body had been stolen, it was too late. We know from informants that Peterson was dissected in an Earth laboratory. I suspect they were looking for the secret of our longevity. I know it's always been a source of envy to you people who live, at the most, a 150 years.'

Informants. That would be otherworlders looking to find ways of wresting the rights to LC3 from the mother planet. Our colonies and those planets which had become independent were ever anxious to get their hands on the energy rods that supplied

Earth with its light and power. Sylvanians never left their home planet, but that did not apply to populations of most other worlds.

'Well, as I said, I know nothing about any dissection, or how we managed to get the corpse from one of your moons. I promise you I will investigate though.'

Inside, I was blazing with rage. What the hell were my bosses thinking, sending me here without being briefed on such a sensitive matter.

'I can well imagine why you're upset, Mr President,' I continued. 'The remains of a citizen of your planet are your – er, the property of your people. Did this Peterson have any siblings?'

'No, he was an only child, but that's not the point, as you yourself imply. Lars Peterson, for all his terrible faults, was one of us and we very much resent the fact that he has been treated like a lump of meat, without recourse to permission from any national of Sylvanus. It's true it happened before independence, and there was a governor in charge of the planet at the time. No doubt Governor Wallace knew of the facts and I suppose he believed that since we were still a colony, it was the right of his government to act without consultation. However, we are still hurt and bewildered by the arrogance behind the incident and would like a full explanation as to the reasons for it.'

6

I RETURNED TO THE EMBASSY feeling chagrined and very unsettled. I could not understand the situation. Olaf Jung was right. It was sheer arrogance. I wondered if Randolph or Charlie knew anything about the business and went to find Randolph in his office. He didn't hear me enter the room and I went up behind him as he was peering intently at a ziMage on the dansefloor of his desk. The coloured shapes were reflected in those stupid spectacles he insisted on wearing.

'I didn't know you were interested in horticulture?' I said.

He almost jumped out of his skin and gestured the ziMage of plants from the dansefloor. It vanished instantly.

'Oh, you know – I was thinking of introducing some vegetation from our own world to Sylvanus.'

'You know, they have enough of their own. There are jungles out there. And they're dead set against any plant that's not endemic to Sylvanus. They want no foreign flora on their world. What makes you think they'd welcome bamboo? That was bamboo you were looking at, wasn't it? It's a very invasive plant and would be most unwelcome, even if they allowed you to import it, which they won't.'

Randolph (who had specifically asked me *not* to call him Randy on an earlier occasion) seemed flustered.

'It was nothing serious. I was just filling in time.'

'Well, perhaps you can fill me in with something else. Do you know of a man, a citizen of this planet, called Lars Peterson?'

He looked at me with narrowed eyes for a moment, before replying. 'Yes, the body found on the moon, Iago.'

'Do you know why I wasn't informed that we had stolen the corpse and dissected it on Earth?'

A smile played about the corner of his mouth for an instant, before he said, 'Weren't you? Oh, I expect it was an oversight. I'm sure you should have been briefed. Maybe one of the civil servants screwed up. You know what a hopeless lot they are. By the way, sir, *stolen* is a bit strong. We were entitled to take Peterson's remains, if we so wished. He had been banished, abandoned by the people here. They wanted no more to do with him and once he had been exiled to Iago, he was no longer a citizen of Sylvanus.'

'Just because a man is put in prison, doesn't take away his right to citizenship.'

'With all due respect, sir, his was not a prison. He had been deported, condemned for life. He belonged to no world. He was, if you like, an outlaw. His people had cast him out for good.'

I let this go. 'And how did we get him?'

'I have no idea, sir.'

'What were we looking for in the dissection?'

Randolph shrugged. 'Again, I'm not privy to that information. Perhaps you'd better ask Mr Johannson, the next time you call him?'

'Shit!' I barked, pleased to notice that I had startled my Chargé out of his complacency. 'What the fuck is going on here?' I quietened my tone. 'Our job here is to keep the Sylvanians sweet. I am Earth's ambassador to this world, and therefore a government representative, but you and I know my most important job is to preserve the agreement between Sylvanus and Earthlight Incorporated, the company that provides our home planet with power. If there's any breakdown in that agreement it would be devastating for the inhabitants of Earth and a death knell for us – you, me, Charlie, and the rest of the staff, personally.'

Randolph had gone pale at my outburst.

'Of course I understand that,' he said. 'We must work constantly to keep the status quo.'

'How can I do that if secrets are kept from me?'

'I don't know. It's not my fault. Talk to Johannson, sir.'

Charlie entered the room before I had fully calmed down.

'What's going on?' she asked, looking from one of us to the other. 'Is there a crisis?'

'Yes,' I fumed. 'I've been kept in a state of ignorance.'

I explained all that had happened in the last few hours and Charlie went immediately to my infopac, producing a word ziMage on my dansefloor. It was encrypted, and had never been decrypted into plain language by the state of the code. I decrypted it now and it indeed revealed the information I was missing, though still there was no explanation of how the body was taken from Iago. Nor did it say what the scientists were looking for in the remains of Peterson, or if they found what they were looking for.

'I'm certain,' I said, 'that package was not in my infopac when I left Earth. I opened all packages and studied them at length. That one was not among them.'

'You probably just missed it,' offered Charlie.

'I can't see how I did.'

'Well,' Randolph replied, 'there were an awful lot of packages, sir. I know I was up nights catching up with them. It's possible this one just slipped by you. It's happened to me before now and I'm a very industrious worker, I can assure you. It could happen to anyone, even someone as assiduous as yourself.'

I wasn't sure whether there was any irony in there, but I let it pass.

'Well, it's not your fault, either of you. I'll take this now and study it and see what can be done to smooth things out. Thank you, both of you. I'm sorry I lost my temper, Randolph. Unforgivable in a diplomat, eh?'

'Oh, no problem. Between friends,' said Randolph.

Between friends it was not, but I left it at that.

7

THE CITY, THE ONLY CITY, on Sylvanus is covered by a massive sti-glass dome. The reason for this is not because Sylvanians loved to be enclosed, but because the equipment and buildings which are necessary to any city do not like to be exposed to the kind of rainfall this planet is subject to. On Sylvanus it rains every single day, usually for around two hours in the afternoons. It is a deluge worthy of a chapter in the Bible, or any other holy book. I have seen famous falls on earth with less water cascading down them than the amount that drops from the sky on one square metre of Sylvanus soil. Which brings to mind something that has been puzzling me for a long time. On the planet Earth, we call the ground *earth*. So on another world, let's take this one, is the ground called *Sylvanus*? I always avoid the dilemma by using words like 'soil' or 'dirt'. One day I'll have a chat with a lexicographer and discover the correct term.

No, the dome isn't there because Sylvanians disliked the countryside, or rather the wilderness, of their world. In fact Sylvanians preferred the wild outdoors and left the streets and buildings behind as often as they could, to walk, ride or whatever in the rainforests outside the dome. Another good purpose for the dome, of course, is that being sti-glass it filters out the harmful rays of LC3: useful if you are a visitor to the planet and have no immunity. The whole beautiful half-bubble was originally constructed to protect the parents of their seemingly immortal children, once they had discovered the hazard of LC3, but it went up too late. By that time the dark cancers were embedded in each and every adult, and the dome was redundant for that purpose.

I must admit, I loved the fact that we could see out into the rainforest. To be on a world with so many trees, whole forests of them, some as tall as city towers, other bushing out, covered in magnificent blooms! It was like being in paradise. I could hardly believe the lushness of the foliage out there, the tree trunks bearing parasitic growths, their boles hidden by tangles of vines. Some of the creepers that hung down from the branches to touch the ground, were thicker than my thigh. They looped and curled from place to place, forming swings and nooses: one could not see where they began or ended. Up high were mosses and ferns, growing from those trunks the tops of which touched the clouds. It was labyrinth upon labyrinth of green vegetation, which every so often exploded into a riot of big waxy blooms and elaborate blossoms, their petals as colourful as the wings or tail feathers of exotic birds.

During my third week on the planet, the President sent a young woman, who told me it was her job to act as my guide.

'Guide to what?' I asked, being distracted at the time by the communications box which had failed to deliver an answer to my question to Earth on the business of Lars Peterson. 'How am I supposed to do my job,' I cried, frustrated, 'if no one will tell me anything? I'm supposed to be an Ambassador, the person who keeps things running smoothly between two major planets, and yet they won't give me tools to work my diplomacy with.'

'I am sorry you are upset.'

I tore myself away from the communicator, to study the person who had entered my office a few minutes previously.

'No, *I'm* sorry. I'm being very rude. That's not diplomatic at all, is it? You said something about being a guide. Are you here to take me somewhere? What's your name? That's a good start, isn't it?'

'I'm called Imogen.'

'A very old name, but a charming one. My name is James, but you can call me Mr Ambassador.'

Her violet eyes widened. 'I would not have thought of doing anything else but call you Mr Ambassador, or more properly, Your Excellency.'

'I know. It's a joke. I do it all the time, I'm afraid.'

She was an attractive person, just a little taller than me, but with a hairless head. Her body, like most Sylvanians, was slightly on the stocky side, made for sport rather than dancing. Yet her eyes were magnificent, a wonderful lilac, or light indigo colour, but wide and deep. The hands did not seem to go with the heavier shape of the torso, but were sylph-like, willowy, with long slim fingers. Her feet were encased in large boots, but I imagined they were as delicate as the hands.

Of course, the Sylvanians would obviously be somewhat different to us Earthians, since their planet – though very similar to ours – would subject their bodies to different pressures and elemental forces. Mr Darwin, from Earth's 19th Century, would have something to say about that, I think. A living organism being shaped by its environment? Or was it Jean Baptiste Larmarck's theory of transmutation? I was never a good student when it came to natural science.

'The President,' she said, ignoring my ill-mannered scrutiny of her Sylvanian form, 'believes you might want to visit various areas of the city, or even go outside. I'm here to show you the way, if you wish to go anywhere.'

'What kind of music do you like?' I asked.

She blinked. 'I'm sorry?'

'Music. I need to know we are soul brothers before I go off with you into the unknown.'

'Brothers?'

'Yes, you're a woman, but you know what I mean.'

'I do like some Earth music, but I'm very old-fashioned,' she said after a short pause. 'Those Sylvanian songs I enjoy listening to are mostly about the forest, but sometimes about lakes and seas.'

'When you say "old-fashioned" are you speaking of classical music, or of folksy type music?'

'Not classical, though I do like someone called Bach. Is that classical?'

'Yes.'

'But the songs I really like come before Bach, I think. They were a quartet called The Beatles from a long way back, several centuries.'

'Actually, Bach came before The Beatles. I too am fond of music from that era. Have you heard of the Rolling Stones? Or Dire Straits? Or Leonard Cohen?'

'No, only The Beatles.'

'So, what's your favourite of theirs? *Hey, Jude*? *Strawberry Fields*?'

'*Polythene Pam*,' Imogen replied, with some animation in her voice. 'I love that song.'

It was my turn to blink. 'Never heard of it. Are you sure it was written and played by The Beatles?'

She looked indignant. 'I know what I'm talking about, Mr Ambassador, even though I'm a provincial from a provincial planet.'

'Hey, I didn't say that. I'm sorry. I've just never heard of *Polythene Pam*, but I believe you, of course I do. I'm no expert on that quartet at all. I've heard their music and I like a lot of it, but my favourite musician and singer is Ragnar Poleski. Have you heard of him?'

'Yes, of course. He died two days ago.'

I felt as if I'd been stabbed in the heart.

'Died?' I cried, accidentally knocking a cup off my desk. 'How did that happen. He was only forty something? Was it an accident?'

She smiled at me. 'He hasn't died. That's a Sylvanian joke.'

I relaxed again. 'A joke? That's not a joke.'

'We think it is. Dying is a very funny thing when you don't have to do it. We're immortal. We always make jokes about other people dying. It's very humorous, especially if they thrash around and moan a lot before they finally expire. I've seen ziMages of people dying. Hilarious.'

'Charming,' I said, wryly, realising I was being taken for a ride. 'Well, Imogen, if I may call you that...'

'It's my name.'

'...I should like to go outside, into the rainforest. I understand I can go out briefly without suffering any ill effects?'

'Better you should wear a protective mantle, then I can show you a lot more. We'll take a tracker.'

I had seen the trackers, ancient-looking vehicles.

'Can't we just jump there in a pod?'

'Mr Ambassador, how can you experience being in the rainforest if all you're doing is jumping over the top of it inside a pod? Using a tracker is bad enough, but I'm thinking you definitely won't walk...'

'*Most* definitely.'

'...so the next best thing is to drive through it.'

'All right,' I said, very reluctantly, 'let's go. I have a free day today, since my bosses back on the old world do not seem willing to brief me on a very important matter.'

Once I was mantled, we took the tracker vehicle out through the exit tunnel to the raw planet outside the dome. Even before I got out of the tracker I felt the stirrings of panic rising in my breast. I had never been in any kind of 'countryside' before this moment. No, wait, I did step outside the lift on Snowdon, but even the Welsh mountain had buildings halfway up its slopes which were visible from the top. Here, in the rainforest of Sylvanus, the sti-glass city vanished within minutes and I was left terrified of the dense greenery that surrounded us. I had enough imagination to conjure up nightmares in those tangles of thick waxy leaves, vines and monstrous trees that were thicker than office tower blocks.

'Slow down a little,' I croaked to Imogen. 'We might be going too far – you wouldn't want to get us lost, would you?'

My driver glanced across at me with a smile playing in the corners of her mouth.

'Ambassador,' she said, lightly, 'we're only a few hundred metres from the entrance to the city. This is cultivated greenery – even manicured, if you ask me. Wait until I get you out into the wilderness, then you can be worried. Are you all right? You look a bit pale.'

I sucked in a deep breath. 'I'm fine. I'm sure you know what you're doing. What...what are you doing?'

'Looking for a glade to stop in so that we can get out and walk around?'

'Oh, do we have to do that? I can see the vegetation quite clearly from here. Is it necessary to leave the safety of the vehicle?'

'It's perfectly safe outside, too. In this area there's nothing out there that can harm you. Not unless you eat it. There's a fungus that can kill you just by sniffing its spores, but it won't jump up and grab you by the throat. Outside, you'll be able to experience the smells and the atmosphere, even with your mantle on. You need to appreciate the wonderful garden we have right on our doorstep. The temperature will permeate your mantle. You may be a little uncomfortable, but nothing too alarming. The only thing that won't penetrate your mantle are the LC3 rays, which will be deflected by that silver coating between the outer and inner layers.'

'How does that work?'

She shrugged. 'Technology. I'm not a scientist.'

'Me neither – and I don't trust anything I don't understand.'

'You must be in a constant state of mistrust then, Mr Ambassador, since we all have to rely on devices we don't understand.'

I cleared my dry throat, not even deigning to reply.

She brought the vehicle to a halt after climbing a hill which had a wooden viewing platform raised above the treetops. I was shaking a little as I left the tracker and we set off towards the platform. It was extremely warm and humid, and I felt a trickle of sweat go down my back. My eyes felt sore as I peered into the deep gloomy holes in the thick foliage, wondering about the darker shadows that seemed to be lurking in there. Incredible odours assailed my senses, some cloyingly sweet, others musty or acrid. I didn't much care for them. They increased my nervousness. There were flighted things too, that zipped from plant to plant, or fluttered upwards on the thermals that rose from the moss and mast of the floor. Surely these were sentient creatures?

I followed Imogen down a narrow path with fronds of plants that overhung the walkway slapping my body. It was an unpleasant sensation. It was almost as if they were attacking me, trying to knock me over. Above us the canopy of the forest seemed to be at least a kilometre away and it was dark – dark as death – shielded as it was by parasol leaves that hid the suns, leaves that were as long and wide as football pitches. I could see spikes on the underside of some of the fronds, many of them as long as my forearm. Curved, wicked-looking, bladed thorns that could pierce a man through like a sabre. There were also tendrils like thin green whips that uncurled and lashed out as if alive, snaking round my ankles, my throat, even my torso. Imogen just brushed these aside as if they were merely an irritant, but I – I tore at them, believing they could ensnare me and wrap me in a cocoon of foul green.

The panic continued to rise in me as I felt as if I were being smothered, swallowed by this alien jungle. Giant inscrutable savages surrounded me: louring trees and bushes decorated with parasitic plants. Was I about to end my life in the maw of a wild vegetable? Had the colonists indeed explored the whole planet and found it to be free of beasts? Perhaps there were green fiends hiding in the green foliage, camouflaged as it were, ready to attack unwary Earthians like me? I desperately wanted to go back to the tracker, but I could see this Amazon striding ahead of me, even bounding on those sturdy legs, crushing seeds, nuts and fruit underfoot without any fear of reprisal from this giant wilderness of untamed plants. Even though I was in a nightmare I could not allow myself to look a fool. Subliminally, I knew I was caught in an irrational place and that my panic was self-generated, but it took all my will-power not to scream and run back to the tracker.

'Here we are,' she said, stepping up onto the platform. 'You can see all over the canopy from here.'

She extended a hand and helped me stumble up to stand beside her on the viewing area, where I swayed for a few moments as giddiness overtook my feeble brain on viewing a world. I was just not used to wide open spaces. They made me feel small and vulnerable, and I teetered on the edge of insanity for a few moments as my vision roved over the vast ocean of greenery whose waves were the wind stirring the leaves. I gripped the rail of the viewing platform and simply stared ahead, my eyes fixed on the distant horizon, hoping she would not sense my discomfort. I had already shown myself to be a lily-livered Earthling.

Imogen was wearing no mantle, just a light overall uniform of silver that reflected the rays of the sun. Her face was glowing. She seemed to be drinking in the atmosphere as if it were a life-giving vapour. Her cheeks were the colour of pink rose petals. Those lilac eyes were alight with pleasure. She had on a beret which covered her baldness, but I was beginning to think that feature of Sylvanians attractive too. I forgot my fear as my eyes roamed over this sturdy but handsome woman for a minute or two, my gaze probably dwelling on her breasts and hips a little too long for good manners.

Of course, she caught me at it, they always do.

'What are you doing?' she asked.

'Nothing. Just…'

'Just staring at my body.'

'Yes,' I said, weakly. 'I was admiring your body – I was admiring *you*. Is that so bad? I was thinking how this place seems to give you vitality, whereas it saps the bejesus out of me. I'm scared – I admit it, I'm scared – I'm uncomfortable and I've never been so unsettled in my life. How can you enjoy this?' I gestured out, over the seemingly endless untamed tangled foliage that stretched out in all directions. 'It's a desert of living vegetable matter. Absolutely disgusting, in my eyes. revolting rhubarb and lettuce. Salad madness. Rebel cabbages marching on civilisation to subjugate the free universe. I shall never be able to face the garnish that accompanies my fried steak again.'

She shuddered. 'You won't get any animal meat on this planet, Mr Ambassador – and if you want to study my body again, ask first.'

I laughed. 'That would be fun. Please ma'am, can I ogle you?'

She looked put out by my making light of the situation.

'It's better than doing it without my permission, isn't it?'

I chuckled again. 'I suppose...' but then something came out of the rainforest and struck my face mask with a sloppy *swack*. It remained stuck there. I jumped and yelled, 'What's this thing?'

The 'thing' remained adhesively clamped to the front of my mask, its tendrils waving just a centimetre from my mouth. A horrible insecty creature that wriggled and squirmed, trying to unstick itself. I brushed at it, wildly, the way you do when you find a spider on the collar of your coat. I wondered if it was one of those killer fungi that she'd spoken of earlier and if so, would its spores penetrate the mantle?

'Is it poisonous?' I cried. 'That yellow stuff coming out of its tail end looks like venom.'

Imogen reached forward and peeled it off like a butterfly from the screen of a vehicle, tossing it back into the forest. 'I've told you, there are no poisonous beasts here, nothing lethal to human beings. No animals at all in fact. Only berrywhisks, dumblers, whistlethistles and trappersnappers. Nothing of flesh and blood. They're all plant-creatures, free-flying, going from place to place to looking for mates to breed with.'

'Mates?' I said. 'Breed?'

'Yes, they're similar to sentient life forms in that respect, but they're still simply innocent plants. They assist in the pollination. We don't have bees here, or other insects, to do that particular job.'

'Berrywhisks,' I repeated while wiping the yellow stuff off my face mask. 'Where did you people get the cute names from?'

'Oh, from a wonderful novel written centuries ago by a writer called Brian Aldiss. A work called *Hothouse*. You probably haven't read it.'

'Why do you assume that? You think I'm uncultured?'

'Yes. You stare at women's bodies like a barbarian. I could see the naked lust in your eyes.'

I gasped in indignation. 'You could not have. I never have naked lust in my eyes.'

'Well it certainly seemed like it. It's not flattering. You should look on me as a competent and efficient personal assistant, trying to help you settle in to a new world which frightens you to bits.'

We were now arguing like a couple of young teenagers and I was finding it fun.

'I do, I do,' I replied. 'Can't you be both? Attractive *and* a good worker? And I'm not *that* scared. I've never experienced anything like this before. I expect if you came to Earth and I took you to New York, you'd feel the same panic amongst all the skyscrapers and masses of people. Yes, and I'd probably take you to a wildlife park and toss you to the lions, then we'd see who was scared and who wasn't.'

She laughed out loud at this, a deep throaty laugh that indeed caused lust – if that was what it was – to rise in me again.

By the time we came to be walking back to the vehicle, I was beginning to conquer my lachanophobia. There was even a slight spring in my step. Perhaps the jungle was not out to get me, after all? Perhaps I was a little paranoid? Then suddenly there were loud explosions and I was struck all over my body by a number of hard missiles. I fell to the ground, convinced that we were under attack. Had I been shot by an old-fashioned firearm? Were there indeed rebels on this planet I had not been told about? The explosions continued, with missiles whizzing around me, striking tree trunks, ricocheting off branches.

When it was over I rose gingerly to my feet, checking my mantle for punctures. There were none, but I knew I had a number of bruises on the tender areas of my skin.

'Are you all right?' asked Imogen, who had managed to zip behind a tree and escape being struck. 'You look a little shaken.'

Again, my manhood was coming into question.

'I was attacked,' I replied, exasperated. 'Of course I'm shaken.'

'It was only seedpods – exploding seedpods.'

I looked down at the soft carpeting humus, to see black liver-shaped bean things, the size of my fist, scattered among the lower creepers. They were already burrowing into the soft mast of the forest floor like moles seeking a subterranean home. It was difficult to take in, this floral world where plants resembled animals. I knew I was going to have nightmares of a peat-hag monster entering my bedroom, trailing drool and dark foul-smelling juices, coming to enfold me in its horrible form: a walking grave intent on the vivisepulture of an Earthman.

'You'll be fine,' she said, casually. 'Absolutely.'

I *would* be fine, once I got back inside the safety of that massive propagating sti-glass dome, where my courage could be allowed to germinate and once again flourish into full flower.

Just as I was recovering the sky let go of its daily motherlode of rainwater. The flood was so dense I couldn't breathe. I staggered to the tracker under the force of a rain that seemed to have joined all its drops together into one almighty torrent. Imogen had reached the vehicle before me and I slid in beside her. She closed the hatch and then started the pump to eject the rainwater that had half-filled the interior. For a few minutes we sat there while the external nozzle had a fierce battle with the downpour to rid us of the water inside the tracker. Then Imogen told the vehicle to return us to the dome.

I was never so glad to get inside that protective glass bubble once more. I had been attacked by green whips and berrywhisks, buffeted by turnip-sized seeds shot from cannons and almost drowned when some damn fool opened the sluices of heaven. You can keep the great outdoors. I came to an appreciation of streets, buildings and nice quiet parks all during the space of one afternoon. The greenery, the vastness, the denseness of the jungle outside the dome was not for me. If this was Eden I had no wonder Eve wanted out. The serpent was a helpful friend, not a foe. Adam needed a toe behind him and Eve provided it.

8

ONE ASPECT OF LIFE ON Sylvanus which I found difficult to get used to, was the fact that there were no children. Sylvanians were infertile for some reason. They had never had the cause investigated because, I was told, they simply weren't interested in the whys and wherefores. Imogen told me they did not miss what they had never had. She, nor any other female – or indeed, male Sylvanian – experienced any feeling of loss, or yearnings, or urges, with regard to having babies. As a single man it did not bother me overmuch, since other people's children are other people's children, but were I married and wanting a family like many would-be fathers, I would have found the situation extremely hard to bear.

Of course, since they believed they were immortal, there was no need for young in the sense of procreating the species. In fact, new human beings were totally unnecessary and would have created a problem over time. If dozens of infants were being born and no one was dying, they would soon run into problems and there would be struggles and wars and all the things that go with overpopulation. The infertility was probably generated by the same transmutation process that gave the locals their immunity to LC3, though it did occur to me that it might be that very element which had sterilised the population. The rays had not given them a deadly disease, but perhaps it had given Sylvanians the gift of shooting blanks, when it came to procreation.

Which led me on to another interesting thought. Did Sylvanians make love? I mean, if the main reason for copulating had gone with the wind, did the desire, the urge, the *lust* to use Imogen's word, go with it? Maybe they were asexual? I had never seen any of them in the shower and though there were one or two images floating around in my head, I had no idea whether they still had the right plumbing for the job. Given that our genitals have two functions they probably did, but it was at least possible that certain physical bodily changes had taken place.

Then again, Imogen had certainly recognised the desire that had been written all over my face, and probably in my demeanour, when I had stared at her longingly. If they did not make love, they were at least aware of the process and could identify it. It was an intriguing question which bothered me a lot during my first weeks in post.

I certainly couldn't ask Imogen or any of the other Sylvanians of my acquaintance whether they made love. They were a very rigid formal people, extremely private, and they would undoubtedly have taken offence at any questions as to whether they shagged. Not only were they a very reserved bunch, they seemed oddly cold when it came to intimacy. There was very little, if any, tactile communication between them. Their smiles were rarely warm or inviting. They did not seem affectionate in any way and treated each other almost as strangers when they met. This left me to wonder whether or not they ever fell in love with one another. I decided, after studying their conventional, conservative behaviour, that men and women on this planet did not form partnerships, either between the sexes or within the same sex. They were simply biological automatons.

I could not have been more wrong.

Two days after I had been outside with Imogen a male Sylvanian stormed past my secretary and entered my office in a very emotional state.

'How dare you!' he fumed. 'You...scallywag!'

I was glad of the big desk in front of me because it looked very much like he wanted to punch me on the nose.

'And you are?' I said, politely.

'Demosthenes Blake. She must have told you about me? Don't pretend you don't know the name.'

'I'm sorry, who is *she*?'

'My Imogen.'

Ah, here we had it. *His* Imogen. The sort of property rights that came with being in love. So, I was wrong. Here was the husband or boyfriend. Certainly not the brother, unless incest was acceptable or rife on this world. He was too furious for that. A brother protecting his sister's honour would not call her *his* Imogen. He would be cool, composed, calculating, and deal me a straight left, desk or not. I had to now calm this irate lover and discover how close was the relationship. Perhaps he was a potential, not yet accepted, or even a mere stalker? That was my hope as I faced up to this bald-headed immortal.

'Scallywag? Interesting choice of a word. I suppose you chose it because you think we use it on Earth? In fact I don't think I've seen that word outside a very old piece of literary fiction. So, I'm a *rascally fellow* am I? Do you mind telling me why?'

Security had entered the room in the form of one of the six marine commandos that I'd brought with me from Earth. As the burly soldier moved forward, I indicated he should hold back for a moment. I needed to understand how serious was the situation I had got myself into by simply *looking*.

'You made some improper advances to my Imogen!' stated the injured boy friend. 'Very improper. You must apologise.'

'To whom?'

'To me, of course.'

'No he mustn't.' Imogen had entered the office and her face was flushed. She looked embarrassed. 'Demosthenes, what are you doing here?'

Good lord, she hadn't even got a short name for him!

He replied, 'You told me he had insulted you.'

Her face was now burning. 'I also told you the Ambassador had apologised to me. It's not your place to come in here and accuse him of indiscretions. I told you that in private...'

Probably to make Mr Blake jealous, a good tool if you wanted to rouse a lover to action and get him to do something.

'...I did not expect you to come charging in here and making a fool of yourself. You will be in a lot of trouble, Demosthenes...'

I was beginning to find the length of that name tedious.

'...and I wouldn't be surprised if you get hauled up in front of the President and forced to apologise in public. Now get out before I really become angry. I'm very upset with you. Go on, get out.'

At a nod from me the marine stepped smartly forward, grabbed the arm of my would-be assailant and marched him firmly from the office.

I now faced my local assistant, my guide, *my* Imogen.

'Indiscretions?' I murmured. 'Not even a hand, or a gesture, nor even a word, but merely a *look*.'

'That's enough Mr Ambassador,' she snapped at me. 'You can see I'm thoroughly embarrassed. Do not take advantage of the situation. You were in the wrong, even if it was merely a look. It was enough to worry me. I should not have told Demosthenes. He has the wrong idea about the depth of our relationship. His and mine, I mean. We are friends, nothing more. We grew up together and he expected we would form a couple.'

'But you don't?'

She stared me directly in the eyes and there was a message in those mauve irises that was unmistakeable.

'I am a single woman, yet to meet my partner in life.'

I have never been so relieved, nay even cheered, to hear such a statement from the lips of a beautiful female of the species.

9

'BEANS AND LENTILS,' SAID RANDOLPH, turning over a flat mashed vegetable pancake with the tip of his knife. 'Banquet?'

The Sylvanians love their banquets and this one was in honour of us, the recently arrived Earthians.

'Oh, get on with it,' replied Charlie, who was wearing a cocktail dress in which she looked absolutely stunning. I was used to seeing her in dark severe-looking suit. 'It's much healthier for you than all that meat we normally eat at home.'

Why is it that women need to state the obvious? At least, I've found that to be the case. Also it seems to me that women are better at change than men and are willing to enjoy foods that might be good for them. Not many men I know are vegetarians, but quite a lot of my female acquaintances definitely are.

'I'm sure these are the beans that tried to kill me the other day,' I said, throwing in my grumble. 'They're the same shape.'

Charlie huffed. 'You said they were much bigger.'

'So they were, but these are probably their smaller cousins, which tars them with the same brush as far as I'm concerned.'

'It wouldn't surprise me,' said Randolph, 'if there are all sorts of killers out there in the rainforest. No one's mentioned anything yet about carnivorous plants, like snap traps, fly traps and bladder traps. *Drosera granduligera, Heliamphora,* plants of that nature. On this planet they'll probably be huge monstrous things that could swallow a man whole. What about a *catapult-flypaper trap*? I wouldn't put it past this place to have one of those the size of an old English oak.'

Again, Randolph had surprised me by his knowledge of plant life, even extending to the Latin names for them.

'You forget one thing,' Charlie said to him. 'There's no animal life on the planet. Pitcher plants and suchlike snare insects back home, but here there aren't any insects to capture.'

Randolph narrowed his eyes behind his glasses.

'Yes, Charlotte, but the Ambassador told us about insect-like plants that whizzed through the air. Perhaps the carnivorous plants on this planet are vegetarians, like the Sylvanians?'

I interjected. 'Contradiction in terms?'

'Well,' he started to attack his bean and lentil pancake as if it and its kind were responsible for as many slaughters and massacres as the human race, 'you know what I mean. There are probably monster plants out there dying to try a club sandwich but would at a pinch settle for devouring a man from the planet Earth. You mark my words, there's more to things here than meets the eye. You won't catch me going outside without a heater in my hand. I'll shrivel the first vegetable that looks at me sideways. I'm pretty mean with a heater, as the boys back at my old school will confirm. should you be at all dubious.'

Olaf, the President, was sitting to my right and was following this conversation with a look of bewilderment.

'Mr Ambassador,' he said, 'you don't really accede to those subjects and ideas you're talking about, do you?'

'It's just dinner table banter,' I explained. 'Please don't take us seriously.'

'Then let us turn to a graver subject. Have you heard anything from your government regarding the dissection of one of our citizens, namely Lars Peterson?'

I put down my knife and fork. I had not been looking forward to this question, which I knew had been coming.

'I'm sorry, Mr President. I have attempted to discover the reasons behind this affair. I'm told it was all a silly mistake. That is, the scientist who carried out the autopsy did it on his own cognisance, without going through the proper channels or contacting the right authority. A full and formal apology will be forthcoming, I'm sure, and as soon as I receive it I'll bring it to you. Lars Peterson's funeral has already taken place and was conducted with all the proper rituals and gravity expected of such an occasion.'

'They are not sending his corpse back to its home planet?'

'They felt it more dignified to cremate what was left of the body, rather than teleport the remains.'

Olaf sighed. 'It's all very unfortunate. I'm afraid there are many here who'll be angry. Yes, Lars Peterson was a criminal, but he was a Sylvanian. It may seem elitist and rather arrogant to people on Earth, but we believe ourselves to be uniquely special. Never before has a group of people lived beyond 150 years of age, and not only that, retained all the youthful features and health of a human on first reaching adulthood. We *are* unique. And Lars was one of us, therefore rare and wonderful.' He paused and cleared his throat. 'You are aware that all Sylvanians are approaching their first half-millennium – we will soon be celebrating our collective five-hundredth birthdays. Not all on the same day, of course, but all in the same two or three years. This has the potential to mar the occasion. What I fail to understand is what your scientists were trying to find? Did they think to discover the secret of immortality? Is that what it was? If so, I can at least understand why they carried out the investigation. We must be envied throughout the known universe for our longevity, for our ability to remain young and immune to sickness.'

'I'm sure it must have been something like that, as you say, Mr President. Jealousy prods us to do many things we later regret. Unfortunately Lars Peterson is now only an urn of ashes. If you wish, I can ask for the urn to be sent here, for any memorial service and interment?'

'That would help, I'm certain.'

'In that case, I'll send a message tomorrow morning at the very latest.'

He managed to look a tiny bit less aggrieved.

'Thank you. I should hate it if something of this nature should interfere with the good relations we have, up until now, enjoyed with your world. You know there are always other governments, other planets desirous of trading with Sylvanus for LC3. For the most part we are reasonably satisfied with the arrangement we have with your government, but I am only the President and must do the bidding of the citizens of Sylvanus, should they find themselves in an uncomfortable position. We are a proud planet. We do not like to be humiliated, nor our citizens, be they dead or alive, to be treated with contempt.'

That was a chilling statement and I made a mental note to pass it on to the authorities back home.

Charlie leaned over and whispered in my ear, 'You handled that very well, James.'

'I don't know,' I murmured back. 'I didn't like what he said at the end there.'

'Oh, it's all puff and bluster. We'll be fine.'

I was glad she was confident on that point. I certainly was not. I believed that President Olaf Jung was serious. We would have to tread very delicately for quite a while. The sooner I got those ashes from Earth, the better. Then we could all have a solemn ceremony, Sylvanian style, and try to put the matter behind us. The Sylvanians hadn't had much practice in dealing with death and I think this business had rocked them back on their heels. Not so much because they were bereaved, but because they were shocked and uncertain. They didn't know how to handle death in the way that we did and they weren't sure they were doing it right. I had learned enough to know they were terrified of being laughed at by other worlds. A fear of seeming provincial and unsophisticated. The country bumpkins of the colonial society. Their stiff conventional attitude was always at the fore. They needed to be sure that they were doing things correctly, in accordance with universally accepted practices.

While I was thus musing on state problems, I happened to look across the room and see my rival Demosthenes talking earnestly with Imogen, who was raising what would have been her eyebrows if she had had any, but in fact was merely a lifting of her smooth pale brows. A pang of jealously went through me. What was this man doing now? Did he think he still stood a chance with Imogen? I chewed my lip. Should I go over and break up this intense conversation?

'Don't do it,' growled Charlie, touching my sleeve.

'Don't do what?'

'Let them talk. You can see she's not enjoying it. Let him dig himself a pit to fall into.'

'I wasn't…' I started to protest.

'Don't be silly,' interrupted my minister, 'it's written all over your face. You can't fool a woman, you know. You're radiating more negative energy than a bundle of LC3 rods.'

'That would be *positive* energy,' I argued.

'Whatever, boss, don't do it. Leave it be. Stay aloof.'

I did as I was told, Charlie being more experienced at this game that I ever was or ever would be.

10

I MAY HAVE GIVEN THE impression so far, that the Sylvanians rarely left the safety of their city dome. Nothing could be further from the truth. They loved being outside in that mess of mangled greenery. They went out there at every opportunity. Some stayed out there for long periods. Almost all Sylvanians owned what they called a 'kuba' in the forest. That was probably a longer word or phrase at one time and I'm told by Imogen it came from the Czech language, but since it was coined by one of the dead parents of Imogen's generation, the origins are now dust. There are thousands of these forest dwellings spreading way beyond the city, way, way out into the tangled wilderness of the rural landscape.

A kuba is a rustic hut, crudely built from split hewn logs, with only the bare essentials for life within. The cooking is done on a charcoal or open wood fire, the beds are as coarsely fashioned as the hut itself out of rude planks and the rest of the furniture likewise. There are no modern conveniences or devices. Imogen explained to me that Sylvanians enjoyed getting back to nature, as she called it, and living rough and ready amongst the trees and plants of their primitive world. Every chance she got she went to her kuba, stayed overnight, or over many nights, and returned refreshed and blooming to do her work.

'Would you like to come and see my kuba?' she said, one day. 'You can take a weekend off, can't you?'

'I'm not sure,' I replied, wondering if this was an offer which was bound to lead to a full-blown affaire. We knew we were attracted to each other and liked to spend time in each other's company, but so far we had made no open declarations. 'Can I think about it?'

The outing would have been tremendously tempting had I not been terrified of going outside into that leafy, stalky, woody place that worried and warped the edge of my dreams. I have to admit too, that I liked a soft bed, good cuisine, and my household appliances all around me. I liked coffee on tap, wine in the rack, toasters, heaters, an entertaining ziMage – in fact all the modern conveniences, contrivances and gadgets that go with a normal city home. I suppose I could do without them for an hour or two, but for a whole weekend? Wow, I would need some iron in my blood for that.

But I could see by her expression that I had disappointed Imogen desperately and I knew if I was ever going to get into her heart, and into her bed, I was going to have to be a lot braver than I really felt. What could happen to me? I could get lost in the forest, a thought that actually made me feel physically sick. I could be killed accidentally by a strange tree or plant whose capabilities for taking human life were unknown to me. That at least sounded, quick even if it was likely to be terminal. Finally, the union between us could turn out to be a disaster. Funnily enough it was this last doubt which worried me most and therefore I realised I was actually falling in love with this stalwart alien female. Alien she was, born on another planet and formed differently to Earth-born humans like me, for she was probably immortal. I decided, in the words of one of my great-grandfathers, to bite the bullet.

'All right then,' I said. 'The very next free weekend.'

'That's this weekend.'

'Is it? Is it indeed? Well then, it must be this weekend. Can we use a jump pod this time?'

'No.'

'All right then, since you're determined to have your planet kill me, we'll do it your way.'

Having once been out into the depths of the heaving maelstrom of greenery outside the dome, I decided to acquaint myself more intimately with a knowledge of the planet's vegetation. I began by studying the native plants of Sylvanus, but since a good section of the local flora had been brought to the planet by the colonists I also later included in my research those plants which had once forested Earth.

Here's some of the strange growths I found which we have or used to have on my rather less verdant home planet:

An Amazonian tree with spikes on its trunk as long as my arm that will happily spear a careless stranger to its hazards.

Quite goodly number of deadly poisonous plants from various types of fungi and on to Oleander, Angel's Trumpet, White Snakeroot, Wolfsbane, Hemlock and a very prettily named *Manzanilla de la Muerte,* or 'the little apple of death'.

There were more, mostly dangerous because of their toxins, but also several 'widow makers' such as the eucalyptus tree known as Black Box which grew in Australia, and the European Crack Willow: trees which let fall heavy branches without warning.

And for longevity, Bristlecone pines, that live many thousands of years, the oldest being the Methuselah tree in California which has lived for more than six millennia.

Welwitschia Mirabilis, which has only two leaves that grow and tangle like two thick, tough, green tongues over a thousand years and eventually spans two metres of ground.

Once I had gained a certain knowledge of plant life on Earth I began a study of the flora of Sylvanus. Here there were killers too. Savage spine-toothed fronds that ate neighbouring leafy growths in the manner of carnivorous beasts. Plants whose sap could burn with the ferocity of acid and could penetrate a protective mantle within seconds. There were trees which shot seeds shaped like sharp thin spears: missiles that could pierce a tracker's doors. There were creepers with loops that would noose a passing human and hang the victim. There were plants that breathed lethal toxic fumes and bushes that had adhesive qualities strong enough to snare you and hold you until you died of thirst. My favourite, if I can call it that, was a tree whose trunk opened up and swallowed anyone leaning against it. You were gone within seconds. There had been attempts to cut the bole open to release the victim, only to find they had dissolved and had blended with the trunk.

Nice.

Now, I understood why plants might eat each other. A sort of struggle for the survival of the fittest in the potato patch. But what I did not understand was why they needed lethal weapons to protect themselves against life forms that had mobility, such as animals and humans, since the planet had no indigenous creatures. Had there indeed been flesh-and-blood walking the planet at one time? Alien organisms that could threaten the greenery? Or had the plant armaments appeared not long after humans had colonised the planet?

If they had, then the process of transmutation was far more rapid on Sylvanus than on Earth. In our exploration of space mankind had found that the influence of a new world on the colonists that settled it could be quite strong and startling. It would indeed be an astonishingly swift genetic alteration in the biological make-up of the plant life, but timescales were particular and peculiar to individual planets, and some very fast adoptions had been noted on other worlds. Sylvanus would not be the first newly colonised planet to throw something alarming in the face of the visitors. It would indeed explain why those born on Sylvanus developed immunity from LC3 as quickly as they did.

I searched the records in the archives of Sylvanus's library, but though two botanists were included in the first group to colonise the planet, they had hardly enough time to begin their research before death snatched them away. Also in the beginning there had been a city to build and the deaths of all the first generation to contend with, before there had been time free enough for people to thoroughly explore the planet and to set out on natural science expeditions into the weird and wonderful rainforests. So there was no way I could find out whether the killer plants had been there before the coming of Earthians, or had developed after their arrival.

11

'WE'RE GOING OUT TO INSPECT the mines,' said Imogen, striding into my office that Friday morning. 'Come on. You sit far too long behind that desk of yours. It's like a fortress. I bet you'd like to build towers on either side of it and arm them with weapons, wouldn't you? I don't know who you think you need protection from. Certainly no one who would want to see the Ambassador from Earth.'

Demosthenes? I thought. But wisely held my tongue.

Why is it that some women – I say this because I don't know all women – assume they know what is in a man's head without any indication from him that it's the case? I have never considered my desk a fortress. I like it, it's a very formidable piece of furniture, but I didn't choose it and I could very well have do with a smaller one.

'Who's we?'

'Me, you, Chargé Ng and Minister Umboko.'

I came from behind the desk and curled an arm around her slim waist.

'Can't it just be me and you?' I wheedled.

She peeled my hand away. 'Stop it, James! This is your work – and mine – this is not the proper time or place for affectionate acts.'

'Affectionate acts? I love your use of language.'

I could tell she was pleased by my teasing, but I knew also that she regarded work as a serious business, not to be confused with play.

'Never mind that. We must go. Please, James.'

'All right, but don't forget to call me Mr Ambassador in front of the other two. I know they know about us, but they're professional enough not to show that they know. However, they're not professional enough to ignore any blatant overt behaviour on our part. We must still be discreet, even if the whole world is aware of our affaire. I could get sent home in disgrace and that would be the end of my career and of our relationship.'

'I don't know what you're talking about. We haven't done anything yet.'

This woman had no respect for superiority or hierarchy.

Once in the vehicle again, mantled up and ready to face the outside world, I began to feel queasy. I had not been outside the sti-glass since Imogen had taken me to the viewing platform. I hadn't enjoyed that trip a great deal. Now I knew a lot more about the dangers in the foliage I was even less inclined to look forward to some fresh country air. Charlie and Randolph didn't appear to be enjoying it either. They were both a little pale and anxious looking. When you've lived in cities all your life, the great outdoors does not seem so great.

'You all right, Charlie?' I asked. I was in the front seat next to Imogen, while the other two were behind us. The tracker was a six-seater and behind us were two more people, two engineers going to inspect the site, Martha and Dominique.

'I'm fine,' Charlie replied. 'It's Randolph who's a bit bothered.'

Randolph turned a greenish-hued face towards me. 'I am not. I'm – I'm just feeling a little delicate today, that's all. Tummy upset.'

'Well don't throw up in your mantle,' I said. 'It's a disgusting way to drown.'

Imogen retracted the caterpillars and punched the Air Cushion keys. Happily we were to have smooth running. Then she programmed the vehicle for our destination. We set off at a moderate speed along a road which had the edges of the forest trimmed back to around ten metres from its centre. It was pleasant enough and the three Earthians relaxed. It seemed we would not be thrashing through undergrowth with long knives, or fording fast rivers, or having to climb trees to ascertain our position. That much was all well and good. True, we went through a tree-lined tunnel that mesmerised me with its passing multiple shades of green, but that was better than bumping along on tracks, the cutters snapping and slicing to clear freshly-grown foliage from the front of the vehicle. It was indeed amazing how quickly things grew on Sylvanus. Yesterday's clear path might be today's impassable jungle.

We travelled for about three hours, the mantles taking care of the bodily functions of those who could not wait, atomising waste without fuss or mess. Finally we came to the outskirts of the mines, an area with a metal wall surrounding it. Within the wall were machines to keep the grass trimmed and the area neat and tidy, working busily away when entered, and mobile robotic devices doing whatever they were supposed to do to keep the place running. The buildings above ground had clean functional lines: sombre grey constructions, their doors sliding back and forth as robots entered or exited. Our two engineers left the vehicle and made their way to an automated control centre. We remained inside, three of us at least concerned about the proximity of highly radioactive materials, despite the fact of our protective mantles.

'What are Martha and Dominique going to do in there?' I asked Imogen. All three Sylvanians were without protective mantles. They were simply wearing the clothes they would wear in the city, despite being so close to the raw radioactive material coming from below the crust of their lethal planet.

'Oh, just some checks. Making sure all the equipment's functioning correctly. They won't be long. In the meantime I'll give you a little tour.'

'Is it necessary to get out?' asked Randolph. 'You could point to things from in here.'

'You're perfectly safe so long as you're wearing mantles,' explained my girlfriend.

She opened all the hatches without waiting for any more concerns.

I got out, followed by Charlie, then Randolph. We stood there and looked around us at the huge site, wondering what the hell we were doing there since we could learn everything we wanted to know by sitting in our offices. However, at least we could report home that we were on the job, making sure that Earth's necessary supply of LC3 was being mined efficiently, since we had 'seen for ourselves' the mines and the teleporting equipment which dealt with the material.

'That huge oblong building over there,' said Imogen striding forth with us goslings trotting behind, 'covers the heads of the bore holes up through which the molten ore is drawn from the planet's core. You don't want to go in there. You'd fry within a few seconds with a nasty sizzling sound. That triangular construction houses the refinery. Again, not a place for human beings, only for tin men. Still a bit too hot for tender flesh-covered officer workers.' The joke was pointed at me of course and I felt the jab. 'The refined material is then sent along channels to an underground chamber where it is left to cool and is moulded into rods. The processed rods are then bundled into sheaves, transported again underground to the teleporting sheds, where they are shipped off to a world I think you all know.'

'You make it all sound so simple and straightforward,' said Charlie, 'yet we know how important it all is to the recipients. I'm very impressed by Sylvanus's professionalism.

'Thank you, Minister Umboko, we appreciate your praise.'

We were taken just about everywhere on the site, apart from inside those buildings which housed the LC3 ore. Imogen said that we would be perfectly protected, but there was nothing in those sheds which would interest a diplomat and his staff. Were we engineers, it might have been worthwhile including those buildings on the tour, but...

'I have an engineering degree,' said Randolph Ng. 'I'd like to go inside one of the sheds.'

'Oh. Well, all right. Do you two,' Imogen asked Charlie and me, 'want to join us?'

'I'm happy to stay out here,' I replied.

'Me too,' added Charlie.

So we let Imogen and Randolph go, while we wandered around trying to look intelligent and thoughtful.

'I didn't know Randolph has an engineering degree,' I said to Charlie. 'I've read his cv from cover to cover and there's nothing in there to indicate any further study after he obtained a Doctorate in Deviousness and Cunning at King's College, London. Why would he lie? What's he playing at?'

Charlie said, 'He's only got a BA and that's in Modern History. Randolph's just making sure they're not hiding anything from us.'

I was mystified. 'Why would they do that?'

'We can't leave anything to chance. You know how important LC3 is to Earth. Everything seems above board here, but it's as well to keep an eye on everything connected with LC3. It's possible they are secretly negotiating with other planets for a better deal than they get from us. That's what we would do, if the roles were reversed. I admit everything looks above board

146

from what we've seen so far, but you have to remember they've only just declared independence from Earth. Now that they're free of any political restraints, they may well look elsewhere.'

'But they owned the mines, even when they were a colony. It's a private enterprise, not a state owned company. You had to be a citizen of Sylvanus to have shares in the LC3 mines, even before independence. Nothing has changed in that respect.'

Charlie nodded. 'And you remember *why* it was not state owned when it was a colony? Because those who discovered the resource and gauged its value did not tell the authorities that a precious and unique mineral lay under the ground. A few of them, unknown to us representing the whole population of Sylvanus, simply bought the land from the Government of Earth, saying they were going to build a satellite town away from the city where they could house malcontents. There were no damn malcontents, James. They knew what they had and they wanted Sylvanians to benefit from it, rather than Earthians.'

'It's what any one of us would have done.'

'True, and anyone who owned the mineral rights now would look around for the best deal, would they not, my leader?'

'Charlie, they have more integrity than the rest of us. They are an honest, dignified people with more honour than we've seen in a long time on Earth, or on any of the other worlds. They wouldn't cheat us and I'm sure they wouldn't go behind our backs. Which is why it's important to settle this business about the dissection of one of their number. They don't understand how we could do such a thing. Neither do I, for that matter. I think we're playing with fire if we start treading on their delicate sense of what's right and wrong.'

'No sense in not checking on them though, is there – that's all Randolph is doing – checking them out. No harm done.'

Later, when we were all done at the site and had returned to the city, I made a date with Imogen for dinner that night.

She said, 'I'll come to dinner, if you'll tell me what was going on at the mines today – Randolph.'

'What about him?'

'He said he had an engineering degree. I don't think he knows one end of a spanner from the other.'

'They're the same, aren't they?' I stalled. 'Different sizes of course, for different nuts.'

'James!'

'Oh, all right.' I decided to tell her the truth. 'He was curious. Randolph is just naturally sneaky and wanted to make sure nothing was being hidden from him. I didn't tell him to do it, by the way, or send him. It was all off his own bat. That's the kind of man he is. A low, nasty, sneaky fellow, who doesn't trust his own grandmother. You get those sort of people everywhere, but especially in the diplomatic service.'

'Huh! What did he expect to find?'

'Don't ask me. I don't know.'

'He works for you, doesn't he?'

I shook my head. 'He works for the Government of Earth, not for me personally. Oh, I'm supposed to be the Ambassador, yes, but my staff are always on the lookout to discredit me and anyone else who'll get in the way of their promotion. If he can find out something that I don't know and report back to Earth, then he'll get the credit for it and I'll look like a dozy fool. He'd like nothing better than to get me replaced, preferably with himself. So if you know of anything that needs to be passed on to my government, let me know before he finds out, will you?'

She stared at me with those violet eyes.

'You people are nasty beggars, aren't you?'

'You don't know the half. We would sell our own children to go one rung up the ladder. You don't join the diplomatic service if you're not fiercely ambitious and don't have the killer instinct. Charlie's the same. She looks as sweet as anything, doesn't she?

But that's acid not sugar in her heart, Imogen. If I were you I'd kick me out of here and never see me again – but I hope you won't.'

'Fortunately, I'm not one of you, otherwise I might.'

'Phew, lucky escape. Now, dinner...'

12

THE WEEKEND EVENTUALLY CAME AND I could find no overriding important worked to be done. Imogen knew exactly what was in my diary and arrived in front of my desk at precisely six o'clock on Friday evening. She looked extremely robust in what she called her 'camping outfit' and she smelled delicious, of strawberries, raspberries or some such sweet fruit. To say I was tempted to make love to her there and then on the soft neocarpet of my office floor would be nothing short of the truth.

'Come on,' she said, 'we've just got enough light left in the day to be able to get to my kuba.'

I tried to look harassed. 'I just have to finish these outstanding problems,' I said. 'It won't take me but an hour.'

Her hand reached for a switch and she turned off my ziMage, and image on the dansefloor swiftly faded.

'Hey!' I said. 'That was important.'

'No it wasn't and you know it. Come on.'

'I need to pack a bag.'

'I've got everything you need already in the tracker. I've even warmed the seat for you. Come on, get into a mantle, it's time to sample a night out in the tropical rainforest.'

I whined, 'Do we have to go away, when all the best things are around us here? Best restaurants, best hide-away hotels, best beds…'

She frowned. 'You *promised*.'

'I know,' I said, 'but what does a promise mean from a diplomat – absolutely nothing. We make promises we don't keep all the time. Now, I was thinking...'

She pointed to the airdoors. 'Now!' she said, firmly.

I rose from my chair, knowing I was defeated. Imogen had the body of a revolutionary guard and the will of a hardened dictator. I was going to enjoy her kuba or die in the experience. I followed her to the vehicle and we were soon zipping towards the exit to the city. Then we were through and out into the green world beyond, where the horizons dripped fronds and mighty trees rose from the ground and formed a dark umbrella with their leafy branches shading the undergrowth.

Once we had the vehicle's tracks out, we sped along the wide dirt pathways leading to the remote areas where Sylvanians had their kubas. It was a world of light and shadow which laced the pathways. It had rained very recently and tall waxy forest ferns glinted and shone in the dying light of one of the huge orange suns as we flew past them. The surface of the path itself was pocked with muddy puddles that constantly splattered the viewscreen of the tracker, blocking our vision. Fortunately, this would instantly be washed away by clear water from the screensprayers. Not that any of this mattered in any way, since the machine drove itself of course and needed no human to watch for obstacles.

However, I liked to see where I was going and what was ahead of me and found this continual bathing of the vehicle in dark-brown alluvium a grating irritant. The jungle became thicker and thicker, rather than thinning out. I knew Sylvanians liked to have their kubas well away from each other, so we would have no neighbours. I believed it was a bad enough to be out in the wilderness, without isolating ourselves even further. Why did these Sylvanians feel the need to be so solitary? There were few enough of them on this world of theirs. If they had been born on

Earth they would find the presence of people a great source of misery, since we had very little elbow room anywhere – at the opera, at the theatre, in a restaurant, even in our own homes. My own apartment on Earth had measured three metres by five. Not a lot of space there and in a building that was hemmed in on all sides by others.

'Are we nearly there yet?' I asked, agitated.

'How old are you?'

I grated my teeth. 'Not as old as you, my love, who are an ancient queen, born before almost all my ancestors saw the light of Earth.'

'There's no need to be rude. Ah, here we are.'

The vehicle came to a stop and the hatchways opened.

I got out and stared around me. All I could see was a mass of greenery, with hardly any light between the layers. Then I noticed a dizzying tree whose limbs had been lopped to form a ladder. Following the trunk up with my eyes I then perceived a roughly-hewn boxy dwelling high up in the branches of the same tree. It looked perilously lofty. It would seem to be up in the canopy brushing the bottom of the sky. Surely the morning clouds would fill the bedroom with their mist? These were mythic regions where no sane man should venture.

'I think I'm going to be sick,' I said.

'Don't be a baby. You go first,' she told me, placing a pack on my back at the same time as soothing me, 'and I'll be behind you to catch you if you fall.'

I began the climb and found the natural ladder easy enough to use. On my way up those free-flying insect plants – the funny names escaped me while I was trying to concentrate on where to put my hands and feet – settled on my mantle and flitted about my mask. They were not as bothersome as I had found them on previous occasions. Some of them were as pretty as butterflies, others as dowdy as night moths. There were spidery types too, that shimmied up the trunk of the tree, and varieties of millipede. It was difficult not to think of them as animal life, they were so very similar to the creatures we are familiar with on Earth.

In a very short time I was standing on the flimsy wooden floor of Imogen's beloved kuba and staring out of the open unglazed window over the canopy of the rainforest. It was beautiful, that scene, and I was indeed grateful to Imogen for bringing me to her secret hideout, away from the throng. I was still not happy being surrounded by foliage, but I could see how it might grow on you – no pun intended.

It was not particularly peaceful. There were no noises of beasts or birds of course, but there was a sweeping wind up there which rustled the dry papery leaves of certain plants, rattled loose branches and encouraged squeaking and squealing from others that rubbed against their neighbours. Indeed many plants of the forest grew so quickly you could hear them forcing their way through competitors for light, shouldering other plants out of the way. Fronds flapped and slapped against stalks, and stalks twisted and choked fronds. It was a battle ground for green dwarves and giants, each fighting for space and sunlight, with no quarter given. Some of the parasitical creepers were merciless in their struggle to overpower their hosts, tightening like boa constrictors and squeezing the sap out of the soft trunks of cycads and tree ferns, strangling them to death with a great power.

'Take your mantle off for an hour,' ordered my hostess.

'Isn't that dangerous?'

'We're far enough away from the mines for you to be safe for that period of time and you can't wear that for what I've got in mind.'

So I stripped off the mantle and we made love, an act which Imogen now threw herself into like a wild beast. I was minded afterwards of a poem by a long-dead writer by the name of

Sackville-West, called 'The Greater Cats'. It is ostensibly about lions and tigers, though there's probably a deeper meaning which eludes a weak brain such as mine. It contains the lines: *'They prowl the aromatic hill and mate as fiercely as they kill...'* This is how Imogen and I went at it that evening, like two lust-filled felines of the jungle and plains. Afterwards I felt washed out, wrung, drained, limp as a rain-soaked petal. We simply lay there naked on that hard bed that had wooden strakes for springs, and held hands while staring at the palm-leafed ceiling. Around us air inside the kuba was littered with flowery insects and butterflies fluttering and flittering on the gentle warm breeze that blew in through the open window, some of them settling on the bark walls and thatched ceiling. The room, the whole kuba, was swaying in the wind at the top of its host tree and I felt as if I had just had the most rewarding experience of my life.

'I love you,' I said. 'I really do.'

'And I you,' she replied, squeezing my fingers.

After a while I began to think about the strange differences between the two of us. I was only now heading towards my fourth decade of life, while Imogen was close to 500 years of age. She didn't look it, of course, she looked younger than me, but what had she been doing all that time? How many lovers had she had in half a thousand years? A score? A hundred? Was I just another tick on a chart full of ticks? How many more would there be? If she was indeed immortal, as she and her kind believed, then I would without doubt be forgotten eventually, lost in a heaving line of lovers that had lost its beginning and had no end. It was a depressing thought that I would have to enjoy the *now*, for there could be no promises of forever with a couple such we were. That was for young couples who lived an ordinary length of life together. I was going to grow old and crusty, my skin turning to blotched papyrus, my bones twisting and crumbling, my eyes to watery blurs, while Imogen remained fresh and healthy as a flower in an eternal spring.

'What's the matter?' she asked. 'You're tense. Didn't you enjoy it?'

'It – the *it* – was fantastic. It was as close to utter ecstasy as I've ever been and I'm sure one day soon you'll carry me beyond it. No, I was thinking – worrying – about the differences between us. You with your – your longevity and me with my shortgevity. I shall grow old and die, and you won't, and that's just a little depressing when I think about it. I'm sorry, I should be pleased for what we have now, but I'm human and I think about the future, and that's where the dark clouds loom.'

She was silent for a while, then she spoke softly in my ear.

'Yes, it is a problem, more for me than for you, because one day you'll be gone and out of it all, and I'll be left with my grief. All I can offer is that I'll be with you until that time. I won't change. I love you, James, as I know you love me. That's a precious thing, not to be thrown away or corroded by dreams of what cannot be changed. We must enjoy what we have and try not to think about when you grow old and die. It's quite a long way off, that time, and though you probably think I will despise you for having a body that's wrinkled and broken, I won't, because Sylvanians love the autumn. I find the red, brown and gold leaves of plants in their autumn season just as attractive as I found them when they were fresh and green. You don't have to stay fresh and green, James, you can take on your autumnal colours and I will still love you.'

That's when I started to cry and wet her breasts with my tears.

13

I HAD MY MONTHLY MEETING with President Olaf Jung the day after we returned to the city. The weekend had been interesting. I have to say I wasn't an immediate convert to life in the wilderness, but nothing terrible happened and indeed, I enjoyed some of it. My cooking on an open fire, something I had never even contemplated let alone tried before now, was probably a disaster. I burned just about everything in the pan on the outside, while the middles of the vegetables remained raw.

Imogen, bless her, ate it all up and said though it could be better she had tasted worse. I didn't believe that, but I wasn't going to argue with her. The food she cooked (we took turns) was naturally superb. I would have eaten it in any restaurant in the known universe and complimented the chef afterwards.

One evening we sat in a grove below a wide hole in the canopy under the stars. I was wearing my mantle, she was in thin loose clothing that wouldn't have served as net for catching insects it was so flimsy. The night sky above Sylvanus is of course completely different to that over Earth. Imogen decided to teach me the names of the constellations and individual stars, but when you are bombarded with labels all at once, only a few of them stick. Sylvanus had mostly followed the custom of naming their stars and constellations after mythological and religious figures, animals or objects in Latin, though on occasion they deviated from the norm. One huge mellow-looking star that reminds me of her now, is Persicum, not mythological or religious that I know of, but is reminiscent of the fruit it is named after which is, I believe, an apricot – no wait, I think I'm wrong, it's probably a peach. Anyway, I'm fond of that star. Very fond.

This brings to mind another little piece of information which I haven't mentioned so far. When the first colonists arrived they brought with them all the fruits and vegetables of Earth. So now on the edge of the city are auto-farms which produce dates, bananas, grapes, apples, oranges and all the other fruit we Earthians are so fond of. In the same way are grown cabbages, potatoes, beetroot and all the vegetables of home. The colonists brought domestic animals with them too, but the last of these died out long ago. The children of the colonists were revolted by the thought of eating meat – a dislike which appeared to be universal amongst them – and once their parents died they separated the male livestock from the female, and eventually the beasts all died a natural death and were never replaced. Veganism did not appear to be so much a choice as a biological aversion to meat as a food. I'm told any child who was forced to eat meat became victim to convulsions. Parents soon realised that they would seriously endanger the health of infants born on Sylvanus if they fed them flesh from any of the livestock. This included dairy products. Even the wearing of woollen garments brought the new worlders out in a horrible rash and was soon discarded.

'You know,' I had said to Imogen while we chatted in our secret glade, 'you are missing a lot by not having animal life on Sylvanus.'

'Such as?'

'Oh, the sight of a leopard running across the African veldt – the grassland.'

'And you've witnessed that often?'

I admitted I'd never seen it. In fact to be fair I hadn't seen many animals at all.

'But I know they're there.'

'Yes, but I can see ziMages of the same creatures and whether one is a hundred miles away from a leopard or several thousand light years, makes no difference, does it?'

When she put it like that, I couldn't argue.

'But what I did have as a child was a beautiful collection of seashells,' I told her, 'which I know you would love. There were spirals and cones, shells like leaves, conches, harps, turbans, oh hundreds – perhaps thousands – more. The shapes and colours were exquisite. They were so shiny and lovely they used to take my breath away. You could not have enjoyed such a pastime as collecting seashells here, on a planet where there was no animal life and therefore no molluscs.'

'Molluscs?'

'The creatures that made the shells.'

'They were live beings – your collection?'

I laughed. 'No, the creatures were dead and gone. They left only their carapaces behind them. Their shells.'

Imogen stared at me. 'Were they killed for their protective houses?'

Ah. Sticky point.

'That I do not know. Some must have been, I suppose. Others perhaps died in storms and were thrown up on the beach, freshly dead, and therefore their shells were in good condition. Yes, I'm sure some of them were deliberately killed, in the way that butterflies and moths are, to preserve their beauty in the name of science.'

'I don't like that, James.'

'No,' I said, 'I realise it was a stupid thing to brag about now. But we have different feelings, most Earthians, to Sylvanians. Oh, there are some like you, down there on my home planet, but not enough to make a difference to scientific quest.'

I didn't tell her that probably most of the occupants of the seashells that ended up in collections such as mine were killed simply in order to own a pretty thing. The ocean's bounty, the aunt who gave me the collection called it. As if they were mineral treasures that could be gathered without destroying life. I was already being stared at as if I were a ghoul and I had destroyed an evening of pleasant companionship and exchange of reminiscences of childhood – the sort of thing that is supposed to be shared by young lovers in order to grow closer together. I was not going to endanger my standing with her any further by admitting that we on Earth were callous with lives not our own.

'So, Ambassador,' said the president, 'you look as if you have something for me.'

My mind swung back quickly to the fact that I was in Olaf's office and had an important piece of information to impart.

'Yes Mr President. I have here an apology from my government, which I would like to play for you. And an urn of ashes has arrived. I shall send it over later.'

'Ah – Lars Peterson.'

I played the image and voice of the President of Earth, Mustapha MacKinley, and when it was finished Olaf nodded.

'Well, we can broadcast this to the city and hopefully it will in part help to mollify the populace. They are still very angry at the complete disregard for the sovereignty and indeed dignity of one of our citizens, albeit a criminal and one despised by most of us. Earth had no right to take him and treat him as they would a piece of meat.'

'President MacKinley does sound very remorseful though, does he not, Mr President?'

Olaf nodded again, gravely.

'You are a very understanding man,' I told him. 'Sylvanus is lucky to have such a fine leader.'

'Are you flattering me, James? Obsequiousness does not become you, even in your diplomatic mode.'

'Well,' I smiled, 'a little over the top, but I do think you are a good man.'

'Let's hope I shall still be here in six months time then, eh?'

I was a little startled. 'What?'

'The new elections, my boy. I am only the interim president, following the Declaration of Independence. Acting President, if you will. I hope they do keep me in office, of course, but there are others who aspire to the position. Your friend Blake for one. He has quite a following out there in the streets. They like the way he rants against your planet for a start. There is a faction amongst the people of Sylvanus who think we should break all traditional ties with Earth and offer our product on the open market, see who is willing to pay the most.'

I was absolutely appalled by this news.

'Demosthenes? My God, that bloody weasel. He's doing it because of me and Imogen, isn't he?'

'You and Imogen? What about you and Imogen? No, I don't think so. I think he has a natural aversion to the Old World and wants us to be a planet that is no longer dependent on Earth for anything. He talks about Earth's imperialism and the yoke of colonialist masters. You and Imogen, eh? I suppose I should have guessed. You're both attractive people. But will it work, James? She's old enough to be your first ancestor.'

I chose to ignore the bits about my affaire with Imogen.

'That's ridiculous. You are the colonials, not us.'

'Well, fortunately there were no incumbents to knock out of the way when our parents arrived, or we would really hate our origins. I don't think he's taken all that seriously and I still hope to go from Acting President to President, so let's not worry too much. By the way, that man you have as your Chargé – Randolph Ng – he sends an awful lot of coded messages without your authority. Did you know that? The traffic between him and your government is voluminous. If I were Ambassador I should be worrying about him the way I'm concerned about my rivals for the presidency. I would be saying to myself, is this fellow a "bloody weasel"? Eh? Just thought I'd mention it, James, Mr Ambassador – and as for Imogen, you have my wholehearted approval. She needs taking out of herself, that woman. Too serious by half. Is that all?'

'I think so, Mr President, and thanks – for the information regarding my Chargé. I take it you monitor our traffic?'

'Only the levels. It would be no good trying to break your individual ciphers anyway. They're unbreakable. As for Mr Ng, I don't trust him. Sly devil.'

'And,' I said, 'I've made a few friends here, since I arrived. I will use all my influence to persuade them that you are the man for the job – the presidency – and let's see if we can't outmanoeuvre Demosthenes Blake in his bid to oust you.'

'I won't deter you from that. I do need support.'

'Good. We'll keep the weasels where they belong – out of the presidential palace and out of your office.'

That evening I sent messages to all the important Sylvanians I had met and had dealings with since my arrival, stressing the importance to their planet to keep Olaf in office and any rivals – and I named Demosthenes – out of public office. Most of the replies were favourable. One or two told me to mind my own business. The latter was fair enough. I was not a citizen of Sylvanus. I really had no right to interfere one way or another and I'm sure my bosses back on Earth would not approve of me getting involved in local politics, but what the hell, you've got to follow your instincts and mine told me Demosthenes was trouble. Once thing my bosses would approve of was keeping the LC3 flowing in one direction – from Sylvanus to Earth – and

I felt that necessitated just a little under-the-covers involvement in the elections that were to come.

14

I MAY HAVE PREVIOUSLY GIVEN the impression that Sylvanians were generally a good looking and attractive people. My enthusiasm for one of them in particular may indeed have led you to that conclusion. However, I am sad to state here that they were among the plainest human beings imaginable, their best feature being their eyes, which as I have said varied between lilac, mauve, purple, violet and all those shades of blue which stem from the primary colour. Their baldness was not the reason for me thinking them generally unattractive, but their pasty, almost *waxy* skin, their very ordinary dull features and their rather angular figures. They had good stature, that much was in their favour, but they walked without fire in their feet: a sort of solid stumpy tread, very determined and totally without suppleness. If you had witnessed an animated, high-backed chair walking across a courtyard, that would be a good impression of a Sylvanian going about his daily business.

Imogen was dear to me, because she was Imogen, not because she was considered beautiful by me or any of my other Earthian compatriots. Whether Sylvanians found each other attractive, I have no idea. It would have been considered very ill-mannered of me to pose such a question. One thing was certain. The longer we were on the planet the more I came to realise that, almost without exception, the Sylvanians were extremely promiscuous. Although many of them had steady partners – there was no such thing as marriage among them – they still had affaires and brief sexual encounters with others. Lots of others, lots of times. This included my beloved Imogen, who expressed astonishment when I voiced my displeasure at finding she had been to a party where they frolicked and made love until the early hours of the morning.

'It doesn't mean anything with regard to our relationship. I love you and only you, my darling. But as for casual sex with no heartstrings involved, we do it all the time,' she said. 'Don't you?'

'My mother does,' I replied, 'but the rest of the inhabitants of Earth are mainly monogamous.' I sighed, then added, 'No, that's not quite true, but indeed we do, most of us anyway, regard promiscuity as unacceptable. It – it arouses feelings of jealously and hurt. We like to regard our partners as special to ourselves alone and if they go with someone else it's considered a betrayal of trust, disloyal, *cheating*.'

She considered this for a while, then said, 'I can see – yes, I can understand what you're saying. But with us, gadding about with people not one's steady partner means so very little in terms of emotion. Yet at the same time there is an intrinsic feeling that it's important and necessary. I don't know why. I wish I could tell you why. I do know one thing, even if I promise you I won't go with anyone else, I'm certain I will break that promise. It's in our nature I'm afraid, darling.' She mused for a while, then added, 'I like that word *darling*, don't you? It's soft and pleasing on the ear. It makes me feel loving towards you.'

I tried to maintain a sternness. 'Imogen, if you…'

We were interrupted by Charlie, whose head had appeared on the dansefloor of the ziMage.

'James, your mother's calling you. Switch to Blue.'

Great, I thought, after finishing my conversation with one strumpet there was another waiting in the queue.

'I'm sorry, Imogen – *darling* – I have talk to my parent.' Then to the caller, 'Thanks, Charlie.'

Imogen called, on leaving my apartment, 'I'll see you for dinner? Tell your mother I think she has a wonderful, understanding son, whom I love with all my heart.'

'Hmm. I'll do that.'

Once Imogen had left the room I switched the ziMage to Blue, the spanspace channel. This was the first call I'd received from my mother since I'd arrived on Sylvanus. Reason being, such communications were expensive in the extreme, since the need to link ziMages over the huge light year distances so that two people could talk to each other in real time involved using an immense amount of energy. Instantly my mother's head replaced that of Charlie's. The dear old thing looked quite animated. Despite her antics, I loved my mother a great deal and actually depended on her for emotional support.

'How are you? You look well.'

'I'm fine dear. You look tired. Are they working you too hard?'

'No, Mother, I have a new girlfriend, one of the locals.'

She smiled. 'Ah, that sounds like a son of mine. Now, James, I don't want you to be upset by what I'm about to tell you, because I know how you get – I'm going to be married again.'

I shrugged. 'That's good.'

'You think I'm a trollop, don't you?'

'Silvia, you're my mother. I have nothing but beautiful thoughts when I think of you. Is it the bishop?'

The image on the dansefloor frowned. 'Bishop?'

'Just before I left Earth you were with a man of the cloth – I saw him briefly on the dansefloor of a public booth.'

Silvia's brow cleared. 'Oh him? On Mars? That was just a one night…'

'Fine, Mother. I don't need any more information except that it's not the clergyman. Who is it then?'

'It's one of your bosses, darling – Frederik Paka.'

My eyes widened a little. Paka was the Head of the Diplomatic Corps and probably the most powerful man on Earth next to the President himself.

'Well, that's a bit too steep for me, Mother. I hope he didn't have anything to do with my appointment here? You know I hate nepotism, even when it advantages me.'

'No, it's a new romance. But he thinks a lot of you. So you don't mind?'

'It's nothing to do with me. I'm not ecstatic, but I'm not unhappy either. I'm sure you'll have a wonderful time together. Just so long as *you're* happy. Is everything else all right? Your health? No more plastic surgery lately, I hope. You look nice, I have to add. Is that a new hair-do? It suits you.'

'Thank you, dear. Yes, I'm as well as I should be, for my age. And what about you? Apart from your extra-curricular activities with – what's her name by the way?'

'Imogen.'

'Curious. Very old-fashioned.'

'Yes, a bit like *Silvia.*'

'Well, older than that, sweetheart. Anyway, how are you faring? I hear bits and pieces about you. Just snatches of conversation in the corridors of power. You know I travel in those circles. It's nice to hear my son's name mentioned by the great and not-so-good. People keep mentioning the word *figurehead*. You're a figurehead, darling. That sounds quite flattering to me. Sounds like you're in the forefront of things. Important, my son. Anyway, I can't afford to stay on here any longer. It's costing a fortune. I just wanted you to know about Frederik. We'll do fine together, and your heritage is safe. He's got his own fortune. Bye bye, love. Look after yourself. Imogen, eh? Anglo-Saxon or Celtic, I think. She sounds lovely. Give her my best regards and say I look forward to a wedding and lots of lovely grandchildren.'

'Mother...' but the image faded and she was gone.

I leaned back in my chair and stared at the blank dansefloor. Figurehead? Yes, a figurehead on the prow of a ship is indeed at the forefront of a vessel ploughing through the waves. But it also had another less impressive meaning. A merely nominal head of an organisation, lacking any real knowledge or power. Figurehead. I would have given a great deal to know who used the word with regard to me – and in what context. Perhaps it was just an innocent remark employed by someone wanting to please my mother, knowing she was within earshot. Many of those government officials lacked any real intellect and no doubt some of them might believe it a compliment.

Then again, maybe the remarks had been intended to convey the business meaning of the word? Was I then just a nominal head of Earth's embassy on Sylvanus? If so, who held the real power? Charlotte? Randolph? Both of them sharing it between them? I was extremely young for the post. Maybe the authorities on Earth regarded me as a sort of acting ambassador, assessing me while I was in the position, receiving reports from my subordinates on how I was coping? *That* would be humiliating. There was no one I could ask. How could I? *Oh, Charlie, do either you or Randolph send reports about my performance as ambassador back to Earth?* Impossible. All I could do was keep alert to any unusual behaviour by my staff.

Then I remembered that Olaf had told me my Chargé was sending and receiving a huge amount of Earth correspondence.

I determined to look at Randolph's activities more closely.

15

WHEN IMOGEN SENT ME A message to say she couldn't see me for a few days I naturally became concerned. There was no tag on the message to say why. No explanation. We had been due to meet the very next day, a Saturday, so on that morning I took a slider to her apartment and called from the street. Her ziMage appeared on the dansefloor in the lobby and she seemed a little angry with me.

'Why are you here? I asked you not to come.'

'I was worried. You don't usually just fob me off with a message. Can I know why? Are you working?'

I hated talking to a three-dimensional image when the person I was conversing with was only a few yards away in the flesh.

She confessed. 'I'm not well.'

I have to admit this threw me.

'But you people *never* get sick.'

'That's not true. We don't get the same sort of problems Earthians and others get, but we do experience certain – what shall I call them – unpleasant episodes. They all go away eventually, but…but this one is unsightly. I don't want you to see me like this. I'm not pretty to look at.'

As I've already explained, Imogen was not 'pretty' at all, though it would be crass to tell her so. Ever since Jocey I've been unimpressed by superficial looks and though it sounds corny my interest has been more in the character of the bearer. Jocey had been, probably still was, a beauty. She had looks that would halt a stampede of rugby players heading towards the bar after a match win. When it came to character though, Jocey had been lacking. She had not been interested in anything beyond her own looks, intellect and desires. Sailing, yes, but that was because she looked good in a sailor's outfit. Imogen on the other hand seemed interested in everything. She had a curious mind and was delightfully enthusiastic about love and life in all its forms.

'Really, Imogen – do you think that worries me? Please give me some credit for being concerned about the woman I love. Let me come up and make you some camomile tea or something?'

The ziMage seemed to hesitate, then said, 'Oh, all right – come on up, but don't say I didn't warn you.'

I took the zip up to her apartment, thinking I would be presented with a red nose and watery eyes. There are no doors on the houses in the city. A dense wall of air keeps the noise out, or in, as appropriate. This barrier of air normally allows anyone to enter or leave a room or building without a problem. You simply walk through it without hindrance. However, for security reasons you can increase the density until the gas turns to a solid impenetrable enough to keep out an elephant. I had to announce myself on this occasion and the device recognised my voice and allowed me entry. When I did so, however, I leapt backwards in alarm.

'God Almighty!'

She began to sniffle, softly, turning away.

'I did tell you,' she said.

I was presented with a face covered in wrinkled grey moss, with two eyes looking at me from within deeply seated pits. There was a mouth, but it was fuzzed with furry hairs. In fact the growth, whatever it was, went even further, covering her ears and the lower part of the back of her head. I had never seen anything so grotesque on a human being, but then I have led a sheltered life. It was as if she were turning into a burrowing animal of some kind.

'I'm sorry,' I said, conquering my repulsion and distaste. 'It was just a bit of shock. Had you warned me…'

'I did warn you,' she accused, 'and you took no notice.'

'You didn't tell me how serious it was.'

I think she humphed from within the growth somewhere, saying quietly, 'It's not serious. It'll be gone in a week.'

'Really?' I said, having trouble keeping the relief out of my tone. 'Just a week?'

'It's only a fungal infection. I caught it from Demosthenes. I've taken the treatment. It'll die off now, but it'll take a few days.'

I didn't make the mistake of asking what she had been doing with Demosthenes to be close enough to her to catch this creeping horror. Instead, I became solicitous and caring. 'I'll make you that tea. I expect you've got to avoid certain foods?'

'Almost everything, if you look at the list, but camomile will be all right.'

The hole that was her mouth fascinated me as it opened and closed: a dark hollow surrounded by grey furze.

She growled, 'Why are you looking at me like that? I'm not a freak you know. It's a fairly common ailment here.'

'Yes, sorry. It's just – never mind. Where does it come from? How do you catch it?'

She waved an arm. 'Oh, there are all sorts of things out there in the rainforest. This is a new type of fungus, but they're all curable with ray treatment and the right kind of food and drink. Demosthenes has been to his kuba about two hundred miles away to the north. He did a trek in a particularly damp area, where there are swamps and marshes. Somewhere out there he collected the fungal infection on his skin and if you're wondering how it came to be transferred to me…'

'It never occurred to me,' I lied.

'…I helped him out of his tracker when he got back. He was already covered in the growth. Much worse than I am.'

A very satisfying image entered my head, of Demosthenes stumbling around blanketed in disgusting grey fungus.

I made her the tea and we sat drinking it and soon got around to our favourite subject: our relationship. It fascinated both of us, probably for different reasons, why we had fallen in love with a totally unsuitable partner. Imogen was almost 500 years of age, while I was a mere tadpole in comparison. Less than a tadpole. The gap was astonishingly wide. Not only that, she appeared to be an immortal, while I had a very short finite time to live. It hurt me that in another 100, perhaps less, years she would have forgotten my name. Sylvanian memories could not possibly hold all the information half a millennium produces. I had tested her and found unsurprisingly that her recall was actually very limited.

'You can't remember the names of your parents?'

'Sometimes I can, sometimes I can't.'

'But for the most part you have a "Sheaf of Memories" that you have to refer to when you want to know something that happened more than a 100 years ago?'

'Yes.'

'Doesn't that worry you?'

She shook her grey-matted head.

'No, it doesn't. What's important is here and now. If we Sylvanians are to live until something really catastrophic happens, something that destroys the whole universe, then we have to concern ourselves with small bubbles in time. Does it matter that I won't be able to recall your name in the future? If you were in love with an Earthian woman, she would be dead also, and therefore neither of you would have memories of the other. She took my hand. 'This is what is important. This moment we're sharing now.'

'Can I catch what you've got?' I asked, aware than my flesh and hers were embracing. 'I mean, is it very contagious?'

She let my hand go with an impatient gesture.

'I don't know. I've never heard of a foreigner being troubled.'

Ah, I was being reminded that I was not one of her kind, not a Sylvanian. I was an alien on her planet.

'I'm sorry, I shouldn't be so squeamish,' I said.

'No, no, you're right. You don't want this stuff growing in your orifices. That's where it goes first, to the areas where it can find fluids. It's not very pleasant, James. Inside, is the worst.'

I was appalled. 'It's growing inside you?'

'Of course. But the treatment will kill it, don't worry. We're quite used to it now. The devices that scour us come from your world. Without them we would be in deep trouble, I think. Do you want to go now? I think it best. Come back in a week and everything will be fine.'

'Perhaps I ought to. I have work to do.'

'See you then, James, my love.'

It was indeed time to go when a thing with a fungus balaclava covering its head called me 'my love'.

16

IT WAS AT OUR WEEKLY meeting together – meetings I had arranged and insisted upon as head of the embassy – that I broached the subject with Randolph Ng and Charlie.

'It's come to my notice,' I began quietly and rather too pompously even for my own taste, 'that the two of you have been sending and receiving a great deal of communications traffic to and from Earth which I have not had sight of. You especially, Randolph. A huge amount. Is there something you want to tell me? Am I no longer the ambassador here? Am I no longer the head of my own embassy? I need to see everything that passes between this embassy and Earth's Government. That is the normal procedure unless altered by the incumbent Ambassador – me – and these rules apply in every Earthian embassy throughout the known universe.' My voice was getting higher as anger overtook me. 'Who the hell do you think you are?' I shouted into Randolph Ng's face. 'What the hell do the pair of you think you're playing at?'

Ng was very red in the face and looked at Charlie, who seemed more in control of her embarrassment. They said nothing at first, simply looking at each other, then at the table top. I waited, fuming, for one of them to start apologising. The apology never came.

'It's like this,' said Randolph Ng, finally find his voice, 'we're – we're not permitted to show you. The subject requires the upmost security and we have been given strict instructions to keep you ignorant of the content of those messages. I'm sorry, Mr Ambassador, but we are under orders.'

I was both shocked and stunned by this statement. Charlie could not look at me.

'Whose orders?' I asked.

'The President's.'

I lost my ability to speak for a few minutes, but finally said, 'I take it you mean the President of Earth.'

'Yes. It comes from the highest authority on our planet.'

I was flummoxed. What was I doing here on Sylvanus as the ambassador if I was not to be in control? Why hadn't they made Randolph the ambassador? None of it made any sense.

Randolph Ng turned to Charlie. 'Minister Umboko, I think you should explain to the ambassador so far as you are able, given the restrictions on us, what is happening here. You can't of course tell him the reason behind it, but you can explain the set up. This is all being recorded of course, so none of us in this room need fear any disciplinary reprisals that are not warranted.'

Charlie stared at the dansefloor of her portable ziMage, then looked up at me.

'I'm sorry you had to find out this way, Mr Ambassador, but this was all planned back on Earth. You are unfortunately a – what shall I call you – a *buffer*. A buffer between the Chargé and myself, and the government of Sylvanus. The fact that you're being kept ignorant of a highly important – immensely important – event that will probably take place during our time here, is all part of the plan. You are the face that the President and Government of Sylvanus sees. You are the man they talk to. If you knew what we know there is the possibility that you might reflect that in your dealings with them. There must be no inkling, not even a facial suggestion, of anything being – well, untoward.'

'Untoward.' I repeated, still absolutely mortified by what I was hearing.

'Yes,' continued Charlie. 'You are the Ambassador from Earth and therefore, you must stay clean, that is completely clear of this knowledge. I'm sure you believe that as a loyal representative of your home planet you must feel now that you could be trusted with this knowledge, but it's not about trust, it's about having you – a very important point this – having you between us and the people of this planet. You are the insulator, if you like. This is no reflection on your abilities as a diplomat and I'm sure you'll go on to become one of the best ambassadors Earth has produced. I have no doubt about it. But in this particular instance you are needed as a clean barrier between us, Randolph and myself, and the populace of this planet.'

'Believe me, Mr Ambassador, you would not *want* to know,' added Randolph Ng.

I studied my own dansefloor. What the hell was going on here?

'Look,' I said, trying unsuccessfully not to blaze the words that came out of my mouth, 'if there is something unsavoury – something very dirty going on here – I want no part of it. What immediately comes to mind is an invasion of Sylvanus to secure the LC3 mines. If that is about to take place, you must tell me now and I'll resign and will no doubt be replaced by someone whose integrity allows them to accept dirty politics. I will not have my personal ethics compromised behind my back. If you two intend throwing me on the garbage patch of history, I will use the rest of my life and my influence to destroy you with every means at my disposal. I have powerful friends back on Earth who will assist me in that enterprise.' I paused before adding, 'And I do hope this is all being recorded accurately.'

Randolph Ng had gone white and I could see his hands shaking, but Charlie was still in command of her emotions.

'Mr Ambassador,' said Charlie, 'you can be assured – I give you my solemn word – that no invasion of Sylvanus is planned.

No such action has been contemplated or even imagined. The Government of Earth is committed to remain on the best of terms with the Government of Sylvanus. What is about to happen is a phenomenon outside the control of mankind. It is barely believable, but it is fact and seems likely to happen. It is best that you do not know simply because you are the face, the front, for this embassy. It is vital that you do not know.'

'Seems likely to happen? Then it's not certain.'

Randolph had captured control of himself again.

'Nothing is certain, Mr Ambassador, not in this life or any other.'

'Don't fob me off with platitudes, Randolph. How certain is it? Do you have proof, if not absolute proof?'

'Yes, we do. We have evidence that leads us to believe this event will take place. It might not. We sincerely hope it does not, believe me, we are aware of our place in history too, but from all the gathered scientific evidence unfortunately it will occur.'

I thought about asteroids and meteors, rough bits of space junk that might damage a planet if it were in their path, all those things that threaten a thing the size of a planet. Was the sun going to go out? Was Sylvanus going to burn up from within, its molten core bursting out of every orifice on the globe? Was one of its moons going to fly out of orbit and threaten the stability of the planet? Were we going to be attacked by alien forces, or the forces of other man-colonised worlds? Was it going to rain acid? Was another ice age coming? Was the vegetation going to wither and die, leaving the surface an untenable desert?

'I really can't know what this is about?' I said.

'No,' said Charlie, 'I'm sorry, James. I know what it looks like, that you're being played for puppet, or a scapegoat, but it's nothing like that at all. You are a respected diplomat, a man with a likeable personality, and the perfect person to keep the truth from becoming known. The truth is, quite frankly, unspeakable, but unavoidable. You would weep to know.'

'And there's nothing we can do to stop it?'

'Nothing.'

Randolph Ng said, 'The next question you will ask, is *when*? We can't tell you that either, I'm afraid. We have a good idea, but we can't be absolutely sure.'

I sighed. 'Because you don't know?'

'We know, but you must not.'

'I see.' I sighed again. 'Well then, you'd better tell our masters back on Earth what has occurred today, in this room. I'll tell them if you like, but I'm sure they'll contact me once they know you've briefed me thus far. This is all very unpleasant, isn't it? I have a bad taste in my mouth.'

'Well,' Charlie said, 'it's not all supposed to be parties and functions. There are sides to the diplomatic life that are ugly.'

'Indeed there are, Minister. Now, I expect you two would like to get back to your normal duties. I want to sit here and contemplate for a while. I've undergone an unexpected shock. It'll take me a while to get myself under control again before having to meet a Sylvanian official who might see through my mask of jollity and bonhomie.'

'Sorry, James.' Charlie stood and left the room.

Randolph Ng stayed, ostensibly sliding the lid of his portable dansefloor back into a protective position, before saying, 'You meant that, didn't you? About destroying us, our careers?'

'I meant that and more. I wouldn't stop at just your careers, Randolph. When I do something, I go all the way. I would make sure your lives would not be worth living, I assure you. You had better be playing straight with me, mister. If not, you are done.'

He smiled, nervously. 'Have you that much power?'

'Frederik Paka is my current step-father.'

Randolph puffed out his cheeks.

'Yes, yes indeed you do have. But *current*.'

'My mother marries a lot, but don't let that give you any false hope. She always chooses her husbands from the political and military elite. Good morning, Mr Chargé.'

'Good morning, Mr Ambassador.'

17

'WHAT'S THAT HAT THING ON your head?' she asks.

'It's called a *David Herbert*.'

'Why?'

'Because the classic writer D. H. Lawrence used to wear one – no, maybe that's wrong, perhaps it's because the characters in his novels wore them. I don't know, I just copy what it says in the script.'

That is not strictly the truth. It is not entirely scripted. We have the freedom to use our own words, expressions and actions, but the rough guide is there to follow or we would lose the shape of the story. I am happy to pluck things from the script when it suits me. As does Imogen, if it seems right to her. This is our entertainment, after all.

We are sitting on the grassy bank of a stream that flows through a meadow. There are beasts in the field behind us. The script calls them cows. Above us are the spreading leafy branches of an ancient live oak, with a squirrel crouched in a fork. Above that is a bright blue sky with puffs of summer cloud decorating its peacefulness. On the ground, near a patch of daises and dandelions, is a white tablecloth covered in food and drinks. A picnic. We are enjoying a picnic in an idyllic setting.

Imogen is wearing a white flouncy dress and I am in a blazer, white flannels, open-necked white shirt and with a brimmed hat on my head. I feel ridiculous but am enjoying that feeling. Indeed, Imogen looks gorgeous and keeps smiling at me. I take a picture of her with a strange box camera out of the 20th Century. I enjoy the sound of the *click* which to me indicates a definite act has taken place. In the background a hawk stoops on something in a distant field, too far away to see what.

I put the camera down and say, 'This is fun, isn't it?'

'Yes, what shall we do?'

'Well, we can eat things, I suppose.'

There is the smell of dung coming from the area where the cows are munching grass. These things have to be authentic, naturally, but such odours put one off one's food.

I say, 'Perhaps I'll just have a drink.'

'Me too. Is that a bee?'

A fluffy looking thing with stripes hovered and swept over the food on the cloth.

'I suppose it might be. Or a – what is it? – a wasp?'

Imogen studies the script closely.

'No, wasps are supposed to be thinner. That's definitely a bumble bee, that shape. It's not dangerous, not like wasps.'

'What next?' she says, after a drink. 'Any ideas?'

I study the script. 'We could play cricket.'

'What's that?'

'I don't know. I'll look in the glossary. Here it is. **Cricket**, *krik'it, noun,* a jumping insect of the family *Gryllidae* related to the grasshopper and locust, the male of which rubs its forewings together to make a chirping sound.'

'How do you play with it?'

'It doesn't say.'

'Well that's no good then, is it? Anything else?'

'We could kick a ball over the field.'

'Sorry, that sounds a bit lame to me, darling. Couldn't we make love instead?'

'We just did that, half an hour ago. You've still got the green grass stains on your white dress.'

She looks. 'So I have. And you can't do it twice?'

'I've got to get in the mood, you know. It's me who does all the work, after all.'

'So, you consider it *work*?'

'You know what I mean.'

She laughs. 'Yes, of course. I'm joking.'

However, the more we look at the script, and the more we seek to find something interesting, the more it seems we have chosen a setplay that is insipid. Eventually I say to her, 'Let's try something else. What do you think?'

'Well, I've always had a yen for deserts. You know, living on a planet which is choked with vegetation, a desert would be a nice change.'

'All right, here we go...'

WE ARE UNDER SOME PALMS by an oasis somewhere on the plains of a country in North Africa, Earth. The script says it is a very dangerous time, because soldiers (me) and their wives (Imogen) are foreigners in this land, colonials, and the local people want to drive them out. Indeed, at this very moment a horde of horsemen with wild hair and flowing robes are charging towards us, waving curved swords. They are firing shots into the air too, with long rifles. They scream and yell at the tops of their voices and their faces are twisted with hate and venom.

'Don't worry darling, I'll protect you,' I say.

'Yes, I know you will,' Imogen murmurs, breathlessly. 'You are my hero, James Ovit. Shall we make love first? They're quite a long way away.'

I draw my sword and stand, legs apart, facing the enemy. I am dressed in an elaborate cavalry uniform with a shining helmet sporting a tall red feather, a tight jacket with two rows of golden buttons, some very, very tight scarlet breeches which must have been responsible for the sudden rise of sexual desire in my beloved, and a pair of black high-topped boots which are so blindingly brilliantly polished I can't look at them for more than a second or two without my eyes hurting. Over my left shoulder is slung a pelisse which is making me feel very hot, but seems necessary to my image of a trooper at his last stand.

'Sorry sweetheart, I think it would take me at least half an hour to remove these riding breeches, and they'll be on us by that time.'

'Who are they?'

I look at the script. 'They're called *Fuzzy-wuzzies*.'

'That doesn't sound very politically correct.'

'No, it doesn't, but I think that's the name of the tribe, or what the colonials – that's you and me, sweetie – used to call that particular tribe of warriors at the time. We would like to change history, but that's not what it's all about. I'm going to have to ask you to stand behind that palm tree until it's all over. Here, take this pistol. It only holds one shot, so you know what to do if I lose the battle.'

'Shoot the bastard who's killed you?'

It gave me a sudden sexual thrill to hear her swear, but the result was a growing painfulness inside my very, very tight breeches.

'No, you're supposed to shoot yourself.'

'Why?'

'In case they rape you.'

'Oh…' she stared at the wild figures charging across the dusty plains, their hennaed hair standing stiffly above their heads like the spiky grass we could see growing around the oasis. 'Oh, yes, of course, if it came to *that*, of course I would shoot myself. Is it likely to hurt?'

'No – there's no pain involved. Otherwise everyone would sue the company who makes these setplays.'

'I don't mind a bit of pain, I just wondered.'

'Well, I'll tell you in a minute…'

The first of the riders reached me and swept downwards with his sword, lopping off my left arm.

'No,' I say, 'just a sort of tingling feeling.'

I slash at the rider as he passes and his head falls onto the ground and rolls into the oasis.

'Yek,' Imogen cries, lifting the hem of her dress.

A second tribesman is almost on me, his horse foaming at the mouth, the horse-sweat flying from its flanks. He has a lance, this one, with a feathery thing decorating its spearpoint. I see the warrior's crazed eyes burning into mine. Hooves thunder on the packed-earth ground as he charges straight at me. My left arm is spurting blood, with Imogen trying to bandage it with a strip ripped from her petticoat. I shrug her off for a moment and lunge at the tribesman, my sword piercing his chest as he lets out a yell of agony mingled with defiance. He topples from his mount and the body rolls against the bottom of the palm. His horse continues on, out into the desert on the far side.

'This is better than picnicking,' says Imogen, excitedly, now redoing the bandage. 'Hold still while I tie a knot.'

Now a whole bunch of mad Fuzzy-wuzzies are on to me and I begin slashing left and right, with bits of body flying everywhere. A lance pierces my left side and breaks, leaving the point in the wound. A club glances off my helmet and strikes my shoulder, shattering some kind of bone in there. Still I battle on, stabbing, slicing, lunging, men falling from their saddles, horses getting entangled with each other. Finally, I have defeated all the enemy, who lie in heaps around the oasis. I myself am exhausted and dying of my wounds, my blood staining the ochre ground, running in rivulets watched by curious lizards. A vulture begins to circle above the trees with glittering eyes fixed on the corpses.

I reach out a bloodstained hand.

'Goodbye, darling. Don't forget to contact my mother – tell her I did my duty.'

'Yes, of course, she's just married one of the top army generals, hasn't she?'

'I don't know. I can't keep up with her. Goodbye. Kiss me, my sweet. Kiss me on the lips.'

Her soft lips touch mine just as I notice the figure of a tribesman getting to his feet, moving towards her.

'Quickly,' I say, as I die, 'the pistol!'

She sees the tribesman, a fanatical creature bent on dealing out a fate worse than death to a Victorian lady, married or otherwise. She lifts the pistol and squeezes the trigger, but the bullet flies from the muzzle harmlessly above her head. Her aim has been poor. She has missed and the tribesman has her in his arms and is whispering in her ear.

'Whoops,' she says, smiling as I fade into death.

WE BOTH TOOK OFF OUR helmets and looked at each other.

'That was good fun,' said Imogen. 'Where did you get the setplays?'

'Brought them with me from Earth. Look, did you miss on purpose, with that pistol?'

'Of course, you dope. I wanted to see your expression.'

A little hurt, I said, 'I was *dying*.'

'Yes, but not really. Oh, come on, James, you have to admit it was funny. A little bit, anyway.'

I laughed. 'I suppose so. Boy, did you see me with that sword? Swish, swish, swish, heads everywhere.'

'Yes, the heads of poor African tribesmen trying to protect their country from invasion.'

'I was just obeying orders.'

'Well, you were very good at that, I have to admit. I think you were born to be good at obeying orders. It's a skill not many Sylvanians have, but seems to be inherent in every Earthian.'

'Irony, eh. Don't you start that, my love. That's the province of an Earthian. Stick to your own territory.'

18

IT IS AN UNDERSTATEMENT TO say that I was uncomfortable with the latest revelations from my two heads of staff. I was actually appalled by the position I'd been put in and I strongly resented being used. A buffer? How ignominious. Here I had been thinking I was a high flier, one of the smartest young diplomats in the service, given a post that many would have exchanged their eyes for, only to find I was an unsuspecting fall guy.

Normally, an ambassador in his embassy is akin to a captain on his ship. He is in a place which by the nature of the work is separated from the forces of the home law. A sea captain's world in ancient times was his ship, itself isolated in a vast ocean, possibly for years. An ambassador's world is his embassy, not much larger than a ship, isolated from authority by unfathomable light years. Both captain and ambassador are endowed with the full power of their governments and therefore akin to dictators. Under normal circumstances I might not be able to hang Randolph Ng or Charlie from a yardarm, but I could castigate them severely without recourse to a proper trial. However, recent events seemed to have undermined that authority. My subordinates appeared to be the people running the ship and I was left impotent.

Whatever it was they were doing behind my back, it smacked of unsavoury practice. Something was rotten in the heart of my embassy and I was not only not allowed to root it out, I was not even to be told what it was. They had been told, *ordered*, to keep me ignorant of some event or plan which it seemed was going to cause great distress on this planet. If this thing ended up with blame being loaded on my back, or if I turned out to be a scapegoat, I wanted it all to be down on record.

I drafted a message to my immediate superior.

To: D. N. Swale, Assistant-Head of Diplomatic Service, Beijing, Earth.

Madam,

I have the honour to be Earth's Ambassador Extraordinary and Plenipotentiary on Sylvanus. I have recently been informed by two members of my staff that there is a secret agenda to which I am denied access. I am told this agenda involves a future event or circumstance which will be detrimental to citizens of this planet, but I am to be kept in ignorance by your orders. I think you will agree this is a highly unusual situation. I fail to see how I can run a successful embassy when my subordinates have access to information which is denied me. I wish to place on record my objection to this situation and I also wish it to be understood that I will take no responsibility for any disastrous fall-out resulting from machinations beyond my ken or control. Should you or any other of my superiors now intend briefing me, it would of course rectify any imbalance of power in this office. However, if I am still to be regarded as a necessary 'buffer' to be kept between my Chargé and the Government of Sylvanus, and am kept in total ignorance of any and all facts and plans in this case, I demand assurances that I will not be held accountable for a failed result.

After this communication you may of course wish to replace me on Sylvanus, a decision which I would naturally accept gracefully.

James Ovit

I didn't want to go directly to Paka, he being my mother's new husband. I received a reply almost by return which was terse in the extreme and to the point. I was to be denied any further information. I was to remain in my post unless ordered otherwise. In all other aspects of the Ambassador's work (apart from this one concern) and with due reference to my position on Sylvanus I was in sole charge and my subordinates – Randolph and Charlie were specifically mentioned by name – were to respect me as their unassailable superior. These orders were to be carried in accordance with the policies of the service. In no way was I to be regarded as less than supreme head of Earth's Embassy on Sylvanus. Only in one particular aspect was I to be kept in the dark, for the sake of the citizens of Sylvanus and Earth. I was expected by my superiors to honour the wishes of those who ran the service and whose ideals, veracity and integrity were as unquestionable as my own.

It was not a satisfactory situation and left me still feeling unhappy and vulnerable, but I decided to accept it for the time being. I could always resign at a later date. My objections were now on record and those records could not be obliterated. Any future court case or admonishment which resulted from ineptitude or neglect on the part of my two staff members would not fall on me. I was no longer responsible for their actions regarding this particular project.

Shortly after receiving the message from my mistresses and masters on Earth, I had an alarming call from Demosthenes.

'Mr Ambassador,' he said excitedly, his ziMage appearing on my dansefloor as I contemplated whether or not to resign my post, 'Imogen has gone missing.'

I knew that Demosthenes was at this time in the middle of a campaign for the Presidency, so I believed his harassed expression and wild eyes were due to his rushing around shaking hands and telling people he was going to improve their lives.

'What do you mean? Missing? Has she not turned up for an appointment with you? She's not here.'

'I mean,' he said, hoarsely, 'she went on an expedition into the hinterland and her pod has returned empty.'

A chill went through me and my stomach turned over.

'Empty?'

'She was on her own. The pod returned on automatic. You can set them to go to any geographical position at any time you require...'

'I know that.'

'Well, in this case she seems to have set it to return to the city at a particular time, but failed to board before it did so.'

'Shit! What can we do?'

'If you'd like to meet me in Brown Square, I'll have a pod waiting and we can both go and look for her. I know what you think of me and I don't blame you, but we have to put aside the fact that we're rivals to find this woman before anything terrible happens to her. Now, are you fond enough of her to meet me or do I go on my own?'

'I'm on my way.'

I called Charlie and told her I would be out of the office for a while, and then closed the dansefloor before taking a slider to Brown Square, named not after the colour of my muddy irises, but because Theodore Brown, the first Sylvanus architect to deviate from Earthian styles, designed it and built it before dying in the arms of his surviving children. Personally I would have called it Theodore Square, a name which was a little more interesting. Brown Square was not flat, but had been fashioned in a sweeping many-pointed star shape and the points of the star lifted in curves to form a shallow bowl. No vehicles were allowed near the square, so I disembarked in a side alley.

I saw Demosthenes on the edge of the square and ran to him.

'Where's the pod?' I asked.

'Over there, in a public shaft.'

We made our way quickly to the pod, a small four-seater. Both of us climbed inside and the body grips closed round us as we sat down in two of the four seats. When I asked why a proper rescue mission had not been set up, Demosthenes shouted back that he had informed the authorities and there was a rescue pod following us. He then closed the hatch and pressed the release. Our pod shot upwards through the barrel and out into the clearness of the air above. Once we were free of the city Demosthenes punched a code into the keypad and we levelled off and zipped over the treetops of the rainforest at a thousand mph. It was almost as unpleasant as hopping through space, but at least we stayed whole and didn't need to be machine-gunned into the ether as a spray of atoms. Luckily too, this vehicle was fitted with what is known in the vernacular as 'sick-suckers' for those who vomited, which soon mopped up my regurgitated breakfast.

'What was is she doing out there?' I asked Demosthenes. 'An expedition doing what?'

'Gathering rare herbs,' he said.

'But she's a P.A., not a grocer!'

'It's more of hobby than a job of work.'

I grunted. 'How does anyone get lost in today's world – with all the devices we have in our arsenal?'

'I know, I know, but things go wrong. Maybe her kit ran out of juice or got damaged?'

'So how did you get to know she's in trouble?'

Demosthenes sighed as if I were asking too many questions of him at a time when we should be worrying about someone else.

'I got part of a signal, which said, *"Can't find pod. Need help. Injury..."* then it broke off, as if something dramatic had happened to the equipment. Look, let's worry about all that later.

Let's find her first and then talk through the circumstances. In the meantime, you need to get yourself mantled if you're going to help me search outside. Are you? There's a one-size in that locker behind you.'

I wasn't altogether happy with his explanation, but decided to go along with what he suggested, having little option at this stage. I took the mantle from the locker and got into it. By the time I was fully ready, the seams all sealed and the anti-mist visor in place, the pod had been landed in a jungle clearing. I guessed we were around 600 miles from the city. Through the porthole I could see the foliage was thick and lush, with huge vines as thick as my legs looping and winding around giant buttressed trees. Somewhere out there was my Imogen and we needed to find her quickly before the tightly-knitted jungle wore her down.

The hatch opened and I slid down the chute to the mossy floor of the forest expecting Demosthenes to follow.

'Come on!' I yelled. 'Let's get started. Have you brought a...'

That's as far as I got. The hatch closed in my face. There was a kick on the moss as the pod thumped up through the middle of the grove into the air above the treetops. As it left I had a very brief glimpse of Demosthenes' face, his expression gloating and triumphant. Then the silver pod was gone, up and away, over the rainforest. I was left standing in the centre of the grove staring upwards like an idiot.

'Wha...' I began, but already I knew what had happened to me. I'd been duped, That bastard Sylvanian had brought me out here presumably to teach me a lesson of some kind. He wanted to frighten me. My anger began to rise almost to rage proportions, but I managed to calm myself after a good think. Demosthenes Blake was in big trouble. You couldn't mess with ambassadors and expect to get away with it. There were ambassadors here from other worlds and they alone would be horrified enough to get this criminal Sylvanian in front of an angry president. Not all ambassadors and consuls were as powerful as me, of course, coming as I did from the mother planet, but they still had the ear of Olaf Jung, who as President could visit punishment on any of the citizens of Sylvanus without further reference to the courts.

I knew better than to go wandering. Imogen was not out there in that tangled greenery. I was sure she was back safe in the city somewhere. I needed to stay calm and steady, remain in the same glade, and wait for the return of the man who had abandoned me – or perhaps a rescue pod. Imogen would surely miss me. We had a date for that night. When I did not turn up she would surely try to get hold of me and then worry when she couldn't. It would not be too long before she put two and two together and ordered her ex-boyfriend to come and fetch me back again. I was quietly confident of that. In the meantime I had to find something to do or I would go bananas surrounded by this vegetable nightmare. I sat on the stump of a broken tree and counted my fingers.

In the late afternoon it began to rain heavily. So dense was the precipitation I felt I was standing underneath a broad waterfall. I found it hard to breathe. Soon the ground beneath my feet was boggy and I couldn't walk around without sinking up to my ankles in the instant marsh. Sheltering under trees offered no respite. The rainwater cascaded off branches and trunks, and used long waxy leaves as funnels out of which it spurted in even greater force. By the time it ceased I felt the whole world must be a soggy ball that needed to be wrung out.

Still I felt rescue would come sooner than later.

When it grew dark, I began to feel uneasy.

19

THERE WAS LITTLE ELSE I could do but spend the night curled up tight in the buttress roots of a wooden giant. When dawn came, grey and shadowy, I began to wonder if indeed I had been missed at all back in the city. I began to feel resentful. I was cold, hungry and though the mantle had taken care of my functions, I felt extremely dirty. Standing in the middle of the glade I looked upwards for the direction of the suns. There were two, one which rose in the north and one in south. Once I had established the approximate direction of the city I began to walk. Somehow I knew it was a foolish thing to do, to leave the area where I had last been seen (albeit by the man who was trying to kill me) I simply could not just stand and wait for rescue. I had to be doing *something*.

I soon found myself battling with the foliage. It closed in around me like a live creature and wrapped itself around my legs, my torso, my throat and my arms. It didn't help that I needed to avoid dangerous plants and trees, like the one which swallowed humans whole. It further did not help that I had difficulty in recognising such plants and trees. Everything green or brown looked dangerous to me. When you have been told that some spiny plants carry a poison on the tips of their spines more deadly than that carried by stonefish or lionfish on Earth – toxins that can kill a man within minutes – you are naturally paranoid about anything that can penetrate skin and treat all thorns and their kind very gingerly. This can make for very slow progress through thick undergrowth.

I struggled, thrashing myself out of ugly twisted bonds and grasping leaves. Those whizzing insecty-plants that Imogen had pointed out, but whose names I had forgotten, flew at me as if I were a magnet for their kind. They stuck to the mantle in awkward places, blocking my air intake and covering my face mask. I scraped them off as best I could with gloved fingers, cursing their parentage. Again it was as if they were live creatures, intent on making my struggle through the undergrowth that much more difficult. At one point a nut the size of a football fell from a thirty-metre high tree and hit the ground with such force the earth shuddered so violently I swear it would have registered at least six on the Richter scale. It had missed me by fractions. There were several bombs of a similar kind and so now I had to look upwards for potential death threats as well as on vines and the underside of leaves. I only had two eyes.

The worst plants were those with thorns. There were many, many varieties. Some had thorns like small fish hooks that gripped my mantle and would not let me proceed before I had spent a great deal of time extricating myself. Others had long straight spikes. Still others had harpoon points with barbs. My mantle was supposed to be impenetrable, but when you're dealing with lethal poisons you don't trust a manufacturer's guarantee one tiny bit. By far the most of these thorns and spikes were on creepers and vines, but others covered the underside of large leaves and the stems and stalks of tall undergrowth plants. They all served to hinder my progress through the rainforest, keeping the speed of my trek down to almost zero. Indeed, by midday I had covered only a hundred paces and was then faced by a green wall of vegetation which would have stood fast as a defence wall for an ancient city. Earth, stone or wooden stakes could not have served as a better barrier.

When the deluge came again, after a day struggling with progress through the thick green tangle of the undergrowth, I gave up and returned to the glade. I was ready to sit down and weep. I had no previous experience of being in the outdoors and here I was actually lost in a wilderness of alien plants. I cursed myself for trusting that vermin Demosthenes. In my anxiety regarding the safety of Imogen I had not even thought to bring a communication device of any kind. If I had thought about it at all, I had imagined we would use the pod's ziMage dansefloor. I had not bargained on the pod not being available.

When I got back to the clearing I saw something that I'd previously missed: a yellow-painted arrow on the biggest tree in the glade. I stumbled off in the direction of the arrow and within a few minutes found a rope ladder dangling from a kuba. Climbing the ladder, awkwardly in my mantle, I reached the dwelling which was lodged in the crown of a large monster of a tree. Entering though the open doorway – there was no door – I found myself inside a well-stocked room with a rustic bed, chair, table and a full larder, including drinks. Clearly I had been meant to find this haven straight away. Demosthenes had obviously set this up and now I was snared like a mouse in a humane trap. I wondered how long he intended to keep me here. Long enough, I suspected, to be able to work on Imogen and cut me out.

I checked the stores and soon realised there was enough to keep me alive for at least two months. He had even thought to supply me with entertainment in the form of zitherbooks, zithermusic and zithermovies. Joy at my fingertips! What a thoughtful fellow. Did he imagine I would shake his hand and laugh it all off as a grand joke when I finally got back to the city? I was an ambassador! An important diplomat who had universal rights. One of those was the right not to be kidnapped by stupid young men (somehow I always thought of the Sylvanians as young people, despite their real age) and kept in captivity. When

I did get back I intended to use all my influence to destroy any ambitions of Demosthenes with regard to any career he hoped to follow. I hated him with a venom. Were he within reach at that very moment I would have beaten him with my bare hands and accepted the consequences.

I sat down at the table and ate some food – all vegetarian dishes, naturally – the mantle's mask being very flexible when it came to such necessary actions. I could even wash without taking the mantle off, since it had a flushing system that would ingest soapy water, swill it around me as if I were a piece of laundry or dirty dish, and then eject the grey water through an exhaust pipe. I make it sound very primitive, but it was not, it was a sophisticated system. One could live and die in the mantle without taking it off for as long as one needed it to stay alive and healthy. Imogen had said that I could remove it for short periods, but I didn't altogether trust her judgement on that account. It wasn't her body that would contract cancer, it was mine. You can be quite casual with someone else's well-being, can't you? I had taken it off once when I was with her, in order that we could make love together, but the sexual urge in a human being will get him or her into all sorts of trouble while it rages. Afterwards, when the urge has been satisfied, only then the worrying starts and you kick yourself for being rash. Only then do you start to wonder whether to get checked out medically.

After eating, I went to bed on the thin mattress that covered the hard wooden slats. It was uncomfortable but I did manage to fall asleep in the end. In the middle of the night I woke to some eerie sounds, like that of a wild birds hooting, or wild men wailing and cavorting. It sent a chill through me and I began wondering if this world had been thoroughly explored before humans had settled it. Perhaps there were aliens here who lived a subterranean life, only coming up during the night? Or animals that crept from holes in the forest However, on investigating it turned out to be only the wind blowing across some bamboo-like pipes that had been sawn and left open-ended. They formed a sort of fan-shaped decoration over the doorway. Each one had a different note, being of a different diameter and length to its neighbours. I ripped the thing away, threw it down into the foliage below, grumbled and then staggered back to my unwholesome camp bed.

In the morning I rose and ate my breakfast, had a shower in the mantle, allowed the mask to shave me, then went outside to see if there was any development on the rescue front. The world simply looked peaceful and untroubled. Things were growing – they grew so fast on Sylvanus you could hear the succulent sounds of their efforts in fighting for sunlight and space – and as usual the air was full of flying vegie-insects, looking for a place to seed and root. They were colourful enough, some as large as small birds and many of them made whizzing and zipping sounds as they travelled through the air. Often they lodged themselves in crevices in the trunks of trees: epiphytes and bromeliads that were not actually parasitic but simply used the bark as a base and then grew into short-stemmed rosettes with stiff spiny leaves that deterred others of their kind from rooting themselves too close.

I breathed deeply, the warm humid morning air filtered of course by the mantle's mask. The air on Sylvanus is richer in oxygen than the air on Earth and always made my head spin in the early morning. In the rainforest around me, the mist curled around the trunks of the trees and played loopy-loo with snaking creepers and vines. Looking up, through the small window at the top of the glade, I could see the sky, a similar blue to that of home. It was usually clear at this time of day, the clouds rolling in around mid-afternoon, prior to the usual downpour later on in the day. I could see no pods searching for me up there. I could hear nothing in the way of a tracker coming through the forest. It seemed I was a forgotten man, easily dispensed with. I wondered if even Imogen were concerned about my absence? Yes, of course she would be, but no doubt that swine Demosthenes had made up a believable story.

'Oh, I expect he's teleported back to Earth for his mother's wedding – you know, it was very sudden, her decision to marry for the seventeenth time?'

Of course, Imogen would check with Charlie or Randolph, and would discover that this scenario was false. Then the three of them would arrange a search party and begin by scouring the city. Once no trace of me was found within the city, they would then start on the immediate surroundings of the sti-glass dome. Then wider and wider. It would be bloody weeks before they reached me here, some 600 miles away from their starting point and by that time I would be half mad. I began to lapse into despair. I knew I couldn't walk out of my prison, but equally I couldn't stay there. I would indeed go insane if I did. All my life I had been surrounded by people. To be alone for a long period of time, even if only a few weeks, would conjure up all kinds of weirdness. I would start seeing things that were not there, hearing voices in the wind, growing more paranoid with every day. I would go quite mad.

Indeed, over the next few days anxiety and panic set in and I spent my hours in feverish contemplation of the sky, hoping and praying for the sight or sound of a pod. Indeed, I did see one or two and my heart leapt with joy, only to be crushed when the vehicle sped away on another compass direction. These craft could have been looking for me, or they might have simply been weekenders going to their kubas for their relaxation time. It was this latter thought that had me doing something I should have done as a child but never got round to it: climbing a tree.

It was easier than I had anticipated. There were many hand and foot holds, especially with the creepers bound so lovingly to the trunk of my giant. Even so I was no athlete and was quite exhausted and out of breath when I reached a height necessary for my purposes. What I needed to see, now that I could stare out over the canopy, was signs of clearings where other kubas might be located. The fierce nature of the plants in the forest allowed for no natural glades. These had to be cleared and kept cleared by human hand. Thus it could be assumed that if I could locate a space in the treetops, it would contain a kuba. That kuba would be occupied frequently or the glade would have grown over and filled itself with invading vegetation. I scoured the near horizons for dark patches, where the greenery had not closed over on itself.

Yes! There it was, not a mile or two away. A clearing! And smoke, blessed smoke, spiralling out of its depths. Thank you, Sylvanians, for your love of getting back to nature! In fact, now that I looked, there were several clearings in the region, but most of them too far away for me to reach in a day and I certainly didn't want to be out in that living forest during the night, with all its slucking and slithering sounds, albeit there was nothing really that would attack me aggressively and harm me physically. I was more worried about my mental state than my body, which was looked after very well by the mantle.

I climbed down again like a twelve-year-old, packed some food and drink into a bag, and grabbed a cutting machine I had since found in a locker at the back of the kuba. The machine still had a goodly amount of juice left in the power pack. I then set off with determination in my breast in the direction of the neighbouring kuba.

Even with the cutter, I found it hard, physical work, shearing a path through that thick jungle. Slicing through vines as thick as my waist took time and energy, and the mantle functioned overtime getting rid of the sweat that oozed from my pores. Rainforest plants do not give up their territory lightly. They fight back with thorn and spike, creepers as tightly bound as old liner ropes, trunks of trees that block the easiest path with their forbidding bulk. If I were a botanist I might have admired the lushness of my surroundings, or a gardener the beauty of the blooms and flowers that filled the air with their perfume, but I was like a crazed lumberjack, working piece-work, anxious to cut down the whole forest before darkness came to spoil my ravagings. In fact, I knew not a single name of any of the flora that I decimated and could not care less that I was destroying life and beauty with every sweep of my machine.

There was, even with the cutter, still danger everywhere.

Remember the old saying, 'If a tree falls in the forest and there is no one to hear it, does it actually make a sound?' Well let me tell you trees frequently fall with the silence of death even when you're there listening intently. One of the biggest killers in any forest is an aged tree breathing its last. The trunk is often so rotten at the base, so soft and soggy, that it breaks at that point with the softest of sighs rather than an audible crack. The rest of the bloody giant is still hardwood of course and several tons of it come crashing down with all the force of a skyscraper being tumbled by a demolition crew.

At one point I stood on the mossy mound with the cutter humming on thin air as a massive cathedral spire toppled and hit the floor close to where I was standing, rooted to the spot by fear of being squashed like a bug. Wild branches flailed and whipped, bringing down the huge boughs of live trees, some of them weighing several tons themselves. Sturdy giants in the path of the faller shrieked with the strains of being struck, quivered, yet somehow managed to bear the weight of their dead brother.

Then all was still except for the whispering of leaves.

'Missed,' I murmured, not too loudly in case the forest had some kind of alien intellect and took umbrage.

This tree-toppling weapon of my green enemy was overt and heavy-handed, but there was also an extremely subtle killer within the seemingly innocent sinuous and serpentine plants. Some perfumes issuing from the blossoms were as deadly as nerve gas. My mantle took great delight in telling me that it had dealt with, filtered, a 'vapour' from a shrub with huge, rather beautiful, bright red blooms that would have killed a herd of elephants and the odd passing rhino. All right, it didn't use that kind of language, but it might as well have done. The mantle's warning was visual as well as verbal. On the right side of my mask a yellow line ascended according to the toxicity of the gas. Once, the line nearly went back on itself when it reached the top of the scale. Wonderful! Killers, killers, everywhere and no place of refuge outside a protective suit.

In the late afternoon I heard the rain coming from a distance, stampeding over waxy leaves until it reached me and trampled on the foliage around me. I judged I was then around half-a-mile from my kuba. I had cut a swathe through the undergrowth that would not fill during the night, no matter how fast-growing the foliage. I retraced my path back to my own kuba and slept fitfully. The next morning I rose, had a mantle-bathe, ate a breakfast, drank a breakfast, and then set off once more on my quest to reach my neighbour. I was frantic to get there before he or she went back to work in the city. Once again the cutter hummed and snicked and snacked at the tangled wall. Before setting out this morning I had climbed my home tree and made sure the path I was cutting was going in the right direction. Indeed, I had deviated a little, but began to correct the course once I was back to hacking again.

Twice during the day I returned and climbed my safe tree, to ascertain that I was homing in on my target. By the time the afternoon rain arrived (set your watch by it) I found myself on the edge of a clearing. I fell to my knees and sobbed for a short while, gathering my faculties and strength of mind, before proceeding towards the kuba. This dwelling was not up in a tree, but on stilts in the centre of a neatly lawned clearing. There were cultivated shrubberies and flower beds in evidence. Clearly the owner of this kuba was not of the same mind as my Imogen and did not let nature take its course willy-nilly, but liked to steer it in the general direction of order and tidiness.

When I entered the kuba, through the open doorway, a man was sitting at a table staring at a portable ziMage dansefloor. A bald naked woman was cavorting on the dansefloor. He himself was eating a lettuce sandwich, completely enthralled by the entertainment. Once, he laughed, lightly, at some acrobatic move by the seven centimetre tall dancer and might have clapped his hands if they had not held the sandwich.

'Sir...' I began.

The man leapt into the air as if he'd been stung by a bee.

'Arrggghhh!'

He stared at me, white-faced, the sandwich lying in pieces on the floor at his feet.

'I'm sorry, I didn't meant to startle you,' I continued, but he pointed towards the doorway. 'Private!' he shouted. 'You have not been invited. Go away. This is a private kuba. Who are you? Why have you come here? This is not a place for you to be.' He turned and switched off the dancer, whose fantastic movements were going to waste. 'Off you go!' he waved at me with pale fluttering hands. 'Out. Out.'

'Sir,' I said, firmly, 'I have been kidnapped. I need to return to the city immediately. I am the Ambassador from Earth. Did you come out here in a pod or a tracker? I have to get back. I've been here nearly two weeks and I'm going out of my mind.'

He stared at me. 'Kidnapped?'

'Abducted against my will. I had to cut my way through the jungle from my captor's kuba to reach you. It was an adventure I could have done without, I can tell you.'

'Abducted? Who would do such a thing?'

'You will find out as soon as you get me back to the city.'

He shrugged. 'I'm not able to do that, not at the moment. I'm so very sorry, who did you say you are, Ambassador from Earth? My dear darling partner will be collecting me tomorrow – there's no vehicle here. She'll be back for me around midday tomorrow. I'm afraid you'll have to wait until then. In the meantime,' he turned and put an ancient kettle on a small wood burning stove that was making the room as hot as a sauna, 'do have some tea. It's lapsang suchong. A burnt flavour. I love it, don't you?' The kettle sang a tune I didn't know.

20

KARL AND SOPHIA, MY RESCUERS, delivered me to my apartment in the city the very next day. I was immensely relieved to shed the mantle and expose my skin to the air, but even more relieved to be alive and well again in a civilized environment. The Sylvanian rainforest was a fine and dandy place to view from a distance, but not one to be trapped in for any length of time. I would not wish it upon my worst enemies – actually, I would – though my very *worst* enemy might possibly enjoy the experience.

I carried out my ablutions and changed into some clean clothes before calling a slider to take me to the Presidential Palace. Once there I demanded an immediate audience with the President. That demand was carried into his office and a short while later I was granted admittance. On crossing the threshold of Olaf Jung's old room my jaw fell in amazement. The man sitting behind the desk gave me a sly smile and requested that I should sit down before I fell down.

'Naturally, you didn't expect to see the likes of me sitting in the President's chair,' said Demosthenes Blake. 'I can understand why you're shocked. The elections took place two days ago and Olaf Jung was ousted in favour of a far better man. Now, what can I do for you Mr Ambassador? Oh?' He let out a mocking cry. 'Of course, let me guess, you've come to thank me for giving you a holiday you didn't expect? In my private my kuba, too? Well don't let it worry you, dear sir, it was nothing. *Da nada*, as the Spanish say. Now, is there anything else I can do for you? By the way, I've requested your removal from the post. I'm expecting an answer from your government very shortly.'

Without warning I stepped forward sharply and slapped the man very hard, first on his right cheek, then on his left, knocking his head first one way, then the other. The action had stung my hand, so I knew it must really have hurt President Blake. Red weals appeared on his face, decorating the shocked and hurt expression. The pain had brought tears to his eyes as he stared at me. I wished I could have struck him with a fist, punching him hard on the nose, but I knew that would have done real damage to this podgy, soft little bastard and I was already in a great deal of trouble.

'You snivelling, whining little coward,' I said in a pleasant tone. 'Is nothing beneath you, even kidnapping a rival for the affections of a woman you can't get to love you?'

He rose from his chair, one hand to his face. I could see his eyes were still misted over with pain. Then his expression clouded over and I could see his hand hovering over a button on his desk. Then he collected himself and sat down again. He stared at his desk top for a few moments, before looking up at me. 'We're even,' he said. 'Let it rest there.'

If he thought that acknowledging he deserved to be struck got him off without further punishment, he had another think coming. I might be chastised for striking him, but he was guilty of kidnapping and the penalty for that, on any planet, was severe. A short prison sentence at the very least, even if he did try to pass it off as a joke. However, it seemed he had anticipated or read what I was thinking, because he came out with what sounded like a prepared speech.

'I expect you're wondering about our laws,' he continued. 'Of course we do have laws against abducting people, especially diplomats who ironically have immunity from those laws, but unfortunately for you they don't apply to presidents, who are above such things.' He leaned forward, his chin on his hands. 'You must realise now why I got you out of the way. Not because of our rivalry. My actions didn't help that side of things in the least. The woman in question has been going frantic for news of you and will have nothing to do with me except to ask me to find you. No, it was for a higher cause I removed you from society. You were rallying support against my bid for the presidency. Interfering in local elections is not something an ambassador should stoop to, Mr Ovit. I think your masters might take a very dim view of such shenanigans. I would not be at all surprised if you lost your rank along with your post.'

'I'm sure you did your best to persuade my government to that end, *Mr* Blake.' I felt despondent, but I wasn't going to let this weasel see it. 'You might be surprised however.'

He laughed, shaking his bald dome of a head.

'Oh, I know you have a whore of a mother who beds every politician and entrepreneur from the Milky Way to Messier 81, but I don't think they're going to take her pleas over the demands of the President of a powerful planet, do you?'

I forced a smile to my face.

'You see, using words like *whore* says more about you than it does my mother, old chum. Your mind is a sewer. And let me remind you that this planet of yours is only powerful so long as you continue to trade LC3 ore with Earth. It's my understanding you want to re-negotiate that agreement and possibly begin trading with other planets. If you do that, you'll have no influence with the mother world at all, and may even invite an invasion of this quiet place with its quaint vegetation and a people who actually depend on Earth for its military defence.'

Again his face went dark with anger.

'Are you threatening me? This conversation is being recorded.'

'How nice. Are you going to broadcast it to the nation? If so I should like to state that I could easily have died out there in the rainforest, where you abandoned me without warning. You might not be impeached for abducting an official of another planet, a diplomat of the highest rank, but your status would plummet. I have been here long enough to know the people of this planet, generally, are good law-abiding citizens who do not subscribe to crimes like kidnapping. I feel you would not be long in your position as President.'

He laced his chubby fingers together, before replying, 'You could be right, but still, I'm having you removed. Once you're gone I can settle down and govern properly. Your presence causes me anguish. I want a man or woman I can deal with. You are not that person.'

The air settled once again. Neither of us were winning this battle of words. I was fairly sure that the Government of Earth was going to recall me now. What was the use of an ambassador on a world which did not want him and would have no dealings with him? My career was in ruins. My mother couldn't save me from this mess, I was sure, even if I wanted her to, which I didn't. Yes, I wanted to stay in my post, but not through nepotism. I was quite sure that up until now I had gained my promotion through merit, despite what others might think, but if my mother intervened on my behalf to keep me in my post, I should have to resign. I did have some principles, some scruples, some ethics – unlike the man behind the desk in front of me. Yes, I had used my mother as a threat against a rebellious subordinate, but that was not nepotism, that was simply using a weapon in my meagre arsenal.

I felt it was time for a bit of reconciliation.

'Look,' I said, 'I'm sorry about Imogen and me. These things happen. I didn't plan it and I know how it hurts, to lose someone you love to another man. There's no victory in it, as far as I'm concerned. I'm not scoring and I hope you find someone else very soon.'

He gave me a strange smile.

'Oh,' he said, using that gesture of open palms, 'After a good deal of thought, I've come to terms with that side of things now. I don't want or need anyone else. I'll simply wait for Imogen. Even if I can't get rid of you from this planet, and I do have high hopes of that, you'll be dead soon enough and Imogen and I will still be here, together, for the rest of eternity, won't we? Mortality will put matters right. You, Mr Ambassador, are a mortal being, while I am not.'

I felt as if I'd been hit on the heart with a brick thrown by a strong man. He was right. Time was on his side. I had to accept the fleeting moment. Our love, Imogen's and mine, was an ephemeral thing. Demosthenes had forever. Ours was a stop-gap affaire, bounded by my short existence in the world. He could stand by and watch me fall to the ground, then step over my grave and take her by the hand. It was a scene which would haunt sleepless hours while waiting for dawns.

At that moment a woman burst into the office, hotly pursued by security personnel.

Demosthenes Blake pushed his chair back.

'Imogen!' he said.

She came straight to me and hugged my head awkwardly in her arms. 'You're safe. Thanks to Life!'

The President waved away the security guards impatiently, then said to Imogen, 'You must go. This is the office of the President. You can't just come barging in here. I'm sorry.'

Imogen ignored him. 'Where have you *been*?' she asked me.

'In that man's kuba. He took me out on the pretence that you were in trouble, then left me there. In his defence there were enough stores for me to survive there until someone came for me, but...'

'Snitch,' muttered Demosthenes under his breath.

'He's a lout.' She turned to her former lover. 'How could you?' she cried, furiously. 'Oh, I could hit you.'

He sighed. 'That's already been taken care of.' He paused before continuing. 'It wasn't because of you, Imogen. He was causing trouble with my campaign. I had to get him out of the way.'

'How democratic,' she said, shaking her head. 'Why didn't you kidnap all the opposition too, so that there were no impediments at all on your path to the presidency?'

He shrugged.

'Come on you,' she said to me, 'let's go and find somewhere with a decent atmosphere to sit and talk.'

At that moment a man came in bearing a message tablet which he handed to the President.

'Ah,' Demosthenes said, smiling, 'your marching orders, I believe, Mr Ambassador.'

He flicked the screen on the tablet. The smile left his face immediately, going somewhere he couldn't reach it. Instead a scowl replaced it. He glanced up at me, then down at the message again, before saying, 'I under-estimated the power of your mother.'

My heart leapt. I was not going to be recalled.

'You mistake your powers of deduction,' I said. 'This has nothing to do with her. I don't know exactly what it does have to do with, but I know there's something in the wind, something in the nature of a scientific breakthrough, or catastrophe, or hopefully an event of the kind the Three Princes of Serendip might chance upon during their travels. I'm not sure anyone knows for sure what it is, but it certainly appears as if certain elements know it's coming. They won't tell me their suspicions, nor point me towards any evidence, but the fact that they're leaving me in my post indicates that it's coming soon, if it's coming at all.'

'How very mysterious,' muttered Demosthenes. 'How very enigmatic. How very fortunate for you. Well, I shall continue in my attempts to get you removed, that will not be down to happy chance, but to my efforts. And if this mumbo-jumbo you've just spouted has any basis to it, then we'll soon see the back of you anyway, since you consider it imminent. Now, if you'll both leave me to my work...' he looked down at his desk again, then added, 'oh, and before you go. The ashes of Lars Peterson...'

'Yes? I gave the urn to your last president.'

'Indeed you did and it was full of nothing but wood ash.'

I frowned, puzzled. 'How do you mean?'

'We had the contents of the urn analysed. There was nothing in there but the ashes of some kind of woody substance. Grass or reed, or bamboo, something of that nature I'm told.'

What the hell were those people on Earth trying to do to me? Giving me these unnecessary problems.

'Sometimes the body is cremated inside the coffin,' I offered. 'Perhaps they did that with the corpse of Peterson?'

'A grass coffin?'

I thought about it, then said, 'The eco-movement is very strong on Earth, now that – ironically – we have only tiny patches of vegetation left to preserve. Coffins are now more often woven from the branches of swiftly-growing trees like willows – and bamboo – yes, now that I think of it often thick grass or marsh reeds as well. Was there nothing else in the urn? Maybe they simply scooped up a handful or two and missed any of the remains of the body?'

'That sounds like a good explanation to me,' Imogen said, coming to my aid. 'Demosthenes? I don't see where the conspiracy lies.'

He shrugged. 'Perhaps you're right. There was a tiny amount of what might have been Lars Peterson amongst the wood ash. I don't know. I just don't trust our old Mother Planet. Don't ask me why. It's in my nature. All right, Mr Ambassador, we'll leave it there. As my former partner has just said, where is the conspiracy? Not, I imagine, in a fistful of dust. Good day to you – both.'

I walked from the office with Imogen by my side.

21

LATER THAT DAY I WAS sitting in my own office, contemplating my position with regard to the current circumstances. It was going to be quite difficult from now on in, working with a president who hated my guts and would do everything in his power to humiliate me. I wondered whether to throw in the towel and just go home, back to Earth, and accept whatever post they had to offer me after my failure as an ambassador. Clearly I was a poor fish in the pool of diplomacy. I had managed to get the back up of the most powerful man on Sylvanus. My job was to keep him sweet, not make an enemy of him. This new president had ideas about putting LC3 on the market for the highest bidder. The one thing that my bosses on Earth did not want to happen. There was no way I was going to influence Demosthenes Blake to think otherwise, so in future I had to think about manipulating and persuading others in his government.

This planet did not go in for a heavy show of politicians: there were too few citizens for that. I knew from meeting the members of the Council that they were, on the whole, a conservative bunch. Most of them disliked change and would want a lot of evidence that floating LC3 on the market would substantially benefit the planet. In many ways they resembled the Quaker movement on Earth: on the whole they believed in simplicity of living, integrity, peace and equality, the four testimonies of Quaker Friends. If the Council believed they were getting all they needed for a quiet life and fulfilment, then the new President would have difficulty in making them change course and venture into unknown waters.

Reviewing this in my head, I began to feel more optimistic. Perhaps Demosthenes could be defeated in his objectives. Certainly there were many obstacles in his way.

'May I come in?'

Randolph Ng was standing in the doorway.

'Yes, Randolph – do come in.'

He stood awkwardly in front of my desk, ignoring the wave I gave him to sit down.

'Mr Ambassador,' he said, a tremble in his tone, 'you went and did exactly what we requested you not to do.'

More trouble.

'Which was?'

'You told President Blake that there was a catastrophe imminent – a catastrophe that threatened this planet.'

'Well, I didn't put it in those words, Randolph. Listen, I was trying to protect myself – protect our position here.' I was suddenly very irritated by him. 'How dare you come in here and accuse me of…what *are* you accusing me of? Disloyalty? Betrayal of confidence? You see,' I said, frustrated now, 'this is just what I was talking about. If I am to be kept in the dark, I have no idea what can be said and what can't. You cannot withhold information from me, simply giving me hints that a crisis is about to occur, then expect me to say the right things. If I knew what all this was about, I could guard my speech.'

Randolph stared me for a few moments, then flopped into the chair at last.

'Well, I've managed to save the situation, I think. I told President Blake that in a panic you had fabricated the whole story in order to save yourself from being accused of using your mother to keep yourself in the post of ambassador. Fortunately he believed me. He thinks you made the whole thing up. Luckily he doesn't think much of your ethics and is quite ready to believe that you will do anything to stay on Sylvanus in order to maintain your affaire with his woman.'

'She is not *his* woman. Nor is she mine. She is her own woman.' I leaned back. 'So, you told him I lied?'

'I said it was a thing you did when you were forced into a corner – to invent a veiled threat in order to worry your opponent.'

'Well, that's very astute of you, Randolph. I appreciate it. Now I shall have a wonderful career as a diplomat. The word will spread that the deceitful James Ovit turns to mendacity when he can't get what he wants by honest and truthful means. Excellent. Would you like a Mention in Dispatches for that brilliant piece of strategy?'

'Ambassador,' he said, slowly and carefully, 'you have no idea what's going on.'

'And that's the plain truth of the matter. I don't. I'm working in a bloody fog created by my subordinates.'

'I can't tell you anything. You blurt it out at the first opportunity.'

'You haven't told me a blamed thing. All you've done is hint at some possible happening about which I know nothing. I'm worse off than before.'

He bowed his head and stared at his feet, before lifting it again and staring me directly in the eyes through those stupid lenses on his face.

'Ambassador – James – I'm going to go out on a limb here. I've been ordered to keep this information from you, but things are becoming a little murky and I'm making a judgement call. Clearly Earth is not going to recall you. They don't think they need to, since the course of this planet's history is probably set and they believe that any change in our situation will only result in causing waves and further instability. We need to act as if nothing untoward is going on – which essentially, it isn't. It's just that since the criminal Lars Peterson was dissected by our scientists we have uncovered a secret about the people of Sylvanus. We have no idea whether they are aware of it themselves. There's no evidence of that either way. But what we have found out makes the situation here very delicate with regard to the LC3 trade.'

Now we were getting somewhere.

'So, what is this secret that's been kept from me for political – or other reasons?'

The look from Randolph Ng was hard and firm.

'Sylvanians are vegetable. Mostly.'

I stared back at him. 'What?' I wanted to laugh.

'Oh, I don't mean they're walking plants, but a good percentage – the majority of their body cells – owe more to the world of flora than to the world of fauna. They're a mix of vegetable and animal, with the vegetable being predominant. A meld. A blend. Something like that. I'm no scientist, James. Suffice to say they've become creatures quite unlike anything we've ever encountered before.'

My mind was buzzing. Could I accept this? Then I remembered the ash in the urn. Grass of some kind. Had that been Lars Peterson?

'But – but why? How? They came from parents who were flesh and blood.'

'Then you have to ask yourself, what is flesh and blood composed of? Look, I've gone through the same scepticism that you're going through now. The same questions were whirling in my head when I was informed of this distinction. But it's not so incredible as you think. Animals and plants aren't that different, James. There are close molecular similarities between our two life bloods. Red haemoglobin in our blood cells and green chlorophyll in plant cells. We're all made of carbon and nitrogren with a few other elements thrown in. Sixty-percent of a human being's DNA is the same as that of a banana.'

'Sylvanians have green blood?'

Randolph stared at me, then said, 'I don't know – have you seen one bleed?'

I admitted I had not.

'Anyway, I haven't said they're vegetable through and through.' Randolph took a pocket ziMage and flicked it. 'Listen, "Ninety-nine percent of the mass of the human body is composed of six elements: oxygen, carbon, hydrogen, nitrogen, calcium and phosphorus. Nought-point-eight-five percent of the rest is potassium, sulphur, sodium, chlorine and magnesium." So, it seems humans are fashioned from minerals. Now, when I look at the composition of plants, I find plant cells *also* contain oxygen, carbon, nitrogen, calcium, potassium, phosphorus, etcetera, etcetera. Are you following? The general make-up of our bodies is similar to the general composition of plants.'

'So, what's the main difference?'

'I'm told that plants have cell walls made of cellulose, whereas animals do not, but the difference is surely marginal. I do know that algae and fungi are not classified as plants *or* animals. They're separate organisms. What do they call them? Kingdoms. That was the word.' He stroked his ziMage and information flooded the dansefloor. 'Yes, here it is – there are six Kingdoms still recognised by many biologists, though there have always been others who dispute the whole system: Bacteria, Protozoa, Chromista, Plantae, Fungi and Animalia. Perhaps the Sylvanians represent a seventh kingdom? – though at one time there were eight, which then dropped back to six.' He let out a long, deep sigh, which I understood to mean he was actually out of his depth. Indeed he went on to say, 'The whole business of sorting through the classifications of *life* is akin to negotiating a rogue asteroid belt in an intergalactic freighter as far as I'm concerned. As I've already said, I know only a little about the subject and merely repeat what I've been told. Maybe the animalia part of them is dependent on the plantae part? I think that's called *mutualism* or *symbiosis* where one side needs the other to survive? I understand coral is a good example? Anyway, there it is, we're told by experts that they're an inseparable mix of animal and plant, and that if one side has problems it will affect the other.'

'So if we spray them with weed killer, the animal in them will die along with the plant.'

'That's rather crude way of putting things, but it would appear to illustrate what we believe to be the case.'

Now it was me that sighed. 'All right, now we go on to a raft of other questions. Why? Why are they walking, talking cabbages?'

Randolph looked very disapproving. 'James, I don't think you should use that kind of language when referring to the inhabitants of this planet. To answer your question, I'm informed by – by specialists in the field that it's probably extremely rapid transmutation. You know their parents were subject to LC3 rays and quickly developed a kind a cancer? Well, while these people were foetuses in their mothers' wombs nature moved quickly to protect them. This was an animal free zone before Earthians arrived. Apart from us, the visitors, it still is. This world of the Sylvanians has some kind of force that comes to bear on the composition of life here. This force – of nature if you like – ensures the survival of its life forms by the use of biological transmutation. It moves swiftly and surely to defend its children and makes, and keeps, them safe. Evolution on wheels, Mr Ambassador.'

'Evolution with rockets on its back, more like.'

It was a lot to take in. However, I trusted our scientists and their theories. Lars Peterson had been dissected, that much I knew for a fact. So, where did that leave us? We were animals on a planet of walking vegetables. Yet, they were enough like us to be able to put aside the differences and to be able to work well together (with one or two exceptions). It was a very strange set-up and I was suddenly aware that my lover was of a different species to me, completely different. Should that make a difference to the way we looked at each other? Dealt with one another? I had to take time to think this out.

'You would think,' I said to Randolph, who was now biting his nails and waiting for me to react to his statement, 'that vegetables would be kind to vegetables. Look how they've cleared the forest to build their city! No compassion for the plants they've cut away. No consideration for their cousins, the trees, that they've hacked down. Surely if they were more vegetable than animal, they'd be sympathetic to their kind?'

Randolph let out a laugh. 'Have you seen the way trees in the forest behave. They'll shoulder a parent or neighbour out of the way simply to get more light. Parasites, like mistletoe, will overwhelm their hosts and kill them without compunction. The plant world is savage, James. Plants take no prisoners. They'll kill each other if it means survival, you can be sure of that. In the same way humans and animals do. No, you can't take that as an indication that they're more animal than vegetable. Plants are ruthless. Watch them fight root and bough for space in that rainforest out there.'

'Hmm, I suppose.' Something else then occurred to me. 'And the longevity? Some trees on Earth live thousands of years. Is this reflected in the long lives these people live?'

'You're getting the picture.'

Apart from my personal feelings, the fact that I was dating a vegetable, I really couldn't see any crisis in the situation. We already knew that the Sylvanians were different from Earthians, by the fact that they lived five times as long and were perhaps even immortal (though I always remained sceptical on that point). This new revelation did not seem to endanger the situation with the supply of LC3. What did it matter if that supply came from walking plants or men?

Unless…unless there was more, something that Randolph Ng was holding back? I could tell by his manner that all was not as well as we would wish it to be. There was definitely something else, something nasty hidden in the Sylvanian woodshed. Was I going to get this out of my assistant? I had to try, though previous threats had come to nothing.

'Randolph – have you told me all?' I asked, quietly.

'No,' he replied, emphatically. 'I've told you too much already. It's possible I could get dismissed for what I've revealed today, but if I told you everything, I would most certainly be recalled and sacked.' He gave me a pleading look. 'Ambassador, please don't ask me anything further. I shall have to refuse to answer and it'll be unpleasant for both of us. I *cannot* tell you any more than I have. Be reassured that the knowledge I do have is in no way harmful to our home planet. Earth is more the observer here than a participant in anything that's likely to happen. When, or if it does, you'll find yourself in a better position without the knowledge of the possible outcome. That's it. That's all I'm prepared to say and I hope you won't persist in your demands.'

How could I? He and Charlie were like rocks. They were impenetrable. I had a choice of course. I could ask to be recalled to Earth. But – damn it, damn it – this was my first ambassadorial post. I was young and as fiercely ambitious as all my kind. If I went back home now I would be sure to be side-shuffled into a dull office job with no future. I would have failed to do my duty as the diplomatic service saw it. The intrigue was killing me, but clearly my orders were to remain ignorant of some catastrophe or other. I knew if I wanted to keep my career path open for great things I had to toe the line and remain dumb.

'Thank you, Randolph. Now if you'll leave me, I'll sit quietly and mull over this conversation. I need a little space to think. It's a bit of a shock to say the least. I'm sure you understand.'

'Completely, Ambassador.' We were back to being formal again. 'Will I see you at lunch?'

'Yes. One o'clock.'

22

FOR A LONG TIME I leaned back in my reclining chair, sitting at my desk and staring up at the sky. I could see puffs of white cloud drifting along over the sti-glass dome above my head. There was no roof on the embassy building. Hardly any house or office block on Sylvanus has a roof, since the whole city is kept at a comfortable temperature and of course no rain can fall within the bubble. The weather has been banished completely from our daily lives, which makes small talk between strangers and casual acquaintances quite difficult. It does make for an unusual environment though and I had come to like it. There's a sort of spatial feeling about it which is good for a troubled soul.

Having made the decision to stay on the planet, that out of the way I was trying to analyse my feelings regarding Imogen and indeed, all my Sylvanian companions. Did it make any difference, this news that they were not true mammals? Were they indeed a new kind of human? Were they human at all? Perhaps being born on another planet and being of a different biological composition made them aliens? I was sleeping with an extra-terrestrial, a creature from outer space, one of those beings that were inscrutable to Homo sapiens and had to be watched in case they had malevolent designs on my home planet, a world which was by definition better than any other.

In my youth I had been obsessed by classic science fiction. The kind of novels and movies which had once been a main entertainment of my ancestors. I would watch antique movies like *It Came from Outer Space; The Thing from Another World; Creature from the Black Lagoon; Target Earth; War of the Worlds; It!; Them!* – dozens more. My childhood image of an alien was a creature with absolutely no compassion, which wanted to steal or destroy my planet. The adult in me had not quite shaken off this prejudice and while I was consciously horrified by my bigotry, my subconscious remained stained.

I thought some more about my feelings for Imogen. Would this news substantially change my view of her, stop me loving her, seriously alter our relationship in any way? What, indeed, had changed now that I knew her physical composition was not what we Earthians would call 'normal'? Surely, as always, what was important was what she was like inside. I'm never sure whether to use the word 'soul' or 'spirit' when speaking of that invisible, insubstantial and indefinable core of human life. 'Soul' has religious connotations which some people find unacceptable, yet 'spirit' does not seem to have the substantial depth of that amazing life-force. I could be pretentious and use words like 'qi' but that would destroy any real profundity. Suffice to say the essence of life is what is important, rather than the shell which houses it.

I couldn't help but compare Imogen with my dear mother. Silvia was a 'normal' human being, but her personality consisted of a turbulent whirlwind of emotions, whereas Imogen was calm, moderate, ordered and composed. One heart could never be satisfied, was full of restlessness and ever seeking something which could not be named: the other thriving on contentment and love. Certainly my feelings for Jocinda Perez, my only other venture into the realms of human passion, did not compare with how I felt about Imogen. My Sylvanian sweetheart had lifted me to a whole new level of emotional experience. What the hell did it matter whether she was white, black or scarlet, had no hair or was covered in it, was vegetable or animal, so long as she was

Imogen? I loved her, deeply, and that needed no analysis or classification.

Looking out of my window, the main square of Sylvanus's only city lay below me. Actually, square it is not. It is in fact a hardwood circular plaza with an unostentatious fountain in the centre and four wooden statues quartering the circle. The statues are of the leaders of the original settlers of the planet: León, Kamala, Deepak and Chung – two women and two men. These works of art are roughly-hewn and barely recognisable as people, but their names appear below their representations so we know who they are. Apart from these chiselled lumps of timber there is nothing but small decorative trees planted at odd distances from each other, which bloom and fruit during the season, providing passers-by with beauty and the odd orange or pear.

That day the square was buzzing with life. Sylvanians, and the odd one or two visitors to this world, thronged the place. A bobbing sea of shiny bald heads moved below me, perfect for a pointillist painter's bird's eye view of the city. Avenues lead from the edge of the square like the rays of a sun. Those avenues seem to serve only to feed people to, or siphon people from, the square. As in all worlds with human life, there are those who dress simply and those who dress outrageously, though on this very conservative planet the latter were few in number. I noticed too that pausing to speak to another Sylvanian was a rare act. This is a society where people are civil rather than polite. Most exchanges are brisk and even sometimes brusque, since citizens of Sylvanus do not tend to waste time with trivial talk. They get on with their lives, often without a smile, and rarely consider idling away precious minutes with a neighbour. A strange mindset, this obsession with making the most of a day, when you consider they believed they were going to live forever.

I thought about Sylvanus as a place to live. It was a pleasant world, despite the dark side of its most precious mineral. Green, wholesome, non-violent. To my knowledge there were no volcanoes or earthquakes. I had never asked about floods, though I was aware that nine-tenths of the planet's surface was covered in water. These were mostly freshwater seas. There were no vast land masses, no large continents, no mountains or even high hills. Only low jungled islands of varying sizes. I had been reliably informed that the basis of all the planet's islands is vegetable matter. Indeed, when the planet had been formed the whole surface had been water – pleasant warm fresh water – in which sub sea plants flourished. This underwater vegetation grew so thick in places it bound to itself and the rotting mass grew more and more concentrated until it appeared as an island above the surface of the water. This build of a land base must have occurred millions of years ago, because so far as I'm aware the ground on which the city is built, the dirt on which I stand daily, appears to be no different to that of Earth's soil and clay. I'm not sure at what point minerals like LC3 were formed, or even how they became what they are, but then I'm definitely no scientist.

BEFORE I HAD BEEN KIDNAPPED, long before, Imogen had suggested and had begun planning a trip to one of the large inland lakes. There were houseboats on those lakes made of reeds, on which one could sail out to seek bays unsullied by other people. There you could moor the craft and spend time doing the things that lovers do, mostly getting to know one another better, sharing childhood secrets and in my case, proving your incompetence at cooking. Now that I'd recently had more than a taste of outdoors life, I was none too keen on this long weekend, but I knew it would wound her deeply if I tried to pull out. It made no difference that I'd been through a traumatic experience. Imogen would only see that as good training and would urge that I got back on the bike I'd fallen off as soon as possible. I could see no other route than going along with what she had long been planning.

In the slider on my way to her apartment I was naturally nervous about seeing her again. I wondered if the recent knowledge I had acquired showed on my face: whether I would act differently and thus reveal the apprehension I was experiencing. A song with the refrain 'a vegetable girl on a vegetable world' was swimming around in my head, until I realised I was paraphrasing something completely different. Women are better that men at noticing apprehension. I often wondered if we males give off a different odour when we're considering an alteration in a relationship. It certainly seemed so in my case.

When I entered the apartment she was busy packing a small backpack. She looked up and smiled.

'Hi, sweetheart,' she said. 'You all ready for the trip?'

My heart melted. I had been prepared to be revolted by this alien woman, but instead I was overcome by a feeling of deep, almost overwhelming love for her. I have already said that she, like all Sylvanians, was not beautiful. Her features were plain and her figure unspectacular. But though she moved without any real grace, her stature was tall and she was sturdy on her feet. These two aspects of Imogen endeared her to me more than any prettiness or superficial surface charm.

Imogen was straight of speech and straight of back. Looking at her I was suddenly reminded of a poem to a girl by one of the ancients – John Betjeman's *A Subaltern's Love Song* – Joan Hunter Dunn was furnish'd and burnish'd by Aldershot sun – shock-headed – wore blazer and flannels – had sports trophies lining her walls. An Amazon. That was my Imogen, a descendant of Joan Hunter Dunn, a woman full of zest and energy, strong in body and spirit, and most importantly, ready to love a man weaker than herself. If these people were more plants than flesh, then my Imogen was an oak, a cedar or a teak.

'Why are you looking at me like that?'

See? What did I tell you. You can't hide anything from them.

'I was just thinking how much I love you.'

'Oh, that's good, now can you help with the packing?'

Practical too. No nonsense. Solid character.

'I'd like you to say it back first.'

'What?' she looked a little puzzled, then smiled again. 'Oh, that. Yes, I love you. Now will you come and help?'

I stared at the small backpack.

'Not this,' she said, slightly exasperated with me. 'There're stores in the other room. We have to feed and water ourselves on the reed boat. Can you carry the boxes I've packed to the chute in the hallway? Just leave them there and I'll come in a few minutes and send them down to the pod.' She stared at me. 'Are you going in those clothes? Sailing needs shorts and shrift-shirt. Have you packed those?'

'Does it matter? I'll be in my mantle.'

'Still, you need to *feel* the part, James.' She turned and sorted through some items of her own clothing. 'You can wear some of mine – here, take these...' she held out a thin shrift-shirt and some baggy shorts, both of which were lilac coloured and had a lace trim.

'If you wanted me to cross-dress for you, I could've brought a ball gown,' I said, flippantly.

She looked impatient. 'Don't be silly. I don't even know what you're talking about. Just pack them – and for goodness sakes, please go and shift the stores from the bedroom to the hallway. I wonder you ever manage to go anywhere. You're always so dreamy.'

'Yes sir, ma'am. I'm on the job.'

I did as I was told and we were soon nestled in the pod and on our way to Lake Chartreuse, named after one of the lakes on Earth. This was of course my first trip outside the dome after the fiasco with Demosthenes. I was nervous, but then I reminded myself I always got nervous when I was out of my favourite environment – the city. This green world always seemed so vast and empty to me, and very very jungly, if there is such a word. A place where flesh and blood is regarded as unnatural. It struck me that it was me who was the alien on this planet, not Imogen.

When we reached the shores of Lake Chartreuse the light green water spread out before us with a stillness that was eerie. It looked as if it had been painted on, bringing to mind Coleridge's ancient mariner though I hoped we were not in for the same adventure as the unfortunate sailor in that poem. A number of largish reed boats shaped like Canadian canoes with open decks were moored either side of a long quay that stretched out a least a kilometre into the lake. One or two other weekenders were busy carrying stores to their craft and occupied with tasks like adjusting the rigging. There was no hold, only a low-roofed reed hut in the middle of each uniform flimsy-looking vessel. I wondered if this was really me. I had never been on a boat longer than twenty minutes, the time it took the ferry to go across Boston harbour where I once lived and worked.

'You know,' I said to my beloved, as I slipped inside a lightweight mantle prior to leaving the pod, 'I think I'd be quite happy staying here, on the boat of course, but tied up to the quay.'

She gave me one of those stares. 'You're going sailing and like it.' Her tone was not unkind, but it was uncompromising.

I lied. 'I don't know what anything's called. You people who like boats seem to feel the need to change all the names of ordinary objects, like the toilets, the back, the front, the kitchen...'

'Heads, stern, bows, galley.'

'There you go! I hope you won't shout at me when in the middle the night I pee in the galley instead of the heads, because I'm sure to forget which is which.'

'Don't be disgusting. Here, carry this,' she handed me a hamper. 'It's the sixth craft on the right. *Hilda May*. I share it with Demosthenes. They're the names of our mothers.'

'Which one is yours? Mother I mean.'

'Hilda.'

'Nice name. But then so is May. All right, I'll carry the bloody basket. Where do I put it?'

'Just dump it on the deck, then come back for more.'

'Yes, Captain Ahab.'

She straightened. 'Don't call me that, my name is Captain Bligh.'

I laughed. 'You *do* have a sense of humour!'

'Of course. Sylvanians all have a sense of fun.' But she said it so seriously, it made me laugh out loud again.

I walked along the quay with the hamper, singing in a dull Germanic voice, '*Sylvanians have a sense of humour, sense of humour Sylvanians have!*' I was stared at by bald headed boat people with expressions of stone.

Once we had everything *stowed* (another nautical term) we cast off from the quay. Progress over the placid lake was courtesy of a small waterjet engine which was out of sight and, because it was so silent in operation, mostly out of mind. I was told we would raise the sail when the late afternoon winds came, bringing in the rain. Oh joy, I thought, yes, the wonderful Sylvanian rain. An open deck and a predictable torrent expected from the sky.

'Is that hut waterproof?' I asked.

'More or less,' came the reply.

'Which?'

'Pardon?'

'Which is it? More or less.'

'Probably more, unless there's an exceptionally heavy downpour, in which case, less.'

Oh joy.

Out on the still waters, there was silence. Once we had gone far enough for the land to appear as a dark pencil line on the horizon, Imogen was satisfied and simply let the boat drift. There did not seem to be any currents, so we just sort of – well – drifted. My girlfriend then smiled at me, as if to say *this is the life*, then took out a scriptola and began to read a novel or short stories, I knew not which. I sort of went into a dreamy state, simply watching the wildlife fluttering over the surface of the water. I say wildlife, but of course I don't mean animal life. They were large seed-butterflies or seed-birds. I was occasionally amazed by an even more awesome sight of a seed with huge wings looking like a giant fruit bat or pterodactyl. Graceful non-creatures that littered the skies with not a whisper of sound in their movements over the flat tranquil surface of Sylvanus's Lake Chartreuse.

My eyes were on an eagle-sized seed with a kernel-body shaped like a banana when something startling shot upwards out of the lake. It was the long green neck and scarlet head of an underwater monster. With ravenous savage jaws it snatched the seed-eagle out of the air and swallowed it in one gulp. Then it was gone, leaving a rings of water glistening in its wake. I jumped at least a metre backwards, shocked by the swiftness and violence of the incident. The creature had had the appearance of a giant serpent, or long-necked Loch Ness monster. Fierce, ferocious and completely accurate taking its prey,

'What the fuck?' I cried.

Imogen eyes left her scriptola and she frowned.

'What is it, darling?'

'Did you see that?' I gasped. 'Did you see…it was a bloody carnivore of some kind.'

'What was?' she asked, mildly.

'That monster out there. It took one of those flying seeds out of the air with its mouth. I've never seen anything so quick.'

Imogen stared out over the lake. 'I don't see anything.'

'No, of course you don't,' I continued in the same exasperated tone. 'It was over in a flash. A long green neck and red teeth. Shot out of the water as straight as a pole. Took the poor bastard out of the air just like that.' I snapped my fingers. 'Swallowed it whole.'

An expression of comprehension swam into her features.

'Oh, one of the *Snatchers*. They're just plants, sweetheart, nothing to worry about. They eat other plants. They're not interested in Earthmen. Too fleshy. Too bony. Of course…'

'Of course *what?*'

'Of course, there are the *Giant* Snatchers, which can take a boat down whole, but I know how to avoid those. My father taught me, oh, several hundred years ago, where to avoid sailing and what to do if I was ever caught in one of the areas where Giant Snatchers grow.'

I gulped. 'You're sure you know what you're doing?'

I was suddenly very concerned for my Sylvanian partner. The Snatchers might not be interested in animals, but though she was probably not aware of it herself, Imogen was strongly, if not wholly vegetable.

'Oh yes. Though, to be entirely truthful to you, sweetheart, I've never been out on the water unaccompanied by an expert before. I used to come all the time with Demosthenes. He knew all the coves and bays where those big ones lurked. And I think I've learned from him.'

Think? She thinks she has learned. Dear sweet life, I wanted to be with someone who actually *knew*, not just thought she knew.

'Maybe we ought to go back,' I suggested. 'I'm not comfortable. Not for myself, or for you. It doesn't seem to me that you know as much as you think you do.'

Her jaw set itself, firmly. 'I'm staying. You can go back if you want. I've been in the wild lots of times and I'm still here.'

Well, I couldn't go back of course and I was unable to tell her what I knew about the composition of her body. I decided in the end that staying was akin to swimming in shark waters in the Pacific, or camping in the Australian desert where some of the snakes were deadly. The chances of actually getting attacked or being bitten were very, very small. People often took that chance, sometimes for the thrill of doing something others might consider dangerous.

23

WE FOUND A LONELY BAY and dropped our anchor there. I sat in a wicker chair on deck and surveyed the curve of the shoreline which swept round us like a live green sickle. It was pleasant and rather picturesque. There was a strand, not golden, but smooth and inviting to the eye. Indeed, we enjoyed quiet waters until the rains came and hammered on the roof of our hut.

When the deluge ceased it was early evening. Some plant tubes then broke the surface. Tubular muzzles with the diameter of old-fashioned drain pipes, they turned out to be cannons and proceeded to fire large beans up into a gentle sky which had done nothing to deserve this bombardment. It was indeed a noisy show, each tube starting with a loud sucking sound followed by a deep thump when it released its ammunition. The beans themselves varied according to which plant had shot them out. Some had little parachutes that opened when they were high in the air and these floated gently away on the back of the evening breeze. Others unfolded leafy wings, sometimes bat-like extensions, others like those of birds, and glided off into an orange sunset. It was a colourful display, a bit like celebration pyrotechnics and despite my resenting the intrusion I watched with great interest.

'Wonderful, isn't it?' said my partner, her eyes full of delight. 'I never stop marvelling at such sights.'

'Well, I would have preferred tranquillity,' I replied, 'but yes, it's quite a wonder of nature.'

We sat outside our little reed hut on the wicker chairs, holding hands like love-smitten youngsters. Together we watched the suns go down on either side of the world, one smaller than the other. Then the stars came out. Always first in the darkening heavens was bright Persicum which shone with such an intensity it almost rivalled the smaller of the two departed suns. There followed a host of others. I knew but few of the names of the constellations, let alone individual stars. Finally the whole sky was encrusted with crushed diamonds. The blaze was sufficient to give the trees shadows until the three moons came out and took over, providing enough mellow light to read by.

'This is so calm,' I said to Imogen. 'I'm just hoping that we're not in a bay where one of those monsters is going to shoot up and swallow us whole. You're sure we're safe here?'

'I think so.'

'Look, I don't want you to think so, I want you to know so.'

She looked at me with mild amusement in her expression. 'Are you afraid, James?'

'Afraid?' I laughed, a little too loudly I expect. 'Me? Of course not. I'm – I'm concerned for *you*.'

'I'm not your responsibility, you know.'

'Yes, of course, but – but still, I employ you. As your employer I'm responsible for what happens to you, aren't I?'

'No – we're not at work. We're on a dirty weekend.'

'Even worse,' I groaned. 'I can see the media now, taking me to task for *luring* my employee out here with evil intent. "So, Mr Ambassador, is this the kind of thing the people on Earth approve of – seducing innocent Personal Assistants who have no choice but to obey the wishes of their boss?" Wonderful. Demosthenes would have a field day with it. I wouldn't be surprised if he had me shot at dawn.'

'James, if I get swallowed, so will you.'

'I'm thinking of my legacy. My poor mother having to stand the disgrace of being the parent of a lewd son.'

'Well, she's put up with that until now, hasn't she, so no change there, Mister Ambassador.'

'Hey! That was uncalled for.'

This inane conversation, which could only have occurred between lovers new to each other, was interrupted by a wave which rocked the boat. Looking out over the waters beyond the entrance to the bay I could see a shape cruising on the surface. It looked like a lemon-coloured submarine: a long lozenge-shaped craft that displaced the still surface water causing large ripples to fan out in front of it.

'What the hell is that?' I cried. 'Is that your president come to check up on us?'

'James, you really are paranoid. It's only another seed carrier. The pods are released from the bottom of the lake and they float to the surface, where they puff themselves off somewhere. Then the pod opens and the seeds settle in the water, floating to the bottom.'

'But it's bloody massive!'

'It has to be. Seed-eating, free-swimming jellyplants will eat most of the cargo before it gets to the bottom of the lake to embed.'

'This is a plant-eat-plant world you live in.'

'Let's just enjoy the evening and our time together without getting too excited by nature and its wonders,' she told me. 'Tell me about when you were a little boy. Were you a tearaway or were you a goody-two-shoes? I bet you were a good little boy, your hair always combed and your socks pulled up.'

'You've been reading too many classic books. No one wore socks when I were a lad. Yes, I suppose I was a bit of a prissy boy. I had my mutinous moments though, when I rebelled and indulged in sedition. I once threw away my comb and mussed up my hair, just to show the world how savage I could be when I got mad. That showed 'em, all right. They didn't mess with me after that.'

'You're silly.'

We sat there the whole evening, talking, exchanging views on love, life and the universe. The conversation was not always so childish. Sometimes we ranged over serious subjects too. I skirted dangerously on the edge of the subject of transmutation. I talked about Darwin and Jean Baptiste Lamarck, from whom Darwin borrowed (along with Wallace) to develop or confirm his theories. However, I failed to ask outright whether my lover suspected she was more vegetable than animal, having so swiftly adapted to Sylvanus's particularly dangerous environment. I wondered if it would even shock her, living on a world where the vegetation was as lively and free-moving as it was on Sylvanus. She would probably be delighted that she was a child of her own planet rather one whose antecedents came from a distant world – a planet she would probably never see.

For her part, she delved into my past delicately but determined to find out what made me tick. She was fascinated by my mother, not because of Silvia's promiscuity – which was fairly common among Sylvanians anyway – but because of her hold on me. I explained that on Earth the mother was a dominant force in the family and a son spent the rest of his life in dutiful recognition of this fact. Yes, I said, there were some sons who broke away completely, cutting the apron strings with determination and thereafter only having occasional contact with the person who gave him birth, but I was not one of those.

'Are you afraid of her disapproval, even when you know her ideas have been fashioned by a different age and time?'

'I suppose. I do like her to approve of me. I trust her judgement on things – she has a better grip of ethics and honour than I do.'

Imogen looked wistful. 'I can't even remember my own mother – I've got ziMage-blots of her, so I know what she looked and sounded like, but that's not the same as knowing what the person is like.'

'It was a long time ago,' I remarked. 'A hell of long time. You couldn't be expected to remember.'

Memory. I wondered just how much Sylvanians did recall of their distant past. Elderly people, like my mother, had told me that their heads were so full of facts and memories gathered over a lifetime, their thoughts were slow to bring them to the surface. Old people aren't stupid, their heads are just so chock full of stuff that they've collected there, they need to process it that much more carefully and slowly. To have almost 500 years worth of junk in one's head! It seemed to me like overload. Then again, not much worth remembering happened on Sylvanus. It was a place where one day was much like the next. Their history was unremarkable and bland. No revolutions, no natural catastrophes, no multiple deaths, no amazing inventions, no wonderful art or writings, not much at all except one day following another with same-ish weather. What was there to remember that was different to what was happening right now?

That night I took off my mantle to make love to her for the first time since I had found out about her biological difference to me. When I touched her skin I was terrified I would suddenly discover it was cold and bloodless, but to my relief it was simply cool and silky. A bit like stroking an aubergine. That felt all right. Then, as we lay locked to one another, our limbs knitted together, I wondered whether her skeleton was osseous, or soft like the pith of a desert cactus. And did it matter? Randolph had said the Sylvanians were *part* animal. If I cut her, would she bleed red blood? Did she have a heart that pumped it round her body? If I rapped her head would it sound like a coconut? I was going crazy with these thoughts whirling round my brain and it obviously showed, for Imogen suddenly drew back and stared into my eyes.

'What's the matter? Are you tired of me?'

'No – no, not at all. I'm sorry, I'm a bit distracted. Work. Randolph Ng has provided me with some information which is a little difficult to analyse. I'm sorry. Now, you have my full attention.'

'You aren't upset with me for something?'

'No, I'm not. I love you. People don't get upset with people they love.'

'Yes they do, all the time.'

I sighed. 'All right, they do – but I'm really fine. Really. It's just work, that's all. Nothing to worry about. Nothing to concern you.'

'Well hurry up and get started then, Mr Ambassador, because you can't stay out of your mantle for too long.'

She was right. Her warning put some urgency into the proceedings, which spoiled our love-making completely. You can't be in a hurry and you can't regard such activity as 'proceedings'. It doesn't work. All the pleasure of passion goes out of it.

'Tomorrow,' I said. 'Tomorrow will be much better, when I'm more relaxed. I'm sorry.'

'Don't be sorry. You can't be expected to perform *every single* time we lay down together. It wouldn't worry me to spend a whole weekend just being together and getting to know one another.'

Strangely enough, I felt the same way.

24

WHEN WE RETURNED TO THE city I was immediately summoned to the President's Office. Demosthenes' face was thunderous when I was ushered in to see him. I thought it was because I had taken his ex-girlfriend away on a dirty weekend, but in fact the reason for his anger was political, not personal.

'Why wasn't I told that man was coming here?' he blurted, spraying me with spittle.

'I'm sorry, Mr President, as usual you've lost me.'

'Colonel Strang arrived from Earth yesterday. You surely knew he was coming?'

'Colonel Strang? I don't know any Colonel Strang. And I was certainly not informed of his visit.'

I was now as angry as President Demosthenes. It seemed my government was going to continue to do things without informing me. What was more, I had a strong hunch that Charlie and Randolph probably *did* know this military person was on his way.

'Well,' Demosthenes seemed to calm down a little, 'he's here on my planet without invitation or prior permission. I would like you to get rid of him as soon as possible. I have a strong suspicion of the military of any nation, but especially of a nation that is not mine.'

'A very healthy attitude, if I may say so, Mr President.'

I too was not over fond of men in the uniform of the Armed Forces of Earth, even though their job was to serve and protect the mother planet and all her satellites and dependencies throughout space. They had a habit of jumping in feet first, getting it wrong, and leaving politicians and diplomats like me to sort out the mess afterwards.

I said, 'I shall find out what the colonel's visit concerns and report back to you immediately. You may be assured I shall look into the matter with the utmost urgency. It is a gross violation of protocol to send an army man to another world without – as you say – going through the proper channels. On behalf of my government I apologise and hope to have a report for you before the end of the morning.'

Demosthenes sighed. 'I think, Mr Ambassador, you too are being dealt with in rather an offhand way. I already know why Colonel Strang is here and I'm surprised that you do not. I would have thought that your subordinates would have contacted you, wherever you were, and informed you of the visit, considering the import of the situation. Please ensure that the colonel is returned to his world within twenty-four hours.'

Underneath I was boiling with indignation at the inefficiency, possibly the effrontery of my staff. Once again I had been put in an untenable position by my subordinates and by my superiors. I seemed to be a pawn in the machinations of both. A person to be kept ignorant of any information. What the hell was going on? Between them they were destroying every vestige of my credibility. It was a shabby situation and I was determined that it should not continue beyond today.

I swallowed my pride, wanting to know before I saw Charlie and Randolph, what was the underlying reason for a colonel on the planet.

'May I ask the nature of the colonel's visit?'

Demosthenes nodded. 'I appreciate how awkward you must feel at this moment, Mr Ambassador, and I feel for you. Believe me when I say I take no pleasure in the humiliation you must be feeling, given that I should be asking the question and you answering.

'Colonel Strang wishes to bring troops here to train. He maintains that our jungles are the perfect training ground for his soldiers. The request was for a whole regiment. I refused. I do not want a regiment of warriors running amuck in our rainforests, thank you very much – how many men and women make a regiment by the way?'

'On paper, 1000 – but regiments are rarely up to full strength. Don't ask me why, it seems it's traditional. It'll be more like 600 to 800. So, what was your answer?'

'I refused permission outright.'

'Thank you, Mr President, I shall attend to the matter straight away – I believe I have the powers to remove the colonel.'

'If you do not, I do.' He paused for a moment before adding, 'I appreciate that we are under the protection of Earth's army. That should we be attacked by a rogue planet, Earth would send its troops to defend us. This is all in the charter drawn up at our independence. It's part of the payment for the cargoes of LC3 we send to your world. However, Sylvanus is under no threat of any kind at the moment, either from colonies of Earth, independent planets like our own, or – yet to be discovered – intelligent aliens not of the human race or form. To my knowledge there is no asteroid or meteor hurtling towards this globe, so no blockbusting weapons are needed to break one up before a collision. I really do not see that we need camouflaged troops infesting our rainforests. I'm sure you understand, Mr Ambassador, and will get your government to understand. This is an independent planet and if we wish to trade elsewhere, we will do it. Do I make myself clear?'

A light suddenly shone in my head. I felt very stupid for not seeing it before, but then I had just returned from gallivanting with a local woman and my vagueness was probably due to the curse of being love. A man in love is not in full command of his senses. He spends half his time dreaming and being, in the words of my departed grandmother, *soppy*. He does not think deeply or even very straight. Half his mind is on his next meeting with his beloved. The other half on the last meeting.

Of course. Demosthenes believed that Earth wanted to place troops on Sylvanus in case the Sylvanian president tried to renege on the current agreement to supply Earth with LC3. And he was probably right. My government was terrified that we would lose the rights to mine LC3 – the effects would be catastrophic for the planet Earth. The lights would go out on Broadway – and the rest of the world too. With troops in place, in case Demosthenes managed to strike a better deal with another world, we would be able to take over the mines by force. Perhaps we would then be attacked, but defenders are in a stronger position than attackers, especially when the defending army is probably militarily the best in the universe: the best trained, the best equipped, the best led.

I left the office of the President feeling very dim and stupid, and not a little humiliated. I was flaming inside. I wanted to strangle Charlie, Randolph, this bloody colonel, all the heads of the diplomatic corps and most of the government of Earth. They were selling my reputation down the river for their own nefarious ends. They were all bastards of the lowest kind and I wanted them to rot in this world before they even got to Hell.

Indeed, there in my embassy was a colonel in full combat uniform. Hard-faced, hard-eyed and probably hard-nosed. He looked as if he'd been rough-hewn out of granite by a non-too-experienced sculptor. Charlie and Randolph were standing talking to him, but they stopped abruptly on seeing me and their faces showed they expected trouble was coming. It was.

'You two, get out of my sight. I'll deal with you later. You sir, get in my office.'

The colonel drew himself up. 'I am...'

'NOW!' I yelled. 'Or do I have to order my marine to march you in there?'

The colonel glanced at the marine guarding my office door and he knew that this man was answerable only to me, not to any visiting officer he did not know, despite the rank. It would have been very embarrassing for him to be forced to do something by a common soldier. He moved towards my office doorway as the other two scattered for theirs. I followed the man through the airdoors into my room.

Colonel Strang whirled on me. 'Now you listen to me...'

'No, I don't think I will. You will shut up colonel and wait your turn to talk. I have just spent the most mortifying ten minutes of my career with the President of this planet because you decided to thrust yourself into my domain without so much as a word of warning. I don't care who sent you, I am Earth's highest representative on this world and I deserve the courtesy of a call before men in uniform arrive here. You were unannounced, sir, and you will apologise for that transgression before we go any further, or I will have you transported back to Earth without any further talk. I am waiting and not very patiently.'

He scratched his shaven right cheek, his eyes blazing, opened his mouth, closed it again, then opened it once more to say, 'Mr Ambassador, I am truly sorry to have put you in an awkward position.'

'An untenable position.'

'Yes – I apologise. But I was ordered here and told to report only to the Chargé before I saw anyone else. Then I heard you were – were on furlough – that is, not in the city, and so went ahead with my orders.'

'Which were to request permission for troops to come here and practise manoeuvres or whatever it is you do?'

'Correct, Ambassador.'

'Which was refused.'

'Yes, by this new President who…'

'Who has radical ideas about trade?'

'Godammit, yes.'

'So, your mission has been a failure and you must return to Earth and face your superiors with the bad news?'

A sort of half-smile came to his face.

'Not exactly, Ambassador. There are certain things I have to do before I go back. We expected this new president to refuse us permission. I need to carry out some surveillance before I return to Earth – and then there's the fact of my luggage.' He pointed to the corner of my office where two huge crates sat. 'I brought it through in the diplomatic bag.'

The 'bag' was a figure of speech. He had transported it to Sylvanus under the wide umbrella of the diplomatic bag, which entitled us to import equipment for the embassy without going through customs and excise, or having that equipment inspected. It was a right to which every diplomat was entitled, even the Sylvanus Ambassador on Earth. Mostly such crates contained communications gear, or sometimes goods not allowable under the local laws, such as alcohol or erotic art.

'What the hell is that?' I asked.

'Truthfully? A teleport terminal.'

I was now all at sea.

'For what purpose? I mean, we already have one. Several in fact. You used one to get here.'

'Yes, but they're all public. This one must remain a secret.'

This time the light in my head was earlier than before.

'You're going to bring the troops in anyway,' I gasped. 'Through the embassy. That's a violation of International Law. I can't allow it. I won't allow it. Those crates will remain closed until…'

'Ambassador, unless you want to be tried as a traitor, you will turn a blind eye to these plans of your government. Drastic times require drastic action. Earth cannot continue without LC3. It cannot. It will die a horrible death. Without this source of power we will descend into utter chaos and mayhem. In which case, we must preserve the status quo by any means at our disposal, lawful or otherwise. The reason we have kept you in the dark is to protect you. I am quite prepared to go down in history as the man who violated diplomatic law. As are your two immediate subordinates. You, however, we need to keep pure and unblemished. When the day comes, the three of us will willingly put ourselves to the sword, figuratively speaking, while you will be held up to the other worlds, the colonies and others, as a shining example of Earth's intention to remain a moral, ethical illustration to all its offspring worlds.'

'You'll go to prison.'

Again that half-smile. 'For a while, until the dust settles. When the talk of the rogue colonel and his accomplices has died down, they'll let us out, let us back into the fold again with quietly-awarded promotions and other rewards, and all will be well again in the universe. Now Mr Ambassador,' he continued in a different tone, almost sounding like an order, 'you have to get me out to the mines, so that I can survey the area, before these cue ball Sylvanians send me back to where I came from.'

'If it's promotion you're after, there's a much easier route. You should have married my mother.'

The colonel looked blank. 'What?'

'Never mind. It's a little joke of mine.'

I needed to get rid of this man as quickly as possible, so I called for Randolph.

'Take the colonel out to the mines, Mr Ng – then get rid of him.'

Colonel Strang was still in the room. The tag on the end of my sentence only caused the corner of his mouth to curl down into a smile.

'Yes, Mr Ambassador.'

'Then I want to see you and Ms Umboko in my office.'

'Yes, Mr Ambassador.'

25

THE INTERVIEW WITH MY TWO subordinates was as unsatisfactory as previous interviews on the same subject. I was told they had orders to keep me out of the loop. I was the buffer, the person who would come out of it all the cleanest. Charlie even told me I should be grateful and she wished she were in my place. She said she felt dirty, but then there was no other route they could take. I would understand, she said, once it was all over. What was about to happen was not at all pleasant.

'And you have orders not to tell me what *is* about to happen.'

'Correct, Mr Ambassador,' replied Randolph Ng. 'I'm sorry, but those are our orders.'

That evening I was due to attend the opera. Puccini's *Turandot*, which I never know whether to pronounce 'Turandow' or how it's spelt. I am an indifferent opera goer, but some of it I can sit through and enjoy. Puccini is probably my favourite composer, though I prefer *La Boheme* to *Turandot*. Mozart is all right, as is Verdi, but I can't stand Wagner. The modern composers, Atonius Harrwud for example, leave me absolutely depressed, in fact almost suicidal. The last one I went to by that particular musician sounded like a bunch of empty cans being dragged along a cobbled street by a bored youth with nothing better to do. It's my belief that composers these days have lost the ability to write music, but then I've been told by my mother that my tastes are old-fashioned.

You may wonder why, if I'm not a great fan, I go to the opera at all. Unfortunately, it's expected of dignitaries of my stamp. An alehouse jazz band is more my style, and I did go to those, but I also had to be seen at the ballet, opera and any new art show. An ambassador is expected to attend cultural activities, whatever they are.

Naturally, Imogen came with me and we had a box in Sylvanus's opera house, designed I believe by a maniac with a desire to create as many angles on the building as possible, but then, as I have just said, I am an old-fashioned man with antique ideas on most things, including architecture.

Imogen seemed unusually excited for some reason, which she herself could not explain.

'I just feel completely happy. I could not be happier.'

This made me feel very comfortable, of course, because my ego told me she was full of joy because she was in love. However, during the interval I noticed that the whole opera house was full of vibrant Sylvanians, chattering away, smiling, waving to friends. This was unusual. Sylvanians, as I have mentioned before, tend to be a rather dour nation, very right and proper, with conservative ideas about demeanour in public. Yet, here they were, a very effervescent crowd. Normally there was a little tension in the air at public gatherings, but tonight the social scene was light and easy, with lots of laughter and even some joshing.

The second half of the opera had many of the audience sniffling of course – me included. I do cry at beautiful music and *Nessun Dorma* always has the tears running down my cheeks. When I looked at Imogen however, she was positively beaming. Surely the opera wasn't *that* good? The sea of bald heads down below were bobbing and bouncing, as if people were enjoying the evening beyond expectations. Once the lights went on again, they all started talking at once. This was completely outside my experience of Sylvanians and I started to wonder if there was a phase of the moons, or something of that nature, responsible for this sudden upsurge in jollity and *bon vivant*.

'I don't understand why you're all so bubbly this evening,' I said to Imogen. 'Where has it come from?'

'I don't know either,' she replied and for a moment she looked worried. 'It's very strange. But does it matter? I'm half-a-thousand years of age and I'm still alive, still healthy…'

'And full of the joys of spring.'

She laughed. 'Yes, I am.'

But then so were all the other citizens of Sylvanus, which was quite unnerving in some way. I suppose I should have been unconcerned. This was a good thing, especially since their territory was about to be violated by the arrival of army troops from Earth. Perhaps they would treat such an invasion with less horror, though I doubted it. However, I did feel a twinge of alarm at their behaviour. Even Demosthenes Blake had a blissful look on his face on coming down the steps of the opera house. He put on a stern face to nod to me, but then beamed at his escort and began chattering to her about something or other.

Imogen left my side and went to speak with him, talking animatedly for a few minutes, before returning.

'Everyone's feeling good tonight,' she mused. 'It must be the stars or something.'

'The moons, I thought.'

'Oh yes,' she laughed. 'The moons.'

'Look,' I said, 'if you don't mind, sweetheart, I've got quite a lot of work to do before I retire…'

'Oh, you go.' She pushed me lightly. 'Go, go, go. I'll find some girlfriends and go out somewhere. I feel like dancing.'

'Well, if it's dancing you want, shouldn't I go with you?'

She grimaced. 'James, you don't like Sylvanian dancing, you know you don't. The last time we went dancing, you fell over three times. You have to be born to it. I don't mind, honestly. I'm happy to go out with some friends and let you do what you have to do. You're an important man,' she touched my cheek with her finger. 'I'm proud of you, James Ovit. I'm proud to be your consort.'

'Consort? Not the word I would use.'

'What would you use? Mistress? Concubine?'

'Lover,' I said, quickly. 'You're my lover.'

'Yes, I am, aren't I?' she murmured. 'Well, lover-man, go and put the world to rights while your frivolous lover-girl goes out on the town to enjoy the shallow delights of the city of Sylvanus.'

I left her and went straight to the embassy without changing out of my glad rags. When I arrived I was astonished to discover the teleport had already been erected and was in working order. Apparently the engineers had begun the work when the office closed for the day and had finished it in record time. The colonel was in attendance.

'I thought you were leaving?' I said, coldly.

'I am. Tonight. But, in the words of a famous general from history, *I shall return.*'

'Bringing with you invasion troops.'

'Don't bother your head with it, Ambassador.' He looked at me sharply. 'Don't judge me until you know what's going on, which you will very shortly.'

'I wasn't aware that an announcement from the President was imminent.'

'I don't suppose it is. This has nothing to do with the President of Sylvanus.' He hesitated a second or two before adding, 'Ambassador, you're about to see a change come over this planet. I'm no scientist, but I've been assured by those that are, that something quite extraordinary is going to happen here. Something very unpleasant. When it happens – expected

249

probably within the next few days – maybe even tomorrow? – we need to have troops here to protect our interest.'

Shades of what Randolph and Charlie had been hinting at. 'What is it? What will happen?'

'That's classified information. You only have to wait. Don't worry, you're safe, I'm safe, all Earthians are safe.'

'The Sylvanians? Something is going to happen to them?'

'I'm afraid so. And there's nothing we can do to stop it. It's as inevitable as death and taxes, Ambassador. I understand you've grown rather fond of a local woman?'

'Yes, yes I have.'

He said nothing but I read tragedy in his expression.

'This – this event?' I said, desperately. 'Is there really nothing that can be done? I have money and influence...'

'Nothing. Please. I've told you because the time is almost here – don't ask me for any more. Just prepare yourself for the worst. There won't be any survivors. It'll be the whole population.'

A short while later, Colonel Strang went back to Earth, using a public teleport. I sat at my desk and stared into space, my mind whirling with possibilities that all seemed ludicrous to me. Surely anything that could destroy the whole population of a world would involve the destruction of any foreigners too? An asteroid or meteor hitting the planet. A core explosion. A sun going nova. They were all hugely improbable scenarios anyway. Then it struck me. Plague. An illness? A deadly virus that would affect only the locals? That had to be the answer.

But in the normal run of things, even that didn't make sense. None of the locals showed any signs of falling ill. Surely it wouldn't affect them all at once? I recalled the nursery rhyme *Ring-a-ring o' roses*. That had been about a plague, the last line being '*All fall down!*' The fall of the dying victims. Yet, that was just a figure of speech. They didn't drop down all at once. The words simply fitted the children's rhyme. There was no sickness that I could recall whereby everyone caught it at once and died together. No, none of it made sense and I began to wonder whether I was being taken for a ride. This hope was soon crushed by the thought that no one had anything to gain by duping me.

While I was deeply mired in these dark unpalatable thoughts the airdoors to my office rippled and then Imogen stood there. She was glowing. Her eyes sparkled and her skin had a fine sheen to it. She flashed a broad smile at me and she seemed very excited. Joyful, I suppose the right word might be. I had never seen her in this mood before. Like all Sylvanian citizens she was normally quite reserved and unexcitable.

'I've been dancing. Now let's go for a walk,' she said, breathlessly. 'It's too nice a night to go to bed and just sleep. Let's just go out and enjoy the atmosphere. Everyone's out there. Let's go and watch the fountains change colour in the square?'

She tripped lightly, almost skipping forward, and took my hand in hers. Her fingers and palm were warm to the touch and smooth as silk. I stared into her face, electric with pleasure. This was not the Imogen I knew. It was a very lovely Imogen, but not *my* Imogen. She frightened me, in this mood, especially after my talk with Colonel Strang.

'Are you feeling all right?' I said. 'You're – you're not unwell?'

She looked surprised and then smiled again. 'No, why should I be?'

'Well, you seem a little – overheated. You haven't got a temperature?'

Imogen laughed. 'No – no of course not. I just feel, I don't know, very happy. It's sort of in the air tonight.' She then said playfully, 'Perhaps it *is* in the stars? Look, there's *our* star, Capsicum. Yours and mine, sweetheart.' She peered through the sti-glass dome at the encrusted sky. 'Oh, just look at those stars, darling. How could anyone not find them beautiful – beautiful enough to fill your spirit with happiness?'

'They're there every night,' I said.

'Don't be a grouch. Come on. You've done enough work. Let's go for a walk through the streets. It's a wonderful night.'

Indeed, the streets were full of Sylvanians in party mood. They were singing. They were dancing. They were full of *bonhomie*. It was like being in a room full of people who had had just a little too much alcohol to drink. Yes, that was it, they seemed intoxicated, but with pure pleasure. I then began to wonder if this was some spontaneous ad hoc festival of some kind. They were on the cusp of a centenary. Their fifth. That would make sense. Every hundred years they might instinctively feel the need to celebrate their continued good health, good life, perhaps with that underlying strong belief in a unique immortality. Maybe the feeling came over them and they just couldn't stop themselves frolicking in the streets, without really understanding why.

I gave in. I just started having a good time. It was impossible not to, with a child-like Imogen bouncing around, pointing at stars, moons, fountains, lights, with such joy in her expression. We met almost everyone we knew and they were all of the same disposition. I tried to bring back my conversation with Strang, take on a serious frame of mind, but it was impossible in the atmosphere of those streets. The jubilation was at fever pitch and I was caught in the elation of the moment. The rest of the night was swept away in a whirlwind of partying in the streets.

When the dawn came, we were both exhausted and we crept back to my apartment, still in a joyous but quiet mood. There I found a message on my dansefloor, telling me I had been recalled to Earth. I was supposed to teleport as soon as possible. Fat chance. There was no way I was going to leave this planet at this precise point in time. Whatever they wanted from me was going to have to wait until I was ready to give it. The last thing I did before falling asleep was to turn off all communication devices, so that we wouldn't be disturbed.

26

OPENING MY EYES AFTER A long sleep which has taken me halfway up the ladder of morning, I stare with astonishment at the face on the pillow next to mine. It is stunningly beautiful. The eyes are closed, but the eyelashes are long and silken on her cheek. Her hair, which now falls from her head in a silver cascade, so invites my touch I can't help myself reaching out and running my fingers through the locks. She wakes at this and smiles at me with full pink lips and teeth that are dazzling in their white purity. Now I see her eyes and almost gasp at the loveliness of them, the colours being rich and wonderful. These are the physical changes of course, but there is also an animation in her features that has never been evident before this moment. I am absolutely captivated and enchanted by her beauty which is so exquisite it frightens me.

'Good morning, darling,' she says, this erstwhile plain woman who has turned into Aphrodite. 'Your mouth's open. Please close it, it doesn't look attractive like that.'

'I'm sorry,' I reply, 'but – but you've changed. You've changed overnight. You're incredibly gorgeous this morning.'

'Whereas I am usually…?'

'Well, *attractive* to me, of course, but look at yourself – you have hair now. Your features have altered. You've always had nice pale skin, but this morning it's positively creamy.'

She sits up quickly, saying, 'Get me a mirror.'

I do what she asks. When I return with my shaving mirror, she's running her fingers through her hair in bemusement. She takes the mirror and I can see how startled she is by her own image. Obviously this has never happened to her before now. I watch her expression as she tries to fathom exactly what's going on. I ask the ziMage for local news and there on the dansefloor is the newscaster, a Sylvanian man whose face I am used to seeing, but this morning he's handsome beyond any surgery or make-up. The same silver hair which has grown on my Imogen overnight, covers his head, though I can see he's made an attempt to cut it shorter. His face is ruggedly good looking. He would make a good ziMage star or celebrity, something of that nature.

He's saying, '…Sylvanus woke this morning to a startling transformation – a change to the physical appearance of all its citizens. Indeed, I have not heard a single instance – please call in if *you* have, because we would love to hear from you – not a single instance where the change has not taken place. The government is as puzzled as everyone else. What has happened to us? Personally, I feel quite well in myself.' He seemed to muse on this fact for a few seconds. 'In fact I feel terrific this morning. So what do these alterations to our physical form mean? Our scientists are working on this weird and wonderful phenomenon even as I speak…'

Then other Sylvanians begin to appear on the screen as the next programme comes on. They are all equally beautiful people with lovely complexions, wonderful eyes and perfect bodies, shoulders hung with a long curtain of that silver hair. They all have this expression of bewilderment, though some seem to be accepting it with a shrug, while others are looking as if they need an answer immediately.

'What's happened?' cries Imogen, in alarm. 'Why have we changed?'

I begin to dress. 'I don't know, sweetheart, but don't be alarmed. All that's really occurred is that you've grown hair. Yes, your features have altered too, but not in a terrible way. In a good way. Look, you haven't woken up and found your body covered in boils, or with some horrible skin complaint. You've woken up and found you're – you're absolutely lovely. There can be nothing sinister in that, surely? I don't for a moment think this change is a bad thing. I have to get in to the office. They recalled me to Earth yesterday. I'm not leaving. Not immediately, anyway. But I have to go in and talk to someone.'

'Yes, yes, of course. Oh, I hope they don't make you go home. We're having such a wonderful time together.'

'They can't *make* me. I shall resign and stay on here, somehow, if your ex-boyfriend will let me. Look, don't come in to work today. Take the day off and talk to your friends. Get a feel for what they think of it all. I'll meet you later at the Café des Artistes? All right. Later in the morning?' I glance at the time. 'No, I mean, this afternoon. The morning's almost over.' I give her a kiss, before moving towards the doorway. 'Chin up, sweetheart. Everything's fine, I'm sure. There'll be a perfectly simple explanation for all this.'

With that I leave my apartment. My slider is waiting at the ramp below. I call the embassy as I speed over streets crowded with beautiful people. They seem to be out on show, saying to the world, hey look at me, I'm something special out of the chocolate box. Yes, they're actually parading, admiring each other, not at all self-conscious and – worryingly – most appear unconcerned at the metamorphosis which had taken place over the last twenty-four hours. Despite my earlier speech to Imogen, telling her not to worry, I'm extremely uneasy. It seems to me, watching this cavorting, that they should be asking themselves *why*, rather than delighting in the change that's taken place so suddenly. Why has this strange metamorphosis occurred overnight, without precedent, without warning, without any rational reason for it?

Charlie appears on the vehicle's ziMage dansefloor.

'Where have you *been*?' she asks, pointedly. 'All hell has been let loose.'

'Hell or Heaven?' I reply. 'Everyone looks like an angel this morning – except you and me, of course.'

'This is no time to be facetious, James! This is serious. We hadn't expected it to happen quite this quickly. You know they're asking you to go home? I think you should. Get to a teleport – now.'

'You have to be joking. I'm not going just like that. I want an explanation first. Why do they want me back on Earth right now, at this point in time? Has it got anything to do with the change in the locals?'

I expected her to say, 'No, of course not.'

Instead she replied, 'It has everything to do with it.'

'Shit! Really?'

'Really. You won't like it, I assure you. Best you stay out of it. Go home, James.'

I switch off. No way. No way am I returning to Earth. Not now. Hopefully not ever. This planet is my new home.

Randolph is waiting for me in the lobby. He nods curtly and leads me through a steadily increasing number of soldiers in combat uniform, presumably arriving through the portal erected earlier. They must have been zipping in at one a minute. They take no notice of me, except to glance and probably note that I am no threat to their operation. Colonel Strang is on the ground floor, surrounded by a small group of officers, no doubt discussing strategy and tactics, things I know nothing about. This is a gross violation of the usage of an embassy and if those people at home think they are going to keep me quiet about it, they've got another think coming. Anger is only just below the surface of my skin, ready to burn holes in anyone who tries to justify this interplanetary crime.

'Mr Ambassador,' says Randolph, 'please sit down. I can see you're upset and you've every right to be, but please don't say anything until you've heard from me. I want to tell you what's going on. It's not very pleasant. Strange and wonderful in a way, but very nasty for those citizens out there in the city. You especially, are not going to like it, considering your – your closeness to one of them.'

'Go ahead,' I say, coldly.

Randolph draws a deep breath and says, 'They're dying.'

'Who?'

'The Sylvanians. Every last one of them. I'm sorry.'

I tried to take this in, my thoughts naturally dwelling mainly on Imogen.

'Dying?' I repeat. 'All of them?'

'Let me explain. You remember Lars Peterson?'

'Of course.'

'You will then recall the fuss caused when one of our doctors performed an autopsy on him? The doctor found something so unusual he called in government scientists, who thoroughly examined the remains and found a high percentage of vegetable matter in the make-up of the corpse.'

'You've told me all this before.'

'I have. But what I haven't told you is they isolated and identified the genus of that vegetable matter. It had a correlation with a type of bamboo found on Earth. There are around a thousand varieties of bamboo known to us. This genus has a number of common names – Fish Pole bamboo, Stone bamboo, Golden bamboo.'

'And the Latin name?'

'*Phyllostachys.*'

My mind is spinning. I'm no botanist. The word *Phyllostachys* means nothing to me. I'm trying to grasp the significance.

'Go on.'

Randolph sucks in another breath before replying, '*Phyllostachys* has a rather unusual life cycle. It lives for a hundred years, then, all over the world, no matter where it is – in someone's garden in England or out on the plains of China – it flowers, then it dies. You don't have to take my word for it. Look it up. *Phyllostachys*. It flowers then dies, no matter where it is, after a century of life as a bamboo plant.'

My mind still spins, but has gathered some intelligence.

'Good God,' I say, as ice forms in my gut, 'you're telling me that the Sylvanians are flowering – and that they will die very soon.'

'They're dying now, Mr Ambassador. We have brought in the troops not to steal the mines from the Sylvanians. There will soon be no Sylvanians. We've brought them in to protect Sylvanus from an invasion by other planets who will see the situation as a free-for-all. Everyone is jealous of Earth and its privileged position of trade. Once they hear that Sylvanus no longer belongs to anyone, they'll send their own troops to try to secure the mines. We'll be here already, to turn them back.'

'I feel sick.'

'I quite understand, sir. Would you like to return to Earth now? I understand you've had your orders.'

I ignore this. 'But a hundred years? These people have lived 500 years.'

Randolph shrugs. 'Different planet. Different conditions. Our scientists examined the cells and with the help of their computers came up with an accurate time period. Half a thousand years. It's sad, but I personally can't feel all *that* sorry for them. They've had five of our lifetimes. A massive bonus. And think, James, nothing lasts forever. There is a finite time to everything. You're just unlucky, falling in love at quite the wrong time in the cycle. I'm not unsympathetic to your pain.'

I grasp at straws. 'But the *Phyllostachys* genus of bamboo must regenerate somehow – surely?'

'Yes, from the root that remains after the plant has died.'

The straws do not hold me up. I continue to drown.

'And of course,' I say, despairingly, 'Sylvanians have no roots.'

This needs no answer from Randolph.

I stare out through the sti-glass dome at a world covered in forests of trees and shrubs, grasses and wildflowers. Some of the trees are as tall as city towers, others bushing out, covered in magnificent blooms. The lushness of the foliage out there, the trunks bearing parasitic growths, their boles hidden by tangles of vines. Some of the creepers hanging from boughs have woven themselves into curtains. They loop and curl from place to place, forming swings and nooses. Up high are mosses and ferns, growing from those trunks the tops of which touch the clouds. It is a labyrinth of green vegetation, which every so often explodes into a riot of big waxy flowers and elaborate blossoms, their petals as colourful as the wings or tail feathers of exotic birds. The Sylvanians have enjoyed this world for 500 years. Now they have to leave it in the way their planet wants them to, has designed them to leave, as one of its plants.

27

I LEAVE THE EMBASSY TO my two subordinates and a colonel with his troops. They have no use for me and I none for them. For the next five hours I search the city looking for Imogen. Already people are dropping to the ground, lying there with bemused expressions on their faces, seemingly not in pain, but life draining from their bodies. I step over and around them. There are too many for me to concern myself with individuals. I feel for them as a nation, but I can't stop what's happening. There is no help for them anyway. If this could have been prevented I believe my own people would have done so, despite their seeming callousness: the plans to take over the mines; the troop movements. This is the destiny this strange planet has devised for its inhabitants and it is inevitable.

I can't find Imogen. She's in none of the usual places. In desperation I go to the Presidential Palace and take the lift up to the President's Office, stepping over bodies in the corridors. She's here, my Imogen, but locked in the arms of President Demosthenes. I go to her in tears to stroke her dear beautiful face. It's slimy to the touch. She's gone and I never got the chance to say goodbye. I realise that as with most sudden deaths the living rarely have the opportunity to tell their loved ones all those things they have regretted saying or doing, or to recount moments that were precious. But still the bitterness comes to me in a nasty flood. I'm desperate for a few words before we part forever. I need to tell her how unique and cherished she is to me.

Time and circumstance are robbers of those balms we need the most in grief.

Demosthenes hugs her tightly. He's still just alive.

He smiles at me and says, 'In the end, I won.'

'Yes, you did,' I say, nodding, the wetness still streaming down my cheeks, 'in the end.'

The President dies as I watch. He's still gripping her slim wrist with his right hand. He's clutching so tightly that at first I can't peel his grasp away. So I take his individual fingers, one by one, and bend them backwards until they break. Each one of them snaps at the base like a raw carrot. Then I take her corpse and lay it out lengthways on the long grey sofa that stands against one of the walls. Hopefully it will be a while before she begins to fully deteriorate, so I stay for a while, simply looking at her, hoping she is happy. Later, I use the President's ziMage to call my mother. She's not surprised to hear from me. Silvia is dressed up to the nines as usual, in a glittering gown covered in silver stars. She amazes me with her longevity and her late-life energy.

'Are you calling to tell me you're getting engaged?' she says, archly. 'I've heard all about your romance from Charlie. Let me see an image of this girl. Is she lovely?'

'Yes she is, Mother. Very lovely. She's – she's resting at the moment.' I turned the ziMage towards my sleeping beauty, giving Silvia a good view of the body. 'What do you think? I don't deserve such a woman, do I?'

'Oh,' says Mother, 'what a catch! Yes, you're very lucky. As to deserving her, you're not a bad catch yourself, young man. Ambassador Ovit.' She peers, myopically. 'Yes, a very pretty girl. My, my, silver hair?' She pats her own copper curls. 'It could be the next fashion. You must be very happy, son. When's the day? Don't wait too long, mind. Am I invited to the wedding? Where is it to be, here or there?'

'We're not sure yet. I'll let you know. I'm coming home, Mother – very shortly. Just a few things to tidy up here first.'

'Oh, wonderful. Look, this call must be costing a fortune. I'm off to a concert anyway. Lots of love, ducky. See you soon.'

I clear down and stare out of the windows. The end is very near. They're dropping in the streets by the hundreds. It's the saddest thing I've ever seen. People – and they are real people – are dying *en masse*, a dreadful thing, the recall of which alone will mar memories of one of the happiest periods in my life. The love of my life lies on the sofa without breath in her body, taken from me by a quirk of botanical science. She believed she would live forever, but like everything else in the universe, her time was finite. Why it had to come to an end just when I came on the scene is a selfish thought, but one which engenders the most acid of feelings in my breast. If there is a Supreme Being anywhere out there, stringing the stars together, he or she must hate my guts. Given with the right hand and snatched back with the left. It was ever thus, was it not, throughout all of mankind's history?

Damn the flowering of Sylvanus.

The airdoor ripples and someone now staggers into the room, a Sylvanian man I don't know. His beauty is beginning to turn fungal. There are pustules and growths on his face and arms. His body has been ravaged by rips and tears, which leak fluids. For some reason this man is dying slowly, rather than swiftly as my Imogen did. Death is creeping over him rather than striking him down. His eyes are full of terror, the foliage on his face, his head, and the normally bare areas of his skin, is revolting. He sees me and with superhuman effort drags himself across the floor and kneels at my feet, his expression piteous.

'Help me,' he croaks. 'Please help me!'

I can do nothing for him. Nor, when I go out into the street carrying Imogen's body in my arms, for the other citizens milling around with expressions of disbelief on their faces, mixed with infinite sadness. Soldiers are moving among them, but they have a duty to do and are having to ignore the chaos to get to their given posts. Nevertheless, they cannot help glancing at the dying Sylvanians with expressions of amazement and horror. Soldiers are human beings too, though their emotions are often locked in by their strict disciplinary code of conduct and a sense of the importance of their mission.

It is now coming on evening and with Imogen in my arms I look up at a bright star – *our* star – Capsicum and ask it some age old questions, 'Why? Why me? Why us? Why now?'

28

THE ARMY HAS TAKEN OVER the mines and have set up defence systems in case any other planet tries to claim them. I have been called by my superiors and told to take over governorship of the planet. They were intending to send someone else, I'm sure, but when I refused to return to Earth they changed their minds. I'm not sure why, but I expect it's because I've been here a while and know the place. Anyone else coming in cold would be fumbling around asking questions and not really in a position to lead. It's not a promotion I enjoy, but I have my duty to do for the citizens of my home planet.

Recently we've had to remove the bodies of the Sylvanians from the confines of the city. Their corpses were swiftly decomposing and the air in the metropolis became foul with the odour. I lost touch with Imogen's body among the mounds of Sylvanian dead. It's now among those they're piling on the edge of the rainforest, great mountains of them, far too many to be concerned with observing rituals or even formal procedures. They're now no better off than decaying cabbages, thrown on compost heaps at the end of gardens, left to rot in the sun and the rain.

Garry Kilworth

Part Three:

MEMOIRS OF A MONSTER

1

'YOU'VE RESIGNED FROM YOUR POST as ambassador?' exclaimed my mother, a little distracted by more important things like getting ready to go out for the evening. 'Why, darling? I thought you loved the diplomatic service.'

'They killed my sweetheart.'

'Well, they didn't exactly *kill* her, did they?'

'They treated her remains like garbage though.'

'But what are you going to do now? You're too young to retire. We can afford it, of course, if you'd like to lay around the house or become an interworld playboy, but I know you'd get itchy feet. You're a doer, not a sitter-arounder.'

'Oh, I don't know,' I replied, listlessly, watching some robotic hair artist do things with the top of her head. Then I added, flippantly, 'Maybe I'll become a hit man for the government. You know, go out and shoot people they don't like. They seem to enjoy destroying life.'

'Goodness, lovely, would you really be suited? Would you be any good at that sort of thing? I seem to remember as a youth you couldn't even hit the toilet bowl when you drank too much. Oh, that's just right,' she said to the mechanical hairstylist, 'you can leave it just as it is.'

'Not yet finished,' muttered the machine. 'Still some to do.'

'Well I like it as it is and you can stop just there, thank you very much.'

The device ceased its operations, but it was clearly a little sulky. I left then, having an appointment with a friend. I actually forgot all about my conversation with Silvia the moment I left the room, but she had not. Unfortunately, she took my remarks about becoming an assassin seriously and passed them on to her latest husband, who duly referred me to Military Intelligence 26H, the department of the government which dealt with 'tidying up' as they called it.

'Tidying up' meant going back into the past and eliminating the mistakes of travellers from a future era. Sometimes that involved permanently getting rid of the travellers themselves when they posed a serious threat to the world of the future and refused to return to face criminal proceedings. The policy was that it was better to remove one fairly useless life when millions of others were threatened.

I had returned to Earth from Sylvanus completely jaded. I was sick of this future world into which I'd been tugged. So I decided to go back to an even earlier time and place, but choosing just when and where was not easy, especially since I had to have a very good reason for going or the Tempus Fugit Department wouldn't let me near their damn time machine.

In every era there are always madmen. These times are no different to any other. Some of you reading this chronicle of my travels through time and space will be aware of a novel written by a woman in the 19th Century. Her name was Mary Shelley and the novel's title was *Frankenstein*. The premise is that the main protagonist gathers together body parts of dead people and joins them together to make a completely new human, into which Frankenstein injects life. Far from being grateful the new patchwork creature is upset because his creator did not forsee the trials he would undergo as a walking *lusus naturae*. Thus there is a monstrosity wandering abroad, creating all sorts of mayhem amongst the decent people of Europe, even to the point of killing them. Naturally Frankenstein. is concerned by this and sets out to uncreate his biological invention, thus acting as God not once, but twice.

Fine, this was the novel, which some students still have to study when ploughing through a degree in Literature. Had the book been left as a novel, all would be peaceful in the Swiss Alps of the 1900s. But that was not to be the case. Enter the madman, from my own period. Josef Linstaph who read the novel as a young man and decided that at last we had the technology to do in the real what Dr Frankenstein did in fiction: make a new human being out of bits of old ones. However, suprisingly enough such experiments are actually illegal in our millennium, so using time travel Josef decided to revisit the 1900s and actually recreate the whole thing in that century, which of course would be much more authentic.

Josef somehow got permission to go back to Mary Shelley's time on a false premise and then manufactured the monster, which promptly killed him, being as upset with him as the original had been with Dr Frankenstein. Thus there is a monster wandering 1800s Switzerland, looking for Percy Bysshe Shelley's wife in order to do the same to her, since it was her manuscript which was eventually responsible for his miserable existence.

Travelling into the future, such as my mother and I had done, did not cause too many problems. Someone arriving from the past simply drops into society as if he or she had come from a geographical location. Time travel to the *past* however, can cause all kinds of havoc, not only with history but with the future too. You could end up wiping yourself or your loved ones out of existence. As one early writer noted, treading on a simple insect like a butterfly in unrecorded prehistory could end up altering the whole course of recorded history. A time traveller to the past has to be very, very cautious and not do something which would gravely affect generations to come – for instance, creating a monster which might then go on to remove many of the descendents of later periods.

When I entered my apartment late one evening my dansefloor was holding a call from a government official. I knew her. I had been on a course with her when I first joined the diplomatic service. Her name was Judy Skelling, now a second level executive in MI33-H, or Miss Havisham as it had been nicknamed. I called her back and her lean attractive personage appeared on my dansefloor.

'James, how are you?' she asked.

'I'm well, Judy – and you?'

'Fine thanks. Look, I understand you want to join us, my department that is, in a somewhat different role to your work with the diplomatic service?'

'Do I?'

'We received a request from one of the council. The word is you would like to take on the task of bleaching.'

Bleaching. Getting rid of stains. *Stains* as in time travellers who do wrong. Killing people.

'Who said that?' I asked.

'I can't say. It would breach security. However, your mother…'

Oh God, that conversation we had while she was being titivated by her robot hairstylist.

'Well, actually, I was being frivolous when I said I wanted to be an assassin for the government.'

'What we have in mind is anything but frivolous, James. There's a potential monster ready to run amuck in the 19th Century. A terrible artificial creature created by someone from our time. We have to eliminate his creation.'

'You're talking about Josef Whatsisname's recreation of Frankenstein's monster?'

'Not a *recreation*. The original was merely a character in a book. We need you to go back and destroy the beast before it goes on the rampage. Really James, I'm not joking. I can see you laughing...'

'I wasn't laughing, I was smiling. Different thing. What makes you think I could hunt down this poor grotesque and destroy it? I've never shown any ability at killing living creatures. I'm not sure I want to. Why don't we just wait until we see that it's harmful? It might be quite benign.'

'It's a monster fashioned from the charnel houses of murderers. I don't suppose it's got a benign cell in its whole body. It was put together in order to send it out to kill as many human beings as it could before it was destroyed itself. James, its hunting grounds are Switzerland in 1818. One of your great-grandfathers was sent to Geneva in that year as a member of the Diplomatic Corps. This was before he had any children. I don't want to alarm you, but you could be gone in the blink of an eye.'

So, it was personal. Silvia and I were prime victims for vanishing without a trace. It seemed I had to go back to the early 1800s and execute the monster created by Josef Linstaph before it had time to run amuck amongst our grandfathers and grandmothers, wiping us all off the face of history.

In the end I agreed to try. I told them I couldn't promise to be successful, but I would certainly join the team they intended sending back to eliminate – that is to say, *bleach* – the ugly historical stain that was threatening our very existence.

2

THE TIME PACK THEY GAVE me before sending me hurtling back through the years would enable me to make short hops back and forth in the 1800s. It was a useful safety device if I got into trouble. If I ended up in prison for any reason, I could hop back a couple of days and then again jump over the top of the dangerous period. The device was only about the size of a man's hand, so it was easy to carry on one's person. It could also be used as a signalling device to the Tempus Fugit Department, who had the ability to recall me without my assistance.

Decked in the clothes of my destination period, carrying a deadly modern weapon disguised as a smooth-bore duelling pistol and with plenty of Swiss coins and notes about my person, I was zapped back in time. Contrary to the beliefs of those who pretended to send me from 1955 to 2055, one does not have to travel naked through time. You can sit astride a powerful jet-zitter and still get to where you want to go in the past or in the future, the bike coming with you.

If there had been any expectation on my part regarding a hue and cry in 1818 Switzerland I would have been disappointed. The monster was not on everyone's lips. In fact I had a hard time finding someone who knew about him. Eventually I spoke in perfect German, injected before I left home, to someone who had heard rumours of a strange, unhallowed experiment in Annecy, a small town not far from Geneva. I hired a horse and rode out towards the town, intending to stop at an inn overnight.

It was the first time I had been in the saddle since riding a heavy farm horse at harvest time in my youth in Essex, England. I hadn't *actually* ridden a Shire of course – it was one of my false memories of the 1950s – but since I *thought* I had, the remembrance-skill was embedded in my psyche. I knew to mount from the left, to hold the reins high and to use my heels to guide the beast along the rough tracks. It was a gentle animal anyway and we got on well together, trotting along paths fringed by very pretty alpine flowers, the birds singing, the breeze soughing in the firs and pines.

In the city of Geneva I had not been an oddity, there being many people of different cultures and races doing business there. Out in the sticks however, I was definitely *peculiar* and I found those I passed on the way eyed me warily, as if I were a government tax collector or an officer from duty and customs. One man on a hay waggon that I stopped and asked the way looked at me as if I were a werewolf or vampire and hurried on by without answering. When a long way ahead he yelled something back, but his French was so thick I understood not a single word.

At the inn I received the same sort of reception, though there were one or two sophisticated types who were, like me, passing through. I spoke to a merchant who was on his way to meet a counterpart from the Americas and enquired if he had heard any rumours about a madman wandering the mountains. He replied that there was a story about a citizen who had appeared naked in a large town to the east, whose twisted tongue spouted nonsense words. Clothes were stolen from a washing line and the stranger had left the main town to run abroad in the surrounding countryside.

'*Danke*,' I said, rising from the table after having bought him another tankard of ale. '*Gute reise.*'

'*Und sie auch*,' he replied.

After a night at the inn I continued on my journey to the small town of Annecy, which turned out to be not much more than a village. There I nailed several posters to trees on the edge of the habitations which simply said:

MRS PERCY BYSSHE SHELLEY WISHES TO
SPEAK WITH YOU. BE AT THE VILLAGE
PUMP HOUSE AT MIDNIGHT.

It was written in all three languages of the Swiss: German, French and Italian and I couched the note in terms that would put off any local youths who took it into their heads that this was a young woman wanting company. The pump house could indeed be swarming with swains hoping to roll a girl in the straw of a farmer's loft. It was doubtful indeed that they had heard of the authoress who had not at this date on the calendar put her name to her famous novel. Mary and her poet had just left Switzerland for Italy, Percy still being very much alive at this date. It would be a few years before it became known that *Frankenstein* had been written by a mere woman and even then there would be those who attributed it solely to Percy.

The monster would know who Mary Shelley was, having been told of his originator by his maker, Josef. I only hoped he was intelligent and schooled enough to be able to read at all. It was entirely possible he was ignorant of learning of any kind and I was going to be faced with a wild boar of a man. I was just beginning to feel fear at the meeting and my hand constantly went to gripping the butt of the pistol beneath my coat. Was I actually going to kill a man, even though he was several dead men brought back to life? The thought was as chilling as it was bizarre. This poor grotesque of a human being was walking straight into my melter.

Having booked a room at the inn, I sat in a corner on my own, listening to the chatter of those quaffing ale and wine, and tearing the limbs from roasted capons, until I heard the clock strike the first of twelve notes. Then I took a dark lantern from the rack by the main door and prepared it for going out into the night.

'You're going for a walk?' cried my landlady. 'At this hour?'

I thumped my chest lightly with the side of my fist.

'I need clean air before retiring. The smoke in here is harmful to my chest.'

She cocked her head to one side. 'Smoke? *Pipe* smoke? That's good for the lungs, that is. The night airs are full of miasmas. It's out there that you'll find things to clog your chest.'

'Still, I have my routine,' I replied, stiffly. 'It's what I've always done and if I don't I'll have difficulty in sleeping.'

She shrugged her bony shoulders. 'If it's what you've always done...'

She helped me light the dark lantern and I stepped outside in the coldness of the Swiss night. It would have been as black as death out there without artificial light. On the ground was a covering of snow that shone in the light of the lantern and the crystalline carpet crunched beneath my feet. I opened a second panel of the lantern and stumbled my way along the street to the pump house, a construction not much more than a thatched roof supported by four roughly-hewn wooden pillars. It kept the snow and rain off the heads of those using the pump.

Once there I closed the panels on the dark lantern and stood in the blackness waiting for my victim, my bootsoles deep in the cold, cold snow. I was unused to weather conditions like these – snow, wind, rain and ice were not tolerated in the future world where weather was controlled and regulated – and I had a frozen hand on the butt of the pistol the whole time, ready to produce the weapon and squeeze the trigger. When I did so, a bolt of energy would be ejected from the muzzle of the barrel and the target would dissolve in front of me. There would be a small pile of ash left, of course, but this would soon be blown away by the breeze.

Nervously I waited and waited. I was no born killer, so all sorts of tangled emotions fought for space in my chest. Rights and wrongs struggled to make themselves known to me and I have to say the wrongs were winning.

There was no moon, so my ears were intent on listening for footfalls. I doubted the monster would come with a light of his own and I had to rely on senses other than sight to note his presence. Once or twice I jumped or started at a noise. Some creature or other, but not my victim. A rat or a cat slinking through the murk of the early morning. Each sound, no matter how soft, had me whirling and peering into the dense gloom. No one came. Either my monster had not seen, read or understood the notice – or he had guessed it was a trap and would never answer the call. In the end I gave up and went back to the inn and to bed. I was disappointed, sure, but also slightly relieved. I had serious doubts about my ability to destroy a living creature, no matter that it should already be dead.

I lay in an uncomfortable, lumpy bed with covers that weighed a ton ruminating on my quest. It was morally ambiguous at best and plain unsavoury at worst. I had always considered myself an honourable man, but I was entering a turbid area with this mission of assassination. *Assassin!* The very word sounded onomatopoeic. Put simply it sounded like a bad thing and could never be justified as good. *Executioner.* At least that had a neutral air to it, the man carrying out the deed being a disinterested tool belonging to those who have ordered the death sentence.

Snores came through the thin wall from the adjoining room and I knew that I was going to have a great problem in getting to sleep. With my mind in a whirl and my ears labouring under that grating sound, there was little chance I could drop into a dreamstate. I rose and went to the window, looking out through the small diamond-shaped leaded panes into the darkness beyond.

Where was my target and what was he doing on this black night. Was he enacting foul deeds? Murder, perhaps? Staining pure white virgin snow with red rivulets of blood? Or worse? What could be worse? Rape, I suppose, was just as terrible. Indeed, was a man of disparate, ill-fitting body parts even capable of performing the sex act? A torso from this tomb, legs from that grave, arms and head from yonder mausoleum, and sexual organs from the Lord knew who or what. Had the monster's maker gone to the trouble of finding a large member to stitch to the loins of his creation, slave to some freakish vicarious notions in his head?

My head whirled and the snores grew louder.

The following night I went again to the pump house, and yet again the night after that. I was beginning to give up hope and on the fourth night simply sat in the inn idling over a glass of porter having lost all enthusiasm for my task. So far as I was concerned my plan had come to a full stop. I had no idea how to contact the monster and get him into my sights and was beginning to feel I ought to go home.

The inn was fairly noisy, as usual, with loud boisterous talk and lewd calls to the landlady and the overworked wench who served behind the barrel-bar. Then suddenly it all went as still as the grave and I looked up to see a tall slim man standing in the doorway brushing drops of moisture from his greatcoat. He took off his hat, struck it against his thigh to remove any snow, and then looked around the room.

His eyes resting on me he half-smiled, giving me a nod, then addressing the rest of the room, said in casual tones, 'Carry on – don't mind me.'

The atmosphere remained slightly tense and silent for a few moments more, then the noise began again, the customers of the hostal having at last lost interest in the tall dark stranger who strolled towards my corner.

'I believe you're looking for me,' he said, quietly. 'You've been advertising all over the village and forest.'

My jaw fell open as I viewed the man who now sat down in an armchair opposite me. He had short dark hair, cut very badly. His lean weathered face held a pair of startling blue eyes that were difficult to stare into without feeling a certain coldness in my bone marrow. The rest of him was fashioned much in the way of a languid youth as he draped himself around the wooden armchair. There was something a little dangerous about his posture. It denoted raw energy ready to spring forth in attack or defence at a moment's notice. I had no doubt of the speed of that potential movement: it would be swift and sure, and undoubtedly deadly.

'You are...' I stopped abruptly, wondering what to call him. I could hardly say *'the monster'* and searched my head for an adequate title, coming up weakly with, '...the person I'm seeking.'

'The unnatural creature,' he said. 'Yes. You were expecting, of course, a lumbering oaf of a fellow, with mismatched limbs and speech that was slurred. A drooling, lummoxing, badly-designed copy of a human being. A horrible effigy of a man smelling strongly of graveyard earth and rotting flesh. A pathetic stumblebum that on the first encounter, draws disgust and contempt from all who see it staggering into view, feelings swiftly replaced by fear as it lurches heavily towards them with great gnarled hands stretched out ready to squeeze the life from their throats?'

'Something like that,' I replied.

'Sorry to disappoint you. Josef is more of an artist than you give him credit for.'

'Sorry – *is?* Not, was?'

'You thought he was dead?'

'I was sure of it. I was told you killed him.'

The monster laughed. 'Why would I want to do that? He gave me life. What's more, he didn't make the mistake of the fictional creator of the original unnatural being. The brain he gave me is from an educated, intelligent man – one with culture and learning. Yes, a lawbreaker of some kind, or his corpse would not have ended up in the district charnel house reserved for serious criminals – to be dissected by so-called doctors – but not a man fettered by ignorance and paranoia. By the way, have you come to destroy me? Josef said they would send someone from the future.'

I stared into those ice-blue eyes.

'Where is Josef, by the way?'

'Alive and well and living in Tuscany. Not in this year, of course, but back in his own time. He said he could return without being caught. I understand he broke your laws by creating me? So, he is a fugitive, but I doubt he'll ever be caught. He has a brilliant mind and will without doubt evade capture. Now, I repeat, are you here to rend asunder what another man has joined together?'

'To answer your question, directly, yes – I have been ordered to destroy you before you destroy future generations. Only fair, don't you think?'

In my hand, under the table, was the pistol, the melter.

'Fair, if I had it in my agenda to destroy those generations of which you speak. However, I'm happy to tell you I have no such intention. Live and let live is my motto.'

'But you are formed from malefactors – creatures who were executed – hung or garrotted for their crimes.'

'My dear sir, one can be executed for stealing a lamb in these times.'

That was true enough.

He said, 'What can I do or say that will put your mind at rest?'

'It's difficult, isn't it?' I argued. 'If it were a case of asking you to perform an act, then it would be easy, but asking you *not* to do something, that's impossible to prove unless a long period of time has passed.'

'Well, you have your hand on the trigger of your weapon, which is pointed at my stomach I believe. Are you going to destroy me – or not?'

My finger tightened slightly, but when it came to the crunch, I could not do it. I just could not do it. Obliterate another being, even if he was a monstrosity, a freak in human form? No. Definitely not. It wasn't in me. I kept thinking of what my mother would say, when she learned what a hero her son was. 'Oh yes, he shot an unarmed creature to death without any compunction or compassion – what a service to the state – what a champion of good over evil!' She would be horrified, I know, and wonder what sort of son she had raised. My finger relaxed. I put the weapon in my coat pocket knowing I would not take it out again in anger.

'Fine,' I said, 'I've failed in my mission and now I've got to go home and tell them I don't think they'll all vanish because I have your solemn promise not to go on the rampage like any other self-respecting monster made of bits of killers. Except I can't do that. I have to take you with me. You may think you're harmless, but you're not of this time – you're not from *any* time at all, having been made out-of-time, so to speak – and you could inadvertently do something to ruin the course of future world history. So, you need to accompany me when I return home.'

'Well,' he said, after a long period of thought, 'be that as it may, I need to take some information with me...'

3

'NOW THAT I HAVE YOU here,' said the monster, leaning forward and piercing my brain with those twin points of ice-blue eyes, 'you could do something for me – something which would help to occupy me for a long time, thus putting you mentally at ease at least for a while, knowing I'm too busy with something to go careering around knocking people on the head.'

'And that would be?'

He leaned back and stared into the log fire that was flaring blue gases after the landlady had thrown more fuel into its heart.

'I want to write my biography – my memoirs. I have a certain amount of information already, having interviewed friends and relatives of those executed murderers who make up the person who is *me*, but I would like to hear from the mouths of the guilty themselves. You could do that for me. You could interview them and perhaps even go on to witness the murder itself. It would be a great help to me.'

I thought about this for a few minutes.

'You are...how many people are you?'

'Six. Six altogether. Legs, torso, arms, head, heart, brain. Only six.'

'You say *only* but that's a lot of research. It would indeed occupy you for quite some time. How are you going to go about it?'

He leaned forward again. 'Ah, well, that's where you come in. Josef told me you would be carrying a device, an engine of sorts that would enable you to move backwards and forwards in time. I have here a list of names,' he took a sheet of paper from an inside pocket and spread it on the table. 'Here are those who make up the complete Frankenstein's monster.' He turned the sheet so I could read it.

I went through the names:

> Werner Straffe – arms
> William Danton – legs
> Louise Leconte – heart
> Christian Geroude – head
> Julius Jules – torso
> Alexander S. Rattringer – brain

'Louise Leconte? A woman?' I said.

He thumped his chest. 'My heart.'

'Well, that's quite encouraging for me, since a woman is not likely to have perpetrated a really violent crime.'

'You would think so,' he came back, 'but this one was a poisoner I believe – she killed three husbands without a flutter of this small beating heart.'

'But not overtly violent.'

'The last husband refused to lie down and die, even after eating potage laced with arsenic, so she took a meat cleaver and split his skull from behind. Otherwise she may never have been caught. It's difficult to explain away why a man with his head in two halves, his brains decorating the tiles, is lying on your kitchen floor.'

I sighed. 'Definitely a *smattering* of violence then.'

He spread his palms as if to say, what can you do?

I sat for a while in thought, drinking, looking around at the other patrons of the inn. There were all sorts in there, from nobles to peasants, poets to goatherds, highwaymen to lawyers.

The mob of drinkers and diners filled the room with noisy talk and clashing tankards, while the serving wench ran around mopping up puddles of ale, filling empty beakers and jugs, carrying platters of food. The landlady helped her on occasion, but more often than not this formidable woman was standing with her arms folded, cackling at some bawdy joke that one of her customers had shared with her. The landlord himself was behind the barrel bar looking as dark and morose as a defeated commander on the bridge of a holed and captured ship. I had not yet seen him smile once, though the coins were clattering in the box behind the counter (folding money went straight into his waistcoat pocket) and for all the world his looked like a lucrative profession.

'I don't think I'm getting very much out of this,' I said, turning to the monster again. 'I don't think you're the type to go on a killing spree, or to start a series of rapes that would shock the whole country.'

'This is true, especially the second set of crimes – I'm not attracted to women at all. I prefer those of my own gender.'

I raised my eyebrows. 'You're gay?' I exclaimed.

He shrugged. 'I am generally cheerful by disposition, yes.'

'No, no – I mean, well, never mind. I still don't see why I should stay here longer simply to do your research for you.'

'You don't think that I have been dealt a terrible hand by Fate and therefore deserve assistance for that reason only? You will recall Mary's monster was rejected and spurned by all, including his creator, and thus his embitterment led to heinous crimes against the society that held him in contempt. I am not actually Frankenstein's beastly conception, it's true, but if you needed an excuse to stay – out of curiosity – then that might be the one you could use to remain here longer. Tell them, when you return, that I am a hideous malformed creature bent on evil and that you were forced to obey my commands or I threatened to go on the rampage.'

'You forget, you're coming with me, whether you like it or not. Although, why don't I use my weapon to obliterate you? It won't make any difference to the future. You were created by a man from another time. Indeed, you are a creature of the world of the future. I could wipe you out and not interfere with the world which is come. Why don't I do that?'

'Because you're a decent human being and unable, when it comes to a fine point, to take the life of another man, be he saint, sinner or even a grotesque like myself, made from the body parts of malefactors.'

He had a point. I was not good at killing things. Even bugs and rodents could dance in my house without fear. What was I to do? It seemed harmless enough, to research this creature's ancestors, if that's the correct term for those legs, arms, torso, head, heart and brain that made him what he was. I had the time and certainly the energy, and indeed it appeared to me at the time to promise to be a hugely interesting exercise. I couldn't foresee any real difficulties or paradoxes. All I was doing was gathering information. Where was the harm in that?

(O what fools, these time travellers be!)

'All right. I'll do it.'

His eyes grew bright with excitement. 'My dear sir, I thank you with all my heart – with all the heart that is, of the previous owner. When can you start?'

'Right away – tomorrow morning.'

He reached out and took my hand, shaking it with the silky palm which I had been told strangled an innocent woman to death.

'I'll give you what information I already have on the six.'

THE NEXT DAY I JUMPED a short way into the past. My first task was to find out where Werner Straffe might be found. I went to the town hall and requested to look through the results of the last census. The Swiss have always been as efficient as the Germans in their records and it didn't take me very long to find the address and occupation of the man I sought. We were three days before Werner set forth to carry out his foul deed and take the life of the woman he loved. The crime of passion is normally the prerogative of those of Latin temperament, but of course we all have the seed of jealousy and revenge in our souls which will flourish when the season is right, and the ugly growth nurtured in the grey desolate hours of early morning. Werner was obviously a man who translated his feelings into actions. He had set forth to destroy the love of his life because he believed she was being unfaithful to him. A story as ancient as the human race, which repeats and repeats as time goes by.

I eventually found Werner behind his cheese stall at the local market.

'Herr Straffe?'

Like the monster, he was a slim man, almost gaunt, with darkish features and a hook nose. His eyes were black and impenetrable. There were only a few wisps of hair on his head. I judged him to be around forty-five to fifty years of age. He wiped his hands on his apron and stared at me knowingly for a few seconds, before saying, 'You're not here to buy cheese. Have I done something wrong? You can check my weights.' He gestured at his scales. 'They are accurate. Are you here to do that?'

'No, no,' I took out a notebook. 'Nothing so serious. I simply want to ask you a few questions. I'm a newspaper reporter. I'd like to do an article on the stall holders in the market. Find out how they came to do what they do. Have you a little time you could offer me? It's almost the hour to pack away your goods and take down your stall. I could help you do that, then take you to a coffee house?'

He stared at me again. 'Why would anyone want to read about a seller of cheeses?'

'I'm sure you haven't been in this trade all your life, Herr Straffe – we all have histories of a kind. Yours will be just as interesting as that of the next man. I've – I've been employed by the council to increase interest in the local market. There are rival markets, are there not, which draw trade away from this one?'

'You have a strange accent,' he said in reply. 'Where are you from?'

'I'm Austrian, by birth. Vienna.'

'Ah, that explains it.' He sighed and looked around him at his unsold wares. 'Well, give me half-an-hour and I'll be with you. You don't need to stay and help. I have my own method of packing and you'd only slow me down. I could do with a coffee, that's certain. However, I'm meeting a young lady at three o'clock, so our talk will have to be over by then. Agreed?'

'Agreed,' I replied. 'I'll see you in the Locust Coffee Shop.'

'My favourite haunt,' he said.

He was ten minutes late, but soon we got down to business. He told me he was born in a hamlet in the Swiss Alps, his father a hill farmer. He was the fourth of five children and the farm could not sustain a large family, so like two of his brothers he left home at around fifteen years of age, first trying for the army at which he was unsuccessful simply because they were not recruiting at the time, and then he made his way down through Italy to Brundisi where he joined a merchant ship, becoming ('After a great deal of being beaten and chastised for not knowing stem from stern or how to hoist a sail.') a deck hand, then a galley hand. Finally, he became a ship's cook, a position he liked, until he was shanghaied in the port of Calcutta and forced to work aboard a British man-o'-war for three years.

'I didn't enjoy going back to climbing the rigging in foul weather and being made to holystone the decks of a morning, but we did take a couple of prizes – French ships when Britain was at war with that country – and as such I was entitled to my share of the prize money. As soon as I could I jumped ship and made my way back to my own country, and here to start a new life. I bought my stall, my first set of cheeses, and so you see me now, a successful businessman with a thriving trade.'

'Thriving?'

'You could say so. I sell some very good cheeses at fair prices. Schabziger, Raclette, oh and Emmentaler of course – but my best selling cheese is Sbrinz. They like their cheeses extra hard in this region.'

Werner Straffe seemed to me to be a nice sort of man, not one who would in seventy-two hours would go out and kill his beloved. It turned out that his 'young lady' was, like him, in her late forties. She was a widow running a boarding house and was relatively well off. Her name was Kate Kleinweiler and she would end her life in an alley close to the market where her killer sold his cheeses. The prosecution maintained he slipped away from his stall for a few minutes, did the terrible crime, then returned to sell his wares as if nothing had occurred. In other words, a callous, cold-blooded killer.

Indeed, he admitted to me that he had a rival for Kate's attentions, a man who sold silk scarves, a man who looked and smelled much sweeter than a cheese merchant. They had exchanged angry words on several occasions, but had never come to blows. Werner was quite proud of the latter, saying, 'I dislike violence intensely. I saw too much of it in the navy. It leads to nowhere but more violence.'

As I have said, he did not seem the type to kill, but then does any murderer fit an immutable profile? Some love their cats yet kill their own mothers without mercy, compassion or remorse.

Some indeed, are psychopaths unable to experience empathy of any kind, and therefore having no emotional feelings do not see any wrong in taking the life of another human being. Werner did not strike me as the latter. He seemed a man quite capable of sympathy, as he talked of his sister who had fallen ill at a young age and had died in the family home. Tears sprang to his eyes on the retelling of a tale over forty years old. I was almost weeping myself by the end.

After three days I had enough in my notebook, I thought, to satisfy the monster when I returned to his time. Now I had to steel my nerves to witness a horrible crime.

At the appointed hour I watched from a high window from the landing of a block of apartments which looked down on the alley. My nerves were jangling. I had no desire to witness this terrible slaying, but the monster had asked me to view all the crimes perpetrated by his body parts. He said it was essential to get a first-hand account of his history. So I stood in the dismal light in a corner between two sets of stairs, one going up to the third floor, the other down to the second. There I waited with a pounding heart wishing I were somewhere, anywhere else.

At about one-ten pm, Kate entered from the right hand end of the alley. She was dressed in a thick coat made of wool and wore a black-brimmed hat. In her left hand she carried a dark bag. My heart was now clogging my throat as I watched her walk slowly up the alley. It took all my strength of will not to shout, 'Hurry, hurry, get to the other end quickly,' but of course the first rule, the main law, of time travelling is that the traveller must on no account interfere with history, no matter what happens we are only allowed to observe, not warn or try to stop an action. Millions of future lives could be affected. The whole course of the world could be changed with just a small alteration in the pattern of what has already been set chronologically.

Then I saw him, coming from the left end, coming at a much faster pace than Kate was moving. As he went to pass her, he suddenly sidestepped, gripped her bag and tried to wrench it from her grasp. She yelled at him, not loudly, but angrily, telling him to let go of her property. He shouted at her, telling her to release it or he would hurt her. Then she started to scream in earnest, calling for assistance, crying for someone to help her fend off her attacker.

That was when he reached out in panic and gripped her by the throat. Kate continued to scream, thrashing with her handbag at her assailant. His fingers must have grown tighter and tighter until at last she stopped screaming and went limp, falling to the ground. The bag was still in her grasp and she fell on top of it, the life having been strangled from her. He made one weak attempt to move her dead body, which was no lightweight, then he gave up and ran swiftly to the end of the alley from which Kate had entered.

I stood there in the dim light coming through the dirty panes of glass, stunned by what I had witnessed.

The killer had not been Werner Straffe, but a young man, a youth with sharp features and hunched shoulders.

'My God,' I whispered to myself, 'Werner is innocent.'

I left the building shaking with shock. Here was a horrible dilemma. I was a witness to crime for which an innocent man was going to die. What was I to do? Stay and give my account to the authorities, thus saving Werner's life, or leave him to his fate? Actually, I knew that I had no choice. Were I to save Werner – even if I did not give up the youth to the law – he might do something within the rest of his life which would destroy what I knew as the future. The law of the time traveller could not be broken. What if they did indeed catch the real murderer and executed him instead of Werner Straffe – and he turned out to be an ancestor of mine, a man who fathered my forefathers? Even were I capable of being selfish enough to damn the rest of the human race, I might still be in danger of obliteration myself.

And indeed, I was not that self-seeking. I cared about humanity. I cared about those who were to come beyond this moment. They had carried out psychological tests on me before I left for the past and were that gene in me which allowed a man to say to hell with everyone else, I'm all right jack, then they would never have let me travel backwards into the past. Thus I had to let a woman be throttled to death in a miserable alley and thus and thus I had to allow a man to go to the gallows who was as innocent of the murder as I was. Indeed, Werner was more guiltless than me, in that I had the ability to intervene in the killing – and did not.

My heart had not felt so heavy since I had watched my own beloved die on a distant planet in the far distant future. It was like a huge lump of galena in my chest, threatening to crush all my other internal organs. Nightmares, I knew, would follow. For the rest of my life I would run the question through and through, even though, as I have already stated, there was no choice. There *should* have been a choice, but there was none. Anyone from my future world would tell me earnestly that it's not my fault and there is no blame attached to me, but that really doesn't help. Still the guilt sits in the brain and will not dislodge no matter how many times I tell myself, or others tell me, that I could do nothing to help. The past must remain immutable.

It would have been honourable of me to stay in the time zone to support Werner Straffe in his last hours before the hangman took his life, to tell him I thought him guiltless and that an injustice was occurring. It might have eased his going just a little to know someone believed his innocence. Probably not a great deal, but just a little. However, I wasn't brave enough to face him. I fled forward in time to the next name on my list, William Danton. I ran away to a period where Werner's execution was an unchangeable event, like the damn coward that I am.

4

THE NEXT ASSIGNMENT GIVEN ME by the monster was to find
Will Danton, but all my researching and enquiries seemed to lead
to nothing. Although I was moving back and forth in time, they
were mere hops and skips of several days, or a week at the most.
The weather was on the turn though and at this point the Swiss
snow had melted somewhat and a little greenery was showing
through the white. I decided to take a walk around a small lake
just outside of the town. The birds were beginning to make
themselves known and one or two flowers poked through the
furze. It was very pleasant to clear my head of all the darkness of
my current task. I was able now to recall my months on the
planet Sylvanus, indeed my very short time with my beloved
Imogen, without falling into a deep depression and cursing
mankind and all its follies.

However, my mood changed once again when I came to a
gloomy building at the far corner of the lake: a place whose dark
shadow even the ducks and swans avoided. It was a square
edifice with small mean windows of thick glass and set within its
aphotic bricks was a double door fashioned from dense wood
studded with bolt-headed iron nails. There was a phrase in
thickly-embossed stone above these doors and the foreign
tongues with which I had been injected allowed me to translate
this epithet, even though it was written in Old French.

It read: CHARNEL HOUSE OF THE DAMNED

This was where some of the bones of poor Werner Straffe would lie, perhaps for eternity, and this was from where those body parts which made up the monster were stolen, freshly dead, on the night that Josef Linstaph came from the future and duplicated the fiction of Mary Shelley, turning it into reality. A sudden thought struck me and I looked around, shuddering with a deep chill. Josef! He had not yet visited this awful house of homicidal felons. I was here before he had taken it upon himself to roam the centuries and commit the heinous transgression of creating life from the worst possible dregs of earlier men and women.

I hurried away from the place. Possibly I could have stopped Josef from carrying out his crime but I had no mandate to do that. It is possible that such an action, killing or harming a fellow traveller, might have serious consequences. What they might be I didn't know, but I was sure I had to refrain from violence even if it was only because I was not a policeman of any sort. Yes, I had been sent back to kill the monster, but that was the equivalent of slaying a dragon or stepping on a bug that did not belong in this particular time period. It affected nothing and should not have an effect on the future. It was all a web of possibilities and probabilities and I was no expert. They had those in plenty in the future and the one thing I did know was I didn't want to meet with Josef Linstaph on the edge of this lake in the vicinity of the black-bricked charnel house from which he was about to remove lumps of human meat.

I went back to the task of finding the whereabouts of Will Danton.

Reappraising the name I realised I was of course not looking for a citizen of Switzerland, but a visitor, probably from Britain or America. In fact after further exhaustive enquiries I discovered that Will Danton was a British businessman with holdings in the sugar plantations of the West Indies. I found a

Mr Danton renting a house on a very pretty slope not far outside the town. It was a log cabin with window boxes and carved wooden elves lining the garden path.

I rang the bell hanging above the doorway, but just then a man came striding down the path to the house.

'Are you looking for me?'

'I'm looking for a Mr Danton.'

He took off his hat and hooked a thick walking stick around his wrist in order to shake my hand.

'Then you've found him. I'm Will Danton.'

'Very pleased to meet you, sir,' I said. 'Could we talk inside?'

When I told him I was a reporter, he let me in and offered me a cup of tea 'or something stronger?' I told him tea would be fine.

He rang a little bell and called out, 'Tea for two!' then smiled at me.

'Please sit down, sir, and we'll go into the history of Will Danton.'

He was sturdy-looking fellow, bullish and, I imagined, probably regarded as pugnacious by those who knew him. There was nothing of the fop about him, his grey hair being cropped short and his clothes rather rustic for a wealthy man. He looked more like a country squire than an entrepreneur. And wealthy he was, for it was one of the first things he told me about himself. 'Enough money to buy half of Yorkshire,' he told me, 'and the change would purchase me the Isle of Wight.' Sugar had made him a fortune, he said, and would continue to do so.

'I'm a plain and simple fellow,' he said, holding his delicate tea cup with fingers as thick as sausages. 'I've never married. The ladies find me a bit on the rough side and they're probably right.'

I found myself glancing at his legs, the legs now owned by the monster, and strangely they were as thick as the trunks of oaks. On recalling the stature of the monster I had the distinct impression that his legs were like those of a greyhound, slim and whipcordish, made for running. However, the monster had had his legs covered in breeches, so I hadn't got a really good look at them. Mr Danton's legs were certainly not those of a fast creature, being fashioned in the style of a boar.

'Surely,' I said, simply to make conversation, 'you would like to be looked after in your old age?'

'Oh,' he said, laughing, 'I have William for that.'

I blinked. 'William? Em, do you have a natural child, named after you?'

He frowned. 'Named after me? My name is Willoughby.'

'Ah, I see – Will is for Willoughby.'

At that moment a tall, slim black man entered the room, carrying a tray on which there were two teacups and saucers, a sugar bowl, several silver spoons, a teapot with a cosy covering it and a small jug of milk. The black man smiled at me and nodded, as he laid the tray on a small table by the fireplace. Then he asked if that would be all and my host told him it would be for the moment.

'That was William,' said my host, 'my house slave.'

My blood ran cold. 'He's not a freed man?'

'Not yet. He wants to be, but I'm afraid if I give him his freedom he'll leave me and go chasing a woman. The silly fellow wants to go looking for his wife, but I sold her ten years ago to an American passing through St Lucia Island, where I have my business. She was pregnant at the time and you always get a good price for a pregnant slave. He's asked me for money to go looking for her, but I won't let him go, not just like that.' Willoughby Danton touched the side of his nose with his forefinger. 'If I keep him, he'll pine for his wife but he won't be able to go after her. I need that boy to look after me. My bones aren't what they used to be. Once I finish my business here I'm on my way to Hong Kong and William will be coming with me, that's certain.'

William Danton.

Freed slaves often took the surnames of their masters, having no recourse to their old-world names. Possibly those in bondage who accompanied their masters abroad also adopted surnames, due to the fact that they needed papers to travel to foreign countries. I knew now what was going to happen in this household and I didn't want to witness it, no matter how much it upset the monster.

Those damn breeches on the monster's legs had hidden the secret of my second murderer, a poor downtrodden African who wanted only to be reunited with his lost loved one, his wife and probably his whole family. No doubt he had the legs of a cheetah and would give his pursuers a run for their money, but in the end – probably with the use of hounds – they would catch him and they would hang him.

5

ONCE AGAIN, I HAD BEEN shaken by an unusual turn of events. I wondered if I was going to come out of this at all sane. The monster surely could not have known what he was asking of me to set me this task, which was swiftly draining my reserves of mental strength. Werner Strasse and William Danton were now taken care of, even though I had found out very little about Willoughby Danton's slave I knew from my readings on the subject that the path of his life had been harrowing. Selling a slave's wife or husband 'down the river' was an atrocious act by a slave owner, but unfortunately more rife than unusual. This time it had led to the murder of a callous master and I'm afraid my sympathies were not with the dead victim.

Louise Leconte was next on my list but I decided to leave her until almost last. I was not looking forward to witnessing a man being hacked to death with a cleaver. So I bypassed the only serial killer on the list and went straight on to Christian Geroude, the head that held the brain of Alexander S. Rattringer. Since this section of the body was simply a vessel, the skull which contained grey matter, it seemed a very unimportant part of the whole. Yes, the head contained the tongue, eyes, nose and ears, four of the five organs that were responsible for the senses, but without its original brain these senses were confused. By that I mean for example *taste* and *smell* are not the same for one man as they are for another, or we would all like the same food and drink, and recoil at the same unpleasant odours. In fact humans enjoy different tastes, different fragrances. So in his case the head and the brain were not acting in concert. The owner of the head might have enjoyed essence of beef, whereas the owner of the brain perhaps despised that fare.

I had little trouble finding Christian Geroude: he was a well-known character in the district. To give him his full title, which I know he would wish me to do, I should call him Lieutenant Christian Geroude of the 8th Swiss Hussar Regiment.

When I first caught sight of him he was swishing through the main street of the town wearing a magnificent uniform of blue and gold, with tassles and embroidered buttonloops everywhere. On his head was a tall dark furry-looking helmet with an embossed emblem in front and a feathery spray sticking up like a white dove's fantail at the back. His pantaloons were dark blue with chamois-leather insides and yellow piping down the outside. Tall, highly-polished boots covered his calves, with silver rowelled spurs at the heel. Round his waist was a white silk sash from which hung a sabre encased in a scabbard covered in black satin and encrusted with the sparkling embedded shards of what looked like crushed rubies. To complete this decorative image was a silk-lined pelisse thrown casually over one shoulder.

I gaped at this glorious bird. He was a creature from another world. A world of wealth, obviously, and aristocracy. I saw a beggar try to speak to him and he kicked the poor fellow's bowl out of his hands. It went flying through the air and struck a woman on the neck, but the lieutenant did not even pause in his stride. You got the impression from his gait that he would have preferred to be on a horse – a war steed of impeccable lineage no doubt – and was having to dirty his bootsoles, and more importantly, his mind by walking through the riff-raff of the town.

I made enquiries about him among the local populace and found he was not a popular man, even among his peers, being arrogant and hot-headed, and thoroughly, inordinately vainglorious. Lieutenant Christian Geroude had fought five duels since becoming an hussar, wounding three men and killing two. He had distinguished himself by showing great courage at the Battle of Golymin while serving with Napoleon's French army against the Russians. (Indeed I have never believed the adage that all bullies are cowards.) Now, apparently, he was fighting his sixth duel against a young man of seventeen summers who had recently joined the regiment of hussars after leaving his father's farm on the slopes of the Alps. It seemed that Geroude took exception to riding alongside a 'filthy peasant' who had somehow managed to weasel himself a commission in one of the most splendid regiments in the Swiss army.

I did indeed try to get an interview with Lieutenant Geroude, but he haughtily declined to meet with me. I sent him a second card with the message that our meeting was highly important, but again he rejected the offer. In fact he told his servant to inform me that if I did not desist in sending him messages he would come out personally and horsewhip me in front of the local populace. I gave up, not being inclined towards a beating from a man with shoulders that were twice as wide as mine.

The filthy peasant's name was Philippe Muraz and when I found him in an inn on the far side of town I discovered a lean pale boy who looked more like twelve years than seventeen. He had pale blue eyes, slim hands and a sort of bewildered look about him, as if he were wondering how he came to be in the world at all. I watched him as he sat at a rough-hewn wooden table on an equally ill-fashioned stool, drinking from a tankard. I guessed that this kind of dining was one of the things Christian Geroude objected to. The fare was not good wine, but ale, the refreshment of the unwashed masses. I could imagine Geroude sneering with contempt on seeing such behaviour and lamenting at the depths the regiment could sink to by allowing such churls as Muraz to become one of its officers.

I sighed. I had no doubt that Geroude was going to kill this young man and then, justifiably in my opinion, be executed for his murder. Duelling was not against the law at this time, but I imagined that Geroude – perhaps accidentally, but if caught in a corner possibly deliberately – would break the rules of the engagement. If Geroude fired his pistol before the appointed time, or lunged at his opponent with his sword at a moment when ordered respite was taking place, he might well go before magistrates and be condemned to death for the murder of a colleague. His seconds would not protect him if his conduct was dishonourable and unworthy of a gentleman.

'How do you do, sir?' I said, sitting on the other side of the table from the young man. 'Do you mind if I join you?'

Philippe wiped froth from his mouth on the back of his hand and nodded at the stool opposite.

'Be my guest.'

I sat down, took a sip of the most disgusting brew I had ever tasted, then smiled at my companion with his unruly straw-coloured head bared of his helmet, which was perched on the windowsill behind him.

'I see you are in a very reputable regiment – the hussars, eh?'

He laughed. 'Reputable? Yes, I suppose it is. It has won several battle honours. However, I seem to be a mongrel amongst pedigrees. I wish my father were not so ambitious for me, but I must obey his wishes.'

'Oh, you're not of aristocratic lineage?'

'Not so's you'd notice. You don't see any of the other officers in this room, do you? Oh, they might be upstairs plunging their members into a bar wench or milk maid, but they would not come amongst the rabble. They would do their business, leave the girl with a few coins, then go quietly out the back door. Any offspring of course would enter the world of foundlings – natural children who would never know their father and perhaps even be spurned by their mother.' He looked around him. 'There'll be a few of those in this room, having survived forced labour and growing up despised and rejected by common society that's no better.'

I made the appropriate expression and said, 'You seem a little discontented.'

He laughed again. 'Yes sir, I do, don't I? Look,' he leaned forward, 'are you a gentleman? You seem out of place here. If you are, you couldn't do me a favour, could you?'

I tried to decide quickly what I was and came out with, 'I'm a travelling poet, but yes, my antecedents are acceptable to most men.'

He looked around him, then leaned forward. 'I need a second, you see. No one else will act for me. They're all on his side in this affair, though most of them hate him as much as I do. Sorry, I'm talking about one of our lieutenants who's challenged me to a duel. Pistols for two, coffee for one. Would you, sir, act for me? I'm sorry, I don't even know your name. I'm being very impolite. My father would give me a walloping if he could see me now. He's a real stickler for good manners, my pa.'

I stared at this callow youth and my heart bled for him. He was so young and innocent and he was going to die on the field of honour very early tomorrow. This cursed Geroude was going to rob parents of their wonderful boy, their rude and rustic youthful child, who was only trying to be an obedient son to a father who wanted him to progress in the wider world beyond the origins of his birth.

'How did you manage to get into such an exclusive regiment?' I asked. 'Don't they usually take only gentry?'

'Yep, they do, normally. But my pa once found a wounded colonel, gored by a boar, in the forest near our farm. He took him home and my ma nursed him back to health. Anyway, the colonel told my parents they could ask anything of him and they told him they wanted their son to join his regiment when he was old enough. To give him his due, the colonel was as good as his word, even though he didn't like it by half, and so here I am, a runt kid-goat amongst high-class wolves.'

'Yes, in answer to your question – yes, I will act for you. Who do I contact?'

'His seconds are Captain Spitzer and Lieutenant Maurer. You'll find them at the barracks. All you need to do – have you done this kind of thing before? No – well, all you need to do is inform them that you are my second and will be at the appointed place tomorrow at dawn. We're meeting in a small copse just south of the barracks.' He reached out and grasped my hand with his slim but surprisingly strong fingers. 'Thank you, sir – and I still don't know your name.'

'James Ovit,' I replied.

'An Englishman?'

'Of sorts – but more of a traveller.'

He stood up, his uniform slightly large for his youthful frame, and nodded.

'I must go now, but again, thank you, and I'll see you tomorrow.'

'Indeed.'

I left the inn a little later and visited the regiment's camp, where I found one of the two seconds, Captain Spitzer. Even though I was treading on very dangerous ground I asked him if there was any way the duel could be prevented. I couldn't imagine young Muraz apologising for his lowly birth, but I felt I needed, as a proper second, to see if there could be a reconciliation of some kind.

Spitzer, with a saddened expression, shook his head.

'Once Geroude has his tail up, there's no stopping him.'

'Well, that's a very unhappy man, I think.'

He raised his eyebrows. 'Muraz?'

'No, Geroude. Possibly he was dropped on his head as a baby and regards the whole world with bitterness, don't you think? Six duels in two years? Something is wrong with the fellow.'

Now the captain's eyes opened wide. 'Be careful you aren't heard – he's not above challenging civilians – and he's nerveless. I never saw a man so cold and calm when delivering, or facing death.'

A psychopath, but the captain would not have understood the word.

'Well, I will see you tomorrow morning. Hopefully this Geroude will pass away in his sleep before then, but I won't place wager on it. You realise that a young boy is going to be shot to death for simply being what he is?'

'I do, I do.' The captain had enough compassion or shame to hang his head. 'Unavoidable, unfortunately. If not here and now, in battle. A soldier's lot, sir. Have you served?'

'Not in the military, but I have witnessed death in different forms. This Lieutenant Geroude. You know him well?'

'Not well, but some.'

'His father?'

'A French duke, but his mother was not the duke's wife – a mistress.'

'A bastard then?'

'Indeed.'

'Surely no shame in that? Kings have been such.'

He nodded. 'No shame, but no gain. In this case lands and titles went to a younger half-brother. A legitimate heir.'

'Hence the interminable choleric.'

The captain sighed. 'I suppose. Look, sir, I've given you information enough to perform your duties tomorrow. In fact, I feel I've overstepped the mark. I would be grateful if you would leave now.'

'Just one more question. Lieutenant Geroude – has he ever been bested at *anything*?'

'Never. It would kill him, if he were.'

'He needs to prove to the world that he is better than his brother and that he would have made a better son to his father than the inheritor.'

'Indeed,' replied the captain, 'he has to be incomparable.'

The following morning I rose incredibly early, which wasn't difficult given the hardness and uncomfortableness of a bed which appeared to have old straw and lumps of turf for a mattress stuffing. I broke the thin ice on my washbowl water and rinsed my face and hands, at the same time noticing there had been a stiff frost overnight: ferns of ice had formed on the small thick windowpanes. It was at such a time that I yearned to be back in the future where houses were warm and beds were soft. However, the breakfast which I had ordered the night before was enough to feed a whole cohort of James Ovits and included sausage, boar meat, thick solid bread, cheese, four boiled eggs, some unmentionable and unidentifiable animal entrails smothered in sauces and a very welcome jug of hot coffee.

Once I had eaten and thanked the kitchen girl for rising so early to serve me (she looked at me blankly since I believe she probably rose at the same ungodly hour every morning) I left the inn and walked to the meeting place. There was indeed a crystalline hoar frost which had turned the grass to white spikes, crisply flattened under my bootsoles. Trees were as stiff and still as frozen ghosts against a grey sky. It was a good day to die, the world being inhospitable and unfriendly. Hungry blackbirds scuttled about on the ground looking for ways to get at the worms under the iron-hard earth. A fox glided by not bothering to even glance at me, it's belly lean and taut. Overhead the heavens were streaked with cirrus cloud like the white brushstrokes of a careless artist. There was a certain visual beauty in it, granted, but the cold was like a metal vice trying to crush my chest.

When I reached the spot where the duel was to take place, I found the captain I had spoken to already waiting, his breath coming out as nosegays of steam. He was wearing a thick cloak to keep out the cold and he first saluted me gravely, then shook my hand. There was another second there wearing a thick overcoat, a youngish lieutenant I think, who simply paced up and down looking very pale and miserable, and probably wishing he had not been asked to perform this duty. Finally there was an older man, perhaps in his late forties or early fifties, who I guessed was the doctor. This man stood by an oak, under branches which occasionally shed white frost dust, and stared at the distant horizon with an unblinking expression.

The young Muraz arrived before his opponent and I shook hands with him and asked him a question which was worrying me.

'What would you have done if I had not acted for you?'

'I would have arranged the meeting myself. I would however have felt a bit like a hayseed with no friends to support me, but I would have met him anyway.'

This satisfied me that I was not going to disturb history in any way.

We awaited the appointed hour, passed it, kept on waiting, and soon I began to believe that Geroude was not going to appear. Then, half an hour late, he rode out of the misty frostlands on his horse, looking as arrogant and contemptuous of the world as ever. When his seconds berated him for his tardiness, he shrugged it off, with the words, 'What, is the boy so eager to die? I think not.' To my mind however, Geroude was playing a psychological game: keeping his adversary on tenterhooks, making him fret, giving him false hopes, then dashing those hopes.

Neither man removed his tunic on such a morning, though I had been told such duels were normally fought in white shirtsleeves, the quicker and easier to see any blood wounds for the doctor to treat. They each chose their slim duelling pistol from a silver-hinged black box lined with red velvet, the youth first since he was the challenged, Geroude taking the remaining weapon as the challenger. They both weighed the pistols in their hands and walked back their seconds with them. I was amazed at the rituals, which were obviously known as well to a farmer's son as they were to a gentleman.

'Do you want me to check it, to see if it is indeed loaded?' I asked, quietly.

Muraz's eyes opened wide. 'Certainly not. That would be incredibly bad form.'

'It's your life,' I said. Then unable to help myself, as I saw this good young life being thrown away, I called to the other seconds, 'Is there no chance of a conciliation? This is not Muraz, asking, it is me. Surely this whole thing is unnecessary?'

The two seconds and the doctor looked towards Geroude, who sneered and then laughed, shaking his head and then attended himself to aiming his pistol at a sapling not far away.

'You should not have done that,' hissed Muraz. 'He will believe it was me and think me a coward.'

'Does it matter?' I growled back. 'You'll be dead and out of it in a few minutes.'

'My honour will still be here.'

I couldn't answer that.

A crow flew over our heads, cawing as if mocking the scene. This triggered the signal for the actual duel. The two men stood back-to-back and were then given the order to proceed. They each took twelve paces, turned and stood with their right shoulders facing their opponent, the youth a narrower, leaner target than the older man. For a long, long moment nothing happened, the world stood still as they simply remained looking at each other. Then Geroude swiftly raised his arm, aimed and fired. I saw something flick the tunic on top of the boy's shoulder. A piece of ragged cloth stood up, no larger than a thumbnail. My heart leapt. He had been nicked, but not hit squarely. I thought perhaps Muraz would now delope and walk away with his honour, leaving Geroude frustrated but unable to do anything further.

That did not happen. The youth raised his arm, took aim, and fired. Geroude flew backwards and fell on the hard ground. The doctor rushed to him immediately and got him into a sitting position. I could see by the blood seeping through the hole in his coat hat he had been hit in the upper arm, just below the shoulder, the ball probably penetrating through almost to his chest. Geroude then stood up and swayed a little, before saying, 'Again! Again, damn you, you fucking pig farmer. Left hands this time.'

'Not a chance,' replied my boy, 'you've had your day.'

'Again!' yelled Geroude. 'Again!'

'Don't be a fool,' said the captain to his man. 'You're badly wounded and you have no cause – no honourable cause – to challenge him again.'

'I will have my way,' snarled Geroude, clearly in great pain. 'I am entitled to challenge whom I wish.'

Muraz replied, 'You stupid man. Don't you realise I could have gone for your head, rather than your arm? I am a deadshot. Most farmer's boys are deadshots. They grow up with a weapon in their hands. I can hit a squirrel in the head at twenty paces, left or right-handed, let alone blow a hole in the skull of a man. If we go again I will surely have to kill you and I'm determined not to do that.' To the doctor he said, 'Treat him and send the bill to me.' With that Muraz, my wonderful youth, took my arm and led me away from the scene, with Geroude still shouting for revenge.

I shook hands with Philippe Muraz, he thanking me for my part, and then went back to the inn wondering how all this squared with the monster getting the head of Lieutenant Geroude on his torso's shoulder. I found out later in the day when Philippe came to me at the inn and gave me the story.

'He hanged himself,' he said. 'They got the ball out of his arm, dressed his wound, and took him back to his rooms. Then later in the day he was discovered hanging from the rafters. Captain Spitzer said it was because he could not stand the shame of being beaten by a man he, Geroude, considered to be inferior in breeding and culture. Anyway,' Philippe Muraz shrugged as if it were all beyond him, 'they cut him down and he's now lying with even lesser men in the charnel house.'

I blinked. 'The charnel house? But he's not a murderer.'

'Oh no, not at all. Of course he's not. But he's a suicide. The priest would not allow him to be buried in the churchyard after committing one of the worst of mortal sins. Only one other place his body could be sent to. The charnel house.' Philippe sat down and slumped. 'What a mess. I never thought the hussars could be like this. I've always admired them for their magnificent panache, their élan. They seemed to me as a child to be wonderful heroes of men with big souls and great courage.'

'Well,' I replied, 'they may have the latter, but not necessarily the former I'm afraid. There is still huge snobbery amongst the aristocratic elite and that makes them into men unworthy of being members of the human race. Will you remain an hussar, or are you going to leave the regiment?'

'Oh, I'll stay. I'll most likely die in battle. Many of us do. But it'll be worth it. My family will be able to boast they had a son who became an hussar and wore a glorious uniform of blue and gold. That's something to be proud of, isn't it? Someone of my lowly origins dying for his country on a thoroughbred horse that most farm boys would never even get a glimpse of in their lives, let alone ride? I think so. I really do.'

And so I left my young hero, not knowing what to say to his simple philosophy.

6

I JUMPED TIME AGAIN, AN even shorter hop than my last one.

My next investigation was on the man who supplied the torso to the monster. His name was Julius Jules and when I looked at the records for the charnel house I discovered he had been a circus performer before committing the crime of taking the life of another human being. I did not discover what his personal skill entailed, it simply said, 'Travelling circus employee'. For all I knew he could merely be one of the men who knocked in the tent pegs to the big top. Then again he could have been a lion tamer or a clown. In fact, after making further enquiries of the clerk who dealt with the court records on Julius's trial, it appears he had been a trapeze artist.

What exotic body parts the monster had! A slave's legs, a cheese seller's arms, a hussar's head and now a trapeze artist's torso. However, circus people tend to be very private folk, easy with their own kind, but not so open with strangers. I found them putting up the big top when I arrived on the scene outside the town. One of the workers, an Italian peasant by the look of him, gave me the directions to the horse-drawn caravan of Julius Jules. I knocked on the door of the van and was told to enter by a shrill voice. Opening the door I was confronted by a man in a dirty vest sitting at a small table eating breakfast sausage. At the other end of the room was a sharp-faced woman, not unattractive, but lacking warmth in her demeanour.

'Yes?' asked the man, cutting a slice of sausage and using the knife to put it into his mouth. 'What do you want?'

'Señor Jules?'

'That's me.'

His hair was thick and matted, looking as if it hadn't been washed for a fortnight. There was a kind of classic Italian look to his features, though he was certainly not young and in his prime. I put him at around forty-five years of age. He could have modelled for one of those busts of Roman gods. Handsome, certainly, and smooth-complexioned. As for his torso, arms and legs, there was a litheness about them, the muscles lean and hard. His eyes were dull however and his mouth tight-lipped and turned down at the corners. I guessed he was something of a drinker who had developed a deeply-jaded outlook on life. He looked bitter and bad-tempered, and I knew from the outset that I was going to get very little out of him.

'I'm a reporter from the local newspaper and I wondered if you would give me an interview – your life story, if you will.'

His wife – I assumed she was such – gave a snort.

'You be quiet, woman,' he said, almost automatically, without turning his head to look at her. Then to me, 'Run away. I'm eating my breakfast.'

'It'll be good publicity for the circus.'

'What do I care about the circus? I'm not the owner. If it doesn't do well, I'll find another circus. There are many. A great many.'

'Wouldn't you like to see your name in print? I've heard you are one of the best trapeze artists in the world.'

Another snort from the woman, this time a lot fiercer.

Suddenly Jules jerked out of his slumping position. He grasped his knife in dagger fashion as his glance flicked back and forth from me to his wife. She was smiling in a sly, supercilious sort of way and then jerked up her head in the mode that Latin people use when they're saying, 'So what? What are you going to do about it?'. He glared at me, wrathfully, his eyes opening wide and dangerous.

'What? What are you looking at her for? Ah, you fancy her, do you? You think you can sleep with my wife without worrying about me? I'll cut out your heart and feed it to the lions.'

'Señor, please, I have no designs on your wife,' I replied. 'This is the first time I've seen her and I looked because she made a noise. All I want is an interview.'

'Get out,' he snarled.

I got out. The man was dangerously psychotic and though I knew he was about to commit a murder today, I didn't want it to be mine. Just because I was a traveller out of my time, did not mean that I was immune from death. I was as vulnerable as any man living in the early 1800s and I could feel the fear tingling down my back as I walked away from Julius Jules and his contemptuous wife. In fact I almost started to run when she followed me and called me back to her side.

'You want to know about *him*?' she said, jerking her head towards the caravan. 'You need to talk to the clown.'

'Clown?' I said in a strangled tone. 'What clown?'

'Bopo. You'll find him over there.' She pointed.

I got away from her as quickly as possible, before an irate husband with a kitchen knife came hurtling out of the caravan in my direction.

I found the clowns near a line of elephants that were swaying gently side to side, as if to some music they held in their heads. The clowns were sitting in a circle discussing politics or some equally contentious subject. They were not fully made up, though one or two of them still had on some make-up, probably from the town before this one. They seemed a rough crew, but when I asked for Bopo a fattish, bald-headed man stood up and excused himself from his friends and work colleagues and followed me to a point beyond the smell of elephant dung.

'Señor Bopo?'

'Just Bopo,' he said in what I recognised as Neapolitan Italian. 'Forget the title.'

I guessed that of course he had a real name and so would be señor something else when being addressed in a formal manner.

'I just tried to interview Julius Jules, but he blew his top and afterwards his wife came to me and suggested I ask you about him. I'm a newspaper correspondent by the way, doing an article on the circus and in particular, trapeze artists. I was hoping to get his life story, but he seemed very reluctant to speak with me.'

Bopo straightened, sucked in his abdomen and puffed out his chest.

'Ah, newspaper? Well, you've come to the right man. Julius and I grew up in the streets of Naples together. I was a hard beginning for both us. We ate what we could steal or find in the gutter and kept warm on winter nights by burning the crates left behind when the markets closed in the evening. We both joined the circus at the age of ten years, before we were arrested or killed by the *carabinieri*.'

'You were in danger of being killed by the *police*?'

'Certainly. Oh, criminals would have sold us into servitude or even slavery, but the police needed to clean the streets of thieves.'

He seemed to think this was the correct way to handle things.

'So, you both joined the circus. This circus?'

'No, no,' he waved a pudgy hand. 'We've been in several over the years. Julius, he was cleverer than me. He learned how to walk the tightrope first, then he went on the horses, you know, acrobatics – finally he took to the trapeze. He was wonderful in his day, but he's getting older and slower now. We have a new young man, from Florence, a beautiful city, no? Well, this fellow

Andreas is much more agile than my dear friend Julius and of course he is screwing Julius's wife, Lola.'

I took a step back, before saying, 'What?'

'You know, they are in bed together – often. Of course, you must not print this in your newspaper. It would be bad for the circus.'

'What?' I cried, stepping back. 'Does Julius know of this affaire?'

'Oh yes, but what can he do?' The clown shrugged, then rubbed some of the white chalky paint from his cheek abstractedly. 'He loves his wife and does not want her to leave him, so he says nothing.'

'Bopo,' I replied, 'surely he is festering inside? Surely he will explode one day and do something to the young man?'

'Oh yes,' replied Bopo, brightly. 'He will do it, sometime soon I think. I have told him the best way is to not catch Andreas when he leaps from the high stand. Julius, I said, you must make as if to catch him, then let him slip from your fingers and fall to his death. Everyone will think it an accident. Even you, though I have told you what I said to Julius, you will be hard put to prove that it is not an accident. Anyway, if you do, I will kill you, and so you have little to gain by doing so and the rest of your life to look forward to, if you say nothing. I know which it will be.'

All the while he spoke he looked at me with those mild, blue eyes, his round face beaming.

'Indeed,' I said, after a minute's silence, 'I shall say nothing – but not for any of the reasons you could imagine. Is there anything else you can tell me about Julius? Any extraordinary event in his life, or yours, that has occurred? I can see you are both dedicated to your profession, which is admirable. Have you done nothing else at all except follow that road?'

He shook his head and shrugged his shoulders. 'Not that I can think of – Julius did once consider joining the army of the

Emperor Napoleon Bonaparte, when that great leader was at the height of his power, but then he met Lola and she talked him out of it.'

'Well then, thank you for your time, Bopo. Much appreciated.'

'You will mention me in your article?'

I nodded, enthusiastically. 'Oh yes, I'll say you threatened to kill me.'

His face lost some of it's sunniness for a moment, then he smiled again and jabbed me on the upper arm.

'Ah, you joke with me. Come to the performance tonight. You'll enjoy it. I'm very funny when I do my act. You'll see.'

'I'll be there.'

I have to be honest, I wasn't looking forward to seeing someone fall from the trapeze and land in a crumpled heap of broken bones. However, I had promised the monster that I would witness first-hand all the murders. I could see that he needed an accurate report for his memoirs and though none of the lives of his body parts had been particularly spectacular, or even very interesting, the manner of their deaths was certainly something out of the ordinary. I just hoped that the monster would not be disappointed with learning that Julius Jules had been a circus performer all his life and had done nothing else, but hey, a lot of people only ever have one job in their years on Earth, me being one of the exceptions.

That evening I went with the crowds to buy a ticket for the show. The big top was full to the brim with excited Swiss, with a sprinkling I guessed of neighbouring nations: Austrians, Germans, French and Italians. These foreigners did seem to spill over into each other's countries. I found my seat, a hard plank about three tiers up from the ring, and studied the glittering surrounds. There were young women wearing sparkles on their costumes, a strong muscular man in a leopard-skin suit, the clowns running around, throwing buckets of shredded paper at screaming children who thought they were full of water and various others.

I recognised Bopo by his plumbob shape only, his make-up thick and bright on his face. He was climbing a balanced ladder that was not fixed in any way or being held, reaching the top before it toppled with his weight and took him to the ground where he rolled over and over, breaking his fall. The children oohed and aahed each time he got to the top of his ladder and pretended to be frightened by the drop below him, swaying back and forth, until once more it went down like a felled tree.

Some of the younger children were scared of the clowns, shrieking and bursting into tears when the clowns came near them. The parents laughed and cuddled their offspring, trying to tell them that clowns were funny, not frightening. A lot of good that did, to be sure, for the kids screamed even louder the next time. I could sympathise with the infants, since I too in my false early years in the 1950s was terrified of these creatures who hid their identities under red and white paint, had huge feet and wore strange clothes that made them look unhuman.

The show started with the ringmaster yelling out what was to come while the tinselled ladies rode ponies around the ring and did all sorts of acrobatic somersaults on their rides. They made the most use of their long white legs and curvy shapes which was probably appreciated by the men in the audience, though the women and children could find excitement in the actual act itself. Next came the elephants, followed by other animals, followed by the lions and their tamer.

During this last performance two burly men stood with long black muskets one either side of the lions' cage looking very purposeful. I wasn't sure whether this was to protect the lion tamer should one of his animals attack him, or whether to assure the audience that if one or more of these savage creatures should escape they would be in no danger because the lion would be shot before it reached them. It all looked very impressive and dramatic, which was obviously the idea.

Finally, we came to the point in the evening where the trapeze artists entered, bowed in their glistering tight vests and stockings, and agilely climbed the ropes to the platforms and trapezes above. There were three of them. I recognised Julius and his wife and the third man, younger and very good looking, was obviously the lover, Andreas, who was about to fall to his death.

My stomach was in a knot, my hands trembled so much I had to jam them between my knees and my heart raced away making me feel a little faint. My neighbour, a thick-headed man with his wife and children, looked into my face and said, 'Ah yes, I too am afraid of heights. It makes you sweat to think of yourself up there, eh? But,' he patted my arm, 'it is not us, it is them, and they are skilful performers. You should not worry for them, friend. They have done it many, many times before.'

'Yes, yes, I'm sure you're right.'

'Of course I am. They will be fine.'

We both then turned our attention back to the scene around us and the talented people above. Many of the other of the night's performers were also crowding into the entrance which the circus artists used to enter into the ring to do their act: the clowns, girls who rode the ponies, the woman with the performing dogs, the lion tamer and his two bodyguards, a few of the drones. Clearly the trapeze was the big draw, the main event, and everyone who was able wanted to watch.

There was no safety net.

With the appropriate drum rolls and music, the act began, and I have to say after a while I was just caught up in the spectacle. These three artists were extremely skilful and had us all on the edges of our seats. The somersaults and catches, twists and spirals, were breathtaking to watch. Each time Andreas leapt from his own trapeze, did two or three twizzles or somersaults, to then be caught by the strong and gifted Julius, my heart was in my mouth. Yet, the grip was always firm and the younger man held on to with great sureness. Each time they did their leap and catch I expected hands to slip, a body to hurl down to the ground: gasps, screams, expressions of horror, pandemonium. Yet the 'accident' never occurred. The act went through all its different phases and the end bows were taken to thunderous applause and shouts of 'Bravo! Bravo! Bravo!' leaving me extremely puzzled.

Julius went slithering down the rope first, reaching the sawdust in the ring, and he took another bow as leader of the team. His wife and Andreas remained on one of the platforms at the top, waving to the crowd below. Then the woman descended, doing little twists and turns on the rope, milking the crowd's admiration. On reaching the ground she pranced around a little, making her last bows, while Andreas stood and waited as the senior members soaked the audience of its appreciation.

While his wife was bending and throwing her arms up, taking the applause, Julius suddenly left her side and walked over to where the lion tamer and his two bodyguards were standing. On reaching them he snatched one of the muskets which was now only being loosely held by its owner and walked back into the middle of the ring. He pointed the weapon upwards, took deliberate aim, and fired. Andreas jerked, toppled, and fell like a sack of wheat to the ground below, narrowly missing Julius's wife. There he lay, a crumpled heap of flesh and bone, seeping blood into the sawdust of the big top's ring.

Gasps, screams, expressions of horror, pandemonium.

I felt sick. The panicking crowds began scrambling towards the exits, getting caught up in themselves, cramming the narrow gaps, trampling on one another. I stayed where I was, knowing the danger of such situations. I sat staring at Julius, who remained as still as a statue, looking down with obvious satisfaction on the man he had murdered. His thin-faced wife was gazing at him. I swear there was a mixture of pride and admiration in her expression. Julius made no effort to escape. When the musket was taken from his hand, he let it go without a murmur. He simply remained where he was until the authorities arrived and led him quietly away.

The circus very soon recovered its composure and its folk calmly went about the business of getting things back to normal. You would not be wrong in thinking they had been expecting something of the sort to happen. The body was removed, the bloody sawdust collected in a bag, and all they while they chatted to each other, mentioning the atrocious slaying they had just witnessed in a casual way, yet talking animatedly of preparations for the next day's performance.

Perhaps they were used to such things? I imagined they were indeed a volatile bunch of people, a little like gypsies: hot-blooded, hot-headed, ruled by their hearts. Jealousy was a prime motive for violence amongst such a group. But why, why did Julius not let his victim fall and claim it was an accident? Why commit a cold-blooded murder in front of hundreds of witnesses? I could only think that he needed to show his wife and the world that he was not a man to stand by and be cuckolded by a young bullock wanting to drive out the old bull. He was a prideful man, one who despised hiding behind deceptive schemes to protect himself from the law. He needed to prove to everyone that he had the courage to do what he felt was necessary to protect his honour, his name, his fiercely-guarded heritage of proud manhood.

Only Bopo, of all the circus people, looked at all distressed. Julius's wife had not shed a single drop of moisture for either Andreas or her husband. Bopo sat on a seat in the front row that fronted the ring with his face buried in his hands, sniffling softly and weeping. I knew he was not crying for Andreas, but for his life-long friend, Julius, who would not be coming back again. When he finally looked up, he gave me an angry stare. 'What?' he said, the make-up running down his face in rivulets, 'clowns can't cry real tears?' His misery appeared deep and embedded. It seemed this fat clown was the only one who cared about what was going to happen to Julius Jules, who would hang just three weeks from the date on which we stood, and even he would have left along with the rest of the circus. When the executioner lets fall the trapdoor on the gallows, this piece of ground on which the crime took place will be a wasteland, with litter blowing across its dreary surface.

7

I WAS GROWING WEARY WITH death and almost jumped back to the monster's time, to tell him I'd had enough and he could either fabricate the rest of his memoirs or give up the project. However, I was so close to the end now that it would have been churlish and cowardly of me. Coward I might be, but I hoped I was not a churl, and therefore went to the records of the court and indeed that ghastly building the charnel house and discovered Alexander S. Rattringer had murdered Percival D. Rattringer on a wild moonless night in February, when the winds were screaming through the mountains and valleys.

Intriguing! A patricide or fratricide, or else a remarkable co-incidence.

It was indeed a fratricide. Alexander, a financier, had slain his brother Percival, a Roman Catholic priest. What had happened here? Mammon taking up arms against the representative of God? Even worse, when I found out that the Rattringers were twin brothers, one who had followed a path to gold, the other the road to heaven.

The killing had been brutal and the surviving brother had almost joined his twin on that murderous night, having been stabbed fourteen times about the body and would probably have died if the assailant had not tried to keep the number of the wounds to reflect the stations of the cross. Alexander in turn had bludgeoned his brother to death with a bagful of coins that he always kept attached to his belt for use in an emergency. Percival died of a shattered skull and Alexander was treated for his injuries, tried, sentenced to death, and was hanged shortly afterwards. Apparently, according to the record clerk's account, the convicted man was so heavy the gallows collapsed at the point the rope broke his neck and a bill for the damage was sent to his surviving relatives.

To kill a priest! That was a crime against humanity, God and the Church, all rolled into one. I did not envy Alexander. If he had gone to another place it was indeed the hot one.

With the address in my pocket I went to the house which apparently the twins had shared since their parents had died. It turned out to be more of a middle-European castle than a house or even a manor. It was dark and gloomy, with witch's-hat towers on all four corners and Norman-arched windows studded with glass that did indeed let in a little light but were impossible to see through. If you were inside and people walked past in the garden, all you would see were blurred shapes with no definition to them. A green mould had covered most of the external woodwork and ivy owned most of the stonework. The whole place had an air of desolation about it, as if it had given up trying to look like a lived-in dwelling. When I used the knocker the sound echoed through the myriad of passageways beyond the door.

The door opened to the width of two centimetres and a voice, probably that of an elderly female, asked what I wanted.

'I'm here to interview the Brothers Rattringer,' I said. 'I'm from the local newspaper.'

A sharp nose now protruded through the gap.

'Which paper would that be?'

No one had asked this question before now, but I was not stupid enough not to have an answer ready.

'The *Zeiten*, naturally, it's the only local newspaper.'

'And what happened to Herr Blumen?'

'Herr Blumen?'

'The reporter who was here last time?'

The flywheel of my mind whizzed round and I answered, 'Oh, Herr Blumen? He's visiting his relations in Geneva.'

The nose sniffed, the door opened wider, and I was confronted by a skeletal-thin figure in a faded grey dress. The eyes were sharp and intelligent as she took in every detail of my appearance. Apparently satisfied she opened the door fully and stepped aside.

'You'd better wait in the library,' she said. 'Third door on the right. Which of the brothers do you wish to speak with?'

'Either of them, if it's possible,' I replied, 'but on preference, Alexander.'

'And the reason for your preference? In case I'm asked, you understand.'

'Financial, though I'm happy to talk of matters of the spirit with Percival, if he is the only one in the house.'

'Matters of the spirit?' She almost chortled at these words. 'Well, we'll see who's in residence.'

I made my way to the room she indicated and indeed it was lined with books on every wall. Studying the titles I discovered that the north and east walls had only volumes on the Christian faith on their shelves while the south and west walls had only tomes on the subject of money matters. Since the whole room was covered in a thin layer of grey dust, including the books themselves, it seemed that they were rarely, if ever taken down and opened, let alone read. Like many libraries of many mansions, the books were there for decoration only, probably to impress any guests with the intellect and learning of the owners of the place.

I didn't sit down on any one of the four winged armchairs. I would only have disturbed the earthworks and any spiders or beetles that inhabited the stuffing. Nor did I amuse myself with looking out of the window, since that occupation was denied me by the bottle-thick glass. Instead I wandered around the vast room, noting that the chandelier was grimy with smoke-black and the candles in its sockets had melted so far down their hoary grease had enveloped the cups beneath. In one corner of the room stood an upright piano. I lifted the lid only to find a metal bar across the keys, presumably there to prevent any unauthorised person from tinkling. While I was thus engaged the door opened and an enormously fat man squeezed through the opening and entered the room. His small eyes stared at me from their depths in a face that had cheeks bulging below them and enormous brows overhanging them.

'You have come to tune the instrument?' he rumbled from the depths of his great body.

'No, no, I was just being inquisitive.'

'Curiosity killed the cat.'

'Yes, so I understand. Do forgive me. It was bad manners. I'm here to interview either Alexander or Percival Rattringer for an article for the *Zeiten*.'

He lumbered towards a chair and sat down with a loud grunt.

'That's all right,' he said, more amiably, 'Do take a seat.'

It was time to stop being fastidious. I did as he asked, aware that my black broadcloth coat was going to need cleaning afterwards.

'So,' he said, 'you're a reporter, eh? Come to interview me?'

I studied the man now buried between the wings of the chair. He was wearing dark clothes like mine, but with no evidence of a clerical collar of any kind. I was certain then that he was Alexander and not Percival. This evidenced, I was just about to ask him a question on the economy of the town, when the door opened again and an exact image of the man in the chair squeezed through the doorway and entered the library wearing a purple cassock and with a massive wooden cross on a golden chain around his neck. Percival, it could be no other, peered at me, then his attention went to the twin brother who filled every tiny centimetre of the chair well.

The two men glared at each other with such intense hatred it shocked me to the core. Clearly these two men only lived in the same house because they had to. Or perhaps it went deeper than that? Maybe the parents had left them the mansion between them and they both refused to let the other claim the whole? So they lived together, each hoping to drive out the other, in order not to give way. I had heard of such things between siblings before and this was no doubt even worse, since these siblings were twins and no doubt deadly rivals. Most twins get on fine together, but over time some twins move into a state of merging, so neither really knows who he is and where the separation comes between him and his brother.

Alexander spoke. 'This man has come to interview me. I would appreciate some privacy, if you don't mind, Percival?'

The tone was silky with an underlying layer of malice.

'You may suit yourself, brother. I just came in to fetch a book…' Percival looked around him, clearly out of countenance and using the excuse of the book to cover his annoyance. He went to one of the shelves and took down a volume from which a dust cloud flew. 'Now, dear brother, I shall leave you both in peace.' Turning to me, he looked into my face and said, 'God be with you, my son.'

Automatically, I replied, 'And with you, father.'

'He always is. He always is. Some may reject him, but I hold him dear.'

With that, Percival made for the door, his purple cassock swishing, and struggled through the opening.

Once he was sure his brother was gone, Alexander rumbled, 'He was wearing purple again – he knows that's for bishops, not ordinary priests.'

'Around his own house is all right, surely?' I ventured.

'*His* house? *His* house? This is also *my* house and I object to someone trying to deceive others with regard to his station. It's pure vanity, which is a sin, though that part doesn't worry me, since I'm a non-believer, an atheist. What does bother me is his audacity, his deceitful nature, his implied mendacity. Bishop! He'll never make bishop. He thinks he'll become a cardinal one day, but he hasn't got the stuff of cardinals. He hasn't got the stuff of bishops. He's lucky they accepted him into the priesthood, but I'm certain they'll never pander to his ambition.' He turned his great head towards me. 'I'm sure you saw through him straight away. A more shallow creature does not exist on the earth than my brother. Vainglorious and pompous, and really without reason. He has a brain the size of a pea...'

Alexander went on and on, maligning his twin, almost foaming at the mouth when he had to use his brother's name. Eventually the housekeeper with the stick-insect limbs came in carrying a tea tray and she snapped at Alexander, telling him not to talk about his brother in that way. Brothers should love each other, she said, and more so if they are twin brothers. She clattered the cups and saucers about, banging the tea pot down to emphasise her opinion that the house should be in harmony – peace and harmony – with everyone getting on famously together. She could not work, she said, in a house where everyone was being nasty to everyone else, and she would leave if it didn't stop and then where would they all be?

'Can you cook for yourselves?' she asked. A rhetorical question, for she answered it herself straight away. 'No. Do you make your own beds? Can you sweep the hallway and beat the carpets? No. Do you wash the windows and get rid of the spiders' webs? No. Can you do the laundry? No. Do you dust the shelves? No.'

No indeed, I thought, and neither do you, madam, as I noted that in the beams of weak sunlight coming through the dirty window panes, the dust motes were thick as sand in a desert storm. We were all breathing dust with every breath we took. The lungs of the inhabitants of the house must have been coated with grey matter. I was trying above all things to take in air through my nose, rather than my mouth, though I doubt I filtered out less than half the detritus that filled the atmosphere.

Once she had gone, I went through the motions of taking out a notebook and jotting down the events of Alexander's life. To say the flow of information was boring would be an understatement. He went into great detail regarding the work of a financier and insisted on giving me the minutiae of the amounts he had made, down to the last penny, on various deals and schemes he had been involved in. I almost fell off the chair several times, having slid forwards in a half-doze, desperate either to stop the drone of his voice or at least to fall asleep. It was a dreadful afternoon, which eventually stretched into evening, until finally he said to me, 'Well, I don't think we can finish today, can we? I'm only halfway through my life. You are finding it interesting material, I'm sure? Yes?' I nodded, eyelids half-closed. 'Very well then, why don't you stay the night with my brother and myself, and we can continue in the morning?'

'That is an excellent suggestion,' I replied, waking up. 'So long as no one minds?'

'My guests are my business and I would like you to stay.' He rang a bell at his elbow and the housekeeper returned. 'Please make up a bed for our guest, Maria. He's staying the night. Oh, and set an extra place at the table, if you will.'

She sniffed. 'Staying, is he?'

'Didn't I just say so? Really, Maria, you're getting a little above yourself lately. Just do as you are asked.'

When she had left the room, Alexander said to me, 'She keeps threatening to leave, but she never will you know. She's got nowhere to go.'

'Has she no family?' I asked.

'Oh yes,' he replied, looking surprised at my question, 'us. My brother and me. Maria is our older sister.'

I almost fell off the chair again, but not this time through mental fatigue.

Next I had to help lever Alexander out of the armchair and steady him before he tottered towards the doorway and, turning sideways, managed to squeeze through once more. Maria then came to meet us with an armful of grey sheets and pillow slips. 'This way,' she said to me, leading me to a winding staircase. 'Be careful not to trip on the rugs. They're a bit ragged around the edges.'

Indeed they were. It looked as if the rats and mice had been at them for many a year.

The house was a maze of landings and passageways. We travelled almost the distance of India before we came to a door which she asked me to open since she was 'bundled up'. The heavy oak door with its iron handle fashioned in the shape of a flamingo swung open to reveal a room almost twice as filthy as the library. I shuddered, knowing I was going to have to sleep in this pit of grime and dirt. Maria half-apologised for the state of the place, telling me it wasn't her fault because she hadn't been aware that I was expected to stay the night.

'Otherwise, I would have dusted,' she said. 'But a little smudge or two won't hurt you, will it?'

She dumped the bedding on the mattress of a four-poster and a cloud of motes flew up. I saw at least two cockroaches scuttling for the safety of cracks in the skirting board. However, I reminded myself that I didn't intend sleeping a wink in this awful house, so I didn't need to worry. Maria made the bed up, then led me to a freezing cold bathroom some three hundred metres away and there told me to wash my hands before I came down to dine.

The plumbing, as can be imagined, was a jungle of lead pipes and huge brass taps, a galvanised bathtub the size of a deckless ship's hull and a giant washbasin made of the same metal with some disgusting hair clogging the plughole. The bathtub's legs were shaped to represent the limbs of some unidentifiable animal with ponderous paws and claws, while the washbasin hung from some precarious-looking rusty bolts fixed deep into the brickwork of the wall. There was no toilet. Only a metal bedpan dangling from three carrying chains on a hook behind the door.

The whole house was a nightmare of monstrous fixtures and fittings that a man who has lived in the future found impossibly ugly and functionally difficult. The huge taps needed the strength of a stevedore to turn them and when they did eventually budge and squeal to an open position there was a lot of banging and clanking in the pipes before the water appeared as a yellowish-brownish slime to dribble into the basin. There was no way I was going to put my lily-white hands into unfiltered water that appeared to be piped from the nearest swamp.

Dinner that evening took place in a large dining-room, with a long table which at each end sat an enormous twin brother. They did not speak to each other. They did not speak to Maria when she brought in the soup, then a platter of roasted pigeons, potatoes and greens, and finally a cheese which was rotten throughout, either on purpose or by accident, which I declined saying I was quite full, thank you. Coffee ended this silent repast, after which we all went upstairs to bed. Except that I didn't actually get in the bed, but sat on the edge of it cursing the monster whose mission I was on and vowing to tell him every detail of Alexander's life story.

I knew from the court records I'd studied that the murder had taken place at around midnight, though I was worried about finding the exact area in a house where the passageways formed a labyrinth of twists, turns and long narrow stretches. At approximately the eleventh hour all the clocks in the mansion, and there were many, chimed the hours mostly out of sequence with each other. I rose and began patrolling the passageways, wondering how on earth I was going to find the killing place. It was as black as death in those hallways and I was glad enough that I had brought along an infra-red flashlight that enabled me to see my past obstacles such as wooden chests, statues and tapestries that had half-fallen and lay at the foot of the walls.

Still, all my searching revealed nothing, and around the appointed hour I was ready to give up the ghost and time-jump away from this hell. Then when I came to a t-junction I heard some noises on the landing above the stairs which led to the servant's quarters. The nearer I came to the spot, the more desperate the sound of the struggle. When I turned a corner, there they were, fighting in the light of a single candle that burned in a window niche. Two huge figures, hardly able to wield their weapons because of the energy they needed to expend in doing so.

I stayed at the end of the passageway, out of sight of both combatants.

Percival was wielding what looked to me like an *aestel*, a pointer baton that was used by clerics and priests to point to words or passages in holy books. It must have been made of metal rather than wood, for he was stabbing his brother in a number of places on his twin's torso without the baton snapping. Each time he did so, he muttered a single prayer such as a devotee might use at a station of the cross. The fat on Alexander's body was so thick however, it was clear that no vital organ could be penetrated by an assailant with the strength of a sick guppy. So that though blood was flowing, it was gently seeping out from shallow wounds, rather than gushing.

Alexander on the other hand, had his bludgeon in his hand and was swinging wildly at his brother's head, making the occasional hit but with little effect since the blows were weak and his brother's skull very thick.

Fourteen times, Percival stabbed his brother and prayed for his eternal soul with each strike.

Fourteen times Alexander struck his twin on the head with the bag of gold and silver coins, each time hoping to open a fracture.

Nothing would have come of this battle and the two opposing forces might have given up, puffing and panting with the exertion and gone back to bed, if the last blow Alexander delivered had not caught his brother on the bridge of the nose.

'Ow,' cried Percival, genuinely in pain. 'That hurt.'

The priest dropped his pointer, staggered backwards clutching his nose, and toppled over the banister rail. He fell like an ox to the stone floor of the servants' quarters below, his head striking first. His skull opened like a coconut hit with a hammer, the blood and brains splattering the walls. Alexander rushed to the rail and looked down on his twin and he let out a howl of anguish.

'Percival!' he cried, distraught. 'Percival, my dear brother!'

The separate fluids from Alexander's two small deep eyes and the fourteen seeping wounds on the body were joined in a confluence of blood and tears.

The only time in his life that Alexander Rattringer had exerted himself was to get out of bed to murder his brother.

I jumped quickly to another time, frankly desperate to be out of and away from the horrible mess that existed in that unholy house. My heart bled for the two mentally-ill brothers, who had been thrown together in a place which could not help but foster animosity between them. What a truly unhappy pair. Now that they had both gone, what was going to happen to their sister, Maria? I was certain she only lived to serve her miserable and unfortunate brothers.

Yet I could do nothing. I was the time traveller and unable to interfere in the past. I could only hope that she would sell that dreadful mansion and use the money to go somewhere more pleasant, more cheerful. An island in the sun. A city with lots of bridges and bright lights. An exotic eastern country with elephants and tigers and splendid princes and boats made of reeds and wild, interesting men.

8

'I THOUGHT I WOULD FIND you here.'

The monster looked up. 'You only left a minute ago.'

Time travel. Yes. 'Of course I did.'

We were in the same inn. I sat down opposite my companion and ordered a cognac. I needed that drink. I was shaken to the soles of my boots with all this death and especially with the hangings. I'm not sure there's a good way to be executed but being strangled or having your neck broken by a rope throws up some terrible images. My head was full of them at the moment. I just wanted to relax and get my nerves settled. I had come from a time when capital punishment has long been abolished. They still hung people in my spurious childhood and I remember reading the papers as a young man and having ghastly images in my head. Murder, of course, should be punished severely in some way, but if you have a law which says killing people is wrong, then executing people must also by definition be wrong.

Anyway, you can't bring back the dead and too many people have been accused and convicted of murder who were completely innocent.

At least – I revised my thoughts on seeing the monster take a long swig of his ale – you shouldn't be able to bring back the dead.

'Well, Alexander,' I said after taking several sips, 'it is you, isn't it?'

He nodded the hussar's head and made a gesture with the cheese-seller's hand. 'Of course. I have Alexander's brain, therefore I am he – mostly.'

'And you have all the memories of your life? I mean, your previous life?'

'Certainly.' He stared at me from within his lean face. 'And so you're wondering if I'm still the self-indulgent man I was before? Whether I am still Alexander the avaricious? Alexander, the man full of hate for his brother? Alexander the murderer? Yes, I recall that man, but being hung is a life-changing experience. You're never the same after dangling from a rope with your neck broken. You smile, but it's true. Of course I don't remember actually *dying* but I do remember my childhood, my youth, my manhood and finally, I most certainly remember killing my brother. However, my regret, my anguish and feeling of bereavement is overwhelming. I wish it had never happened and – you must know this – it was in the end an accident. I was enraged with him enough to want to hurt him, but not to end his life like that.'

'He tried to kill you.'

'Percival didn't have the strength. He wanted to hurt me, but I doubt he wished me dead. Now, my sorrow is still very fresh,' his eyes misted over and he wiped away a tear, 'so you'll forgive me if I don't dwell too long on my departed twin brother. It may seem strange to you, but I mourn him all the more because we were rivals and enemies, than I would a brother I loved and cherished. One cannot go to the former and say one is sorry, while with the latter there is no need to express regret or ask for forgiveness because the departed one knew he would be missed.'

'I have no desire to pursue the subject. However, I would like to remind you that you also have a sister…'

He smiled. 'Ah, Maria. We treated her abominably, worse than a servant, though she was quite capable of giving us both a tongue-lashing. You will be pleased to learn I have been to the house in the guise of a lawyer. I encouraged her to sell the property and move to Vienna, where she has established herself in a smart little white-stone town-house with a maid and a Pug called Pinkie. Both dog and mistress have grown a little fat on cream chicken and iced cakes. Maria now visits the opera, concerts and has become quite a society lady, going to *kaffee und kuchen* of an afternoon with newly made friends of the Austrian aristocracy and spends weekends by the Danube.'

'Yes, I am pleased to hear that.'

'And I was pleased to learn that her experience with us, her slovenly brothers, caused her to treat her maid with great kindness. Now,' said the monster, rubbing his hands, 'you have all the research notes for me? I'm eager to get started.'

'No quite,' I replied. 'I have to go back. It's a question of the heart.'

He looked dismayed. 'You haven't done the Leconte woman?'

'Louise. No. But I will. My last duty to you. Then it's over. I will spend the night here, and then I'll go back and do this one last favour for you.'

He looked relieved, 'Thank you, you have no idea how important this is to me. As Alexander I did very little to further knowledge or art, or in any way add to the progress of condition of mankind. All I did was shift paper bullion from one place to another, each time making more and more profit, and each time congratulating myself on being wealthy. Of course my book will not be a literary sensation. I am no intellectual. But my quirky experiences will be of interest to some people, I'm sure.'

I was by that time and with the brandy adding its soporific effect, half asleep, and I bid him good night and went upstairs to my room.

The next morning the snow lay crisp and even on the ground and I set off back to the time of the murderer Louise Leconte.

In the human psyche, in our imaginations, the heart has magical and mystical qualities. There are still many among us who believe the heart is responsible for our emotions, especially love and hate. I have no idea where the emotions really lodge, but I expect the brain has something to do with it. Still, it is hard to shake off the opinion that the heart is merely a pump sending blood coursing through our veins and is not the primal engine of our feelings, any more than we can thoroughly reject the persuasion that the blood contains more than the imprint of our genetic line. We still look on blood as having defining qualities of kinship and race. We still talk of 'pure' and 'bad' blood and think this viscous red fluid – whose practical work is merely to supply essential nutrients to our bodies and carry away the waste element – contains the ingredients of good and evil. We still often believe that the blood of our ancestors, the blood of our nation, is superior to others and defines us as a people different to, and even better than, those who live on the other side of the border.

Myths are stronger than truth when it comes to finding an identity.

So, like many others, I carry with me the mistaken idea that the heart is the house of the soul and therefore a mystical organ. Such a feeling is hard to shake off. The heart of a woman being even more mysterious to me, women in my opinion giving more importance to their emotions than men. Intuition, a sixth sense, a gift for the paranormal, the psychic or premonitions: these to me have always been primarily the province of women, men being more down to earth and pragmatic. I am probably wrong – most men are wrong about most things regarding women – but here I am stating my own singular opinion on the matter while I am off searching for a murderess who hacked her husband to death with a chopper.

I cut to the chase. This one was going to be easy to witness. All I had to do was stand in the garden of the cottage owned by the couple and peer through the curtainless window. It being evening, a dark one at that, the scene inside that kitchen was clearly lit by a lamp. I stood by a dark laurel bush which I hoped, if the light from the lamp fell upon my form, would constitute some sort of camouflage by breaking up my shape, my silhouette, and give me some time to escape into the dark.

There was a cold wind blowing, which swept along the valley, and with the snow under my boots I knew it would not be long before I was frozen.

I had arrived just at the right time. M. Leconte was sitting at the kitchen table staring down at his potage. I could not hear the words, but I could see him beginning to remonstrate with his wife Louise. His arms flew in the air and he kept pointing at the plate full of stew and his mouth was opening and closing with shouts. She on the other hand was wiping her hands on an apron and giving as good as she got, yelling at him and gesturing towards the corner of the kitchen where stood the range on which she had undoubtedly cooked his meal. Finally, I saw him pick up a long sleek knife whose edge glinted in the lamplight. He threatened her with it, swishing it around her head, and narrowly missing her throat.

Next M. Leconte pinned his wife against the hot range I spoke of above and put the point of the knife to her throat, nicking it so that a globule of blood appear, which seemed to delight him. He then stepped back, laughing, and she flew off the range, beating her smoking rear with her hands and crying with the pain. It was then her third husband made his fatal mistake. He turned his back on the injured woman and walked towards the door. In an instant she had the meat cleaver in her hand and brought it down with all her force on the back of his head. Bizarrely the cleaver stuck deep in his skull and she let go of it. With the weapon of his destruction still protruding comically from his skull Leconte staggered forward, then turned and stared at his wife in bemusement, seemingly puzzled about something. She stepped back, looking frightened. Finally, he took one more step towards her then crashed to the ground, smashing a kitchen chair to kindling on the way. Louise screamed, looked towards the window probably wondering if anyone had seen, and then she ran from the kitchen, came hurtling out of the front doorway, and finally – still wearing only thin clothes and with her apron flying – over the fields beyond.

I went to the court records and found that Louise was captured two days later, still wearing the uniform of the 1800s housewife. She was taken half-dead with exposure first to a hospital, then to the jail. Tried for murder she put up a spirited defence, telling the court she had acted in self-defence. Naturally they took little notice of her protests, she being a woman who had defied her husband. Even if he had threatened her with a knife, he was still the man of the household and to be obeyed in all things. Right was on the side of the man and no doubt, the records said, she had goaded him into his actions and caused him to lose his temper.

Louise Leconte, I learned, was actually of Spanish birth, and so the court decided she should be executed in the manner of her nation. She was garrotted a week after sentence had been passed. A horrible way to die, but as I have already written, is there really a good way to be executed? It was a time of course when life expectancy was short, people were dying of starvation in European cities, of typhus and other diseases, and indeed life among the lower classes was a cheap thing, difficult to hold onto unless you were lucky. I consoled myself with this thought, even though I was aware that it was cold comfort. That, and the thought that there had been two other husbands who had died in mysterious circumstances: poisoned according to the monster who it has to be said was a man of his time and therefore had received opinions as to the low status and untrustworthiness of women. I remained, despite my need to believe she was guilty of such crimes, still slightly open to the idea of co-incidence. There was no mention in the court report of the potage being laced with arsenic, as the monster had stated. As far-fetched as it seemed, perhaps Louise was innocent of the murder of the first two husbands? There are more things in heaven and earth than dreamed of in the monster's philosophy.

'Well, here are all my notes,' I said to the monster, now back with him, 'and I think you have a fine strong healthy heart there. Louise Leconte survived two days out in the mountains in winter and still lived to be strangled by the state.'

'Thank you. However can I show my gratitude?'

I peered into his lean and handsome face. The head of an arrogant hussar, but still it was a countenance which could turn the heads of women. Or, as I recalled an earlier conversation, a certain type of man.

'As I told you earlier, I don't think I can leave you here,' I said to the monster. 'You are, you will admit, an aberration, and since all the parts that make up the essential you are pieces of dead people's flesh and bone, you should not be walking around.'

He raised his dark eyebrows. 'You are going to kill me?'

'No, I'm going to take you back to the future with me.'

'When is that, I wonder?'

'The year 3704 AD.'

'Will I still be able to publish my book?'

'Oh yes, we still read, some of us. Perhaps not as many as did used to, but then the population is much larger and spans the galaxies. You could be famous on several different worlds. Funnily enough, they're still called books. They might be in an electronic form, or delivered by some other device, audio or written, but we still cling to the nostalgic idea of books as books. Indeed, there are eccentrics among us who still like their reading in paper form, just as there are those who continue to ride horses in a time when travel can be flashed through. We continue to hold on to remnants of the past which were once essential, but now a pastime.'

'So be it, but tell, have you enjoyed the experience of being my researcher?'

'In a word, no. I grew old very quickly doing it.'

'Never mind, I'll pay you lots of money if I ever become rich.'

'No need,' I said. 'I have a rich mother. Silvia, my dear mater, insists on pouring the stuff into my pockets, even though I earn a great deal myself.'

'Oh well, some other reward then.'

'I'll settle for watching what they do with you in the future.'

So WE RETURNED TO THE far distant future. It took me some time to persuade the authorities that the monster was harmless and was better suited to be in the 31st century, but I am after all a trained diplomat with strong persuasive powers. Once settled in the monster wrote his autobiographies* and became a famous author and celebrity. He was lionised by society on several planets, many of whose populations wanted to claim ancestry to at least one or more of his body parts. A large number of women especially were convinced their distant relative provided the monster with his heart. Wreaths were laid on various mountainsides, none of which had anything to do with the Swiss Alps, as a mark of mourning for Louise Leconte. Men looked to the aristocratic countenance of the monster for their ancestry, and those with fast legs, a love of cheeses, a skill with high swings, to a bloodline that stretched back way beyond any fractions of ownership, not even bothering to think that there were thousands of great-grandparents, all with an equal stake in their being, which might account for any talent they had for athletics or guessing the variety of a cheese.

And so ends the account of the sometimes falsely-imagined travels through time and space of me, James Winston Ovit: I hope you have enjoyed the ride.

* *Memoirs of a Monster: My Autobiographies* will be available in all good bookshops and online and other outlets in September 3706 AD.

On my way to Samarkand
memoirs of a travelling writer
by Garry Douglas Kilworth
http://www.infinityplus.co.uk/book.php?book=gkiomwts

Garry (Douglas) Kilworth is a varied and prolific writer who has travelled widely since childhood, living in a number of countries, especially in the Far East.

His books include science fiction and fantasy, historical novels, literary novels, short story collections, children's books and film novelisations.

This autobiography contains anecdotes about his farm worker antecedents and his rovings around the globe, as well as his experiences in the middle list of many publishing houses.

The style is chatty, the structure loose - pole vaulting time and space on occasion - and the whole saga is an entertaining ramble through a 1950s childhood, foreign climes and the genre corridors of the literary world.

"Kilworth is a master of his trade." —*Punch*

"Garry Kilworth is arguably the finest writer of short fiction today, in any genre. " —*New Scientist*

"Kilworth is one of the most significant writers in the English language. " —*Fear*

**For full details of infinity plus books
see www.infinityplus.co.uk**

CPSIA information can be obtained
at www.ICGtesting.com
Printed in the USA
LVHW01s2004170118
563092LV00001B/246/P